AN
UNLIKELY
COVEN

"Hi, Mik, I'm Joan,"  walking forward and offering a hand.

Mik stared at it, d ... ppearance," they said. "I'm ... really. A bad life."

"We've all been th ... gic can be tough on humans, but the adverse effects will fade in a few hours." Any creature would get magic poisoning from a high enough dose of raw magic, but humans had the lowest tolerance.

"Oh no, sorry, wow, I really didn't explain *anything* on the phone, did I?" CZ said with a wince and a laugh that bordered on delirious. "This isn't because of the Night Market—this is a reaction to their own magic."

"You're a witch?" Joan blurted. She'd assumed human based on how sick they seemed. "Did you channel past your limits?"

"I'm not a witch," Mik confirmed. "I don't remember much, but I remember that. I am totally human."

Joan made meaningful eyes at CZ, *explain what the fuck this is* eyes.

CZ performed a stupid flourish. "Joan, let me introduce you to the human who recently ascended to witchhood: Mik Batbayar."

Mik, to punctuate this point, threw up in their trash can.

AN UNLIKELY COVEN

Book One of the Green Witch Cycle

AM KVITA

orbit

orbit-books.co.uk

ORBIT

First published in Great Britain in 2025 by Orbit

1 3 5 7 9 10 8 6 4 2

A CIP catalogue record for this book
is available from the British Library.

ISBN 978-0-356-52751-2

Printed and bound in Great Britain by Clays Ltd, Elcograf, S.p.A.

Papers used by Orbit are from well-managed forests
and other responsible sources.

MIX
Paper | Supporting
responsible forestry
FSC
www.fsc.org   FSC® C104740

Orbit
An imprint of
Little, Brown Book Group
Carmelite House
50 Victoria Embankment
London, EC4Y 0DZ

The authorised representative
in the EEA is
Hachette Ireland
8 Castlecourt Centre,
Dublin 15, D15 XTP3, Ireland
(email: info@hbgi.ie)

An Hachette UK Company
www.hachette.co.uk

orbit-books.co.uk

For the Raft, who kept me afloat in the fallow years

ACT ONE

ONE

Joan Greenwood's grand homecoming was ruined by the fact that no one remembered to show up.

Nearly seven years after she fled for college, then her master's degree, Joan stepped off the train at Grand Central with all the fanfare of a slowly deflating balloon. Her duffel bag felt like the heaviest thing on earth, and her ratty sneakers nearly twisted her ankles as she trudged up the stairs from the platform. Moving with the approximate grace of a bike with a flat tire, she wove through the crowds flowing out onto the street.

There, she found no car waiting, no parents loitering, no sister waving amid the swirl of New York City.

This was no great surprise to Joan, but she had expected better anyways. When her father had said he'd send a car, she'd believed him. She scanned the street and hoped to see his ghost chauffeur idling by the curb.

Her mother had offered to take her out for lunch, and Joan had browsed restaurants in the area.

Her sister had said they'd meet up and take the witch subway back home together.

Joan had believed each of them.

Her aunt was too busy to even pretend, and that, in the end, meant she was the only one who had not, for the millionth time, let Joan down.

People shouldered past her to exit into their splendid lives. With a huff, Joan found a corner to wait on, out of the way, in case they were running late. But her phone held no notifications, and the minutes aggregated into despairing blocks of time. Joan didn't even want to be back; she hadn't ever really *wanted* to come back. Everyone assumed she would return, and as she ran after jobs post-graduation at respected witch architecture firms, she was repeatedly met with surprise.

I just thought you'd be returning to the city. An endless variation on this, until Joan began to suspect that it wasn't so much that everyone had made assumptions as it was that her father, Merlin, had spread the word behind her back.

Joan was returning to New York. Period. End of sentence.

She allowed her eyes to prickle and burn for precisely four seconds, breathing in the smell of food vendors and car exhaust and dirty cement, hating that it felt like home in a way New Haven and Yale hadn't, even though she'd only been back nine times in seven years. Hating that it felt like home because it *was* home, and no matter how far she ran, for how long, she was always going to end up here.

Alone.

At Grand Central.

Disappointed.

You should have known better, she thought, because this also meant she owed CZ five bucks.

"So? I assume if you're calling, it isn't good," CZ said on the phone as Joan gathered herself, telling her eyes to unprickle and unburn, even though they did neither, because nothing ever went the way she wanted it to.

"No one showed," Joan replied, crossing the street and really starting to sweat in the growing June heat. She valiantly fought the strap on her shoulder as it began to slip off. Her bag held her entire life.

"I'm sorry, Jo," CZ said. "I can be there in like five. No, two— the light just changed."

"Two? Why are you around Grand Central?"

CZ was suspiciously silent.

Joan stopped in the middle of the sidewalk and was rewarded with several pissed-off heckles from the people around her. "CZ—"

"Forty-five seconds!" he said, and then hung up.

Less than a minute later, CZ had located a bewildered Joan on the sidewalk and was weaving toward her, a wide grin on display, slightly elongated canines betraying his vampire heritage. A smile split her own face, wide enough to make her cheeks burn. That was the kind of guy CZ was; he smiled and you had to smile back.

"Jo!" he said, throwing his arms wide—they were *really* blocking the sidewalk—and Joan responded with a laugh, opening her arms so he could scoop her up, lifting her off her feet like she was a child, like she still housed every innocent thing she'd already lost.

"CZ," she said into his neck, and if it was a little teary, who could blame her? And if she squeezed tight enough to choke out anyone whose heart beat faster than twelve beats per minute... well, then he was kind enough not to comment on it.

He swung her a little before setting her down, patting her shoulders. He was tall and Black, with his hair cropped close to his head.

"I know this is a terrible day for you, but for me? Personally? It's so nice to have you back in the city," CZ said sincerely, which reminded her of how quickly he'd arrived.

She punched him in his extremely well-toned bicep, earning herself a set of stinging knuckles. He rubbed at the spot, pouting.

"It's one thing to bet on my family not coming; it's a whole other thing to be so confident I'm going to be abandoned that you show up and wait for my inevitable call," she scolded. They'd been friends, best friends, since freshman year of undergrad, and each of the nine times Joan had visited New York in the last seven years, it'd been to come home to him.

"You keep enough faith for both of us," he said, tucking Joan under his arm so they could continue walking. "Not my fault I can't stand the thought of you out on these streets, alone and so, so small."

"I'm not that small."

"Small and weak."

"Is this supposed to help boost my spirits?"

"You're a cat that I have lovingly taken home from the shelter. Oh! Bonus to returning—you can finally get a cat."

"A cat as small and weak and abandoned as me," Joan said, and flicked another tear from her eye, because even though the joking was fun, it kind of didn't matter how old you were, fifteen or twenty-five—abandonment was still abandonment.

CZ planted a kiss on the top of her head, furthering his *small* theory, but only because he was over six feet and she was merely five ten.

"You hungry?" he asked. "We can go somewhere, or we can go to my new apartment. You owe me five dollars."

"Yes to everything," Joan said.

"They're not going to be furious you didn't go straight home?"

CZ asked, knowing better than to pose such an obvious question but asking anyways, to be polite, because CZ was a LaMorte vampire the same way Joan was a Greenwood witch; they both lived at the whims of their families.

"They absolutely are," Joan said, disappointment morphing into annoyance in the safety of CZ's arms. "I just don't care at the moment."

CZ squeezed her shoulder. "So bold! Bets on how long it lasts?"

She huffed a laugh. "One hour, max."

"I'll be the optimist this time, then, and say two."

An hour later they were leaving the café they'd stopped at—because even if her mom hadn't remembered her, Joan's restaurant research didn't need to go to waste—so Joan could have a huge, late lunch and CZ, who did not consume human food, could watch her eat with a vaguely disgusted look on his face. It was familiar and comforting and meant absolutely everything to Joan as she tucked into her messy sandwich.

Once she finally reached her family, she would not be allowed to dine so sloppily. There would be napkins in laps. She'd have to fix her posture. All meals would be spent contemplating which utensil would best allow her to gouge her own eyes out. She had to enjoy it while she could as the minutes counted down.

The café had been almost entirely human, though there were plenty of magical creatures who worked service roles, hidden in plain sight. CZ was chattering in that way he did to keep Joan's mind off things. About his pack, something his brother, Abel, had said, and a fae he'd met recently at the magical underground market run by Moon Creatures, a classification of magical species encompassing the fae and vampires that were tied together by fabled connections to a single mythical ancestor, Empusa.

"Do *not* hang around Times Square. There's a new information broker there who frolics with pigeons—nasty—and the pizza place on 42nd that you liked closed."

"Kill me now."

"And there's a new witch family gaining power, the Proctors or something. They're cutting deals left and right in the Night Market, but jury's out on if anyone likes them or just their money. Oh, and that witch who can create new spells—Grace something— she's being courted by all the New York elite, but she's based in Brooklyn."

"Dad can't be happy about that," Joan murmured. Merlin collected interesting people like they were coins, keeping them in drawers until the time was right. The ability to create new spells was quite rare, and Merlin would be extra pissed off if Grace ended up working for Wista Redd, the High Witch of Brooklyn, rather than Merlin's sister, Valeria, the High Witch of Manhattan and Head Witch of New York State.

"Your dad isn't happy about anything," CZ said. "That's what happens when you're a dickbag."

Joan didn't correct him—Merlin was the king of dickbags, and half of Joan's life was playing out fictional arguments with him in her head, thus keeping her therapist in business—and CZ continued, cycling through the most pertinent changes to the witch world before swapping into the vampire one, then the fae one.

There were myriad magical creatures, but only three factions with populations large and organized enough to hold political sway. Witches, who were the smallest group at thirty million worldwide, set the laws that kept the magic world hidden and regulated trade across the human-magic border. Then there were vampires, who numbered sixty million, and the fae, who were over eighty million, both with lobbyist groups and microgovernments. The rest, the ancients—dryads, harpies, banshees, a thousand other creatures with different names across different cultures— were old magic, and mainly unconcerned with the human world. They kept to themselves and ranged in population from only a few dozen to less than a hundred thousand worldwide.

CZ had moved on to a story about his brother's new boyfriend when time ran out for Joan.

Her phone vibrated incessantly, and the caller ID showed her sister, Molly, which was smart, because Joan might have been a bitch and sent her father to voicemail if he'd been the one to call.

"Mol," Joan said by way of greeting. CZ raised an eyebrow, checked his watch, and then dug in his wallet to hand her back her five.

"I'm so sorry," Molly said, loud over the din in the background. "I just realized."

Over an hour late? CZ mouthed at her with exaggerated movements.

"CZ met me," Joan said in reply, turning from CZ so she wouldn't laugh outright on the phone.

"Of course, oh good," Molly said, and the noise started to dim. "I'm really sorry, I mean that. It's, well, it's been kind of a morn- ing at work. With the family."

"It's midafternoon," Joan said.

"It's been kind of a morning and midafternoon, whatever. Are you close? Aunt Val's—um—well, I think you'd better come. There's been an event."

"And people want *me* there?" Joan asked incredulously, and she hated the note of wanting that seeped into her voice. She was the child who refused to come home, the one who had received all the finest training at witch prep schools but *still couldn't cast actual spells*.

"*Well*." Molly drew out the word.

Which answered her question perfectly.

"Tell me even a single one of them remembered I exist and I'll come home right now," Joan said. "Tell me Mom or Dad or Aunt Val said, just once, 'Where's Joan?' and I'll sprint uptown. Gods, an *event*. Whatever the fuck that means."

In the high-drama world of Joan's family, that could indicate truly anything: Someone had gotten the wrong napkins for the latest witch soiree. Merlin's watch had gone missing and tracking spells weren't working to locate it. Perhaps New York was caving into a magma bath and the Greenwoods, as the family in charge of the state, were responsible for pulling the earth back out.

Molly's silence was a death knell. No one would leave Molly at a train station. She had recently started a position at the family's investment firm.

She sighed loudly over the line. "Jo—"

"Don't make excuses for them," Joan said, and CZ wrapped a hand around her arm, squeezing sympathetically.

"Joan, I'm only saying this over the phone because I suspect the news is going to hit everyone else in like an hour, and CZ's going to know, and he's going to tell you anyways, and I know he's listening right now with his super vampire ears, and I'm evil and rotten and my ancestors are ashamed of me, but, Joan, come home now. There's been a rumor—"

Joan snorted. "A rumor."

"That we've spent all morning verifying," Molly continued. "A human who managed to ascend to witchhood via some kind of spell. The whole magic world's talking about it."

A wave of horror smashed through Joan's body, leaving the hairs on her arms standing upright in its wake.

That was impossible. A complete nonstarter—witchhood was inherent, not gained. Credited to a single shared ancestor, Circe, earning them the classification Sun Creatures. And only witches could cast spells or channel magic; ancients and Moon Creatures had innate magic that tended to manifest in physical abilities, like speed, heightened senses, or fae shape-shifting.

Humans were entirely unmagical—the softest, weakest species and nothing more to witches than moneymaking sheep to herd. The magic world operated beyond the sight of humans to hoard resources, not out of fear.

Hearing this was like being told the sheep had turned into Godzilla. It was just not possible, not without threatening every structure and hierarchy that witches held so dear.

But impossibilities didn't earn her a call from her sister. Impossibilities didn't send her family scrambling to verify it.

CZ drew back and pulled out his own phone. Joan knew who he was calling without seeing his screen—his older brother, Abel, heir to the powerful LaMorte pack in Queens.

"You're sure?" Joan whispered.

"Every source we have is saying the same thing: A human managed to become a witch and is now casting," Molly said.

CZ whipped around, eyes wide, before responding to his brother on the phone, too far away to be audible. That was all the confirmation Joan needed.

"Come home, Joan," Molly said. "Now."

"On my way," Joan reported, and the line went dead.

TWO

They parted at the mouth of the subway station with promises to call each other later that night and recap their respective families' level of sheer alarm, CZ heading toward the human side to take a train to his pack's headquarters in Queens and Joan heading uptown via the HERMES transport network to the Greenwood Mansion, her heart lodged in her throat, strangling her half to death.

As she fumbled in her duffel bag, fishing for the black plastic card she hadn't used in nearly a year—dredging the horrible depths of her disorganized packing job and dislodging Chap-Sticks, receipts, a small lotion, pens, more pens, an endless stream of pens—she was left to parse *why* exactly Molly's phone call had unsettled her so.

On the surface, it was obvious why this news would send the Greenwoods straight into a panic. If humans started becoming witches left and right, they'd need to be properly taught and acclimated to witch society somehow, which would be a burden on the magic world's infrastructure. If it was a spell that made this happen, then the Greenwoods wouldn't want that power in any random person's hands—they'd want to control how the witch population grew, and when, and who these newly turned humans were loyal to.

There would be those in the witch world who viewed this as a threat to their power. Joan, however, cared little for the power of witches. That was the byproduct of not being able to cast herself, an affliction entirely unheard of before her birth—sometimes children were born without the ability to channel magic and were thus deemed human, but no one had been born *with* the ability to channel, indeed an unusually strong ability to channel, yet completely unable to control the magic with spells. Without the power to form magic into spells that could influence the world, Joan's ability to channel was utterly useless. Like drawing breath but never actually processing the air in her bloodstream—inhaling without breathing. She had been forced to find other ways to define herself, and an architecture degree, grad school, they had all guided her forward.

She located the dingy card and jogged down the steps, swiping the card through a nondescript seam in the wall tile and stepping through an invisible barrier with the surface tension of a bubble. The moment she was through, the noise of a thousand commuters faded.

Inside the HERMES 51st Street Station, a large, polished lobby greeted her. Anywhere there were major transit systems, witches had hacked them, creating mirror realms over human stations and using portals instead of trains to move faster. Witches were entwined deep in human history and innovation.

Joan navigated quickly to one of the four lines, picking the one she thought would move fastest and, as always, somehow managing to select the slowest. She tapped a foot impatiently, pulled out her phone, and put it back. There was no reception here. Too much raw magic charged the air, and though it was present everywhere, latent in the world, anywhere witches concentrated, it could sicken humans and mess with electronic signals. Magic was only manageable when schooled into spells.

Around her, all types of witches murmured to one another scandalously. Apparently, Molly hadn't had as much of a head start as she thought, because as Joan shuffled forward behind an East Asian man and a South Asian woman, she could hear their excited whispers.

"It can't honestly be true."

The woman scoffed. "If it were, someone would have figured out how to do it by now. Why today? Why now?"

"Something old that the historians unearthed? Or a hobbyist? I don't know," the man guessed. "Or a new spell."

"They keep track of spellmakers. If it's new, then the person behind it would be a fool to send it out to the public without letting the Greenwoods know."

"Unless the Greenwoods *do* know," the man said with a waggle of his eyebrows. "Who's to say they're not the ones behind this?"

"Valeria seems too competent to leak it."

Dad would, Joan thought. *Anything to try and destabilize Aunt Val so he can get named Head Witch of New York.* The fast way would have been to challenge her to a Scales Law duel that granted the winner their opponent's social title and property, but doing so would weaken the family.

"Merlin might." The man's voice hushed here, and he glanced around fearfully without actually noticing Joan, which was fine; she was kind of a recluse, so people likely didn't know her face that well. Plus, it had been seven years, and in that time, Joan had cut all her ringlets to her collarbone, gotten a septum ring, nose ring, cartilage piercings, a couple of tattoos—

"Next," the attendant called, and the man and woman stepped forward to show their black cards and identify a destination. The HERMES system was nationwide and extended from the local subway portals to secret airport-like buildings that could pop you across state or country lines.

No one around her seemed overly concerned with the news; it was still just a rumor. To them, maybe it wouldn't make a difference at all if humans could become witches. Maybe it was the dawn of an amazing new age, a way to shift the demographics to favor their kind and force a closer merger with the human world, though witches tended to enjoy the exclusive club that was the magic world.

Why did Joan feel so concerned, then?

If Joan were a good little soldier, she'd already be thinking about telling her family the news had hit and people were gossiping that the Greenwoods themselves were behind it. Joan liked to think she was not a good little soldier, even though she was currently on her way to the Upper East Side because her older sister had said *Jump!* and Joan had replied *How high?*

"Hello?" said the attendant, an androgynous white person with perfectly coiffed blonde hair. Likely for at least the second time.

"Right, sorry." Joan fumbled her card out again, nearly throwing it at them. They were clearly not paid enough to put up with her nonsense, and they swiped it nimbly out of her hand and held it to the magicked tablet that registered her identity.

Their eyebrows shot up. "Joan Gre—"

"Madison, East 63rd," Joan interrupted, with what she hoped was an apologetic smile but maybe was more of a feral grimace. *Please do not out me in this subway station, dear gods.*

"Of course," the attendant sputtered, turning to the massive mirror behind them, raising their hands to cast in a few quick movements that helped shape the spell they were forming.

Joan stepped through the mirror, in one side and out the other, entering the next station with the feeling of walking through mist.

Shaking off the odd, small feeling of vertigo that resulted from changing locations so abruptly, she hustled up the stairs, really starting to feel grimy from the hours-long train ride, then the sweating around New York City. The Greenwood family mansion (one of several, but the main one) was around the corner, and when she arrived at the front gate, she needed only to put a hand on it for the powerful wards to recognize her and open up.

It was her aunt's house, technically, and the central working hub of New York witches, though the whole Greenwood family lived there. All the (many) windows were lit up as she approached through the small front courtyard, though the only person outside was George, Merlin's ghost chauffeur, sitting on a bench and going fuzzy around the edges the moment a breeze shifted through him.

"Miss Joan!" he said excitedly, standing up.

"George! Is that a new bow tie?" she teased.

"Did you just get in? Who picked you up?" he asked, wearing the same dark blue bow tie he'd probably been wearing for thirty years at least, his suit crisp, his gray hair slicked, and his mustache well oiled. Merlin didn't like to be reminded that George was dead, so he was in a mostly corporeal form, with colors solid enough that he couldn't be seen through.

"No one," Joan said cheerily. "Well, CZ. I was completely forgotten about until Molly called."

"Ah," George said sympathetically. "Welcome home, then." Ghosts didn't classify as a specific magical species, as everyone died eventually and almost no one really wanted to, so they tended to hang around for ages until the universe recycled them. Magical creatures, though they lived much longer than humans, moved on the quickest, since their magic usually got folded back into the worldwide magical currents long before humans did.

Joan hopped up the first step to the door. "How bad is it in there?"

"Judging by the number of people who have come and gone… quite," George said pleasantly. "But, of course, the spells are meant to keep me from overhearing."

"If only magic worked on ghosts," Joan said dryly. But it passed right through them. No body, no way for magic to manipulate it.

George gave a little bow. "If only, Miss Joan."

Joan shook her head with a laugh and hopped up the remaining stairs to the door before placing a hand on the knob.

But her hand wouldn't turn.

The moment she crossed the threshold, their problems would become hers. She was here to serve the family and whatever the family was wrestling with. She'd been eighteen when she left for college, and she'd never had any real responsibilities, being so young, but what contact she'd gotten from her parents over the years had been clear: *We paid for your degrees, so now you return home to do as we say.*

"Miss Joan?" George asked politely.

"Sorry, George," she replied softly. "Cold feet." Another breeze made goose bumps rise on her arm.

"I think often, Miss Joan, about how few things there are in this world that cannot be undone."

Joan whipped around, searching his face for some deeper meaning, but it was perfectly composed, as always. George was unwaveringly committed to Merlin in death, as he'd been committed to Merlin's father in life. Joan had spent years trying to worm her way into a joking relationship with him, and what they had now was as far as he had ever seemed willing to go.

But that statement hit her like a truck.

There were so few things that could not be undone. She stepped over the threshold. She . . . could step back one day. One day.

She could do that; she could change her mind later.

Carved into the stone above the door, the Greenwood family logo looked down on her, a coffin with a scythe in the background, wrapped in ivy.

Joan pushed the door open.

Inside, witches bustled from one side of the grand lobby to the other, their voices joining in a murmur loud enough to drown out the edges of Joan's thoughts. The two-story lobby was framed by double curved staircases on either side, and as the door shut resolutely behind her, no one paused in their various quests.

There were menacing-looking witches watching everyone, dressed in matching black uniforms. Likely a private defense company that had been contracted by the Greenwoods to guard the house, which was a truly terrible sign of what was to come. The average witch knew only a small amount of offensive magic and certainly wasn't trained for physical combat. These witches looked lethal.

Well, now that she was here, she would need to get things over with: find her family, listen to them talk at and over her for a while, retire to her childhood bedroom upstairs, sob in the shower, call CZ. A nearby potted plant stretched its leaves out to her in her agitation. It wasn't real witchcraft; the magic in plants just liked Joan a lot.

If she knew her family—and despite her recent best efforts, she thought she did—they would be in Valeria's study on the first floor.

Joan shoved through the crowd, stepping past expensive vases, priceless wall art, and the grand chandelier to fight her way to the wooden double doors of the study.

"You can't go in there," a sharply dressed witch said, half stepping into Joan's way.

Joan shied back in frank shock. "Why not?"

"The Greenwoods are having a private meeting," the witch said impatiently, tucking their long black hair behind their ears. "Wait out here."

"The Greenwoods are having a private meeting," Joan repeated faintly. She clamped down on a *do you know who I am?* because that was obnoxious, and this assistant or whatever was just trying to do their job. But come on now, this was a bit ridiculous, wasn't it? Did she have to be on some sort of guest list to roam her own childhood home? Worse, was she so entirely unrecognizable? She'd passed portraits on her way over, an endless stream of stately oil paintings. Grandparents, great-aunts, distant cousins. Down the hallway Joan could see her mother's portrait done in deep brown skin tones, her father's pale face staring down at her, Valeria's stately grace and eternally gray hair, Molly's springboard curls and brown skin—but not Joan.

"Okay, can you please move?" Joan said, trying not to be mean but really starting to reach the end of her roughly one-inch rope.

The witch looked alarmed. "I said—"

"Pardon me," a voice said behind Joan. "I think we're meant to join that meeting?"

Joan whirled to find a frankly gorgeous Black woman behind her, dressed in a neat dark blue button-down and black pencil skirt, sensible heels on her feet. Her box braids were pulled back into a matching blue scarf. Her lips were a respectable dark red. Her chin was held high, which gave her a commanding enough aura that her complete lack of height was less noticeable.

She was looking at Joan as curiously as Joan was looking at her.

Beside her was a white woman with orange-brown hair, dressed in very expensive-looking clothing. She barely glanced Joan's way.

"Ms. Collins, Ms. Ganon," the doorkeeper said, "we've been expecting you. Please step in." They nudged Joan out of the way, knocked, and opened the door, ushering *Ms. Collins and Ms. Ganon* inside.

Joan came to her senses in time to wedge her foot in the door as it closed—which, *ow*—and bodily shoulder the outraged gate-keeper to the side so she could palm the door back open.

"Ma'am!" the witch cried, wobbling before they lifted their hands, settling into the start of a binding spell Joan could recognize on sight alone—even if she did suck at casting, she still knew all the standard spells by heart.

"Oh my fucking god," Joan ground out, shoving the door open wider to reveal the study. "Someone tell this person I am a Greenwood."

Inside, Valeria, Head and High Witch of New York and Manhattan, respectively, was sitting behind her massive wooden desk in a lovely gray suit. Her lips quirked in the ghost of a smile as she looked at the door, and Joan, the flustered attendant, and Ms. Collins, who had wheeled in alarm, though this Ganon woman was scanning the room.

"Francesca, darling," Valeria said, "you don't know Joan, my niece?"

Someone, presumably Francesca, gasped like she'd been shot in the stomach, but Joan's pride kept her from turning. Pride and maybe some animal instinct that knew better than to put her back to her father, Merlin Greenwood, who was standing behind one of the large leather armchairs, gripping it like it had personally wronged him, his salt-and-pepper hair looking a little run through.

"Joan!" Molly said, rising from the couch where she'd been sitting next to their mother, Selene. "Sorry, I forgot to warn everyone you were coming."

"She should have been recognized on sight," Selene said disapprovingly, her wavy black sew-in gathered neatly over one shoulder.

"Forgive Francesca; she's new," Valeria said. "And you, Joan, never come home."

"I am so sorry!" Francesca said, on the verge of a wail, and Joan wouldn't have been surprised to find Francesca had fallen to her knees in outright horror at the faux pas, but Joan still wasn't turning around; she was accepting a hug from her sister, who was wearing neat beige work attire that blended in perfectly with all the wood and leather in the sizeable study.

"Hey, Mol," Joan said softly, pulling her sister to her chest, avoiding eye contact with their father over Molly's back. "Can you maybe euthanize me real quick? Preemptively."

"Sorry again," Molly whispered.

"Joan!" Merlin said, straightening. "You're back in town?"

This was the first knife to Joan's ribs.

"You're early, aren't you?" Selene said with a frown, another knife.

"I sent you all my information," Joan protested weakly.

"She's perfectly on time," Valeria said. "You two forgot about her."

"So did you," Merlin replied, a bit petulantly.

"I did not. I simply never made any promises to her in the first place." Valeria rose from her chair. "Come here, Joan."

Joan obediently separated from Molly to hug her aunt, becoming acutely aware of her own griminess as she pressed against her aunt's silk shirt. "Sorry," she muttered generally, because it seemed the safest way to cover her bases.

"You really should have showered before coming here," Merlin said, having made no effort to cross the room to her. "You look a mess."

"Merlin," Selene sighed, rubbing her forehead in irritation, but also not moving from her seat. "Joan, you should have called. I'd have sent a car."

Ms. Collins cleared her throat. "Should we come back?"

"Nonsense," Valeria said, having already left Joan to sit back down. "We need your expertise, Grace. When we called Fiona in, she insisted you come with her. She says you've studied with her?"

"I did, back home in Atlanta," Grace confirmed. "She tutored me in spellmaking."

Fiona smiled, wire-rimmed glasses glinting on her face. "My best student."

Grace... why is that name familiar?

The room resumed their work as if the youngest Greenwood child hadn't just returned home to build a life here after seven years away.

Joan let her bag slide off her body, ignoring Merlin's disapproving glare when it thumped onto the Persian rug.

Valeria forged on. "Fiona's been throwing around the word *prodigy* like it's nothing, but you did always have a flair for the dramatic, didn't you?"

Joan, staring at Fiona Ganon's back, watched it stiffen.

"I don't use the word lightly."

Valeria's smile was icy. "I assume you've both heard about this ascended human?"

Grace kept darting nervous glances Joan's way as Joan noisily took a seat in an armchair, but Grace cleared her throat and addressed Valeria. "I have heard, yes. At least, the rumors of a human who seems to be attracting magic."

"We have eyewitness reports of a human channeling magic into some sort of light spell last night before disappearing into the Night Market. We are beyond the scope of rumors," Selene said dryly. "Witches on the scene confirmed a spell signature that indicated the human had been cast on."

"Our top priority is, obviously, ascertaining how this happened," Valeria said, picking up the threads. "A new spell? A freak accident? We need to know, and we would like you to stay close by, should you have any insight into how one might achieve these ends."

"Do you?" Merlin said. "Have any insight?" There was a sharp, suspicious gleam to his eye. "Perhaps Wista Redd employed you to—"

"Enough, Merlin," Valeria cut in. "This is not an accusation."

Merlin threw up his hands. "Maybe it should be. We've been getting nowhere all day—no one can point a finger, but everyone knows a finger must be pointed."

"So, you're looking for both the human and the witch who must have changed them? I can assure you, I did not write such a spell," Grace said. *Grace. Grace, Grace, Grace who has ties to Wista Redd in Brooklyn*—oh, *CZ mentioned her.*

"Neither did I," Fiona said. "I got into town only an hour ago."

"All we have is your word," Selene said apologetically, always smoothing over what Merlin had done. "We know Fiona, but you, Grace, are a new player on the scene."

Joan gnawed on her knuckle to avoid letting out a scream. Selene made meaningful eye contact with her.

Joan removed the knuckle from her mouth, a chastised toddler.

She had to quietly get through being in this room. Despite the fact that she wanted to crawl out of her skin expeditiously. Time away had lowered her tolerance, she could feel that acutely. Merely existing in here made her a bit winded. Her body still knew what her mind had tried to bury—looking at Merlin, she saw every screaming match they'd ever had. Every school play he'd ever missed, every senseless comment that had hurt her feelings. Looking at Selene, she saw every time her mother had apologized on her father's behalf, then proceeded to tell Joan it was easiest to just do what he asked.

Fiona leaned into Grace subtly, a small signal sent.

"I will submit to a truth spell," Grace said, her voice carefully level. Rehearsed, like she had expected this. Smart. Or maybe completely naive, to expect this and still walk into the room.

"Perfect," Merlin said, rolling back the sleeves of his dark gray button-down, "I'll do the honors." His eagerness rubbed Joan precisely the wrong way—as did his personality, his dismissal of her, the fact that he had forgotten his own child was coming into town—and she felt she might burst as waves of familiar ire crawled up her chest. She was so, so mentally unstable. Her previous commitment to silence vanished into thin air.

"No, no," Joan said, just to be a complete dickhead. "Let me."

"I see your time away hasn't cured you of your poor sense of humor," Merlin replied.

"No, I remain deathly ill in that regard," Joan said.

A smile flickered across Grace's lips before she crushed it like an ant.

"Be gentle, Dad," Molly said with an apologetic smile in Grace's direction. A smile Grace did not return as she faced Merlin's magic with her spine ramrod straight.

Joan watched with her arms crossed tightly over her chest as her father's fingers danced in the air. He muttered a string of words under his breath as the truth spell took shape. The most advanced spellcasters could manipulate magic without moving or speaking, but Merlin certainly wasn't among them.

Not that Joan was in any position to judge.

Magic, latent in the air, thickened into threads and flowed toward him to be caught and manipulated by the bounds of the spell. Unlike most witches, Joan could see it without the help of spelled glasses. Like ghostly hands around Grace's neck.

"Grace Collins," Merlin said, "did you write the spell that produced witchhood in a human?"

Grace's voice came out of her in a burst. "No."

"Do you know how to craft a spell like that?" he continued.

"Only the basic considerations—you need to first grant them the ability to channel magic, then teach them to shape it. The former is, as far as I know, an impossibility on any sort of permanent basis. Spells fade, eventually, as they use up their magic manipulating the world."

Words pushed at Joan's lips. *And on a temporary basis?* she wanted to ask. Could someone temporarily grant themselves the ability to attract magic? But she was not going to help her family with this quest; she was still trying to puzzle out why she cared at all.

Valeria spoke up to tack on a question. "Do you have knowledge of anyone who might be able to create a spell like that?"

"Not specifically," Grace said. "Any spellmaker could write it, but I can't think of one who might have possibly solved the problem of how. No one was publishing research on it, at least."

Merlin did not look particularly strained by the spell, likely because truth spells weren't so far off from persuasion spells, which were his specialty. Grace, on the other hand, was gripping her handbag so tightly, it was pushing the blood from her fingers.

"Let her go," Joan cut in.

The room looked at her, as if remembering anew she was even here.

"She can handle it," Fiona said. She was vaguely familiar to Joan; perhaps they'd met before. If the family wasn't making *her* undergo a truth spell, then they must have worked with her rather extensively in the past.

"If you have no more questions," Joan added. "It's not good for her, and I can't imagine you're winning her favor by forcing her to do this. I thought we wanted her to work for us."

"She submitted willingly," Merlin said gruffly.

Valeria waved a hand, and Merlin released Grace after a few moments of deliberate hesitation, just to prove Valeria didn't control him (even though she did). Grace sagged, looking for a moment like she might collapse entirely under the strain. But as Joan prepared to lunge out of her chair and catch the woman, Grace straightened.

Fiona kept her chin high. They were close, Joan could see that, but not close enough for Fiona to look anything less than perfect before the Greenwoods.

"If I learn anything, you will be the first to know," Grace said to Valeria.

Valeria hummed a pensive note, sitting back in her chair. "I want you to recreate it."

"Valeria," Selene said chidingly. "We agreed that wasn't a path we wanted to go down."

"That was several hours ago, when we thought our informants might turn something up and we could squash it or buy it off this rogue witch," Valeria said. "This is now. Someone's already cracked it, and I cannot deal with a spell I do not understand. We're well past simple containment. Grace, recreate this spell. You will have whatever resources you need at your disposal. Fiona claims you will be better positioned to do such a thing than she is, but she'll help you. Or not; I don't care which of you it comes from."

Grace's lips pressed into a line. She slid a glance Fiona's way. "I don't feel that sort of magic is to be messed with."

Merlin clucked his tongue, a patronizing smile on his face. "Leave the repercussions to us, Ms. Collins."

Grace's hard gaze settled on Merlin, unflinchingly. Joan was beginning to feel like she wanted to befriend this woman, and quickly.

"She'll do it," Fiona replied. "Her abilities allow her to see and predict the movement of magic; it's one of a kind and makes her spellmaking more advanced than mine."

"Of course I will," Grace said in acquiescence, giving Fiona another meaningful look, and the moment Valeria dismissed them, Grace was out the door.

Fiona hesitated a moment longer, gaze tracking to Joan curiously, but Valeria sent her an impatient glance. "We'll be in touch, Fiona."

Fiona's mouth snapped shut. She nodded, once, and left.

Joan had seen enough social climbers to recognize one on the spot.

"She wants an official place in your employ," Selene said, once the doors had closed behind them. "You know that."

"If she can solve this spell for me, I'll give it to her gladly," Valeria replied. "We are our reputation; we cannot risk this spinning out of our control. Whoever holds that spell could gain unimaginable financial, political, and social power."

"Hell, if she can solve the spell, *I'll* make her rich," Merlin said, fingers drumming. "If we can control that sort of magic, we control the humans entirely. An endless supply of people grateful to the Greenwoods for giving them power."

"That is not what we'll use it for," Valeria said. "We won't be growing the witch population recklessly."

Merlin huffed. "Like how the vampires can turn anyone they want, on top of biological procreation? They outnumber us two to one. Don't get me started on the fae population. They have a million kids each, all guaranteed to possess abilities and, worse, outlive us."

"Then it's a good thing we're not at war," Joan said sharply. Merlin wasn't the only witch who nervously eyed the vampires' ability to turn humans, but with the power and money he wielded, he was one of the most dangerous. It was a small mercy he wasn't technically in charge here, but there were plenty of people like him across the witch world. In California, witches trained in offensive magic and operated as a sort of police presence, enforcing witch rules on other magical creatures.

"Don't be naive, Joan," Merlin dismissed, not even paying her the courtesy of looking in her direction.

"The vampires keep track of their own population, produce very few biological children, and there are rules about turning humans," Valeria said.

"Rules *we* set in place," Merlin countered. "Rules that they could, at any moment, decide to stop following."

Joan groaned, loud enough to make a point, and rubbed her face.

"Maybe you want to go upstairs and shower, my love?" Selene said, not unkindly, but still a clear indication that Joan was absolutely not needed here.

Joan kept rubbing her eyes, and eventually her family settled back into their discussion about next steps, but her brain was humming with new information. *I don't feel that sort of magic is to be messed with.*

Was *that* why this news had freaked Joan out? Some feeling that they were messing with cosmic forces whose consequences could be vast? No, that was too abstract.

Her family was in a real, genuine tizzy with this news, the house was full despite the evening hour, and they were calling in spellmakers, both people they'd worked with before and random witches who had no track record of loyalty, to do things like craft forbidden spells. And it was in such contrast to the HERMES and the buzzy but generally nonchalant way the news had hit all the regular magical creatures in this city. Exciting, but not disastrous.

Joan sat up straighter.

That was it. She didn't have some personal fear of the repercussions of this power. No, as Joan looked around at her bickering family, she saw why this news unsettled her—because she didn't know what her family would do.

Because Merlin was already talking about turning his own personal army.

Because Joan wasn't afraid of what humans might do with the ability to become witches or what another witch might do with this magic—she was afraid, very specifically, of what lengths the Greenwood family would go to in order to protect, to *grow*, their power.

Shit.

THREE

Joan excused herself from the room after fifteen of the longest minutes of her life, swinging by the kitchen to raid the well-stocked pantry for whatever dried fruit was Selene's latest obsession and then getting in the shower.

She stood under the spray, contemplating her family's alignments. Valeria, at least, had said she didn't intend to turn humans into loyal followers en masse. She could typically be trusted to keep her brother in check. But Joan had been away for a long time, and Merlin had spent his life obsessed with the Greenwood legacy. This was a major carrot dangled in front of him.

She exited the shower. Her childhood bedroom was a patterned green, and it looked like something out of *Architectural Digest* rather than the mind of a ten-year-old because Joan had only been allowed to pick some colors, not the actual furniture. Children ruined interior design, her parents had explained to her—in vaguer, more passive-aggressive terms than that, but the message was clear. This would always be the official Greenwood residence, not so much the warm, fuzzy home of a kid.

She had a queen bed as the centerpiece and a small balcony off to the side. The adjoining bathroom was also green and respectably large. By the time Joan emerged from her shower to pull wrinkled pajamas out of her duffel bag, the house was still buzzing very faintly with noise.

It was abominably early, but she'd rather be crushed in a trash compactor than venture back into that hellscape downstairs, so Joan got into bed and closed her eyes, just for a second. She'd had a very hard day and deserved a moment of rest.

She woke to darkness outside her window and her phone vibrating on her nightstand. She'd been awake only a second ago, and the level of disorientation she was now experiencing forced a despairing groan from deep in her chest as she slapped around, trying to pull her phone to her ear. Her watch indicated it was one AM, which was embarrassing, because it had been no later than five thirty when she closed her eyes.

Words wouldn't form in her mouth, so she kind of made a high-pitched questioning noise, like a particularly fucked-up bird.

"Oh, finally," CZ said, panting slightly, which meant he was really in a bind, because he truly didn't need much air. "I need help."

Another bird noise, this one slightly more formed, but still unintelligible to anyone who wasn't her best friend in the whole entire world.

"You didn't call me, so I assumed you were sleeping, or dead; I didn't know which you'd find preferable. Anyways, I went on with my life after meeting with my family and took a little stroll around the Night Market and— No don't touch that, okay, okay, sit tight—" CZ's voice muffled as he talked to someone in the background.

Joan managed to coherently say his name and hoped she'd tacked a question mark onto the end.

"I need you to come over," he said. "I have committed crimes the likes of which the world has never seen."

That woke Joan up. She threw the covers off her body, darted a glance at the door, and still cupped her hand over the phone to shield her voice. "Murder, CZ? On my first night back? Really?"

"Not murder—TRASH CAN, THROW UP IN THE TRASH CAN—something worse."

Joan scrambled to get out of bed, looking desperately for a pair of pants. "*Worse than murder?* Also, who the fuck is there?"

"The person I stole," CZ said.

Joan set her phone down on the dresser to shimmy into her joggers, leaning toward it to whisper-scream, "You stole a person!?"

"Get here first, answers after you arrive, and hurry up. I need to go clean up vomit," CZ said, and hung up the phone. He texted moments later with his new address.

Though she was utterly bewildered, Joan's hesitation was nonetheless brief. CZ called, she answered. This was a law of the universe. The only uncertainty was how to get out of the house. It sounded like people might still be awake, which made sneaking down the corridor risky. The only other way out was . . .

Joan rifled in the back of her closet and was relieved to find her rope was still in its little, innocuous box, left between several sketchbooks and her clarinet from when she'd been forced to pick up the instrument for two years until her parents begged her to stop making such gods-awful noises.

She pulled the rope out triumphantly, and the movements returned like muscle memory—throw open the balcony doors, tie one end to two of the metal bars, swing her leg over the banister.

She'd snuck out in high school this way many a time, mainly to wander the grounds and sketch because she didn't really have friends to party with. After Joan twisted her ankle once and made enough noise that Molly had caught her, Molly had then been so kind as to charm the rope to make Joan semi-weightless when on it, and thus less likely to crash down to her untimely death.

Time had eaten away at the spell, dwindling the amount of magic that had been pushed into it during Molly's original casting. Luckily it still held, though it was less effective.

Joan was grateful for it as she lowered herself into the hedges, remembering only when her feet hit the carefully manicured mulch that she hadn't jammed shoes on. She pulled herself back up to gain a pair of sneakers.

By the time she was darting around the house for the side gate, she was enormously sweaty from all the stress. Joan was reaching for the handle when a voice cut through the courtyard.

"You know you're an adult, right?" Valeria said, and Joan yelped, effectively annihilating her stealth mission. Valeria was sitting on a stone bench, entirely shrouded in shadow. Her gray hair was unbound, loose around her shoulders.

"You just sit out here? At one AM?" Joan gasped, clutching her chest like she was one hundred and eight. "Shouldn't you be in bed with your wife?"

"Ronnie gave up waiting for me on nights like this long ago," Valeria said. "Don't deflect—as I was saying, you are an adult. If you'd like to leave at all hours of the night, you can exit through the front door instead of over the balcony on that ridiculous old-fashioned rope."

Joan straightened her hoodie self-consciously. "You know about that?"

Valeria's returning look was long-suffering. "I know about everything on these grounds."

"Do Mom and Dad?"

"This isn't their house," Valeria said. "Technically. All the spells are keyed to me. What they don't know won't hurt them. Besides, I thought it was funny. A rope, Joan? An honest-to-Circe rope? What are you, a pirate swinging from the mast of a ship?"

"Better than a string of bedsheets," Joan grumbled. "I'm going; don't tell anyone."

Valeria's chuckle was soft. "It's good to have you back in town, Jo. But don't worry, I won't hold my breath waiting for you to say it back. Be careful out there."

Joan nodded her agreement, unsure if Valeria could even see her through the darkness, before slipping out the gate, orienting herself toward Hell's Kitchen, and taking off.

Joan hadn't been to this apartment before. It was new, the result of a pay raise at CZ's soulless, corporate Wall Street finance job. And generational wealth.

She knew it had been a little bit of an *event* in his family when he moved—his brother lived close to their parents and aunt in Queens, as it was their pack's home territory. But CZ had insisted on carving out a life for himself away from their long shadow, and it had taken him here.

The exterior looked like every other New York apartment building in the area, and Joan texted the moment she hit the front door to be buzzed up. The response was instantaneous.

As she climbed the steps to his unit, sweating even worse than before, her thoughts began to catch up with her. CZ had kidnapped someone. Likely for good reason; CZ wasn't prone to making bad decisions. He was silly sometimes, sure, naturally rather nocturnal, and he could drink you under the table, but he was a good guy, Your Honor, and she'd testify to that effect on the stand.

Before she could knock, CZ was practically ripping the door off its hinges, a wild look in his red-brown eyes.

"Finally."

"I can't run at superspeed," Joan said, stepping inside without preamble. "Oh my god, this is so much space."

"I know, right, and it was a deal. I feel like it needs a renovation, blackout curtains, whatever—you'll have to design it for me, Mister Big Man Architecture, and find me some nice plants to liven the space up," CZ said, gesturing at the entryway, the kitchen bordering it, the living room beyond. It was a warehouse-esque space with exposed metal rafters and impossibly high ceilings.

"If you dodge the federal kidnapping charges, absolutely," Joan said.

"Right." CZ closed the door, then locked and deadbolted it. "Mik!" he called. "Come out!"

Well, the person was at least not chained up, another point in CZ's favor. A likely indication that it wasn't a full kidnapping. She'd present this evidence on the stand beside her testimony. It was unclear if this would be a witch trial or one set in the human world—maybe a vampire one? She'd need to be prepared for all legal systems.

From the block of rooms at the back of the rectangular space, someone shuffled out of a doorway, a trash can in their hands.

Their head was shaved close, their skin a very light sun-darkened brown, and their cheekbones high, rounded, and flushed red.

They were dressed in a hoodie Joan could recognize as CZ's and boxer shorts that Joan guessed were also CZ's.

Joan turned to CZ, eyebrow raised. "A hookup?"

"What, no," CZ said, walking to Mik's side and gesturing at them. "Joan, this is Mik. I found them at the Night Market and had to lend them some clothes after they threw up on theirs because of the magic."

"Hi, Mik, I'm Joan," Joan said, walking forward and offering a hand.

Mik stared at it, dazed and sweaty. "I'm sorry for my appearance," they said. "I'm having a really bad night. Or week, really. A bad life."

"We've all been there," Joan assured. "The market's magic can be tough on humans, but the adverse effects will fade in a few hours." Any creature would get magic poisoning from a high enough dose of raw magic, but humans had the lowest tolerance.

"Oh no, sorry, wow, I really didn't explain *anything* on the phone, did I?" CZ said with a wince and a laugh that bordered on delirious. "This isn't because of the Night Market—this is a reaction to their own magic."

"You're a witch?" Joan blurted. She'd assumed human based on how sick they seemed. "Did you channel past your limits?"

"I'm not a witch," Mik confirmed. "I don't remember much, but I remember that. I am totally human."

Joan made meaningful eyes at CZ, *explain what the fuck this is* eyes.

CZ performed a stupid flourish. "Joan, let me introduce you to the human who recently ascended to witchhood: Mik Batbayar."

Mik, to punctuate this point, threw up in their trash can.

FOUR

This was, maybe, the worst-case scenario.

"I'd rather you'd killed someone," Joan said, pacing the floor.

"Hey," Mik said weakly, a bag of wrapped ice on their forehead as they reclined on the couch.

CZ stood protectively over Mik with his arms crossed. "Trust me, I also would rather I killed someone."

"*Hey*," Mik said, louder this time.

"Of all the people in New York to bring home, you chose some-one witches are *desperately* searching for?" Joan said, pointing viciously in Mik's direction. "My family wants them bad; they want to know how to replicate the spell."

"My family is also looking for Mik, as are the fae, most likely," CZ said. "Maybe even people beyond the regular Sun and Moon Creature split are looking for Mik. I don't know! Maybe the fuck-ing dryads are looking for them! I am well aware of how hunted they are. Witches aren't the only ones interested in the ability to grant casting magic to another species."

Fuck. That made sense.

"It's my fault," Mik said. "I begged CZ for help. I was...very disoriented. I don't remember anything that's happened in the last week. My name is Mik, I'm from New Jersey, I come into the city regularly. I work in book publishing. I heard about a magic market that happens in Owl's Head Park at night, which was a total joke, but my coworker managed to score us an in, so I thought—okay, maybe it's a really cool market, I wonder what sort of tricks they're playing to make people think it's *magic*. I went a week ago and then"—Mik made some exploding gestures with their hands—"poof. Gone."

"Until tonight," Joan prompted.

"Until last night. I woke up in a strange tent, no coworker to be seen, stumbled outside, and just kind of took off running. I didn't know who was after me or whatever? But I had a feeling someone wanted me, and I had to get out. And I freaked out, and it had been so dark in the tent, and, like, a bunch of light burst out of my skin and everyone was looking at me, so I ran and hid. I moved every time someone got close. For like a day, but then I was getting hungry from all the throwing up, so I was looking for food and trying to figure out how to get out of the damn market because maybe my parents could help? And I ran right into CZ."

"Casting magic is nullified within the Night Market," Joan said. "How did you cast a light spell inside the borders?"

"It's not totally nullified for them," CZ countered. "But whatever they were doing was pretty tame, until I got them out of the market bounds and things kind of exploded."

That was its own question, tacked onto an increasingly long list of them.

Mik went on, their tone growing in urgency. "Do you think my friend is dead? She wasn't even really a friend, more an acquaintance. But I got out, and one moment I was shoplifting some food—"

"Fae food," CZ muttered. "I thought I was rescuing some hapless human from dancing all night. I'll never be merciful again."

"You save humans from the market all the time," Joan muttered back.

"And then CZ was showing me out of the market," Mik continued, a worryingly frantic gleam in their eye. "And telling me to go home. But as soon as we crossed the boundary, I got scared and...I don't know, *reached* for something, and it felt like a tornado was funneling into my body, but I had no idea what to do with all the energy, and then I passed out, and when I woke up, CZ was carrying me. I threw up on myself."

"Nightmare, by the way," CZ said, wrinkling his nose. "I guessed that they were indeed casting based on the way Mik described it as funneling energy. Then the nausea—that happens to you too!"

It was true, when Joan attempted to cast, she usually felt a great gust of energy flowing through her before her spell broke and she got nauseous. And now that Joan focused, she could see the way magic was curling curiously around Mik, attracted to them.

"It's not necessarily casting," Joan murmured.

"You're going to be pedantic right now?" CZ said.

"I'm just saying. Casting is the part where you manipulate magic into changing the world, through spells typically. Mik is mostly just channeling, like what I do. Do you know spells, Mik?"

"Maybe some rhyming stuff from books. Is that real?"

"No." Joan hesitated. "Mostly no. How did you make the lights burst from your skin?"

"I said, 'I wish it wasn't so fucking dark,' and then something happened—ah!" Mik slapped at their arm, where a tiny orb of light was emerging. Joan's gaze snapped up to where an unsteady tide of magic shifted toward Mik.

"That's ridiculous as fuck, is that a spell?" CZ asked.

"Mik, say *never mind*," Joan instructed, watching magic wind through Mik. This was actually rather fascinating, and for just a second, Joan wondered if a spell like the one on Mik could grant *her* the ability to cast properly.

Another orb emerged; Mik scratched at their skin. "Never mind, never mind! I really don't want this—oh, I'm gonna be sick again." They gagged, but the light snuffed out.

"Spells are containers for our desires," Joan said. "Words, gestures, they create an impression of our will, and witches have found that certain words, in certain orders, under certain conditions, can produce consistent results with magic. Hence learned spells. But usually any witch will have a special affinity to a type of magic, and magic will respond to your simple desires without having to use a formal, preestablished spell."

"So Mik has a light spell affinity, probably," CZ said. "Mik! Congrats!"

"Can we get back to the story?" Joan said. "All this happened, and you decided to bring Mik here. Here, of all places."

"The fuck else was I supposed to do, leave them half dead on the ground, throwing up, while magic swirled around us like a homing beacon?" CZ protested, looking meaningfully at Mik. *I was saving my own ass* was the implication, and that was probably true, though Joan was suspicious. CZ did regularly save humans from a prowling vampire or teasing fae. But she couldn't believe he was silly enough to save *this* human while knowing they were also now a witch. Probably. Maybe.

He was such a softie.

Joan sighed, scrutinizing them both. "Mik, setting you loose in the world seems like a bad idea. Going to my family isn't an option."

"Or mine." CZ paused a beat too long, dredged his next words up from the bottom of some deep well. "We need to figure out how to reverse it; it's clearly making them sick, and it was against their will," he said miserably. "We should figure out who did this to them, before they do it to some other human."

Help them. CZ wanted to *keep* helping them. *Keep* harboring them. Protect them from several of the most powerful magic factions in the city. Find out who *made them a witch*.

"Cane," Joan said warningly.

CZ threw his hands up, helpless, flustered. "Well, now that they're here, how am I supposed to kick them back out? They are seriously unwell."

"I am," Mik said. "I am so unwell." Their eyes were big and beseeching. "I'm unwell and I can't go home to my parents like this. Right? I can't, right?"

Joan searched desperately for a way out. Helping Mik would be throwing their lot in with a sinking ship, and Joan and CZ weren't particularly capable people, something they'd spent many an evening lamenting, Joan drunk and CZ regrettably sober. They were second children, and though CZ did his best to help his family where he could, it was his brother who would be in charge one day.

But what *were* they supposed to do with Mik? Pack them a lunchbox and put them on the street corner to wait for a bus that would never come? Little more than blood in the predatory water of New York City? They were sick. They were sick and—and Joan didn't want her family to be the one to find them.

Against her better judgment, Joan was feeling curious herself about what this spell could do.

So maybe it was empathy here, and maybe it was because CZ already seemed rather implicated, and maybe, just maybe, it was selfishness too.

"Cane," she groaned.

CZ, clearly having gone through all five stages of grief before Joan even arrived, and having landed on helping Mik, sensed her crumbling resolve and latched on.

"It's fine, it'll be breezy. We find out how to undo it and never tell anyone about this ever. You're unemployed, you've got time," CZ pointed out. "And my apartment is warded."

Joan's glare could melt steel beams. "Uncalled for. I'm between jobs."

"Unemployed with a trust fund," CZ said. "So, you're helping? I'd really like you to help me, because the more we talk about it, the more certain I am that I can't throw them out onto the street at this point, pesky morals and all, but I also really don't know what the fuck to do here. At least you managed to help them when they did the light thing."

Mik moved the bag of ice back over their eyes. "I've probably been fired by now for missing a week of work. Maybe it's not that bad? Could I go home and grab some clothes and stuff, buy a plane ticket? Disappear off the face of the earth? I don't know."

"Mik, I really don't mean to scare you, but you will be more than fired if the people after you get their hands on you. They will dissect you," Joan said, and saying it out loud was the final nail in her coffin. Her family wasn't touching a hair on Mik's shaved head. Not one tiny little stub of hair.

"Tell me you don't mean that literally," Mik said, sitting up.

They hugged their arms to themself, fingers digging into the flesh of their biceps. "What the actual fuck are witches doing?"

Anything, anything they could. Joan had seen her family screw people over again and again. Humans, Moon Creatures, ancients, even other witches were all pawns for the Greenwoods to move across a board, to use and discard. No one wanted to be the one who lost the Greenwoods their five-hundred-year legacy of power, so anything was fair game. Even holding a human against their will and tormenting them with magical experiments to reverse engineer this spell. Joan had watched Valeria and Merlin ruin reputations, run families out of the city, mandate that vampires turn new vampires only within strict quotas, and even put attendance limits on certain fae revels to keep too many of them from banding together at once. All in the name of order. Power.

"You have no idea what kind of awful things they'll do to stay on top of the magic world," CZ said bitterly. The Greenwoods had kept their boots on the necks of the LaMortes for centuries. "Plus, you can't afford to keep channeling magic and making yourself sick."

"We should keep you here," Joan continued, before swallowing past the tightness in her throat. "At least until I determine if my family can come up with a counterspell or a cure or whatever, and then I'll steal it. Just . . . give us some time. Stay here."

"But—"

"Mik, I know we haven't known each other long, but I'd like to think we're friends now," CZ said.

"A stretch," Mik muttered.

"And as your friend, I am asking you to give us a few days. I know maybe you can't parse the magnitude of how fucked we all are, but Joan and I are *really* fucked if we're found harboring you, and we have no idea what happens if someone else finds you. But, at minimum, if whoever took you originally gets their hands on you, they will probably continue whatever sick experiment they started. So. Stay inside. It's a nice apartment—isn't it a nice apartment, Joan?"

"It's dusty," Joan said. "But nice."

"Dusty but nice!" CZ exclaimed.

Mik, after a long moment of silence, grunted. Joan chose to believe this was acceptance and waved CZ over so they could whisper by the door.

"Okay, you need to subtly ask around the Night Market to find out what happened to Mik and their coworker a week ago," Joan said as they bent their heads together.

"And you need to use your big, sexy brain to figure out how to undo this, before the magic poisons them and makes them puke their organs out," CZ said, bobbing his head along vigorously.

"I am not qualified for that," Joan said. "And I can't cast anything that will undo this spell, not without chaotic, sets-fire-to-things consequences."

"But you've gotta know something? What leads does your family have?"

Nothing, apparently. They were spinning their wheels; they didn't even know that this rumored human-turned-witch was someone in their early twenties who clearly hadn't wanted this. They were looking for a witch and human like they might be in cahoots, when they should be looking for a solo witch with completely unknown intentions who was willing to kidnap to reach their goals.

All they had was . . .

Grace Collins, the spellmaker. And if pressed, maybe Fiona

could be motivated to help Mik, if Joan could promise her the right things. But Grace was apparently the more skilled of the two.

"I've maybe got something," Joan said begrudgingly.

"Perfect, keep me updated," CZ said. "I'm heading back to the market before it closes to see if Mik's disappearance made any ripples. You stay here and watch them."

"What? I have my own house I snuck out of," Joan protested, but CZ was already putting shoes on. It wasn't fair; he'd had too long to think this all through, and Joan's feeble brain was only now catching up.

"Mik, Joan's gonna take care of you!" CZ called out. "Be back soon!"

Another groan.

"Have fun!" CZ said cheerily, and shut the door in Joan's face.

Joan risked leaving Mik alone long enough to run to a twenty-four-hour pharmacy to get anti-nausea meds and whatever food she could get her hands on, since CZ's fridge was mainly décor. Décor filled with blood bags he got on ration via one of the many vampire bars that regulated blood distribution. Joan felt it was best Mik not look in there.

After a very brief crash course on the magic world and spellcasting specifically *This shit is real?* Yes. *You're like an actual witch?* Yes. *With a broom?* That's a myth. *But you cast spells.* Witches do, yes, but I specifically can't control my spells, so I usually avoid them. *That sucks.* Thanks—they watched TV while waiting for the meds to kick in and swapped backstories.

Joan was the misunderstood artist child of a prominent witch family; Mik was the second-generation immigrant child of two humans from Mongolia whom their parents had pinned their hopes and dreams onto, before they failed them by going into publishing.

Mik and Joan argued at various housewives in the show, then passed completely the fuck out before CZ returned, almost entirely empty-handed. Two missing humans wasn't a big deal in the market. Humans went missing all the time—dinner for a vampire, a toy for the fae. Victims of their own curiosity. Truthfully, Joan wasn't optimistic Mik's coworker had survived. But everyone was still buzzing with the news that some human had ascended. Rumors were beginning to spiral out of control. Mik was the greatest con artist of their generation. Mik actually wasn't a witch. Mik was a four-headed rat that had been blasted with magic by accident one evening and mutated.

Joan was quite fond of this last theory, and even Mik found it a little funny.

The next morning, Joan traded off the babysitting shift with CZ after confirming Mik's nausea had faded, fairly certain they'd be okay so long as they stayed calm. They seemed to channel only when upset, like their body was unhappy with the world and reached out to magic to change it until Joan managed to distract them or talk them down. All they had to do was keep Mik temporarily calm. And around enough light that they didn't panic and accidentally summon more orbs.

And locked up in a strange man's apartment.

Joan returned to her own family with haste.

She entered through the front door this time and marched straight for Molly's room, only to find it empty and bare. Unlived in.

It was almost eight AM, and enough of the house had risen that Joan could go down to the kitchen, corner the chef—very nicely—and ask about Molly's whereabouts.

"She's likely at home, Miss Joan," the cook said, pulling out a container of oatmeal.

"She's not up there," Joan countered.

"I mean her home in Tribeca, with her boyfriend." The chef was too familiar with the Greenwoods to be much bothered by Joan.

"Molly moved out?" Joan blurted in shock. "And in with Nate?"

"A few months ago," the chef said, finally sparing the youngest Greenwood a pitying glance.

Oh, Joan was terribly out of the loop. She was so out of the loop, she didn't even know what the loop was.

"Do you have an address?" Joan asked, and waited impatiently for the chef to write it down for her before she ran upstairs to brush her teeth, change again, and pull up the rope still dangling from her balcony. She fled the house as she saw her father emerging from his suite, his eyebrows furrowing at the sight of her.

"Joan, where are you off to?"

Nowhere was her best and most pedantic answer.

"Did you eat breakfast? I'm about to eat; we should chat about your job prospects."

"I'm busy."

"Doing what?"

"Meeting CZ."

Merlin's face transformed into something long-suffering, the beginning of an argument about who Joan spent her time with that they'd had one thousand times already. Didn't he ever get tired of hating absolutely everything Joan did? Everyone she chose to hang out with? Couldn't he, just once, say she had done something right?

Worse, why did she keep giving him chances? She still lived with the family, despite how much she ragged on them. She still accepted their money. She still yearned to find her place among them. She still hoped when Merlin opened his mouth, he might be saying something perfectly normal instead of starting a fight.

"There are some people I want to introduce you to tonight who might be a better use of your time than running around the city with your vampire."

"I'm busy," Joan repeated, and luckily some random witch in her family's employ walked past, distracting Merlin long enough that she could book it out the door.

In Tribeca, Molly's town house was on a quieter side street, and Joan stormed up the steps to pound on the door.

Molly's boyfriend of over a year—at least Joan knew *that*—answered, a puzzled but kind smile on his face.

"Joan? Welcome back," he said. He was in work attire, a businessman like Molly. His family owned some hospitals, Joan thought. His curly hair was only a few shades darker than his warm-brown skin.

"Thanks, Nate," Joan said, heart still beating a little too fast from talking to Merlin. She really needed to schedule an appointment with her therapist. "Is Molly home? I need to talk to her."

Nate shifted out of the way so Joan could step inside. It was a very cute house, tastefully decorated in warm tones, and Joan fought against her admiration so she could remain pissed off her sister hadn't told her about this.

Molly was sitting at the breakfast nook, nursing some coffee, when Joan walked in.

"Uh-oh," Molly said, putting down her phone.

"You didn't tell me you moved out," Joan accused, trying not to sound sulky or get too distracted by the gorgeous tile backsplash in the kitchen.

"I didn't think you'd come back to New York if you knew," Molly admitted.

"And what did you think I'd do once I got back and realized?"

Molly shrugged. "I don't know, I thought you'd be in too deep to leave at that point. You *are* in too deep, right?"

Joan had joint custody of a magical fugitive, so yes, she was in way too fucking deep, but she wasn't going to give Molly the satisfaction of admitting that.

"I'm off," Nate said, leaning down to kiss Molly's cheek. "Joan, I hope you come over for dinner sometime soon?"

Joan really could not be mean to Nate, who clearly was obsessed with her sister, as she felt the dynamic should be in a straight relationship. "Maybe," she grumbled. "Probably. Yes."

"Wonderful," he said, and gave her a half hug on his way out the door. "And the party thing tonight, I'll see you there? We can catch up."

Joan made big, pitiful, questioning eyes at Molly.

"She'll be there," Molly answered. "Dad's orders."

Nate huffed a little laugh. "Sorry, Joan," he said, and made his final exit.

Molly was still looking after him with a sappy expression on her face when Joan snapped her fingers. "I fucking hate people in love," Joan grumbled.

"Of course your single ass does," Molly said, rising to bring her cup to the sink. "Is everything okay? Normally you're passed out until at least ten AM."

"What's this party?"

Molly's back was turned and her wince subtle, but Joan still saw it.

"What, Molly?"

"There's been another event."

Joan groaned. "I can't handle more events. We aren't even finished with the first one."

"News hit California," Molly said, sitting back down and leaning forward, the charm necklace she always wore swinging from her neck. It was filled with luck magic, Molly's specialty. "They're sending someone to watch us."

Joan levied another mighty groan, for the drama of it all, and sank into the chair across from her sister. New York was the most powerful witch state in the US, but California was a close second. The population density of magical creatures was high there, and a number of institutions, academic or otherwise, sported some very impressive witch thinkers. The Wardwells, who ran California, hated the Greenwoods with a mutual passion. Joan was pretty ambivalent on the topic, but it made everyone around her snippy, which she'd rather avoid.

"Who're they sending? Poppy?" The High Witch of LA and Head Witch of California was, Joan would freely admit, a woman she didn't want to meet in a dark alley. Or a lit one. Or at all. California's witch patrol system was everything Joan despised, a malignant evolution of human policing that fell victim to its same inequities.

"Astoria Wardwell," Molly said. The daughter, then, heir to her mother's empire. "It was Poppy, but we negotiated them down to Astoria last night while you were asleep. Official word is they're here to help."

Joan had absolutely not been sleeping, but she wasn't going

to reveal she'd been harboring precisely the person everyone was searching for instead. "And unofficially, they're here to figure out the spell before we can."

Aunt Val had said she didn't intend to use it to turn humans, she wanted to understand it to stop it, but California had not and would not make any such promises. Joan wasn't sure what she wanted here—was it fair to wipe knowledge like this spell from existence? Deny humans the chance to cast? It was making Mik horribly sick, but maybe another spell could cure that. Or maybe humans wouldn't care, and they'd kill themselves with magic poisoning in their quest for power. Scores of untrained humans, suddenly casting—that was dangerous.

Who was Joan to decide all this? Whatever the moral implications, she would leave that to smarter people to puzzle out. She could get an ethics lecture from Abel wearing his professor hat later; what she needed now was to focus specifically on helping Mik. She could do that, she could conceptualize that—one innocent person in need of Joan's help.

Molly blew out a breath. "I've been named Astoria's babysitter, and in the interest of cordiality, we're throwing a get-together tonight to welcome her to New York."

"And try to intimidate her," Joan muttered. Gods, now they were going to have New York *and* California after Mik. "I need Grace Collins's phone number. If you don't have it, I need you to secretly get it for me."

Molly's eyebrows rose inquisitively. "Why?"

Deny, deny, deny. "No reason."

Molly's eyes said, *You can't fool me*, but Joan wasn't the teenager she used to be. She'd grown at least a little bit of a backbone in college, so she kept her mouth shut.

"I'm not giving it to you without a reason," Molly said, which was what Joan had been afraid of. She flitted through her most compelling lies, ready to roll one out with all the fluent charm of a Greenwood: *I want her to write me a spell, something innocent to help me figure out where I should be applying for jobs. I think I can convince her to help us; she looks around my age, and I'm a bit of an outsider, so maybe she'll trust me.*

But she didn't have to use any of them, because Molly, bless her heart, jumped to her own conclusions.

"If you think she's hot, just say so," Molly said. "I'm not entirely sure that's a good enough reason for me to get her number for you—I mean, if you were a man, I'd definitely call it stalking—but I really want you to find someone."

For once in Joan's life, her gayness was working out *deeply* in her favor.

"Yes," Joan said slowly, like a robot. "Grace Collins is a smoke show."

This was true, but simultaneously, Joan didn't actually feel attracted to the woman. She was beautiful, but like a work of art, and Joan didn't want to kiss art. Well, not totally true—there was something beautiful about a Zaha Hadid architectural drawing or an Auguste Toulmouche painting that maybe she did want to kiss. With tongue. Respectfully.

Grace Collins was neither of those; she was a Kehinde Wiley— gorgeous, fascinating, a *liiiittle* too photorealistic for Joan's tastes.

Molly was still talking about how Joan needed to open herself up to the world, date seriously, find love like what she and Nate had, all in a well-meaning though kind of patronizing manner. When Joan had come out, Molly hadn't even blinked, which maybe wasn't a surprise considering Valeria's lesbianism and the fact that most witches didn't follow human religions. Or any religion. Hard to worship other beings as gods when you had the power of one. When you were reportedly descended from one.

Even among people who valued biological children to pass witch traits down to, witches followed power, and power set the structures of their world. It mattered what you could do more than how you loved or who you were, so much so that even interspecies children who could cast were given access to training. CZ had a couple of witch-vampires in his pack.

"Molly?" Joan interrupted. "The number?"

Molly sighed. "I'll text you. I have to go to work. I'll see you tonight? Find something to wear or let me know if you need help."

Hmm, Joan was supposed to be babysitting Mik tonight, but she was likely going to attract Molly's suspicion if she showed up abruptly, asked for a woman's number, then cited vague plans she couldn't reschedule, all after a single day back in the city. Especially since Molly knew that Joan's plan for her return was mainly to fall into a deep depression and lie in bed for weeks until she rotted away and died.

Which, perhaps, explained why Molly was so desperate to believe Joan was trying out dating.

This was also, unfortunately, probably what Merlin had been trying to tell Joan that morning when he'd said he wanted her to meet some people.

"Thanks, loves yah," Joan said on her way out the door, skipping down the steps feeling much better about her prospects. At least in terms of solving the Mik problem. In all other, broader aspects, her issues had tripled, top of the list being California's forthcoming presence. Joan had sort of known Astoria, once. They'd gone to one or two summer camps together as children when they'd all been learning to cast, then again as teenagers when they'd all decided they hated themselves, as teenagers often did. Astoria had been eternally silent, a rule follower Joan had never been able to provoke into laughter. Fierce, but quietly gentle, and in the end, uninteresting to Joan.

While Joan hadn't seen Astoria in nearly a decade, she'd heard plenty of rumors about how the other woman had changed. Astoria Wardwell was a highly trained machine now, her mother's bloodhound.

Their timeline had just shortened.

FIVE

Joan got the text from Molly with Grace's number not even an hour later, accompanied by a warning to not come on too strong. Also, please make sure to find a suitable outfit for tonight, Mom is worried you're going to wear jeans.

Joan promptly texted Grace: Can we meet up today?

And was rewarded about thirty minutes later with: who is this?

Oh sorry, Joan Greenwood, we met yesterday? I'd love to take you out for coffee? I can meet you wherever you want

Perks of being unemployed.

*Unemployed with a trust fund.

respectfully, I don't need a minder, I promise I will report on my findings the moment I have them.

Joan: Ono coffee date

She elected to skip over the minder accusations, because maybe if Grace felt like this was an order from the Greenwood family itself, she wouldn't be inclined to blow her off, as Joan would be inclined to blow off a stranger who had somehow procured her phone number.

Joan had to wait another twenty minutes before Grace replied.
i can do 12:30. Buy me lunch

After a trip back uptown to shower and take intense psychic damage from her father, who tried to corner her into another conversation about the Manhattan architectural firms he wanted her to interview at, Joan took the regular subway to Brooklyn, because she had time to kill and because, if she was being very, very honest, she didn't particularly enjoy watching witches cast.

She was old enough that she'd long ago accepted her own shortcomings, but after extensive therapy, she knew she hadn't necessarily *forgiven* herself for them. Even if she, long before her parents and aunt, had given up on herself—spitefully, hopelessly—she still saw people around her doing incredible things and felt acutely what she could not do.

Mik was a long shot. Maybe if a very smart person reverse engineered the spell on them, they'd uncover the basic mechanics of a witch's power and determine why Joan could channel but not cast. And, critically, fix it. And maybe then Joan's depression would be cured and her skin would clear and her crops would flourish. Or maybe the parameters of a spell geared toward granting a human the ability to channel magic could not realistically explain why a witch could channel but not create spells strong enough to contain the magic she pressed into them.

Joan was going to choose to live in the optimism though, if only privately, and quietly, and with a little hopeful thrill that she fostered in her like a tiny orb of light.

She hopped off at the 36th Street station, found the café Grace had picked, and realized she still had thirty minutes to kill.

Enough time to order a chai, pull out her sketchbook, and idly draw as she tried to determine her next steps.

What was she actually going to *ask* Grace? *How do you undo this mystery spell?* The Greenwoods had already asked that, and Grace didn't know yet. *What are the potential side effects?* Seeing Mik, Joan had a pretty good grasp on them.

"Ordered without me?" Grace said, appearing behind the chair in front of Joan suddenly enough that she yelped and sloshed her drink a little.

Grace raised an eyebrow as Joan dabbed at her hand with napkins. "You had a clear line of sight, how did you not see me coming?"

Joan fumbled with her sketchbook, hastily closing the scene on the café drawing, and checked her watch to confirm that no, it had not been thirty whole minutes, Grace was fifteen minutes early.

"I make no excuses for my idiocy," Joan said, putting on a weak smile. "Thanks for meeting me. I ordered a drink to kill time."

Grace thumped into her chair. "Well, I ordered food, so now you're behind."

Joan grumbled as she rose, because she did not, as a rule, miss meals. "Okay, power play."

Grace's smile was utterly beguiling. "Like forcing this meeting was a power play?"

A laugh burst out of Joan, soft and surprised. "Be right back."

After ordering, Joan slid back into her chair and steeled herself for the coming conversation. Sincerity, she would try that before the many tricks she'd seen her family use to get what they wanted. "This meeting was not meant as a power play. As you will likely learn, I have very little power in my family. I needed to talk to you. Off the record."

Grace was sitting neatly in her chair, in a way that almost reminded Joan of Valeria's impeccable elegance. Her braids were tied back in a dark green headscarf this time, and she was in stylish work attire.

"Off the record," Grace mused. "What is this about? I'm not inclined to do any more favors for the Greenwoods. I only did it in the first place because Fiona's been on me to try and establish myself in the New York scene so I can settle into an area of research and make a name for myself, like her."

Hostility toward Joan's family, she was used to that. It was intriguing, though, that Grace would take so bold a stance without a family to back her. Joan had asked around the house as best she could that morning—Grace Collins had been born to two humans, one utterly unmagical and the other with sleeper witch genes, who never manifested the ability to channel. They ran a pizzeria, and her entire family was in Atlanta, Georgia, not here. If Fiona hadn't noticed Grace and taken her in, she wouldn't be on the radar of New York at all.

"I thought you hadn't picked a borough to work for yet," Joan said.

Grace tapped her fingers. "Who says I'm going to work for any borough? I have a chemical engineering degree; I can easily work only in the human world."

Huh. A spellmaker shunning their gifts to stay out of the witch world? Grace Collins was only getting more interesting.

"Time's ticking," Grace said, as their food was delivered and she picked up her sandwich.

Alright, fuck it. Joan was getting bogged down in the big picture, trying to play politics when she should be focusing on the details. In architecture, when Joan hit a dead end in one perspective, she swapped to a new one. *Forget plans, try elevations. Forget drawings, try models.* "Forget how the spell was made. My family asked you a string of questions yesterday, but what did we forget to ask you?"

Grace stopped eating. "What are you getting at?"

"You're a spellmaker, we are not. And I won't fall victim to the same ego that fuels my family. What did we fail to ask you? I'm sure there's something." Joan could already think of one thing; she'd thought the question herself—Grace said it was impossible to pull off this spell long term but hadn't clarified its potential temporary possibilities. If she was right, maybe whatever this was would wear off Mik eventually.

Grace's long hesitation was filled to the brim with obvious suspicion, but she answered anyways. "Power source. A spell like that is a constant drain, and you'd need to find some way to keep it automatically renewing. You're fighting against the human's basic nature by granting them the ability to attract magic, casting ability aside. There would have to be some constant level of magic expended. Maybe with enough effort, you could take a look at the magic patterns in New York and see if there was somewhere it was all funneling. The city's in constant chaos, eating up and spitting out magic, but a spell this complex *and* this consistent, if tracked over time, might be visible."

This was terrible news for hiding Mik, but— "Did you tell my family this?"

Grace shrugged, picking up her sandwich. "Like you said, no one asked."

"And you…aren't worried about this ascended human? Enough to try and track them down? Or the witch who made up this spell? We have no idea what their motives are." A new thought dawned on Joan in a burst of brilliance. "Or you're working for someone else, helping them find the person first."

"I can almost see the lightbulb above your head," Grace said with a snort. "But no, I'm not double agenting the Greenwoods. I have a greater sense of self-preservation than that. I personally don't care if a human became a witch. It doesn't pay my bills or put food on my table. I'm sure the witch did it for the chance at money—a spell like this could make you a modern-day king, with the right bidders, but that's so boring. Whoever did this was a genius. How *does* one make a human attract magic?"

Grace launched into this topic with a curious gleam in her eye. "That's interesting to me. While magic twists unconsciously through witches at some low level at all times, humans are never permeated."

"Because it makes them sick?" Joan said, prompting her on as she ripped into her own sandwich. "The body's natural defense against something that makes you unwell?"

"Right. So if humans have some level of protective barrier, then witches have a much more porous one. To make a human a witch, you'd need to punch a bunch of holes in that barrier to allow magic to flow through. That's how you unlock channeling, and casting is just a matter of learning spells, like all witches do."

Didn't mean the spells would *work*.

"But that doesn't solve the fact that humans aren't made to process magic." Grace was clearly energized by the thought, which didn't seem like the actions of someone ready to give up spellmaking to work in the human world.

This all meant something profound to her.

"It's an interesting reframing of the problem," Grace theorized. "If we keep breaking it down into smaller pieces, the question isn't how to get a human to cast, it's how to get them access to magic. And it isn't just how to get them access to magic, it's how to make it so they can tolerate it."

Okay, here went nothing. Joan focused intensely on her food to avoid looking at Grace and seeming too eager. If they couldn't "fix" Mik entirely, they could at least help make it so their life wasn't so miserable and sickening. "And how *would* one make it tolerable? Do we at least know the answer to that, if not any of the other bits?"

Grace didn't look amused, not at all. "What are you up to?"

"Lunch, mainly."

"You're here for my help."

"They're innocent questions."

"I kind of doubt *you're* innocent though."

"You wound me, Grace Collins. I'm wounded," Joan said, even as her mind danced a little jig, looking for a rip cord to get out of this conversation.

Joan was two seconds from spilling her drink on herself so she'd have an excuse to skitter away like a bug up a wall when Grace's flinty stare flicked away, her displeasure melted into something more accommodating. Joan had seen it many times—people giving up on trying to figure her out.

"Reducing the harm of magic instead of blocking it entirely?" Grace's fingers were back to drumming; her gaze had become distant, far off, as she returned to Joan's question. "In some ways, that's an old question. Magic poisoning doesn't just affect humans—it can rip through a witch too if they channel more than they're naturally built to. No one's answered it though. The pain we feel is the body's method of saving us from potential death; it's critical. That's Fiona's research interest, and she's on the cutting edge of it, but even she hasn't cracked it. It's hard to imagine some random did it before us."

"Us?"

Grace snapped back to the table abruptly, gaze clearing. "I work with Fiona a lot. I think she's hoping that if she never cracks magic poisoning, I will. But nonetheless, you're the first person to ask me these very good questions."

Joan gave a nervous laugh, aiming for *oh, you know me*, instead of *I am hiding a person in Manhattan*. "I'm an outside-the-box thinker."

"Makes sense," Grace said. "What with your own unusual magic."

Joan was piling dirty napkins onto her plate, longing for a moist towelette to wipe her greasy fingers. "What about my magic?"

Grace waved a vague hand. "You don't have any barrier at all. A current of magic does not enter you and take a new shape; when a current of magic enters you, it exits in the exact same form. Fi and I have never even heard of anything like this."

"How do you know that?"

"I can see and predict magic without the intervention of magical tools."

"Huh," Joan said unintelligently. Though Joan could also naturally see magic, she couldn't see herself from a third-party view and had never seen herself cast successfully, nor paid too much attention. She hadn't heard this about her channeling before and had no idea what any of it meant. But that wasn't her priority at the moment; Mik was.

Grace had taught her two key facts: Someone could track Mik with enough effort, and Mik must be somehow linked to some broader power source or perhaps even the caster themself. Maybe they could follow that thread back to the source.

Grace sighed, clearly mistaking Joan's furious hamster wheel thinking for disengagement. "I'm boring you, and my lunch is nearly over. My best guess is that the way to reverse or mitigate the effects is the same as stopping the spell as a whole—seal the witch's magic. We have the spell for that. Essentially, a team of witches can thicken that barrier so the subject can't channel. If you can locate this person, you can seal them. But I've told your family all this already, before they made me trek all the way to the Upper East Side. So has Fiona, so have all the spellmakers the Greenwoods have called up. The other problems, how to keep the magic from corroding a person, they're all secondary to this fix. I know it doesn't help track down the witch who did this, but it would undo whatever was done to this human."

It took Joan's brain, stumbling toddler that it was, an embarrassingly long time to catch up to the implications of Grace's statement.

"If it's that simple, why are they making all this fuss about figuring out how the spell works?" Joan asked, dread settling in her. Valeria had said . . .

Grace gave her another Look. One that was equal parts confusion and exasperation. "Is this a test?"

"I am genuinely asking," Joan said, desperately afraid of the answer. "If they know how to undo it, why do they need the spell recreated at all? They can seal people to control the consequences of a spell like this being released."

Grace rose from the table. "Why do they need a spell to turn humans into witches? Gee, I don't know, Greenwood, maybe to *turn humans into witches*?"

Valeria had claimed—and Selene had said . . . but Merlin. Merlin had stated the obvious. It didn't make sense why Valeria would say they weren't going to recklessly turn humans and then commission the spell.

But maybe the operative word had been *recklessly*.

Valeria didn't do anything without careful consideration, but that wasn't a guarantee she was never going to do the thing.

And with California after the spell, it seemed all the more likely Aunt Val's restraint had been little more than a stall. Grace could be lying, but as Joan sized her up, every horrible thing her family had ever done stacked the scales. It was much more believable that the Greenwoods really were looking for a way to capitalize on this spell, no matter what they'd said last night. Hell, since Joan had left the room yesterday, they'd also planned a party and determined Astoria Wardwell would be coming to town.

Joan wasn't necessarily the first person they'd tell if they had plans to use the spell to create loyal followers. It didn't even seem like they cared about motive. Grace could chalk it up to a witch wanting to sell the spell for incredible wealth, but if that were the case, wouldn't they have gone public by now? Mik was an escapee, and the spell on them was unfinished, but even a partially finished spell would be worth an incredible amount of money. It made Joan think there was something else at play.

"Grace," Joan said, as the other woman turned away. "Do you think it's right? Doing this?" *Do you think it's okay?* Because for Mik, it seemed like torture.

Grace lifted a shoulder, dropped it. "I told you all at your house—I don't think this is magic to be trifled with. But I don't set the moral code of the witch world, people like the Greenwoods and Wardwells do. The rest of us are cogs in a machine; ethics don't factor into my ability to turn."

"But they should," Joan said. "It should be your choice."

Grace pulled her purse up higher on her shoulder and snorted. "Like working for the Greenwoods is 'my choice'? No, Joan. When your family calls, the magic world bends. It doesn't matter if I work for Manhattan or Queens or Brooklyn—I'm only free if I stay out of the witch world entirely." She gave a half wave. "I'm only free if I coven break and turn my back on everything. This has been profoundly interesting. See you around."

"Wait—Grace, those aren't your only options," Joan said, standing in a rush. Coven breaking was a serious split from one's family, community, or state at large. The term covered both a self-imposed, informal exile and something more official.

"Is this where you say I could work for you specifically?" Grace called over her shoulder, not breaking stride. "Pass. You're clearly after something, and I don't like being used."

No! Joan wanted to scream, left behind with her crumbs and her doubts. This whole lunch soured in her mind. She had forced that woman to come here and talk to her. It hadn't been kind. It had been all sorts of desperate. Joan *was* using her, but Joan didn't have a choice in the matter. She had to dig herself and CZ out of a Mik-size hole. She had to dig Mik out of their own coffin. Her hands were tied.

That was probably what Merlin told himself so he could sleep at night.

Six

~~~~~~~~

Joan stayed out of the house for as long as she could.

She'd have stayed away for eternity if it had been possible, but Molly's indication that Joan's presence had been requested at the evening's party was reinforced with a call first from their mother, then from George, because Merlin didn't debase himself by talking on the phone.

She was taking her shift at CZ's, watching Mik sleep, as the clock ticked down.

Mik had, reportedly, woken up, eaten, watched TV, re-organized CZ's entire apartment, attempted a breakout, been thwarted, and was now sleeping again. Joan had quietly cleaned CZ's kitchen so the space seemed a bit more livable, running her hand over the raggedy money tree CZ was rapidly killing on the counter and watching it perk up under her fingers.

Mik was still sleeping by the time she finished with all that, so Joan sat down.

They were wrapped in a knit blanket on the couch, the TV low, snoring in a super ugly, kind of adorable, deliriously funny way. Joan recorded a video. Or two. Then second-guessed herself, because they really didn't know each other that well and maybe this was bullying.

A socked foot dug into Joan's thigh. "Where are you going tonight? CZ said he'd be home early to take over." Mik yawned, stretching obnoxiously as their shirt rode up to reveal a cute stretch of soft belly. "You can head out if you need to."

"What, so you can make another escape attempt?" Joan said half-heartedly. She was not CZ; if Mik ran, she didn't possess the strength to stop them. She could *maybe* cast and blow up the whole building.

"Yes," Mik said. They flopped onto their back. "No. How was your meeting with the spellmaker?"

"Only sort of helpful. I mean, the good news is I think we know how to fix you, we need to seal your magic, but that usually takes four witches in tandem and I'm just me," Joan said. "Bad news, apparently, you're probably a constant magic suck, and once someone else figures that out, they can generally track your location. Sort of medium news—that might mean you're linked to whoever did this to you."

"Then can't I surrender myself to witch authorities? Won't they strip me of the magic?" Mik said. "And then follow that thread back to the source?"

Joan patted their foot. "If you'd asked me that yesterday, I'd have said yes. Today, I'm thinking it's less likely. They'd probably follow the links back to your kidnapper—"

"Original kidnapper."

"Original kidnapper, instead of us, the secondary kidnappers," Joan corrected. "But I'm not convinced they'll seal you and set you free."

"You think they'll guinea pig me."

It wasn't a question, so Joan didn't answer. Joan herself might benefit from Mik being guinea pigged. It was an intoxicating thought.

Mik rubbed their eyes. "I want to see you cast."

"Oh, I can't cast," Joan reminded them quickly. "Things backfire. Spectacularly."

Mik leveraged themself up, sitting crisscross on the couch. "Last week, I'd never seen magic. I was a perfectly ordinary person. Boring, even, and I barely had any friends, and I wasn't a part of anything, and I thought I could disappear and no one would notice."

They took a deep breath. "Now my memories are a mess, and I live with a vampire, and magic is *real*. I mean, that's like the coolest thing that could ever possibly happen to me, and it's also apparently the worst. I don't know if anyone missed me or noticed I was gone besides my parents, and I don't want to think about it. Let me see what happens when you try magic, please. One itty-bitty spell. It'll make me feel better if I'm not the only messed-up witch. I mean, my grandmother had, like, premonitions, and she claimed she made the hens lay better eggs, but that's the closest I've been to real magic. That I remember, at least."

Joan had long ago stopped giving people demonstrations of her ability or lack thereof. People *always* wanted to see for themselves. The Greenwood curiosity.

But Mik, sleep-addled Mik, was a human, mostly, and the apartment was empty, and while Joan hadn't been the one to do this to Mik, a weird mix of guilt and pity churned in her, leading her to make bad decisions. Like track down Grace to try to help Mik. And this, as she cleared the coffee table of everything but a loose receipt from the pharmacy she'd gone to last night for their meds.

"Keep the vomit bucket close," Joan muttered, and Mik dutifully picked it up, hovering beside Joan as she leaned forward over the receipt, concentrating.

She'd attempt a little origami, maybe set the crane she'd make flying. It was an easy, low-level spell they taught to five-year-olds. And, critically, it did not involve any combustible magic. Joan had made that mistake too many times.

She breathed out, settling into stasis as she hovered her hands over the receipt. The hand movements the spell required helped her focus on guiding the magic, which swirled in agitation over the receipt as Joan forged onward. She thought of Grace's assertion that Joan had no barrier, that magic moved through her at all times. It was always at her fingertips, sparking around her, and she so rarely let it rise. She breathed in, and magic funneled into her body, an icy rush that flashed along her veins and made her feel invincible. She breathed it in and held it like a breath.

Trying to be cautious, she pushed a little bit of magic into the spell to actualize her intentions and held the rest within her. She finished with a small flourish.

The magic rushed into the paper, folding it rapidly. Mik's face shone with awe, and Joan couldn't help the bubble of happiness that bloomed in her chest. That was her, she was doing that, she was changing the world around her. Magic felt like a cool river on a hot day, soothing her and reminding her simultaneously of the great currents that fueled it, the lakes and oceans it flowed into. She wanted to bathe in it forever, and for a second, she was buzzing with the very fabric of the universe.

But only for a second.

Her magic didn't properly portion itself—only a sliver was needed here—it funneled into the spell, making it swell to outrageous proportions despite her efforts to hold it back. The magic in her unraveled like yarn, gaining speed.

"Oh fuck," Joan said, scrambling back on the couch. She saw the moment the spell burst, too weak a container for the amount of magic slamming into it.

The paper disintegrated at an atomic level, reassembled itself just as fast, ripped into shreds, and then bumbled itself together in a perversion of the original folding. Then the ball took off, shooting across the room, bouncing off a wall and taking a new angle.

"Not planned?" Mik said with a yelp, defending their head as the ball rocketed toward them at roughly Mach 5.

"Not planned!" Joan yelled, letting loose her own shriek when she was sliced across the arm. The ball returned to bonk her on the head, then took off again, whipping around the apartment. But that wasn't even the worst of it; the worst was the nausea that grabbed her by the gut. Joan released all the energy in her on an exhale and bodily cut off the magic greedily funneling into the spell. Dizziness overtook her. She scrambled for the bucket, letting a thin stream of bile into it. She could channel more magic than she could handle, and it made her sick every time.

Mik was cursing, vaulting behind the couch and crouching in a defensive position. Even though Joan had stopped pouring magic into the spell, the paper was still full of the energy that had already streamed into it, and it wasn't running out of steam.

She knelt on the floor, carpet digging into her knees, spitting into the bucket as a CVS receipt assaulted her continuously.

"Can I trap it?" Mik yelled, army crawling to the kitchen with the receipt tearing after them.

Joan groaned, spat again. "You can try. It'll tire itself out eventually."

Mik started making sobbing noises, and Joan stood up in panic, worried they'd had an artery sliced by paper.

They were laughing. Uproariously, in great peals of mirth that were punctuated by the occasional "ow" and "please have mercy."

"I'm being killed via paper cut," they howled. "This is incredible. Magic is incredible."

"I *told* you it always goes wrong!"

Mik only laughed harder.

There was the sound of the door unlocking, and CZ walked in with several ginormous grocery bags. He promptly dropped one to snatch the magic ball out of the air. It struggled raucously in his grip, but he held on to it without issue.

"What the hell, guys," he said. "My apartment!"

His throw pillows were on the floor, his curtains askew. The paper ball had knocked the loose mail off his counters and only now gave an angry dying buzz before going still and disintegrating in his hand. He sighed and dumped the ashes in the trash.

"What was the goal?" he asked.

"Origami," Joan said, fumbling her way to the bathroom to wash out both her mouth and the bin she'd baby barfed into. When she walked back out, CZ was leveraging his grocery bags onto the counter as he talked to Mik, who was up off the floor and, on the whole, looking much cheerier than Joan had ever seen them.

"I didn't super know what was good," he said, shrugging off his coat, "so I got every food Joan likes."

"You could have asked them," Joan said, but Mik didn't seem to mind, already rummaging through a bag and producing some chips.

"Quiet," Mik said. "I want it all. Turns out vomiting your guts up makes you hungry. As does being assaulted by paper."

CZ walked over to Joan and dropped a kiss on her head. "You ready for your thing? Feeling okay?"

"No," Joan grumbled. She hadn't even found an outfit, like Molly said she had to.

"You never are," CZ said. "Go, confront your aunt about her illicit plans to reverse engineer a magic-granting spell, eat some canapés, come back here."

"Easy," Joan said, gathering her phone from where it was wedged in the couch, because it was getting to be time, and while her family likely wouldn't notice if she was late, they would notice if she didn't show up at all.

"Speaking of family," CZ said too casually, "can we please ask Abel for help? If anyone knows if this spell is something brand-new or very old, it'll be him and his stacks of occult knowledge."

Joan, midway through jamming her phone in her pocket, paused. "CZ, you're seriously telling me you called me before your brother?" Since vampires were often infertile, there was a large age gap between Abel and his brother. Over fifteen years. But they were close nonetheless.

CZ slumped onto the couch. "Is that really so unbelievable? Of course I called you. Only you would be reckless enough to become an accomplice, no questions asked."

Joan's eyes burned with unshed emotion. "Babe."

CZ gave her one of his prettiest smiles. "Babe." His expression dropped too soon. "And also, I was a bit ashamed to go to him."

Joan knew the rest—CZ had long tried to measure up to his brother, heir to his pack, a leader to the community, and acutely felt that he was falling short. Asking him for help rather than being able to handle things alone…Joan gave him a sympathetic grimace.

"You should find out at this party or whatever if there are other witches you trust who can come seal me," Mik said, crunching noisily in Joan's ear.

Joan jumped with a little shriek at their stealthy movements. "What the hell!"

Mik crashed into the couch next to CZ. "You have to have friends, don't you?"

CZ winced, flashed Joan an apologetic smile. "You're looking at him."

Mik snorted. "I'm so fucked, then."

"Not fucked," Joan said, regaining control of her heart so she could pull on her light coat. "I'll figure this out," she muttered. Molly felt like an option, but not a good one. Joan wasn't completely sure she could trust her not to let something slip to their family, and even if they recruited her, they'd still need three more. Better to find them all at once so no one could leak the news early. "And yes to Abel."

He was a classics professor at Columbia, teaching standard mythology and translation classes to humans while serving as a leading expert in magical lore to those who knew better.

They definitely needed his help, at least in determining if this was a new spell or something old. They'd passed *in over their heads* roughly three crimes ago.

Joan returned to the Greenwood house to find a golden-yellow jumpsuit laid out on her bed with a blue sticky note on top that read *Knew you weren't gonna find something to wear.*

And Joan knew it was Molly without a second thought. She donned the jumpsuit, a bit grumpy that it fit perfectly, and walked downstairs amid the growing swell of party noise.

The house looked almost the same as always: Polished wood. Priceless art. Expensive furniture. But everything seemed a bit brighter, like it was shimmering slightly, likely Selene's doing. She specialized in illusion magic and could make any space look grander.

An increasingly large swarm of witches was passing through the front door, smiling at one another with false warmth and engaging in verbal sparring sharp enough for Joan to willingly slit her throat on.

She couldn't linger on the stairs without drawing attention, but being swallowed up by the crowd felt impossible. Her hands started to sweat; she rubbed them on her thighs.

Come on, Joan. It was a simple party. It was every party she'd ever been to. She was just going to walk around. She was going to get skewered and cooked by every witch in the building who could spot weakness from ten miles away and would want to know what the youngest Greenwood was up to.

Nothing.

Some bad things.

Well, arguably, some good things that were bad only because they were in opposition to her family.

Joan watched said family navigate the foyer. Merlin was laughing boisterously with a group of men. Molly was surrounded by a semicircle of friends. Valeria was across the room with her wife, Ronnie, speaking with an old family friend.

Ronnie turned and caught Joan's gaze, her eyes a light, almost-unnatural blue. Aunt Val and Ronnie had been together for over thirty years, but Ronnie avoided witch society as much as she could, so Joan rarely saw her. She leaned down to whisper something to Valeria, whose eyes flicked to Joan briefly before resetting on the person in front of her.

Which reminded Joan why she was here. There had to be some other solution to this crisis, one that didn't make witches even more powerful gatekeepers than they already were. She was going to confront her aunt about what Grace had said and do what she could to convince Valeria that thinking ethically about the repercussions of this spell and the concept of humans turning into witches was what was important here. Not racing to get the spell before California to turn a fleet of loyal followers. It would help if Joan could effectively convince Valeria that the spell was unfinished and not worth using—that it let the human channel but didn't grant them a tolerance to magic. They couldn't scale it up without making a lot of people very sick.

But Joan couldn't reveal how she knew that the spell had side effects.

She'd try it all anyways, and then she'd flee into the night and figure out her secondary problem—how to find a witch to help them track Mik's magic back to its source, without asking any pesky questions. As the receipt had proven, Joan herself was not the one for the job.

She'd just taken another step when the room hushed, then surged, stopping her in her tracks.

Because there, entering now, was Astoria Wardwell.

She was dressed in a tailored black suit with a red vest peeking from underneath her jacket. Her hair was down, curling around her shoulders, a deep brown shot through with warmer highlights that matched her brown skin. A decade could change a lot;

a decade could apparently change *everything*. Last time Joan had seen the Wardwell heir, they'd both been fifteen and awkward, with acne and bodies they were so clearly uncomfortable in. Joan had been a year away from coming out to her family. Now Astoria was broad shouldered and fucking tall as hell. Joan's gaydar started screaming at her so loudly—*I mean, what straight woman wears a suit that well?*—that she barely noticed the much shorter, slighter woman behind Astoria. Skin pale, hair dark, features sharp. The two Californians were rapidly folded into the party, pulled in every direction by witches vying for their attention, equal parts starstruck and curious about the interlopers.

The short woman stood slightly in front of Astoria, steering conversations as Astoria looked broodily across the crowd, scanning it like a predator, until her eyes lit upon Joan.

And stuck.

And stuck.

Joan couldn't look away.

"Joan Greenwood, back among the wolves," said a woman with incredibly red lipstick, breaking Joan's concentration and drawing her down the last two steps.

Her gaze followed Joan's, and she smirked. "If my son stares any harder at that Wardwell girl, his eyes might pop right out." She gestured toward the crowd watching Astoria. As if they were old friends. As if they were anything to each other.

Joan stopped a waiter to white-knuckle a flute of prosecco. She sipped it as a hot flash of repulsion overcame her. "Someone should remind him not to ogle. Who are you?"

A Greenwood never admitted they didn't know anything. Joan knew every rule of the witch world; it was why she was so excellent at breaking them.

The woman laughed that stupid fake laugh they all employed so confidently. "Janet Proctor," she said.

Ah, the Proctors were money magicians. They likely had little raw power but a great deal of subtle control over fickle things. They were, apparently, cutting business deals with Moon Creatures. And, apparently, had become important enough to be invited to the welcome party for Astoria Wardwell.

Joan noted that neither Grace nor Fiona seemed to be in attendance. They were useful enough to work for the Greenwoods, but not respected enough to appear among them.

"I hear you have trouble casting," Janet was saying, a sly smile on her lips. "Is that so? My children, they were late bloomers, but now they're such strong casters."

"Can I help you with something, Janet?"

A Greenwood never showed impatience.

"You can, actually," Janet said. She fluttered a hand to her chest, as if scandalized by Joan's directness. "This plan of your aunt's... raiding the Night Market. Is she really so desperate? The business that would be disrupted—well, isn't there another way to get what we need out of the Moon Creatures? I could certainly work my own contacts, if the sway of the Greenwoods is slipping— Valeria! It's wonderful to see you."

Joan's arm was caught by her aunt, polite but a little rough.

Valeria smelled faintly of lavender. "Janet," she said neutrally. "I need to borrow my niece."

Sound had dimmed in Joan's ears. What the hell was Janet talking about, raiding the Night Market? It was unthinkable—a violation of Moon Creature sovereignty. It was a plan straight out of California.

Joan twisted like a heat-seeking missile, hoping to catch sight of Astoria, but Valeria's grip was unyielding. Unable to find Astoria, Joan focused her nuclear capacity on her aunt, attempting to incinerate Valeria with her mind. Her mouth was halfway through launching the first word of the admonishment swimming to life in her brain when Valeria squeezed, hard enough to really hurt, cutting off Joan's speech with a small, pained whimper. The currents of the room shifted, sweeping Janet off to other schemes. The Greenwood matriarch, still strong-arming Joan, pulled her along to the back terrace. The stone balcony was drenched in roses, gaudily so, supernaturally vibrant.

"Where have you been all day?" Valeria asked. "Why were you in Brooklyn with Grace Collins?"

"Can you unhand me?" Joan said as forcefully as she could manage through gritted teeth.

Valeria let go with a noise of scorn deep in her throat, and Joan shook out her arm finally, mercifully.

"You were having me followed?"

Valeria shook her head and snapped her fingers, refilling Joan's champagne glass with prosecco and taking it from her hands. It looked like some sort of time magic variation, turning back the clock on the cup to mimic a previous state. Her specialty. "You children are constantly underestimating me."

Joan rested her hands on the railing, the roses and thorns alike tangling with her fingers in glee. She slipped them off and shook her hand, blood welling from a cut. "I have some concerns."

"Don't you always," Valeria muttered. The world gusted, an uncharacteristic chill for early June. "What is it this time, Joan?"

Valeria's tone grated. Joan worked to tamp down on her frustration. "Grace says she told you how to reverse this new spell. You seal the person's magic. But you want her to recreate it anyways, why? You said we weren't going to use it to turn a bajillion humans."

Please don't say what I think you're going to say.

"No, that's your father's ill-founded idea. I have no intentions of pursuing half-baked plans. There must be systems in place before such a thing can happen," Valeria said. "Ways to train these new witches. We have to think through who gets turned, and how. This is not a move to make out of rabid fear. We are not *afraid* of the humans or the vampires or the fae, in the same way the predator does not fear its prey. Fear begets recklessness, and we are at the top of the food chain. Even without the numbers in our favor."

There it is.

Valeria was working herself up a little bit. "Do you have any idea how many people covet our power? We are one major event away from mass unrest. The Greenwoods are a very small family, and our reputation protects us. If people didn't trust *and* fear me, we'd have witches invoking the Scales Law to duel me every other day."

"Why not make it illegal, then?" Joan countered. The duels were a relic of a time when titles and land were more formal, but a powerful relic nonetheless.

"You, who's always railing against our authoritarian rule, want me to take a foundational witch custom and make it illegal? One of the only checks on our family's power? Make up your mind, Joan."

Chastised, Joan couldn't come up with a good response. Witches were suckers for custom and tradition, and duels were rare because those who won tended to be those with more thorough witch educations, and the already rich and powerful could afford those educations. Power was in settled lines these days; it was a suicide mission to try and challenge them.

Valeria continued, refilling and draining her glass again. "No, we'll be careful here. We need to determine how this spell might impact the balance of the magic world and its intersection with the human one. All answers to be determined once I know the exact parameters of this magic. Its costs and consequences. And whoever this witch is who wrote it, I'll need them in my employ."

Even after all they did to Mik? It's not finished, Joan wanted to tell her. *It makes you sick.*

Valeria's gaze was eagle-eyed. "Why do you look guilty?"

Joan straightened. Denying was easiest, but the Greenwoods were born liars; she'd been doing it since she was eight and Merlin had told her to stop crying in public. "Because you didn't say we weren't going to do it, you said it was a question of when. The magical world's social and economic stratification will worsen if you swell the witch population. You may not feel guilt about that, but I do."

"And why do you feel this magic should be suppressed?" Valeria asked. She always seemed to be debating Joan, but it was a falsehood in itself—Merlin shut you down fast when you didn't have a chance. Molly was a people pleaser, and she made sure to actually consider your viewpoint. But Valeria's methods were insidious; she'd argue you into a corner just to make you feel heard, but her mind wasn't changed by other people. She was the great Valeria Greenwood.

As Grace had said, when the Greenwoods spoke, the magic world bent unquestioningly toward them.

"Janet Proctor says you're eyeing the Moon Creatures," Joan said. "And the Night Market. Tell me that part isn't true, at least."

"We know the transformed human was casting within its borders, and they're likely still being harbored there. It would be the perfect place to hide; not enough witches go there to recognize something going on, so casting magic might go mostly unnoticed."

A jolt seized Joan. They were closer to Mik's trail than she'd thought, which meant they were closer to CZ's than she'd thought. Joan had family protection, but Mik and CZ weren't witches—if they were discovered, Mik could be taken and CZ exiled or heavily sanctioned or really anything the Greenwoods might deem appropriate, despite the influence of his family. Even if the LaMortes did shield him, it would be a huge blow to witch-vampire relations.

"Casting magic is negated within the market's wards; it's not just unnoticeable. Why would you look there?" Joan said, and to her own ears, her tone sounded level, a fact as disturbing as it was reassuring.

Valeria refilled her glass again. "You think no one's clever enough to have figured out how to get around that? I can think of three options off the top of my head—pocket realm, portal to another location, ward nullification in a small area of effect. Think, Joan."

Joan *was* thinking. She was thinking so hard, it felt like her brain was going to burn to a crisp. It wasn't that she was opposed to this magic; it was that she opposed how badly everyone seemed to want it. "You're trying to race California to the spell. You don't know what it might do—"

"Do you, Joan?" Valeria interrupted, eyes narrowing. "Do you know what this spell might do?"

"Of course not." It was smooth, so smooth, easy. Joan injected some frustration into her tone. "But we should slow down. Everyone's trying to figure this out, not just witches and not just New York. We should think about the repercussions of this, what could happen if a place like California gets a spell that can swell their ranks. They're already essentially a police state—"

"Exactly, Joan, *exactly*," Valeria said. "That's why we'll get to it first, because I am the lesser evil here, because casting magic in the hands of Moon Creatures will drive the magical world to war. Because this spell in the hands of Poppy Wardwell and her daughter will drive the Moon Creatures even further into the dirt."

Scorn roiled in Joan, sharp and cresting. "But this magic in the hands of Valeria Greenwood, well, all will be right in the world."

Valeria sighed. It looked involuntary, a true bit of exasperation. "What on earth is behind this latest act of rebellion? When will you settle into your place here? You're impossible, so much like your father. In the end, it's always nothing but posturing with you two."

Joan might as well have been slapped in the face for the impact it had on her. Her fingers clenched the banister; her clothing felt suddenly too tight. "What?"

"Joan," Valeria said, clearly struggling to say it patiently. "I absolutely adore you. You are strong-willed and curious and have been that way since you were a child. But you're also twenty-five, and I am nearly three times your age, and I know what is best for the magical world. Please trust that with this spell in hand, I will make the right decisions. Stop trying to work against us all the time and put your head down. You don't always have to fight."

Joan's fingers curved and straightened. It was all too easy to cut to the core of her. *You're like your father.* That shouldn't have stopped her in her tracks as thoroughly as it did. But for all

Valeria's great evils, she still spoke to Joan like a person, and so Joan had always preferred her aunt and her straightforwardness to her own parents.

"It's not just about what you do with this spell, Aunt Val. It's about what you're willing to do to get there. I know you can be a decent person. Leave Moon Creatures alone. Do not invade the Night Market."

"I won't sit idly by," Valeria said.

"Then *defend* Moon Creatures from people who think it's their right to invade the market," Joan countered. "And promise me that when you figure out this spell, you aren't going to use it for the direct benefit of the Greenwoods and crush the other magical factions of this city beneath your heel."

Valeria's eyes softened uncharacteristically. "A promise, Joan? That's what you think still holds power? We aren't children."

Joan's eyes burned with frustration. Everything she said was wrong and naive. All she was in the eyes of people like the Proctors was the weakest link in the Greenwood family chain.

"When are you going to do it?" Joan asked. "Invade the market."

Valeria looked genuinely pitying, which after everything shouldn't have felt like such a sledgehammer to the chest, but it did. It did. "So you can warn them? I don't think so."

"You can't even trust me with family secrets?"

"Don't make me answer that."

Joan blinked away the tears prickling at her eyes. "I'll see myself out," she said coolly.

"This is your own home," Valeria protested.

But it wasn't, not really. Joan walked through the wide-open French doors and melded with the crowd.

SEVEN

J oan reentered the party feeling deeply unenthused.

She headed for the door as spite dug its claws in deeper, began its transformation into righteousness. Joan didn't know what the future held, but she had to beat her family to sealing Mik, before they followed the trail right to CZ's doorstep.

And now, she also needed to figure out who had done this to Mik to protect Moon Creatures. If Joan could use the clues from Mik to deliver this person to Valeria, then Mik and a whole bunch of Moon Creatures would be spared.

On the downside, Joan would be delivering the spellmaker to her aunt, to use in ways she might not agree with. She didn't want to protect whatever sick bastard had done this to Mik; it was only because, in Valeria's hands, this power was dangerous. Joan, in a fit of bloodlust, thought she'd rather eradicate the spellmaker from the earth, but she shook the thought out of her head before it could take hold.

She wasn't having much luck making it to the door. They'd entered the dancing portion of the night, a rare break from the endless small talk. The foyer had cleared in a circle, and couples were dancing together in easy spins like it was the 1800s. Molly and Nate rotated around, laughing. Valeria and Ronnie joined in, swaying, Valeria looking totally at peace, like she wasn't planning to forgo all diplomatic relations and enact the equivalent of invading Canada by storming the Night Market.

"Excuse me," a voice said at her side.

Joan, having been stopped by the dance floor, dragged her gaze from her family, and it landed, instead, on Astoria Wardwell.

"Would you like to dance?" Astoria asked, one hand out.

Her face was unreadable. She'd shed her jacket at some point, and the sleeves of her dress shirt were rolled up her forearms, revealing a neat constellation of small, jagged scars. Her hair was set off beautifully against her warm skin. Her eyes were thickly lashed and exquisitely hazel, and she was so tall that Joan felt positively weak in the knees. Astoria Wardwell, legendary fighter, heir to the Wardwell estate and future Head and High Witch of California and LA. She wasn't just hot, she was beautiful. Like, Owl's-Head-Park-at-sunset beautiful. Like, the-Met-at-night beautiful. Gorgeous enough that her face belonged in magazine ads. She had a perfect little beauty mark above her lip and there was a tiny curl fluttering by her forehead.

"Shit," Joan said. Fifteen seemed so long ago. Had Astoria always been so good-looking? Impossible—Joan would have developed a violent crush as a teenager if so.

Astoria's hand receded. "No, then."

Joan grabbed it, despite herself. "Definitely yes," she said, and winced. Her desperation was surely showing. She saw a beautiful woman and her brain became a nonsensical place.

There was a scar in the corner of Astoria's mouth that tugged it down slightly in a perpetual frown. She led Joan onto the dance floor, and the two assumed the position of a waltz.

"Who's leading?" Joan asked, trying to remember how to waltz.

Astoria responded by taking the lead, moving them into the first steps as they joined the fray. The music was live and mostly violins, a band tucked away in the corner. Astoria had a couple of inches on Joan, but not too many, and the pair slotted together easily.

Too easily. Joan's breath was getting a little wispy, and her thoughts were definitely running away from her. "How are you liking New York?" she asked, scrambling to find something to say.

Astoria was analyzing Joan, her gaze scrutinizing. Joan hoped she didn't have something in her teeth.

"It's cramped," Astoria said. "And I've only arrived. I heard the same is true for you, that you're freshly back in town."

Joan stumbled a step, and Astoria held tight, sweeping her along. Her Greenwood body remembered enough to hang in there, but only so long as she didn't actually think about the dance.

"I just finished grad school," Joan said.

They kept gliding. "At the same time this new magic popped up?"

Joan's brain hit a brief dial tone before she could form a reply. "Is there an accusation in there?"

"More of an observation."

"You must have heard I can't cast," Joan said, "much less spell-make. You think I wrote and cast a spell on someone against their will?"

"Is that the Greenwood theory? That the human is an involuntary participant, not themself the source of anything?"

Oh shit. Joan was not excelling at this subterfuge. There wasn't a specific reason to keep this information from her own family, except for the fact that she accidentally had.

Astoria's grip on Joan tightened. "More than a theory? Do you know for sure?"

Maybe this was for the best; maybe this would get people more focused on Mik's torturer than Mik themself. Word spread fast in the witch world. "That's my personal theory."

Astoria stopped looking directly into Joan's face, which was helpful, because Joan couldn't think when Astoria was looking at her. "You had an argument with your aunt."

Joan fumbled another step but caught herself this time. She had the sinking feeling she was being pumped for information.

Astoria nodded her chin toward the French doors. "I saw you two walk out. You came back in looking upset. Am I right, then? You argued? What about?"

"Private family matters," Joan said through clenched teeth.

"Private family matters, in a family you've only just returned to after seven years out of state," Astoria said.

Joan very deliberately stepped on Astoria's foot.

Astoria's attention snapped back down to Joan, mouth a tight line.

"Next time you ask me to dance, Wardwell," Joan said, "you had better want to dance with *me*, not my family name."

Joan let go before the song ended and darted back to the edges of the crowd. This was not the most disastrous party she'd been to, not by far, but after seven years of freedom, it was wearing her down faster than ever before. She was tempted to try some origami again and see how these witches fared against a storm of vicious paper balls.

"Sorry, did she come on too strong?" Joan looked down to find the other California witch standing next to her, a friendly smile on her face. Yeesh. These people appeared out of nowhere.

Joan should have said, *How about you both leave me alone*, and instead asked, irresistibly curious, "Does she do that a lot?"

The woman laughed. "She's very to the point. It's one of her best qualities, but I think it makes it tough for her to make new friends."

Astoria was now in a discussion with Merlin, her brow furrowed.

"Was that her trying to make friends?" Joan asked.

The woman stuck out a hand. "Wren Dahl-Min," she introduced, as Joan paused for long enough to be rude, then shook the hand. "I'm here as Astoria's sidekick."

"I thought she'd been sent solo."

"We're a package deal," Wren said.

Joan raised an eyebrow.

"Not like that," Wren said. "Just best friends, which I know sounds juvenile, but it works for us. Joan Greenwood, right?"

"Is this where you attempt to pump me for information too?" Joan said.

Wren's face fell into a frown as she looked at Astoria. "No, that's not why I'm in New York."

"Right."

"I mean it, I'm here for her," Wren said with a tilt of her head. "Trust me, my only interest in this new spell is its application to Moon Creatures."

Cherry on top of the godsdamn sundae. "And that's supposed to make me trust you? I doubt I make the news too much, but my best friend—best friend like it seems Astoria is your best friend—is a vampire. I have no interest in further worsening the power divide in the magic world," Joan snapped.

"You're misunderstanding me," Wren said with an apologetic smile. "My focus isn't on keeping this magic from Moon Creatures; it's on giving them the ability to cast."

The ability to cast…spells. The thing Valeria had said was liable to cause a magical civil war. Well.

That was new.

EIGHT

Joan's head whipped around like one of those inflatable guys in front of a car wash, trying to ascertain who might have overheard, but the two of them had a little circle of space around them.

Joan was a little bit of a radical, sure, but she wasn't enough of one to talk about Moon Creatures casting at a witch party. She might mention it in a one-on-one or behind closed doors, certainly. To herself in the mirror, late at night, in a soundproof room.

"I heard about your best friend, the LaMorte vampire," Wren said, nonplussed by Joan's cartoonish panic. "I thought you might hold similar values. Values that are certainly rare among named witch society."

Joan tried not to look like she'd been run over by a car. "I...Is this a trap?"

Wren shrugged a little. "No, but I guess there's no way for me to really prove that. Just know, Astoria might be here to do what her mother says, but I am under no such constraints. There's no reason only witches should cast—it's an incredible ability, and I don't believe in whatever genetic deterministic bullshit currently dictates things. I also don't believe in the disgusting, fearmongering police system that Poppy Wardwell runs in California. If you feel similarly, we might help each other. And if not, well, then it would be bold to accuse a guest witch here with the heir to California of saying all this. Publicly."

Joan performed another evaluation of Wren, scanning her from head to toe. "How are you both trying to get on my side and threatening me?"

Wren sipped her drink. "It's an art I unfortunately had to hone running in the same circles as Astoria. We met when we were only three, you know. Grew up together. A friendship like that... sometimes your values diverge, but you find ways to stay together."

"Does she know you're trying to convince me to help you give casting magic to Moon Creatures?"

Wren downed her glass, glossy manicured nails clinking against the cup. "I better go rescue Astoria. She can't hold a conversation that isn't about fighting tactics or swords. Or romance novels." Her face was soft, fond.

She turned to Joan, flashed her a bright smile. Her dark eyes had a gorgeous iridescence to them. "We'll run into each other again."

Her tone did not indicate a question, and Joan was left baffled as Wren slipped into the conversation Astoria was having. Astoria visibly sagged with relief.

Hmm.

"I still can't believe Poppy let her come," Molly said, sidling up and poking Joan in the side. "How did the thing with Grace go? Will there be a second date?"

"Let who come?"

"Wren." Molly looked at Joan expectantly, and when Joan

failed to deliver whatever recognition she was looking for, elaborated with a sigh. "Because of the whole fae thing?"

Joan absolutely could not connect the dots.

"Wren Dahl-Min is half fae, half witch," Molly supplied. "She was adopted by a witch family as a kid. But Poppy's a purist about her inner circle. Astoria must have lobbied hard to bring Wren. Are you avoiding my Grace question?"

Joan focused in on Wren's nails, a little bit too long. Her ears, just slightly pointed. Both signs of the fae. Adopted into a witch family . . . Joan wondered, rather rudely, what had led to her being put up for adoption. Mixed kids weren't always accepted by their birth families, depending on the species, and witches were usually eager to get the children into witch training as soon as possible.

"Joan. Please. Grace?"

"Did you tell Aunt Val about it?" Joan grumbled, swatting Molly's still poking hand away.

"Was it a secret?"

Yes, absolutely, and also . . . "No, but I don't think it's going to work out."

Molly deflated. She looked stunning in a dark red dress, her hair pulled back into a knot at the nape of her neck. "I'm sorry, I hope you keep trying."

Joan kept her eyes glued to Astoria and Wren, trying to puzzle out their presence and apparently diverging interests. Wren Dahl-Min, half fae herself, wanted to give casting magic to Moon Creatures. Astoria Wardwell represented the desire to use casting magic to oppress Moon Creatures further.

Maybe in the race between New York witches, California witches, and Moon Creatures, Joan was on Mik's side, but she could also be on the side of Moon Creatures. It would fundamentally transform the magic world if vampires and fae could cast too, if they could manipulate others the way witches so easily did, nudge the stock market in a certain direction, grease some political palms, create wards on their own. Not that Joan felt people should be manipulated. But it would make it impossible for witches to do something asinine like invade the Night Market. Which could happen at any time, apparently. But not tonight, not while witches were getting drunk uptown.

And she had CZ right there with her, if they found the answers first. She could give them to him or Abel. To the LaMortes.

"Joan?" Molly was saying, voice fuzzy in Joan's ear.

"I'm going to go," Joan said. The world sharpened. "Mol, if the family tries to go after the market, I need you to stop them."

Joan might as well have asked for Molly to rip the sun from the sky, reverse the tides, alter the orbit of the planet—but she asked anyways, because she could. Because if either of them had a chance, it was Molly.

Molly's gaze was sad, the corners of her lips slightly down-turned. "What are you going to do, Jo?"

Joan leaned in, bumped her sister's shoulder. "Plausible deniability, Mol. Promise me you'll try."

Molly hesitated a moment before bumping Joan back. "I can only stall. You know the moment they feel really backed into a corner, they'll do whatever they think they have to."

"I know," Joan said. "I'm going to try to fix it before they hit that corner."

She patted Molly on the shoulder, snatched another glass of prosecco, and downed it as she walked out the door.

In Hell's Kitchen, Joan entered CZ's apartment to find him standing on the kitchen island with a fistful of popcorn in his hand and Mik, mouth open, below him.

The two of them froze comedically upon her entrance.

Joan broke the silence. "You have a kidnapped person and didn't lock your door?"

"No one ever comes by!" CZ protested.

At the same time, Mik replied, "Isn't he kind of an apex predator?"

Which was so blissfully normal after the string of conversations she'd had at her family's house. Joan was overwhelmed with the desire to gather them both into a hug and kiss their faces in gratitude. Instead, she joined Mik by the counter and opened her mouth.

CZ plucked out a popped kernel and threw it.

Joan was no athlete, but she was a pro at this game and caught the popcorn to raucous cheers. She bowed dramatically at the waist.

"CZ," she said without preamble. "I need you to get me into the Night Market."

The cheers cut off. Mik shuddered. CZ tossed the popcorn back in the bag and scrambled to grab Joan by the arms.

"Why, what happened?"

Joan gave him the rundown. The Greenwoods thinking of invading the market for answers, their knowledge that Mik had stumbled out of there, Astoria Wardwell's presence in New York, and Wren Dahl-Min's odd proposal.

Mik rubbed at the stubble of their shaved head, agitation rising. "So we're no closer to having enough witches for a sealing spell *and* they're getting closer to us?"

CZ was staring contemplatively out the window, like he was in an old movie, but Joan knew him well enough to know he wasn't being faux dramatic. The usually ever-present humor had dropped entirely off his face.

"It's a risk," he admitted. "Giving us casting magic. You don't know what we'll do with it any more than you know what your aunt will do with it."

"Actually, I think I do have a good sense of what Aunt Val will do," Joan said. "And Merlin. And California. The gamble of Moon Creatures is feeling best to me; at least in the uncertainty, there's *some* possibility this doesn't all go totally sideways. If I were a spellmaker, maybe I could study Mik right now, but that's not my wheelhouse, so we need to either get a spellmaker on our side or find the original one."

"You want to join up with Wren? What if it's just a way of weaseling into your trust?" Mik said. "Do you know her?"

No. Before today, Joan had never even heard of Wren. "I think this is a 'rock and a hard place' kind of situation," Joan admitted.

"A rock and a hard place with my life liable to be crushed between them," Mik muttered.

CZ rubbed his chin, turning from the window. "Alright, I'll go back to the Night Market and look around again. I haven't been able to retrace Mik's steps exactly, but I'll try. Abel can probably meet me there, and he'll be able to help. I filled him in on the phone. He is not pleased with us."

"Probably for good reason, and me too. I'm going," Joan said. "I can help you cover more ground."

CZ was already shaking his head. "Absolutely not, the Night Market is no place for witches."

"Witches go there," Joan argued.

"Not Greenwoods."

They quickly descended into a sharp little bickering match, interrupted only by Mik.

"I'll go, then," they said a bit snappishly. "I'll be able to guide you best; it's *my* footsteps you're trying to retrace."

CZ and Joan wasted no time before uniting in a shared cause.

"And what happens if you accidentally get upset and suck some magic in again?" CZ said, opening his fridge and pouring himself a glass of blood. "Or get scared of the dark? If people start reporting a weird magical fluctuation in the market, or worse, see you casting again with their own eyes, it will only strengthen Valeria's case."

"Or what if whoever kidnapped you takes you back?" Joan added. "I can't protect you, and CZ can only do so much."

"Yet another reason why *you* shouldn't attend," CZ said to Joan. He tipped the glass back, and Joan absently handed him a napkin to wipe his mouth.

"I'm going if I have to walk to Owl's Head myself and wander around until I hit the market wards," Joan said. "I'm not taking a backseat on this one, not with so much on the line." *Just like your father*, Valeria had said. *All posturing*. Not tonight—tonight Joan was going to grab the world in her fists.

Mik's voice pitched toward a shout, gaze sticking to the red-tinged glass CZ set down on the counter. "Can you two stop talking like I'm not here, and grown, and capable of making my own decisions? If I want to put my fucking life in danger, I sure as hell will—oh no."

Mik lunged toward the kitchen sink as magic in the room shifted, drawn toward Mik in their agitation. The sharp scent of vomit pierced the air.

Joan and CZ avoided eye contact, both with each other and

Mik, as Mik rinsed their mouth out and rested their forehead on the cool counter.

They looked small there. Hunched over, skin flushed, and arms braced around their head. They couldn't keep letting magic funnel through them like that—it would kill them. And Mik didn't know how to control their channeling. Joan could try to teach them, but that was a Band-Aid at best.

"Both of you go," Mik said, on the edge of tears. "And leave me alone for a while. I promise I won't break out, and if I do, I won't snitch on you two. But if I don't get some alone time, I'm going to begin to act out in a way that would have gotten me swiftly institutionalized in the 1800s."

This was very hard logic to argue with. Worse, Joan didn't *want* to argue with it. She didn't want to keep Mik here, being watched by strangers, even though it was safest. If it were her, if she had been the one to get kidnapped and transformed... if it had been Joan who had woken up alone and scared in that market, she'd have lost her mind much faster than Mik seemed to be losing theirs.

One glance at CZ revealed a look of guilt Joan assumed she was mirroring.

"Two hours," CZ said finally. "We'll be back in two hours, three max. Okay?"

Mik did not respond, only curling tighter in on themselves.

"Mik," Joan said, thinking back on their prior conversation. "If you disappear, we will notice. Okay? We will notice, and we'll be devastated. We're doing everything we can to make sure that doesn't happen to you. When I get back, I'll try to help you control your channeling."

Still, silence.

Properly sobered, Joan followed CZ out the door.

NINE

Joan had never been to the Night Market before.

For a witch, going to the market meant giving up any means of personal protection. Channeling was suppressed by the wards, and as such, witches at the market were little more than humans. Out of their depth and surrounded by both predators built to drain the blood from other beings and tricksters like the fae aiming to trap them in eternal servitude.

In Brooklyn, they approached Owl's Head Park from the south, and CZ stepped confidently onto a path leading into the trees. During the day, the park was an entirely normal place for humans. At night, a warded section unfolded for the magical world.

"One more time," CZ said.

Joan huffed a breath. "Don't talk to anyone, don't touch anything, don't make eye contact. Definitely don't drink any of the pretty fae drinks."

CZ gave her a long-suffering glare.

"Fine," Joan amended. "Don't drink anything, period, and

especially not from the fae; they will turn me inside out and laugh."

CZ shifted, crossing his arms as he stared into the shadowed trees. He was in a black hoodie and dark pants. He could walk around the Night Market because he was a vampire. Better, a LaMorte vampire, and his mother ran his pack. To outsiders, the Night Market was a spooky place full of illegal dealings and illicit goods. To CZ, it was like a big family bazaar, in the way that all vampires were family to him, and even the fae wouldn't mess with him. There were rules here, but none of them protected humans or witches.

"Bad fucking idea," he muttered. For the thousandth time.

"There isn't a better one," Joan said. "We're losing our head start in this race. We keep needing a witch or three to help us, and we have precisely none."

"It really be two dumbasses deciding the fate of everything," CZ muttered.

"Only if these two dumbasses find this witch first," Joan replied.

Rubbing a nonexistent headache at his temple—vampires didn't get sick, a fact Joan, who did get sick, loathed with a passion—CZ started forward, stepping between two trees.

Similar to the HERMES stations, Joan met slight resistance as she passed through the wards, an elastic film pressing against her body. She gasped, but CZ's grasp was steady.

On the other side of the trees and wards, Joan stumbled slightly. Magic remained around her, but it was like she was in a winter coat and the cold couldn't penetrate.

A clearing spread out before them, grass defiantly lush beneath their shoes. It curled over Joan's Vans, making her steps a bit tougher, like she was walking on sand. Multicolored tents had been erected, and it looked rather like a farmer's market, just at night. People chatted at the stalls, and various magical creatures wheeled bikes around, putting odds and ends in the baskets up front. Music was playing from somewhere, and sound washed over her as she entered this new world. To her right, a fae was peddling an array of pretty pink drinks in tiny bottles. It was a cash-only market, and to her left, a grizzled human was dealing out hard bills like an ATM. *See*, Joan tried to say with her eyes. *A human is safe here, I'll be safe here.*

CZ wasn't paying attention to her. He'd grabbed her hand to weave through the tents, but it was slow going because people kept stopping to greet him.

Vampires especially melted from the sides to throw him laughs, clap him on the back, and ask about his parents, aunt, brother, or job. CZ responded in turn, asking about children, how sales were going, passing jokes left and right.

Joan's chest warmed at the sight, CZ surrounded by people who loved and knew him. For all he worried about not being useful, and all the guilt he'd started carrying around when he moved out of LaMorte territory and into Manhattan, he was still a vital member of his pack.

Joan attracted some stares, but that was the extent of it. Every time someone asked about her, CZ brushed them off easily. Witches sometimes came to the Night Market, but they didn't come to hold sway. They came to buy or to sell illegally. Cursed magic objects changed hands. One stall they passed was selling antique mirrors, but none reflected the world around them.

Joan leaned up to whisper at CZ. "We're going to where you found Mik?"

CZ's face was grim. "Abel will meet us there."

A fae brushed past Joan, close. CZ snarled, all predator, with his fangs flashing in the dim light of the market as he pulled Joan toward him. The fae backed off with a start, Joan's phone tipping from their hands. CZ caught it and handed it back to Joan, who—well, of course she'd gotten pickpocketed. She probably looked like an easy mark. She *was* an easy mark.

"Alright, big guy," Joan said, pulling CZ back and tucking her phone into her pocket, deeper this time. "Let's just get through this."

CZ put his fangs away. "Bad *fucking* idea, this whole thing," he said, but steered her forward.

The Night Market must have benefited heavily from witch magic, despite the clear aversion to them, because it never ended. The clearing stretched large and deep around them. Even the wards smothering Joan's magic and making her chest tight must have come from witches, even if they were witch-fae or witch-vampires. It was all casting magic.

Joan tried not to stare too hard at everyone around her, instead letting CZ pull her ahead.

But the air was charged tonight.

She caught herself staring down alleyways, watching shadows morph before her eyes.

"Cane!" Abel called, as they approached a gap in between two tents. He was tall and broad, taller and broader than even CZ, his skin dark and his hair in short little twists. They had the same smile, Abel and CZ, wide and guileless, and Joan saw both on display as they dapped each other up, CZ's posture straightening a little.

"And Joan," Abel said kindly, pulling Joan into a hug. "I hear you've managed to get yourself into trouble already. So soon after your return too."

"I couldn't run the risk of life being too boring," Joan returned with a laugh, as they pulled apart. "How're the students?"

"On summer break now," Abel said. "Just in time for all my attention to be occupied by the...situation. I've done what research I can."

"Do you know where this spell could have come from?"

Abel shook his head. "I know people were theorizing it was an old one, but I can't imagine a historian uncovering this in some archive and not taking credit for their find, and no archives I know of have reported anything missing. There's no history of humans being granted casting magic, this would have come out of nowhere. My knowledge isn't complete—"

"—but it's pretty comprehensive, nerd," CZ mumbled.

Abel cuffed him across the back of the head. "But it's extensive, and unless someone somehow made a completely unforeseen discovery in some very obscure archive or archaeological site, there is no historical precedent. I suspect we're looking at something new."

CZ rubbed the back of his head and sighed. "Well, we've kind of been operating under that assumption, but I guess this more distinctly confirms some sort of spellmaker did this. Let's hurry through this so we can get Joan out of here," he said.

Abel and Joan put on their best listening faces.

"I was here," CZ explained. "I'd been hanging out with Jeremiah and was heading home for the night when I saw Mik standing there." He pointed way down the gap in the tents they stood in. "They didn't seem okay."

"What kind of not okay?" Abel asked, arms crossed as he contemplated the information.

"Shaky, haunted. And I know humans get tormented here all the time, that's just the way things go, but something felt different here. They turned and started eyeing the fae food, and I've seen that go wrong too many times, so I walked over..." CZ started walking down the gap, and Abel dutifully followed. Joan had made it only a few steps when she felt a whisper across her back.

She whirled, clamping a hand down on her nape, searching for the source of the sensation, but there was no one there. Her eyes saw nothing, but her body was sounding all sorts of alarms. The grass waved frantically at her feet. There were eyes on her back. Eyes on her front. Eyes, watching from everywhere.

CZ called her name distantly, but Joan was frozen in place, reaching out with every single one of her senses to try and determine what had just happened.

A heavy hand landed on her shoulder. She inhaled a gasp, and her breath frosted in the air, even in the warm night.

Her mind fractured like a kaleidoscope, spinning through images. The party uptown, taking the N to Brooklyn. Hell's Kitchen—

"Jo, what is it?" CZ said urgently, and his voice rang like a thousand bells, and Joan's lips were numb. She couldn't think or breathe or—

There was a rush of warmth, and the pressure in her mind cut off abruptly. Sounds resumed at a normal cadence as she heaved in a breath and blinked frost from her eyelashes to find Abel holding her shoulders and CZ several yards to her left, holding the wrist of a woman who was furiously talking at him.

Joan blinked again and the image crystalized.

CZ, fangs out, eyes an incandescent red, hand rising to grasp the woman's throat.

And the woman—not just anyone.

"Grace?" Joan said around a dry mouth. She lurched forward, Abel moving with her. "CZ, don't hurt her."

CZ paused, thrumming with violence. "What the hell just happened?"

Grace snatched her wrist back, rubbing it unhappily. "Someone fished around in Joan's memories. I stopped it. You're welcome."

"Grace, what are you doing in the market?" Joan gathered her wits, leaning heavily on Abel, who was scanning their surroundings.

Grace gestured violently at her tote bag, which was full of produce and a couple of books, each wrapped and kept away from the other. "Shopping. I live around here, I just met up with a friend. What are *you* doing here, getting sucked into a mind-invasion spell? Someone pocket realmed you. I had to step into the realm to undo it."

Valeria had mentioned there were plenty of ways around the wards, for someone skilled enough.

"I . . ." Joan trailed off. "From afar?"

"No, they'd need to be close—"

Abel's reassuring weight disappeared as he whizzed off. Joan stumbled and was righted by CZ tucking her behind his back.

Joan wiggled forward. "I'm being so rude," she said a bit breathlessly. "Grace, this is my best friend, CZ. CZ, this is Grace Collins, the spellmaker I was telling you about. Grace, I appreciate you saving my life. Or my mind."

CZ winced. "Sorry I manhandled you as thanks."

Grace's chin rose proudly. Her gaze very obviously flicked up and down CZ, who in turn gave her his own once-over.

Joan took advantage of CZ's distraction to completely escape his protective stance.

"Whoever it was, they aren't close by anymore," Abel said, appearing in a rush of air and startling CZ and Grace apart.

Grace recovered quickly. "It was advanced work, and I've never seen the spell before. Why do you have someone hunting you?"

"Can you use what you saw to figure out who cast it?" Joan asked urgently.

Grace's eyes flickered between the three of them. "Another Greenwood favor?"

"If it helps, you can count it as a LaMorte favor," Abel said. "And your discretion would be similarly appreciated."

"How do we know *she's* not the spellmaker who did it?" CZ asked. "There aren't that many in the world. First, she's conveniently summoned by the Greenwoods, then shows up here? I told you not to come with me, Joan. I don't know why you never listen."

"I know you're very worried about me, so I'm going to let that comment slide," Joan said.

Grace hefted her tote higher on her shoulder and put her other hand on her hip. "First of all, I've been in New York for years, I wasn't 'summoned' here, so take the bass out your voice. Secondly, Joan Greenwood comes to me outside her family to ask me a series of abstract questions about this new spell, then shows up at the Night Market, where people are saying the spell originated, and is attacked by an exceptionally skilled witch who rifles through her memories. Leading me to believe that, one"—Grace held up her fingers to punctuate her points—"Joan is not acting on behalf of the Greenwoods and might actually be acting in opposition to them, and two, that you, Joan, know something about this spell. Something others are desperate to know. Which maybe makes sense as someone who can't cast herself."

Joan sputtered. "Meaning what, exactly?"

"The chance to gain casting ability would be of particular interest to you," Grace said. She ended her monologue in a huff, glaring them all down, her words such a rapid assault that Joan felt like she was being slapped repeatedly.

"No!" Joan cried out at the final insinuation, at the same time CZ burst into surprised laughter.

"You think *Joan* created the spell?" he asked incredulously.

"Or someone Joan knows well," Grace said firmly. "It makes sense."

"No, it doesn't!" Joan interjected. "Well, maybe it does! But it isn't true—we just—" Joan looked at the LaMorte brothers helplessly. Joan *had*, in the privacy of her own mind, ruminated fairly extensively on whether Mik's spell could help her fix her own issues. But she had never uncaged the thought, and she'd only acted on it as far as it coincided with her urge to help Mik. She knew better than to pin her hopes of finally regaining status in her family on a half-baked spell cast on a human.

"Not my problem," Abel said, raising his hands. "Witch business belongs to witches."

CZ was bent over, palms on his knees, laughing even harder. "Joan! An evil mastermind! Do you know how many times I caught her burning her bagel in the dining hall in college because she can't even use a toaster?"

"They're all different!" Joan snapped. "The settings vary, and sometimes one minute on one is too much or too little!"

"It was the same dining hall every time, Joan! Same toaster!"

"Guys," Abel chided. "Please focus."

"I wonder what your family would think about all this," Grace said coldly to Joan.

Joan slapped CZ on the back, hard, but it only sent him deeper into his fit of laughter. "Do *not* tell my family," Joan said.

Grace, to her credit, only stood straighter. "Or what? You're gonna throw around your privilege and bury me? I have no interest in protecting people trying to mess with magic like this. You have no idea what the repercussions are, and with your family history, I can only assume it's a mess of ethical dilemmas ignored for the sake of power."

CZ straightened, dusting off his clothes and letting out one last amused sigh. "This has been a real pleasure. I've never seen someone so fundamentally misunderstand Joan. It's beautiful, really."

"Grace, I need you to forget everything you saw tonight," Joan said urgently. "Not for my sake."

Abel winced. "This is coming off as a threat, Joan."

Joan waved her hands. "No! No, no, it's— CZ, help me."

CZ shrugged. "I don't know her well enough to know if we should trust her, and I have no intentions of kidnapping or killing her to keep her quiet. Her presence here is still suspicious to me."

"So *now* you're drawing a line," Joan snarked without thinking. "Maybe you should have made a no-taking-people rule *before* you took— Oops."

Abel rubbed at his temples. "I can't believe you guys haven't been caught yet. It's honestly so sad to listen to this. Either send her away or bring her into this fucked-up little group of confidants. If she's the one behind all this, she deserves to win at this rate, because the two of you are just fumbling around, bumping into things."

Unfortunately, Joan *needed* Grace. Well, any spellmaker, or really any witch who could cast, but Grace was both. Joan needed to know who had rifled through her head and how to undo the spell on Mik. She needed witches for a sealing spell, and Grace now had some information to hold over Joan's head. Very dangerous suppositions that could really mess up Joan's life—and, more importantly, CZ's and Mik's.

What Joan knew about Grace was hearsay and instinct. Grace didn't seem to want to be involved in witch politics, and she was willing to break from the whole witch world to stay away. She wasn't even from the city, though she'd been here several years. Her mentor was encouraging her to establish herself, but she resisted. She shopped at the Night Market like it was no big deal, indicating she clearly had no problem being in community with Moon Creatures. She didn't feel that this magic should have been messed with in the first place. If Joan didn't do something, Grace could turn around tomorrow and tell Valeria.

Joan wasn't proud of it, but she suspected the best way to get Grace on their side was to make her complicit. Staring her down hard, Joan felt, in her heart of hearts, that Grace was not the one who had just been in Joan's head. That touch had been freezing cold, and Grace was warm, vast.

Joan would have to trust her gut here.

"We know the human who was turned into a witch," Joan confessed. "We have them, and they're not well—the magic, it makes them sick. It happened against their will, and we're trying to track down who did this to them before my family catches up to us." Joan looked at the brothers. "Before either of our families catches up to us."

Grace's eyes were wide and round and dark, drinking in the lights of the market. Her hand fell off her hip; her mouth lost its tension. That was surprise on her face, genuine surprise, Joan was sure of it, and it morphed into horror moments later.

In that transformation, Joan saw the heart of Grace Collins—this was not a woman playing the game of witches. This was someone who genuinely cared. This person, despite reason, *believed* Joan.

Grace's gaze turned flinty. "How can I help?"

TEN

Clustered together in an alley, Joan, CZ, and Abel filled Grace in on what little they knew.

Grace was tapping her foot, face unreadable. "You definitely need a witch to help you," she said. "You'll have to take me to Mik, and I'll do what I can to suppress the magic a little, and then we can figure out how to determine if there's still some sort of tether in place. Or I can try to rummage around in their memories like someone did in Joan's."

Joan relaxed with each confident word Grace uttered. Grace clearly possessed the ability to stop another attack. CZ looked absolutely starstruck by the woman.

"Wait," Abel said suddenly. "Someone rooted around in Joan's head."

The three of them looked at him questioningly. He grabbed CZ's arm to usher them all rapidly through the market, walking backward for a second to hiss at them. "Someone rooted around in Joan's head, a head that knows exactly where Mik is at this moment, totally alone."

CZ whirled on Joan, and panic had transformed his face. Mik, all alone. Mik, being taken again. They had known each other a sum total of two days but—

"We can't let anything happen to them," CZ said.

"Human subway's an hour, but if I take the HERMES, I don't know how to bring them back with me, and I'm not—I mean, if there *is* an intruder, I don't think I can…" Joan trailed off in a bit of a breathless gasp as the four of them picked up speed, now running for one of the boundaries of the market.

I don't think I can protect them. Joan wasn't like Grace, who could cast, or Abel and CZ, who could rip a person apart.

She couldn't protect the people who mattered to her.

Desperate tears welled in her eyes, an overload of frustrated helplessness. "How fast can you run there?" she asked CZ urgently.

"Less than twenty minutes," CZ said. "But where do we bring them after? My apartment isn't safe anymore."

They burst through the wards, moving at a dead sprint for the witches and a casual jog for the vampires, ignoring the alarmed looks they were getting. The park was deep and endless in the darkness around them.

"My apartment," Grace said without hesitation, and listed an address nearby in Bay Ridge. "My wards are strong. We'll meet you there. And be careful."

If Grace was the spellmaker behind all this, they'd be delivering Mik right into her waiting hands.

But Joan didn't know where else they could possibly move Mik.

CZ sent a questioning glance in Abel's direction.

"I'm not sending my little brother into potential danger alone," Abel said. "Mom and Dad and even Aunt Lila would kill me. I'm with you."

CZ's fingertips brushed Joan's bare arm lightly in reassurance, and then the brothers were gone.

After pausing so Grace and Joan could put their hands on their knees and gasp a bit in tandem, Grace led the way to her nearby apartment.

It was on the fifth floor of a building in Bay Ridge, and they were both wiped enough that they took the little elevator rather than attempt the stairs.

"Hanging out with vampires makes me feel like shit," Grace grumbled, fanning herself with a hand.

"Tell me about it," Joan said, slumped against the wall. "You know, I used to run track in high school?"

"And how long ago was high school?"

"Long enough that I'm wheezing in an elevator," Joan said, straightening as they hit the fifth floor and Grace exited, walking down the hallway to an apartment that fizzled with magic.

Joan concentrated for a moment, narrowing her eyes, and magic manifested like a golden web on the apartment. She whistled low, impressed, distracted at least for a second from the thought of Mik being snatched. "Those are some kick-ass wards."

Grace didn't look back as she opened the door, but there was a clear smile in her voice. "All my private tutoring had to be good for something. When Fiona visits, she does her best to poke holes in them. Mik should be safe here for the moment."

"Fiona comes by often? You must be close." Joan had run all her tutors off, eventually.

"She has an apartment in the city, New York's better for finding odd magic jobs, but she remains based in Atlanta," Grace said, flicking on a light in the entryway and making room for Joan to step in. "And we *are* close. My dad is totally human, and my mom doesn't have magic, though her parents can cast. It meant a lot of my exposure to the spellmaking world came through Fiona. I wouldn't have had half the opportunities I've had if not for her. She works really hard, you know."

There was something accusatory about Grace's tone. "I never said she didn't."

"Tell that to your aunt. Fiona's been gunning for an actual job for years. Spellmaking isn't particularly lucrative unless you work in academia, which Fiona hates, or as a private contractor for corporations, and those positions go to people with family connections," Grace said bitterly. "She can only make a living by pulling in jobs here in the city, but she can't afford to live here full-time either and has to rent it out half the year."

"Grace, I know my aunt is watching you two closely. If you help with this spell, I'm sure she'll help Fiona get placed," Joan said. She was pretty used to people taking out their Greenwood family grudges on her. It went hand in hand with being the least intimidating Greenwood.

"Sorry," Grace said after a beat. "I guess that was a lot. It's just…I know Fiona can be a bit cold, but underneath she's one of the best and most generous people I know. I'd do anything to help her. We used to dream of this city together. I gave her a stupid snow globe of it, some tourist nonsense, back when I was still a kid in Georgia, and she used to bring it out all the time to show people."

"It's no problem." Joan toed off her shoes, massaging her still-burning thighs. The apartment was actually fairly well sized, with a hallway that bent at an angle with a few doors off it, and a kitchen and living room in front of her. It was very sparsely furnished. A window at the back of the kitchen showed, way off in the distance, the Verrazzano-Narrows Bridge lit up in the night.

"Water? There's no use standing there worrying," Grace said, stepping into the kitchen and placing her produce bag on the counter. "They'll probably text soon to confirm if they have Mik. Can CZ run back with them?"

Joan shuddered. "A piggyback ride from CZ at high speeds is a harrowing experience, but yes, it's possible." She had mainly done it drunk, so hopefully Mik would fare better sober. Joan accepted the glass of water, and the two of them stood there in the kitchen, leaning against the counter.

Grace seemed unconcerned with the silence, so Joan settled into it, her mind beginning to drift. Someone had clearly connected Joan to Mik, which was a distressing thought. Joan didn't think she'd left any obvious trails—Grace was her loosest end, and she was now part of the inner circle.

"Oh!" Grace said, thunking her empty glass down on the counter. "My roommate!"

Joan came back to herself, dreaming suddenly of yet another person who might rat them all out. "Should I tell the boys not to come here?"

"No, she won't mind, and she can keep a secret— There you are, Billy."

Grace was looking over Joan's shoulder, and Joan spun around to see a ghost floating in the entryway to the kitchen, hair dark and wild around her, eyes golden and shaped like a hawk's.

The ghost, Billy, watched Joan curiously. "Finally," she said, "I've been waiting so long." Then she phased through the wall behind her and disappeared into nothing.

"You get used to her," Grace said with a smile. "She's a freaky little fucker, but she came with the apartment, and the haunting rumors kept the rent absurdly low, especially for a three-bedroom. Two thousand a month."

"*Three* bedrooms for two thousand—" Joan began, maybe a few pitches too loud, when her phone buzzed, and she fumbled it out expeditiously to see a text from CZ.

Got Mik, they're fine.

Very Grumpy

On our way

Joan: thank jeebus. Pls hurry

CZ: I am breaking world records rn

"They're fine," Joan said, glancing up at Grace, who was frowning. "Are you upset that they're fine?"

"No, of course not. But it does make me wonder…this person had a head start, so why didn't they grab Mik?" Grace asked. "What stood in their way?"

"Or who," Joan said. "Two powerful vampires might be enough to deter a singular witch. Or…we're assuming that the person who invaded my mind was after Mik specifically, but we don't know that for sure. They could be after something else up there." Joan rapped her knuckles on her skull.

"You *are* a Greenwood, I guess," Grace said. "I'd jump into your head if I found you in the Night Market and wanted to know what your parents and aunt were up to. What are they up to?"

Joan reclaimed her glass of water. It was a weirdly reassuring thought that she might have been attacked because of her last name and not because someone knew about Mik. "I'm really taking a swing trusting you. You actually could be an ingenious villain who has just had everything you ever wanted handed to you on a silver platter. Mik's coming here; I'm about to spill family secrets."

"That's true," Grace said, in the no-bullshit way Joan was coming to know and like a great deal. "You have absolutely no way of knowing if I'm trustworthy, but it kind of feels too late to back out now. So, while we wait for your vampires, please let me know what your family is planning next. I promise I won't tell anyone else, if that helps. I keep my word."

A promise. *We aren't children, Joan.*

But Joan didn't want to live like her aunt did, always on the lookout. Joan still wanted to believe people could make promises to one another and keep them.

So she picked up the threads they'd left off on in the market and told Grace absolutely everything she could. By the time she was done, Grace had buzzed to let the LaMortes into the building, and then they were knocking on the front door.

Grace answered it, and CZ and Mik fell in through the door in a flurry of thrown elbows and curses, from where they'd clearly been wrestling a bit outside the door.

"Grace!" CZ said, straightening and brushing off his shirt. "Beautiful apartment."

"Where's Abel?" Grace asked.

"Broke off once we hit Bay Ridge. Mom called him in for something, what with him being so important and everything."

Joan gave him a look, the one that was supposed to mean *You are not your brother, and that's a good thing.*

CZ let out a breath, one that meant *Sorry, didn't mean to get too down.* "He'll link up with us tomorrow. Said he might have a trinket for Joan."

"A trinket?" Grace asked.

"I love trinkets," Joan said happily. Abel collected magic arti-facts and occasionally passed on rings and bracelets and other jewelry to Joan if they ended up being unmagical or empty. Half the rings on Joan's fingers now were from Abel.

"Something about a mind ward, just in case," CZ said.

Mik coughed conspicuously. They were dressed rather ridicu-lously in one of CZ's baseball caps, sunglasses, and a scarf, like a very obvious spy in a movie. They ripped the layers off, sweating.

"Hello, I'm Mik. The source of everyone's problems these days," they said, sticking out a hand that Grace shook. "Sorry you've been pulled into the crime ring."

"Don't worry about it," Grace said. "If I go down, I'm taking Joan with me, which her family won't like at all, so there might be some level of protection there."

"Smart," Joan said.

Mik made to remove their hand, but Grace held fast, giving them an intense stare.

"Whoa there," Mik said, yanking their hand again.

CZ made his way into the kitchen to stand next to Joan, lean-ing down to whisper at her. "We trust her?"

"Mostly," Joan whispered back. Magic danced around Grace, caressing her body. "I think she's about to cast. Mik, hold still."

Grace's lips moved soundlessly, and her free hand floated up to twist in the air, where it hovered for a moment before her fists closed around a thread of magic that ran into Mik and she pulled.

Mik made a keening noise, and CZ tensed, but Joan held him back with a hand as Grace pulled out more threads of magic.

"There," Grace said, blinking herself back into reality and finally dropping Mik's hand. "That should help."

Mik examined their hands. "I feel way lighter," they whispered. "What did you do?"

"I can't do a full seal on my own," Grace said. "I could dim the magic a bit. We'll have to try the magic tracing and the memory stuff tomorrow, I think. It's been a long day for me; I'll admit I'm tired."

Mik's fist bunched in their scarf. "Joan said you'd need four witches for a seal."

"I could swing it with only one other witch, if they were really powerful," Grace said. "But two more would be safest. It might seem counterintuitive, but it takes an enormous amount of magic to strip it from someone else, and you usually need multiple people to net that much energy and then come up with a spell powerful enough to shape it. Come in, did CZ and Abel explain you'd be staying with me for a little?"

"Ish," Mik said. "Mostly they were zipping around, grabbing me and running. But I gathered the gist. Thanks for opening up your apartment."

"She has a ghost roommate," Joan added.

"I don't know what that means," Mik said cheerily, wandering into the living room, which had a TV and nothing else. "Did you just move in?"

"A few weeks ago," Grace said. "Didn't do a lot of furnishing."

"Oh, I can help with that," Joan said with no small amount of relief. She was standing there twiddling her thumbs. She pulled a credit card out of the back of her phone. "Here, Grace, as thanks for your help, and Mik, as apology for your house arrest, feel free to engage in some retail therapy, on me."

"There's no need," Grace said, eyes narrowing. "I don't need charity."

"What's the budget?" Mik asked, accepting the card. They shrugged at Grace's glare. "I've decided to embrace the fact that I am crashing on people's floors. Whatever. She's offering."

"The budget," CZ said with a little laugh. "Nice one."

"I'm really quite wealthy," Joan said. "Spend away."

"Then why were you acting impressed by my rent?" Grace grumbled, snatching the card from Mik's hands to examine it, like it might start spitting out money on the spot.

"Because that's damn good rent in New York," Joan said. "Not that I'm trying to deny my privilege."

"Unemployed with a trust fund," CZ said.

"Unemployed with a trust fund," Joan agreed. "Okay, I, for one, am so tired. Can I sleep at your place tonight, CZ? I don't know if the party is still raging at mine."

"Are we sure it's safe?" CZ asked. "I was contemplating crashing with Abel."

"You can both stay here," Grace said. She cleared her throat awkwardly. "If you want. I'll conjure up mattresses for now, if you don't mind sleeping without bed frames. We'll resume our escapades in the morning."

"Oh, we don't want to be a bother," Joan said.

At the same time, CZ waved his hand and replied, "Joan and I can figure out our own stuff, thanks though."

Mik leaned toward Grace. "They're such a unit. They talk in unison all the time, and when they're not doing that, they kind of look at each other and somehow communicate telepathically. Is that a vampire thing?"

"It is not," Grace said. "And I didn't offer to be polite. I have two more bedrooms: Mik can have one, the happy couple can have the other." There was a curious note to the last part of her sentence.

"We get that a lot," Joan said. "But we're not together."

"Tragically, Joan has turned down all my advances," CZ said in a bad fake British accent.

"I'm a lesbian," Joan said. "And he has never been attracted to me; he's lying. He once referred to me as a 'sister' while hitting on some guy, which feels pretty damning."

"Why I oughtta…" CZ said half-heartedly, faking a punch.

"We're still cool to share a room though," Joan said. "If you really meant it about staying a night. We'll figure something out tomorrow. No need to conjure something, especially something as big as a mattress; we can sleep on the floor. We don't want to drain your magic even faster." Witches could, in theory, conjure up any sort of physical object but were typically limited by size. The larger an object, the more magic it took to create and the more magic it drained to keep the spell active and the object manifested. Once that magic ran out, it would fizzle out of existence.

Grace was chewing on her lip, gaze darting between CZ, who was still talking in that terrible accent and posturing himself across the kitchen, and Joan, who was still in the jumpsuit Molly had laid out for her.

"I don't say things I don't mean," Grace said, "and no guests of mine will sleep on the floor." She pivoted, waving everyone down the hallway so she could assign rooms. "My mother would beat my ass if she heard I treated a visitor like that."

Each was totally empty, but clean and without cobwebs. Grace explained that Billy didn't sleep and so had elected not to choose a bedroom for herself, instead appearing in the apartment at random. She then conjured up king-size mattresses for both rooms, despite heavy protest, looking a bit weary after the fact, and after showing them the two bathrooms, she sent them all off to bed.

CZ didn't really sleep more than about three hours a day, but he was content to scroll on his phone with a borrowed charger for hours on end, so Joan curled up at his side, back pressed to him.

Faster than she'd thought possible, she was asleep.

ELEVEN

Joan dreamt of a garden, halfway up the mountain on a strange small island, and woke to an empty mattress beside her.

She rolled, the taste of salty ocean air fading, and was met with a pair of golden eyes.

"Good morning," Billy said, leaning over the mattress to stare down at Joan.

Joan's yelp was involuntary and loud, and her bladder was so full that she feared she'd pee right there in that bed.

The door slammed open to CZ, Grace behind him with a spatula in her hand, wielding it like a weapon.

Joan thumped back on her pillow. "False alarm," she said. "Billy scared me."

Billy had her arms folded, one hip cocked to the side as she looked at the two of them in the doorway. "I think it's about time you all get your little show on the road," she said. "Metaphorically—Mik really shouldn't go anywhere."

Grace lowered her spatula and turned back to the kitchen, grumbling. "Nag."

"You have work!" Billy said, drifting through the wall to follow Grace.

CZ offered Joan a hand up. He didn't really sweat, but both of them were grimy from the events of the previous night. Joan realized as she stood up—but luckily before she stepped into the hallway—that she was dressed in only her underwear and one of Grace's borrowed shirts.

"Clothes," Joan mumbled. "Then peeing."

"Grace is making pancakes," CZ offered.

"Then pancakes," Joan added, yanking on last night's jumpsuit. "Then Grace does the memory thing?"

"Then Grace and I go to work," CZ finished, leading her out the door. "And you?"

"I don't know," Joan said truthfully, stepping into the neat little bathroom. She'd been blowing off job interviews her dad had set up because she was determined to find her own thing, but it felt like it fell to the bottom of her list of worries when she had a house and didn't pay rent and someone else bought groceries, and oh, she was currently trying to figure out how to keep Mik safe.

She exited the bathroom after splashing water on her face and, back in the kitchen, accepted a plate of pancakes from Grace, blowing her a kiss, which Grace made a show of slapping out of the air. Mik was already chowing down on their own stack, seated crisscross on the floor of the living room.

"You need a dining table," Joan remarked, sitting beside Mik. "And a couch. Please. Oh, and plants!"

"Joan pretends to choke to death in any room without plants," CZ said.

Joan dug into her food. "They make a real difference in oxygen levels."

"Everyone's a critic," Grace said. She pointed her spatula at Mik, who was scrambling to pull out Joan's credit card. "*No. Don't even think about it*—I don't need a load of brand-new garbage. I intend to thrift what I can."

"I respect it. If someone would allow me a device, I can get on my thrifting sites," Mik said, licking syrup off their fork. "I'm kind of a savant at finding stuff secondhand. Or I was, before my whole life ended."

Joan paused with her second bite of pancakes partway to her mouth and looked up to see Grace and CZ already exchanging a meaningful look. Mik had stumbled into CZ's arms sans phone or computer, and CZ didn't exactly have spares, and it had really been less than three days in total since he'd found them, so Mik had not had access to a device in that time. They'd all agreed it was likely best they didn't contact anyone from their old life (yet) and tell them they were alive.

"I promise I won't text my parents," Mik said, sitting straighter. "Despite the fact that they're probably out of their minds with worry. Look, I know I've made some escape attempts."

"Several," CZ said.

"And I know I've been vocally against my lockup," Mik continued, unbothered.

"As anyone would be," Joan reassured.

"But I'm feeling better about the whole situation, so I'm going to be better at being a team player while we sort this out," they finished. "Stockholm syndrome is setting in."

"That's not real," Grace murmured. "Cops made it up to be sexist."

Now Joan and CZ were doing the telepathic-communication thing.

Grace is so smart and sexy, Joan imagined CZ was saying.

Is Mik trying to trick us? Joan asked back.

CZ shrugged. *We're easily tricked.*

Grace stepped in again, turning back to the last of the pancakes she was flipping. "Last night CZ had to literally run to Manhattan because we thought you were being attacked, as a result of Joan being attacked, and now you're in some stranger's house in Brooklyn, where that stranger is preparing to delve into your memory. And all that is making you feel better about the situation?"

Mik got up to put their plate in the sink and leaned against the counter, arms folded. "Yup," they said, popping the *p* at the end. "When it was just CZ and Joan, I knew you guys meant the best, but I could see how panicked you both were, and that didn't inspire a lot of confidence. No offense."

"None taken," Joan said.

"Sooo much offense taken," CZ countered.

"But Grace and Abel seem to have a better handle on things," Mik said, and at least their tone was a bit apologetic. "We know what the next steps are. So I'm giving you all a week where I am the picture of obedience. I can be trusted with a phone."

Grace's matter-of-fact tone really helped her live up to the *has a better handle on things* reputation. "Let's see if we can get you out of here in under a week, then." She set down her spatula and approached Mik. "Let me try taking a look at your memories to see if there's anything we can uncover. And Joan and I will have to figure out if there are any witches we might be able to trust to come over and do a sealing. Fiona feels like an obvious choice for me."

"See," Mik said. "I am but a baby bird Grace has taken under her wing."

"Ungrateful," CZ grumbled, sidestepping Grace and heading to the sink so he could start washing the dishes, a loathsome task.

"Oh, I'll handle that—" Grace started, looking alarmed.

"Don't be silly," CZ interrupted. "You are saving the life of my dear friend Mik."

"Still a stretch," Mik said.

"And you let us crash here last night. I'm doing the bare minimum."

If Grace's skin weren't so dark, Joan was roughly 99 percent sure she'd be blushing. Joan glared at the two of them, sizing them up. She would love to see CZ fall into a romance; he deserved it. And Joan admittedly did kind of worship the ground Grace walked on. But would they work together? They were in the shy early stages, much too soon to tell.

"I think they'd be a good match," a voice whispered in her ear, and it was a testament to Joan's adaptability that she only shivered as Billy faded in and then rapidly out.

Mik regained Grace's attention with a pointed little smirk, and Grace scowled, bringing her hands up. "This shouldn't hurt, but it might feel a bit weird," Grace said. "Hang in there."

She began casting a spell that looked vaguely familiar to Joan, likely some standard memory spell meant to find any blocks. As it had last night, magic danced around Grace, gleaming like bells as she wove a sort of crown and placed it on Mik's head.

Joan couldn't see the effects of the spell beyond that, but both of them closed their eyes and stood there, Grace's hand gentle on Mik's face.

Enough time had passed that CZ finished with the dishes and was drying his hands when tears began to pour from Mik's still-closed eyes.

"Is that normal?" CZ asked Joan, tensing like he was prepared to rip them apart.

"I don't know, but—"

"They're fine," Billy said. "And nearly done." Billy leaned in close to Grace and Mik, admiring them from different angles. "I always love to watch Grace cast. Joan, isn't it beautiful?"

"I can't believe she's considering working in only the human world and leaving spellmaking behind," Joan grumbled. "She really is a prodigy."

"She's seen too much cruelty among witches," Billy said. "If you'd watched your mentor kicked to the edges of high society, disrespected constantly by families like the Greenwoods, and kept on the brink of poverty, would you want to join this world? She's not alone. So many witches just like her, talented in all sorts of magic, are never given a proper place in your community."

That was fair, the Greenwoods were miles away from the normal everyday concerns of working-class witches, and Joan had no illusions about how much her family was *liked*. But she also didn't want Grace to have to give up something she clearly loved, a field she could likely make a real difference in, because Joan's family had ruined everything.

"Are you a witch?" CZ asked Billy.

"I'm a ghost," Billy said.

"No, I mean . . . before you died."

Billy's eyebrows rose. "I'm dead?"

CZ grimaced. "No . . . of course not . . ."

"I'm messing with you," Billy said. "I was a witch of sorts. Now I . . . I can't touch magic like I used to, not dead as I am. It runs through me like the wind, harmless." She gave a little smile, meeting Joan's gaze. "Oh, here we go."

Grace removed her hand as both their eyes flew open. Mik dashed at their cheeks, laughing a little self-consciously.

"Crying?" they said. "In this economy?"

Grace remained totally silent. Joan didn't know her well enough to read all her facial expressions, but there was a pinching to her brows that Joan didn't much like.

"What did you see?" CZ asked, hand drifting up slightly like he could offer some sort of physical comfort to them both.

"Glimpses, not much," Mik said. "Entering the market, the... the *wonder* I felt. And I was shopping for little odds and ends to take home, I remember that, and then there was someone touching my elbow, and it felt so cold, my breath was frosting. I turned around to see who it was, and then my vision blacked out."

They took a steadying breath. "From there, it's just darkness, and then I wake up in a tent. It looks lived in. I'm on a bed, and the walls are dark blue. There's another bed and lots of books, leather-bound journals. Mice in cages. There are, like, strips of sheets tying me to the bed, but one of the knots has come loose, so I get out. I get up and I stumble out and, well, the rest is history."

Breath cold enough to frost. That sounded familiar.

"Grace? What about you?" CZ asked.

Grace was staring through them all.

"Grace?" Joan said cautiously, moving closer to the woman. When she hesitantly touched Grace's arm, it was cold. A line of frost burst across her skin under Joan's fingers.

Grace moved the moment she was touched, grabbing her own arms to give herself a hug. Magic rose like a shield, settling on her skin in a layer that wiped away the frost.

"What? Oh, I saw the same. The rest of the memories have been stolen," Grace murmured. "Erased entirely. I can't recover them."

"Are you alright?" Joan asked, looking around to see if there was a blanket or sweater or something to hand to Grace, but Grace shrugged her off, stepping away to grab her purse off the ground and sling it over her shoulder.

"I have to go to work," Grace said. "Mik, my computer's in my room, and there's a sticky note on it with my password. Feel free to do what you want. We can try to figure out your magic further once I get back; I don't want to be late."

"Are you sure you're okay?" Mik asked, clearly as uneasy as the rest of them at Grace's strange behavior. "I won't even comment on the terrible security system that is putting your password on paper right on your computer."

"Peachy," Grace said, yanked her door open, and left.

"We trust her, right?" Mik asked into the resulting quiet. "Because that was suspicious as hell."

"I'm inclined to believe a brilliant criminal would have lied better than she did," CZ mused. "And would not do the computer password thing. What is she, sixty-seven?"

Joan couldn't help but agree with both sides. Something had clearly upset Grace, but this was too obvious to fully believe. The same person who had gotten Mik delivered right to her couldn't be silly enough to blow it all because she couldn't lie.

Joan was very thin on proof of Grace's innocence other than her instinct though.

Her phone buzzed, and she pulled it out as Mik and CZ melted into a bickering match over the proper way to fold and hang a kitchen towel, cleaning up the rest of the kitchen. Joan, distracted by Mik's frankly absurd assertion that it should be folded into a square, answered without thinking.

"Jo," Molly said. "Can you come save my life?"

Joan blinked rapidly, focusing on her sister's voice. "What happened to hello? Good morning? How are you?" People couldn't keep calling her and saying stuff like this.

"I need you to come to my house right now, please," Molly said. "I will owe you one trillion dollars and my firstborn."

"I don't know if now's a good time," Joan said, eyeing Mik, who was folding and refolding the towel with exaggerated movements. "And you already owe me your firstborn from the last deal we made."

"Joan," Molly groaned. "Uncle."

Joan pulled the phone away from her ear as if she would be able to see Molly through it. Neither of them had cried *uncle* since Joan left for college. It had always been their tap-out move, less *I give up* and more *please, I need you to help me, no questions asked*.

They'd used it for help climbing out of the house in the dead of night (Joan). To get everyone to leave them alone so they could listen to music in their closet instead of doing homework (Molly). To rescue each other from conversations with their parents, one sister valiantly sacrificing herself to their parents' ire to save the other. At witch parties, funerals, and stuffy meetings. And then they'd grown up, and it had felt silly to call on someone else to fix your problems. Molly had gone to college first, two years Joan's senior, and left Joan behind.

"I'll be there in half an hour or so," Joan said, and hung up the call.

Mik was hitting CZ with the kitchen towel now in a fit of rage, but CZ caught it, looking at Joan, well versed enough in her tells to catch the simplest shifts in mood. "All good?"

"Molly needs me," Joan said. *I wish I knew what for.* "I'm heading uptown, probably on the HERMES. You're going to work? Mik, you're going to be okay?"

Both of them nodded dutifully.

"Be careful," Mik said.

"No more getting sucked into pocket dimensions," CZ added.

"I will try my best. Do you think that's a real risk?" Someone on the HERMES would notice if that happened, most likely. Joan would need to stay around witches who could save her until she reached her sister.

She couldn't be scared of her own city. New York would devour her.

"Hopefully not," Mik said. "But if so, run back here; Grace swears by her wards."

"Great," Joan said. She looked a mess, she smelled, her phone was almost out of charge, and she needed to brush her teeth, badly. But she'd worry about this after she made it to Tribeca.

"Be good, kids," Joan called, and she fled as fast as Grace had.

TWELVE

Joan knocked on Molly's door, already tired of this day, and it swung open to reveal none other than Astoria Wardwell.

Astoria looked perfectly crisp in a black muscle tank and those really cool pants with lots of pockets and straps, except her straps were filled with little knives. Her hair was French braided down either side of her head. She was, somehow, even more gorgeous than she had been last night. Effortlessly beautiful.

Joan looked like the rats of New York were on the brink of naming her their queen.

"You don't look very well," Astoria said with an entirely neutral inflection. "Did you have a bad night after stepping viciously on my toes?"

"What are you doing in my sister's house?" Joan asked, self-consciously running her hand through her curls and nearly getting her fingers stuck in a snarl.

"We were invited over for breakfast," Astoria said.

Wren popped around Astoria's shoulder. "Joan!" she said. "What a nice surprise."

Astoria moved aside unconsciously, making room for Wren in the tight space. "You two know each other?"

"We had a little chat last night," Wren said. "I think we'll be fast friends."

Joan gave a confused smile as her reply, because she wasn't at all convinced that they were going to be friends and that Wren wasn't trying to manipulate Joan into giving up all her secrets, which were many and dangerous. Joan was susceptible to manipulation, especially by a pretty woman. If Astoria tried it, she'd crack immediately.

"Is Molly in there?" Joan asked, trying to look everywhere but at Astoria. "I need to see her."

"Oh, of course, look at us, blocking the doorway. Come on, Story," Wren said, and tugged Astoria's massive bicep to move her out of the way.

Joan stepped in, brushing past Astoria with a smirk. "Come on, Story," she mocked, because she couldn't help it. Astoria looked too good not to be taken down a few pegs, and Joan had never been particularly demure.

Astoria grumbled as she shut the door. Joan couldn't pick out specific words, but Astoria even grumbled cutely.

Joan toed off her sneakers and found Molly in the kitchen, leaning on the counter as she spoke furiously into the phone. When Joan walked in, Molly looked up and abruptly cut off the conversation with a few words of deflection.

"Thank Circe," Molly said, grabbing Joan's arm and pulling her in to whisper in her ear. "Work's a mess; I need you to watch the Californians for me."

"What! You can't pawn them off on me," Joan hissed back. "I have obligations."

"You are unemployed and freshly back in town," Molly said.

"There are people I need to catch up with."

"You don't have friends; it's just CZ, and I'm sure he's at work right now."

Joan's unemployment was actually causing her a fair number of problems. *You're unemployed*, CZ had argued, *you have time to help me babysit Mik.*

You're unemployed, Molly was arguing, *you have time to help me babysit the Californians.*

Joan was going to get a job out of spite, because they were all grown, weren't they, and they shouldn't all need babysitting.

"Jo," Molly said, hushing her voice a bit and darting a glance to the dining room, where Wren and Astoria were chatting. "You should know that Mom and Dad are not pleased you left the party so early last night; I'd avoid them for a while if I were you. Mom's gone lawyer mode talking about how you don't have the right to leave, and Dad's convinced you're doing it specifically to spite him."

The thought of her parents being angry with her made her feel like she was thirteen. She *was* spiting them, but all of them, not just Merlin, and she was doing it quietly, in a not-so-in-your-face way. Merlin being on to her elicited a weird panic. Her parents' voices echoed in her head like ghosts, rattling around hard enough to kick up loose memories.

Do you have to embarrass us all the time? You make me feel like a bad mother.

Stop crying, you're giving everyone the wrong idea.

Her hands started to get clammy; her breathing thickened. Fuck, she was twenty-five with bigger problems. Why did it still feel like this?

She shook her head bodily, like the physical action would be able to crush her anxiety. It was hopeless, but it gave her enough clarity to refocus on Molly as best she could. *Breathe in, then out.* She really needed to find a therapist in the city.

Molly leaned in even closer. "Also, you know you kind of smell? Why are you still in your clothes from last night?"

Joan looked down at the yellow jumpsuit. "You're criticizing me while asking me for a favor?"

"Oh!" Molly gasped, loud enough that Astoria and Wren looked over. "Is this a walk of shame?"

Joan's face flushed with the power of a million suns. "Shut up!" she snarled at Molly. "No, it isn't." She held up defensive hands toward both Molly and the Californians. Wren was looking quite amused, and Astoria was as impassive as ever.

"I had a sleepover with CZ." Technically true. "And then you called me and I came running."

"Sure, Joan. CZ's a convenient excuse. I'm so glad you got some!" Molly said gleefully. She grabbed her keys off the counter. "This is such good news. You've completely turned around my day."

"Molly, please shut the fuck up," Joan said, following her sister around the kitchen. "Your obsession with this is becoming incredibly concerning. Guys, please don't listen to her."

"We're not hearing a thing," Wren sang. "Congrats though."

"Congratulating someone on having sex, that has to be embarrassing," Astoria remarked.

Joan made a slashing motion across her throat in Astoria's direction, and Astoria cocked an eyebrow.

"I don't think you can get close enough to shut me up," Astoria said.

"I'm wily," Joan said as Molly gathered her purse. "I'm like a cat, I will claw you to shit."

"I'm a dog person," Astoria said. "Wouldn't know, so the threat doesn't scare me."

Of course Astoria was a dog person; she seemed like the sort of person who trained hunting dogs and then raced them to the kill. All muscled and ferocious looking. No, Joan only respected cat people. Maybe rat people. Not ferret people.

Molly had taken advantage of this back-and-forth to scurry into the hallway and slip on her shoes.

"Hey! You!" Joan yelled, chasing after her sister and skidding a little on the chevron hardwood floors. She backtracked three steps to turn a plant in the window that was starting to grow lopsided, and its leaves tickled her hand. "I never agreed to this."

"I called *uncle*," Molly yelled back at the end of the hallway, already closing the door behind her. "I owe you!"

The door shut with a horrifying finality, and Joan banged a fist into the wall, but lightly because she didn't want to actually risk the drywall and she wasn't really that strong.

"Gods damn it," she muttered to a framed picture of Molly and Nate on a hike.

"We're not that bad," Wren called from the other room.

"In fact, we don't need an escort at all," Astoria added. "I promise we can make it around New York City on our own. Your aunt has already tried to pack our schedules with various meetings to keep us occupied and unable to meddle in her affairs."

Joan peeked hopefully around the corner. "So all I have to do is drop you off at some meetings?"

"Oh no," Wren said conspiratorially. "We declined all of them. We have other plans."

"Plans I assume I am supposed to stop you from enacting," Joan said miserably, walking dejectedly into the room.

"Probably," Astoria said.

Wren slapped her arm lightly. "We don't need to be at odds with each other."

"You can say that all you want, doesn't mean I believe you," Astoria said. She canted her body language toward Joan. "Wren says you aren't a Greenwood lackey and might be convinced to defy your family."

Joan crossed her arms, then consciously uncrossed them. Defensive body language wouldn't help here. She glared at Wren, as if she could read the woman's true intentions on her face alone. Grace felt like the maximum leap of faith Joan could take right now.

"Why? Are you trying to turn me over to the dark side? Make me a spy for the Wardwells? Because I should warn you, I do not like Poppy Wardwell or the way your state is run."

"Well, neither does Wren," Astoria said easily. "Join the club. And I'd never make *you* a spy."

"I could be a spy," Joan said. Who was Astoria to say what Joan could or could not be?

"You'd break in seconds."

"I would not." Astoria had no idea how many secrets Joan was holding right this very second. "What about you?"

"I could easily be a spy."

"No, I mean where do you stand on your mother's policies?"

Astoria took a beat to answer. "I see the logic in both sides."

Wren rolled her eyes. "I'm not going to have this fight right now. It's never-ending."

A rare flash of emotion crossed Astoria's face. If Joan were more generous, she might have marked it down as hurt. "I'm trying."

"I know," Wren said, putting a hand lightly on Astoria's

shoulder. She cleared her throat. "Joan, do you need some time before we begin?"

Joan felt like she was not supposed to have seen that interaction. It was too late to avert her eyes though; she had spent it staring both of them down in complete confusion.

She could press.

Her family would press—the chance to further a clear fission between the two interlopers from California? Priceless. Her family would squirrel away this information and feed it to Valeria to use as she deemed fit.

"Begin what?" Joan asked, following Wren's deflection. "Time for what?"

"Take a shower first, and you can find out," Astoria said, and perhaps Joan imagined the relief in her voice. "Against my better judgment."

"Astoria," Wren warned.

"Your wish is my command, Wren—just make her shower first."

Astoria was making Joan regret being nice.

"You do whatever Wren says?" Joan said, maybe a little meanly, but only because telling someone they needed to shower outright was a bit rude, even when it was totally true.

"Yes," Astoria replied. "She's way cleverer than me. I'm just a big guy with a sword."

"I don't see a sword," Joan sniped back.

Astoria put out her hand and cast without words or movements. A silver sword materialized in it. Gorgeous and sharp. "Better, Greenwood? I don't issue empty threats."

A warm shiver danced its way down Joan's spine. *A big woman with a sword. Kill me now.* "I've yet to hear a decent threat out of you, sweetheart."

Wren put her head on Astoria's shoulder briefly, laughing as Astoria's face flickered with outrage at Joan's taunt. "Go on, Joan, we promise we won't run away."

"And if we do, you'll just say we dastardly, devious Californians overpowered you and fled," Astoria said. "You can then go about your day as normal."

This felt like a win-win for Joan, so with a last suspicious glare in their direction—and a deliberate effort not to think too hard about what it would feel like for Astoria to overpower her, grab her bodily, wrap her big hands around Joan's wrists—she went upstairs to raid Molly's closet.

After a shower, which Joan wasn't too proud to admit did cure her depression, she thundered back downstairs in a borrowed blouse and jeans. Joan would never choose a blouse for herself, especially one with all these little bows at the cuffs and collar, but Molly's options were limited. This was, without a doubt, the most casual ensemble Molly owned.

The entire affair had unfortunately taken Joan a full thirty minutes, because she was forced to hand-wash her underwear and then throw it in the dryer for as long a cycle as she could spare. The glamorous life of Joan Greenwood.

Downstairs, Wren and Astoria were, surprisingly, still in the house. They sat at the dining table with a large piece of paper between them covered in scribbles.

Joan paused in the doorway, watching them, a portrait of long-standing intimacy. *We've known each other since we were three*, Wren had said, and Joan could see it in the easy way they occupied space together. Wren's finger traced something on the paper, and Astoria watched her intently, like the whole world revolved around whatever it was Wren was saying. Astoria replied, and Wren nodded along animatedly, their heads bent toward each other.

Just friends, Wren claimed, but Joan thought Astoria looked at Wren like they were something more.

Unrequited love, that was a knife to the heart. Joan felt an unexpected burst of sympathy for Astoria Wardwell. She shoved it down quickly; that was like feeling sorry for a snake that was actively strangling you.

"You're not as stealthy as you think," Astoria said without turning around. Her sword had disappeared. Joan kind of missed it, in a twisted way. None of her friends carried swords.

Joan stuck her tongue out at the back of Astoria's head. Wren, who'd been sitting opposite Astoria, stifled a laugh at the action.

"I'm not trying to be stealthy; it's my sister's house," Joan said, walking over and plopping into a chair on the other side of Wren.

Astoria gave her an appraising glance. "Those clothes don't suit you."

Wren smacked her arm. "Astoria!"

"What clothes *would* suit me, Wardwell, since you're apparently a fashion expert?" Joan shot back. "Something made of knives? A giant pointed dunce hat? I can't wait for your next scintillating insult."

"Something with fewer ruffles" was Astoria's serene reply. "Can we start?"

Wren shuffled the papers together and stacked them neatly, revealing a printed map of New York at the top. "Ready when you are. Joan, we'll explain after so it's harder for you to mess us up."

"You underestimate what a rascal I can be," Joan muttered. The paper was clearly important; she could snatch it away and scamper off. Knock Wren's chair out from under her. In a rare turn of events, the wishes of her family were aligning with her own—the Californians could not be allowed to make progress in tracking down the spell that had turned Mik.

Astoria's answering flick of her eyes was accompanied by an amused twist of the mouth. "I'd never underestimate your ability to annoy and pester."

Wren heaved a put-upon sigh, but she was smiling too, wider and more genuine. Not like Astoria's bare twitches of emotions. This close, Joan could see the faint jewel-tone shine, the too-large irises of Wren's dark eyes, more hints to her half-fae heritage.

"You're in a rare funny mood, Astoria," Wren said. "Joan, I should invite you around more often, soften her up."

"I'm always funny," Astoria protested.

"Hard pass," Joan replied. "Unless you can bring the sword back."

Astoria smirked. "Women only want one thing and it's disgusting."

"Shut *up*, Wardwell, oh my gods," Joan said, and she hated that a laugh broke free from behind the iron bars of her will. "Get on with your thingy so I can figure out how to ruin your lives."

Astoria looked all too smug as she lifted her hands to cast.

Wren's movements mirrored hers as magic began to swirl up around them, like a sandstorm kicked up in the desert. They moved beautifully together, and Joan squinted a little to clarify her vision. Magic shifted as it was drawn toward Astoria, taking on a silver hue. The longer Joan watched, the more she noticed that they weren't casting the same spell in tandem—they had broken apart one spell. Astoria was the one drawing in the vast majority of the magic, and Wren was there as a support, helping shape the actual spell to hold it.

Perhaps Wren was not a particularly powerful witch? She didn't seem to be attracting substantial levels of magic to herself, but her movements were highly refined. She was an adept spellcaster, and she'd scaled the magnitude of the spell to match the quantity of magic Astoria was pulling in. Her casting ability seemed to far outstrip her channeling. Joan had never, not once, seen someone split magic like this. It hadn't even occurred to her that it was possible.

Joan blinked, and the patterns of magic coalesced above the paper, making a shimmering map in roughly the shape of New York City and its five boroughs.

Astoria's and Wren's hands stopped, and they leaned in, peering at it closely.

"You made a map?" Joan said, also trying to get a better look. "That glows?"

Wren scooted her chair to the side to make more room. "Ink magic's my specialty, though I admit I normally do temporary tattoos with status-boosting effects to help us in fights, not magic maps. In LA—well, all over California—we have a series of magicked maps that track the way magic flows across the state. When something causes a blip, like a huge upsurge caused by magical creatures gathering, an attack of some kind, and so on, it shows up on the maps. Then the witches on call get deployed to investigate."

"This is a simple version of that," Astoria continued. "We don't have the time or resources to make something that can pick up on or parse the nuances like we do in LA, but this, broadly, shows us the way magic flows in New York City."

Oh no.

"Before we left, we consulted with some of our own spellmakers," Wren said, watching Joan's face closely. "They surmised that a spell large enough to turn a human into a witch might be a constant drain on the magic in the area."

Joan made her numb lips move. "You're trying to find a magic vacuum." *Don't give yourself away. Channel every ounce of Greenwood in you into lying.*

"Exactly," Wren said. The magic signature of New York swirled, folding in on itself. Tiny rifts formed and were smoothed over. Bright spots flared and then darkened.

"Where's this?" Astoria asked, pointing her finger at a spot in Brooklyn where the magic had gone dark. And stayed dark.

Wren furrowed her brow and wiggled her fingers slightly, and the map on the paper shifted, the ink rearranging to reveal Brooklyn in greater detail. The words hadn't yet formed labels, but Joan knew the area like the back of her hand.

Bay Ridge.

The entire borough on one piece of printer paper wasn't making for enough specificity to pull anything like a street number, but Wren seemed more than capable of making the map home in.

Joan had no idea how to undo this spell—she was as much a failure at casting counterspells as she was at producing the initial magic—but she had to disrupt the map, and fast.

"Isn't this area where the Night Market is?" Wren mused. "Poppy said it was in Brooklyn, most likely in a park. Its nullification wards might trigger a dead spot."

"Greenwood? Is that correct?" Astoria asked.

Joan's tongue tangled in her mouth, which was suddenly completely dry. She pried it open and took a breath. She couldn't allow them to narrow down to the Night Market *or* Grace's apartment—both trails led to Mik, and the former might add fuel to the whole *invade the market* idea.

"The market is in Staten Island," Joan said smoothly.

Astoria gave her a calculating look. "I doubt my mother's intel is wrong."

"Your mother isn't a New Yorker," Joan replied. This was a small delay, no more. Everyone in New York knew the Night Market was in Brooklyn. Almost everyone knew it was in Owl's Head. They only had to ask one magical creature outside the Greenwoods and the other richest families and someone would tell them the truth.

"It's probably a good place for them to hide," Wren muttered to herself. "In the market itself, the wards would cover the magic vacuum they were producing."

"Can you make the map clearer?" Astoria asked.

Whoever was behind the spell on Mik, Joan already knew they had been in that market, and now that Wren mentioned it, it was probably for precisely those reasons—to hide the effect of funneling so much magic in.

And while the Owl's Head rift was much bigger, Joan knew what she was looking for and could see that there were two rifts on the map: one indeed over Owl's Head, and another one over Grace's apartment. If they zoomed in, they would see both.

Magic vacuums.

What if Joan could produce another one, then, one large enough to skew the entire map?

She couldn't counterspell, that was a fact. But one thing she'd always been able to do was draw in enormous amounts of magic.

If she formed it into a spell, the two witches next to her would know instantly, and it would likely go awry, as always. And if she held it in her, she'd get sick.

But if she just *funneled* it, funneled it and released it back into the room simultaneously, maybe she could create enough movement over the whole map that she could distract them, at least long enough to lunge around Wren and burn that paper.

She'd never done it before, and if she gambled wrong, she was about to risk projectile vomiting all over both of them. Which would be embarrassing, but at minimum would likely distract them from their spell.

For Mik.

Joan drew a breath in as Wren's hands hovered over the paper again, working to zoom in.

Magic responded to her like air.

She drew it in, in, in. Not too fast but not too slow, letting it fill her insides, watching it shift in the room itself. And just as it seemed like it might fill her, Joan exhaled, expending magic back out in one stream, asking nothing of it, trying only to be a vessel through which it might flow seamlessly.

Like Grace said it tended to.

Like Billy said happened to ghosts.

Magic shifted, pulled toward her siren song, releasing back into the room only to be pulled back in again, and the map flickered.

Astoria sat up straighter. "Something's happening, zoom back out."

Wren did so quickly, scaling back to the borough, then the city, to see magic across New York heading subtly in the direction of Manhattan. It made waves that crested over the whole city, sloshing over the rifts in Brooklyn.

A cold sweat broke out on Joan's lower back as she concentrated,

Astoria and Wren's puzzled and rapid exchange of words fading out.

She was doing it.

It was like she was channeling the city itself.

Deep in the back of Joan's mind, something opened its eyes.

It was ancient, eternal. Joan felt its attention on her like a patter of rain across her face. It nuzzled closer, intrigued, and the more magic Joan drew in, the more solid it became in her mind. A formless, vast *thing* made of magic itself, so much so that it had gained some level of sentience.

Green Witch, it breathed.

Welcome home.

ACT TWO

THIRTEEN

The sound of Astoria's chair shifting brought Joan back to the present, shattering her concentration as Astoria stood up, hands raised as if to cast again.

The voice disappeared.

Joan's grip slipped, and magic slowed. The map started to stabilize as whatever Astoria was doing shored up its edges.

What the hell had happened? Joan had never channeled in a cycle at that scale before—she'd never thought such a thing would be useful, probably because she wasn't typically faced with the need to neutralize a magic map. Probably because she'd never really thought of magic across the entire city as having a pattern. Definitely she'd never imagined that if she did that, magic itself would look at her.

"It's fixing itself," Astoria muttered at the map.

But that wouldn't do.

That map ran on magic. It was magic, and Joan might not be able to dismantle it, but if there was no magic, it wouldn't run.

She could see its fraying ends, so she reached out mentally, picked at a corner, and sucked in, releasing the structured magic back into the formless air.

The magic blinked out.

"What the hell—" Wren began, and Joan took this as her chance to lunge past her, half standing to slap her palm down on the paper, whispering softly under her breath.

Astoria's hand came down on hers. Bigger, stronger, rough and scarred. Her hand curled around Joan's to pry it off, but it was too late.

Joan smiled sweetly up at Astoria as the paper beneath her burned away, the result of a tiny light charm that, as always, went haywire the moment Joan cast it, overloading the spell and making it burst into a little flame.

"Sorry," Joan said, her heart hammering. "Did you need that?"

She fluttered her eyelashes a few times, smiling pleasantly.

Astoria's face was a mask of shock, and her fingers curled further around Joan's, as if her body hadn't gotten the message and was still trying to stop Joan's shenanigans.

Joan looked at their entwined hands pointedly, then up at Astoria. She aimed to knock Astoria off-kilter the best way she knew how: being a shameless flirt.

"At least buy me dinner first, sweetheart. I'll take flowers too. Dahlias are my favorite."

Astoria's fingers stopped their movement. Joan watched the words process on her sweet little face. This close, with only a foot or two of space between them, Joan could smell Astoria's cherry soap, count her lashes, feel the cool flutter of her breath. This close, Joan could read Astoria like an open book. Surprise, then confusion, then a dawning realization.

Then amusement.

"You need someone to buy you dinner before you can even hold hands?" Astoria said in a low voice. "No wonder your sister was celebrating your walk of shame."

Joan curled her fingers into a fist, thoughts of ancient magic beings scattering. "You're not being very inclusive right now. It's Pride Month, you know. There's going to be a parade soon."

"Joan Greenwood," Astoria said softly, and her voice was so lulling. Joan felt herself drifting away on it. "What are you hiding in Brooklyn?"

Joan took an embarrassingly long time to register the question, deep as she'd fallen into Astoria's dark hazel eyes. She blinked, jerked back, and the dizzying sense of attraction was broken.

Astoria removed her hand from Joan's as they pulled apart, revealing a delighted-looking Wren sitting beneath and between them.

"Oh no," Wren said. "Don't let me interrupt this. Ray is going to kill himself when I tell him how hard you've been flirting, Astoria."

Ray? A boyfriend? Had Joan's gaydar been wrong? That was horribly worrying. A sinking feeling settled in Joan, which was stupid, because she hated Astoria Wardwell and all she stood for. She hated Astoria's mother, and she hated Astoria's smugness. Her muscled arms. Her sword. The beauty mark by Astoria's mouth. The scar in the corner of her lip. Yes, this burning feeling was hatred.

"I'm not flirting," Astoria said. "And you were right."

"I usually am," Wren said.

"Right about what?" Joan asked. "And who's Ray?"

Wren brushed the ashes on the table into a neat pile. Joan had scorched the wood. Maybe she could blame the mark on Astoria so Molly wouldn't get mad at her.

"My boyfriend," Wren said. "Our friend."

Astoria took this pronouncement a bit like a punch to the gut, bending slightly and then sitting back in her chair, her poker face back on. Wren didn't seem to notice.

Joan's unrequited-love theory was only gaining strength, and it was worse than that—Wren was in a relationship. With a mutual friend.

"And I'm right about the fact that the Greenwoods know something," Wren continued.

"Wren suspected if we let you in on our plan, you'd stop us the moment we started to get close to something good," Astoria said, back to being the picture of nonchalance. "We know your family is withholding information from the broader witch community. You've confirmed there's something about the Night Market in Brooklyn we should be investigating."

This was probably very bad news for Valeria, and it was certainly even worse news for Joan, someone else realizing the Night Market was the origin of Mik's creation. Joan flashed back to Janet Proctor cautioning the Greenwoods not to give in to the growing witch sentiment that they should storm the market. That would be disastrous, but it was at least a few steps removed from Mik themself. Selfishly, in the grand scheme of things, hearing that they hadn't realized there was a rift above Grace's apartment too was a huge win for Joan. Even if she had stupidly only drawn further suspicion to the market.

"Though I'd like to know how you messed with our spell," Wren said excitedly. "I didn't see or sense you cast. I've really never heard of a witch doing complex counterspells without moving or speaking; that level of talent usually only ever stretches to common, uncomplicated spells."

"Especially surprising, considering we heard you can't cast," Astoria added. "Was that a lie New York whispered into the world to hide you until some later moment? You're more formidable than I thought."

Joan leaned past Wren again to claim the pile of ashes, scooping it into her hand so she could walk to the kitchen and dump it in the trash. Giving her room away from Wren and Astoria. *You're more formidable than I thought.* Rumors of Joan must have been more pitiful than she'd known.

They didn't even know she had done something deliriously, unspeakably cool by sucking the magic right out of their spell. She'd messed with the magic currents across all of New York.

"Not a lie," Joan said. "I can't cast at all. I had nothing to do with your spell going wrong. Maybe look inward."

When she looked up, Astoria was rubbing her temples, and Wren had propped her chin on her hand, looking curiously at Joan.

"You're a good liar," Astoria said, and Joan chose to interpret her tone as a begrudging compliment. "You put people at ease so effortlessly."

"And you're a master manipulator," Joan replied, and she surprised even herself with the current of anger that ran through her words. "I've apparently played right into your hands. Did you orchestrate Molly needing to run out so I'd be called in? Try and get the weakest link to snap, and all that. Like you both tried last night."

"I have no ulterior motives with you," Wren said. "I've made my intentions very clear, and I won't lie to you. We did perhaps nudge a few things to get your sister out of the house."

Astoria gave Wren a measured glance, then redirected the full weight of that heavy stare on Joan. "I've also made it clear what I'm here for. My mother wants this spell. I have been sent to get it for her. You know that. But neither of us thinks you're the weakest link. At least, not anymore."

But they weren't the same intentions, Wren's and Astoria's, were they, and Wren's gaze held a dare in it. *Try and reveal me*, it said. *See what happens.*

"What remains unclear are *your* intentions, Joan," Astoria continued. "As I said, Wren is completely convinced you do not want New York witches to gain sole control over this new magic. So, are you an extension of your family, or do you have your own thing going on?"

Oh, how that question had always plagued Joan. Who was she, without the Greenwood name? Was she no one and nothing, or did she have her own things going for her?

Joan didn't, in whatever form the future took, want New York, and her family especially, to gain and maintain full control over this new magic, no. But confessing that here felt like high treason. Trying to argue with her aunt was one thing, but publicly acting contrary to the family's interests and loudly professing this to two Californian witches was another. It was betrayal. It was a line she wasn't ready to cross. She wasn't quite sure she'd be forgiven, and it dawned on her that, despite everything, she *did* want to be forgiven. She wanted to be forgiven of every crime she'd ever committed against her family, serious or not, and to have her portrait up in the hall, and for people to recognize her at the door of her aunt's study. She wanted to feel important.

She wanted to *be* important. And the thought felt dangerous, pathetic, and best left alone.

Joan straightened in the kitchen, crossed her arms, and cocked her head at the door. "I think it's time you leave my sister's house," she said.

Astoria's smile was razor-sharp, barbed wire and broken glass and the dangerous crush of the tide. "Don't make empty threats, Greenwood."

Joan felt, in that moment, that she was perfectly willing to burn the house down with all of them in it. That was how Astoria made her feel, like she was dangerous too. Like she had power too.

Wren stood, breaking the tension between them with her hands on her hips. "Stop it, you two. Joan, does this mean you're setting us loose in the city to do what we want, or are you still taking your babysitting duties seriously?"

"I assume you'd much prefer the former," Joan replied, unsure yet what her plan was. Being by Astoria made her want to shed her skin and destroy everything, but Molly was going to be so pissed off if Joan abandoned her post.

"No, I'd actually much prefer to spend some time with you," Wren replied. "As I've said, I think we're on the same side."

"Do you honestly? You *really* still think our goals are aligned here?"

Wren put out a hand to pull Astoria to her feet. "I do. Show us New York, if you want, take us to an endless stream of your favorite coffee shops, we won't mind. Do whatever makes you feel best so you can trust us."

Us, she said, but she still hadn't said it out loud in front of Astoria: *I want to give Moon Creatures the ability to cast.* Joan couldn't trust Wren until she knew she wasn't aligned with Astoria, and as far as Astoria had admitted, she was nothing more than her mother's puppet.

Wren was consistently light and positive, but there was an iron depth to her when she evaluated Joan. Joan remembered what Astoria had said, about Wren being the clever one here. Wren pulling the strings to get Joan today instead of Molly. Wren being convinced, somehow, that Joan would side with her desire to give casting magic to Moon Creatures.

Wren was, of course, right. Joan knew that at this point, but she still didn't know if those were Wren's true intentions or a masterful obfuscation. Wren's cleverness was only providing evidence for her capacity for betrayal.

"Come on, then," Joan said, making her decision. She'd have to run with this whole *friends close and enemies closer* business. "I know just the coffee shop."

Joan took them to four coffee shops, five bookshops, several parks, and then a street food vendor, where they happily ate street meat. By the end of the day, Joan was fairly confident she had succeeded only in tiring herself out.

Indeed, partway through, Wren had been seized by a great enthusiasm for New York City, begging to be taken to both Times Square and the Statue of Liberty, which had left Joan forging an unfortunate alliance with Astoria, who refused to go to either location.

Each time Joan had suggested their next destination, eyeing them pointedly as if to say *Retire to your hotel room at any time*, the devilish glint in Astoria's eye had only flashed brighter, and Wren had only gotten herself worked up further.

The unfortunate result of which was Joan was really starting to like them.

"We do have to meet your aunt for dinner," Wren said

apologetically, after making them stop at some cheesy merch shop so she could purchase a classic ı ♥ NY shirt.

"Oh nooo," Joan said, leaning heavily against a wall. "But we were having so much fun."

"We can always continue tomorrow," Astoria deadpanned, adorned in blinking sunglasses shaped like the Statue of Liberty's crown.

Joan reached out absently, pushing the glasses higher up Astoria's nose, where they'd been slipping. "Only if you orchestrate Molly's absence again."

Astoria went rigid, and Joan realized what she'd done. How familiar that touch had been. She snatched her hands away, and they both went back to watching Wren, saying nothing as she babbled about key chains to bring back for Ray.

Joan dropped them off at the Greenwood Mansion, walking barely farther than the gates to see them in, Molly's warning looming large in her mind.

"I'm pretty sure you can attend this dinner," Wren said, pointing at the door.

"Indeed, Miss Joan's presence has been requested," George said, bowing low ahead of them. He'd been the one to answer the gate to let them all in, since Wren and Astoria weren't keyed to the wards like Joan was.

"Miss Joan," Astoria said with a snort.

"Story," Joan shot back.

"Your mother and father have been asking for you quite urgently," George added. "Though Miss Molly assures them you are quite alright. They insist you attend dinner tonight. Quite emphatically."

Oh, Molly. Joan owed her a life debt. "I'm busy tonight,

George. And no one wants to see me get into an argument with them while we have guests." They'd deploy Joan's mother for a fight with guests over—Merlin was harsh and to the point, but Selene was a maestro in a debate. She'd practiced law at a top firm up until about four years ago, when she'd left for reasons Joan didn't fully understand but suspected had to do with Merlin's controlling tendencies.

"I would love to see an argument," Astoria said. "In fact, it would make my night."

Joan flipped Astoria off, swinging open the side gate. "Rot in hell, Wardwell."

"Hopefully with you by my side, Greenwood," Astoria called back, before the Greenwood Mansion's yawning doorway ate them alive.

Joan returned to Bay Ridge on the human subway, relishing the long ride.

As she took the elevator up to Grace's apartment, two pizzas in hand, Astoria and Wren's general pleasantness couldn't distract her for long from the issues at hand. A semisentient force that Joan had flirted with by cycling magic. Grace's odd behavior that morning.

Mik let Joan into the apartment. CZ wasn't around, which was devastating, because Joan was itching to catch him up on her major magical triumph. Grace was shut in her bedroom.

"She came home after work, said she needed to work on the spell to see if I have a tether to whoever did this to me, and shut the door," Mik whispered. There was still no kitchen table, so they set the pizza on the counter, and Mik ate straight out of the box.

After the coffee shops and a sweet treat at each one, Joan wasn't very hungry, but she pulled out a single slice for herself and bit into it, a queasy feeling rolling in her stomach.

"She seems nice though," Mik said. "I mean, I like her. I just get the feeling…"

"She's got a secret," Joan finished. "Or a couple, something to do with what she saw in your head."

"We don't really have a choice in trusting her though?" Mik said, and there was a clear question mark at the end. *Did* they have a choice?

Joan, unfortunately, knew the answer was no. "Let's have her do this tether-tracing spell and then decide from there. CZ texted to say he had a family thing and can't be here with Abel until seven thirty or so, but then we can get this going. At least if something goes awry, we'll have them."

Mik grabbed another slice of pizza. "TV in the interim?"

They watched more housewives make terrible decisions and backstab one another as Joan very quietly did some tiny magic cycles, practicing letting go of magic as soon as she touched it. It went against instinct—normally, she held magic in and tried to proportion it in little bits into her spells. It was how she had been trained and, when they realized her spells were bursting, retrained in an attempt to get her to push less magic into her castings. She ran the trials. If she held magic in for longer than three seconds, she started to feel nauseous. She could really fuck up any magic map she wanted if she kept practicing, but more pressingly, she might effectively be able to cancel out spells by yanking magic from them.

With Mik's eyes glued to the screen, Joan concentrated on looking them over, as if she could unravel the spell on Mik here and now, but there were no loose edges to pick at. The haze of magic on them was airtight, bending at the corners like it was slipping from this reality into the next. Joan tried anyways, trying to suck in more magic from Mik, but the spell didn't so much as flicker. Odd.

It was seven twenty when Grace finally exited her room.

She looked tired. She'd clearly been chewing on her bottom lip. Grace was so far from the polished, put-together person Joan had come to know these last few days that she scrambled to her feet like she might physically be able to help.

"Are you okay?" Joan blurted out. "I brought pizza."

Grace gave a tired smile as she opened the box and put a slice on a plate, eating it cold. "Fine. When are CZ and Abel coming?"

"Within the next ten minutes. Grace, are you *sure* you're fine? Because you don't really look it," Joan said.

"Thanks."

"And we've been relying on you a lot. I understand if that's taken its toll and you need another day to rest or something, or help? You mentioned Fiona might be willing to help us seal Mik? We don't know each other that well, so maybe you don't trust us if something *is* wrong, but we have no interest in running you down." It was only when Joan said it, her rambling pouring out of her, that she really consciously registered that worry—that in the same way Joan wasn't sure about trusting Grace, Grace wasn't sure about trusting Joan.

Grace set her pizza down on her plate as a strange look crossed her face. "You know what the stakes are. For all of us. Your family and Fiona have already checked in with me twice to see if I've made progress on recreating the spell on Mik. I can't deflect forever."

Mik leaned back on their hands, their head resting on their shoulder. "As the person facing the highest stakes, I don't mind another day if you need it, Grace. I really do appreciate all you're doing for me."

Grace's plate hit the counter with a thunk. "Why are you being so nice to me? You don't even know me. I could be…I don't know. I could be downright evil. I could kick puppies in my free time."

"I kind of think you're supposed to be nice to everyone," Joan said. "At least until they're proven puppy kickers, then you rip them to shreds."

"Mercilessly," Mik added.

Grace bit her bottom lip hard, like she was holding in tears. Joan didn't think she'd done anything particularly moving here, but Grace looked ready to burst. "Guys, I—"

A knock on the door cut her off, before it swung open to reveal the LaMorte brothers. They stepped inside and respectfully took off their shoes, calling greetings.

"Everything alright in here?" Abel asked.

"Grace, did you have something to say?" Joan prompted, turning back to the woman who had finished off her pizza and was scrubbing furiously at her plate.

"Nothing," Grace said. She finished and dried off her hands. "Okay, let's start."

FOURTEEN

~~~

They gathered in a little circle in the kitchen, looking at Grace expectantly.

They'd been on the brink of something when the LaMortes arrived, but Joan felt the fragility of that peace. She didn't want to push and risk Grace freaking out. She wanted to...extend Grace some trust and hope she did the same for Joan.

Gods, it was like she was six again, trying to make friends on the playground.

Abel held up a finger just as Grace looked like she was about to begin and fished in his pocket. "One second, sorry," he said, pulling out a battered metal coin on a length of twine. He tossed it to Joan, who fumbled the catch and had to be saved by CZ's deft reflexes.

Joan examined it in the light. The metal was old, with engravings she didn't recognize.

"Mind ward," Abel said. "It's decent. Thought maybe you should keep it on you for the next while, until we're sure no one else is going to try to get into that devious head of yours." His gaze slid to Grace. "I'm sure you can make one but thought this might be less of a drain on your resources."

"Thank you," Grace said, her voice cracking slightly. She cleared it. "Both for the faith in my abilities and the thoughtfulness."

Joan slipped it over her head. "What Grace said. And thanks especially for not picking something ugly. I half expected you to show up with a clown mask that you were going to tell me was a powerful relic I needed to keep on me at all times. What a horror that would be. A cruel and unusual punishment. Dare I say, diabolical even."

"I played that prank precisely once, Joan, and it was years ago," Abel groaned.

"It was once too many," Joan replied, tucking the charm beneath her blouse, because yes, she was still wearing it.

Their jokes were easy and familiar, and it helped crack some of the thick sheet of tension lying over all of them. Joan wasn't any use casting, or running across New York, or fighting anyone off, or anything. But she could put people at ease. Effortlessly, according to local grouch Astoria Wardwell.

Oh! She still hadn't told CZ about the cycling. She made meaningful eyes at him, and he looked at her, confused, mouthing, *What?* Joan could tell the entire group, they were holding a lot of her secrets, but this felt new and exciting and useful, and she wanted some time to practice it first before she showed off.

Joan sighed. "Go ahead, Grace."

Grace beckoned Mik closer, pulling them into the center of the semicircle of friends in the small kitchen.

"As discussed, I'm going to try to see if there's some sort of tether on you, either to the spell's caster or to whatever source of magic is keeping the power of the spell running."

Mik saluted. "Godspeed, soldier."

For a third time, Joan got to watch the beauty that was Grace Collins casting. This time though, none of the movements were familiar. Joan had a fairly extensive knowledge of spellcasting, but she couldn't recognize any of the motions Grace made, and the words she spoke were cobbled together from several languages, only some of which Joan had enough passing fluency in to understand. *Unravel* and *reveal*. *Trace* and *follow*. Magic bent in toward Grace, snaking through her arms as she moved them, trailing from the tips of her fingers as they danced through the air.

Thickening into a band around Mik's waist, a single thread led out from them, toward the door. A few more seconds, and that thread strengthened, weaving into a braid.

Grace opened her eyes, and they glowed golden. Her gaze snapped to the magic leading out the door. "You see it too, Joan?"

Joan hummed a confirmation.

"I'm not sure where it goes," Grace said distantly. "But I don't think it's far. We'll have to follow it ourselves."

"I don't see anything," Mik said, looking down at themself.

"Neither do I," CZ added.

"I'll lead," Joan said. "Grace, you take up the rear."

They pulled on their shoes and fell in line out the door.

Their little duckling march took them down the stairs and out onto the street, where the thread took a sharp right. It stretched a number of feet ahead of them, but only manifested a farther distance when Mik stepped forward. Joan prayed Astoria and Wren weren't running their map again, because they were extra exposed right now.

They walked, CZ and Mik making nervous jokes at each other as Joan led them down the sidewalk, across streets, past stoplights, her eyes on that golden rope. There was something alluring about it, something that faded out the rest of her consciousness. The gold shimmered. In its sparkle Joan saw the endless twists of eternal magic. She could reach out her senses, just so, and touch it with the back of her hand, like petting a small bird.

The eyes in the back of her head opened again.

Joan, they whispered.

We see you.

Joan snatched her hand back, shaking, and stumbled to a stop. She found herself on a familiar path in a familiar park. The golden rope disappeared between two shadowed trees, and at her back, CZ narrowly avoided bumping into her.

"Whoa, what happened? Did it disappear?" he said, hands coming down on her shoulders as he swerved around her.

Once was maybe a fit of delusion. Twice made her think something was trying to talk to her. Something older than anything she'd ever seen or experienced.

"No, it's still there," Grace said, stepping up.

The bush next to Joan unfurled new leaves.

"Is that normal?" Mik asked nervously, pointing at it.

"It's a Joan thing," CZ said. "Don't worry about it. She agitates plants."

"She agitates the *magic* in plants," Grace corrected, peering at the bush. "Probably a side effect of her weird symbiosis with natural magic. Joan? Why did you stop?"

I'm losing my mind.

No.

There's some magic in New York I've never seen or heard of before.

"Abel," Joan said. "Is New York alive?"

CZ groaned. "What the actual hell are you saying right now?"

"Philosophically?" Abel asked. Joan turned to him, and he looked at her patiently. "Like metaphorically? Or do you mean something else?"

"Magically," Joan said. "Folklorically—I don't know."

Abel gave her a searching look. "Depending on the story, it might be."

"Sorry to be a hater, but is this directly relevant to the magic at hand?" Mik asked, staring at the trees with wide eyes. "Because isn't this the way back to the Night Market?"

Joan broke eye contact with Abel. "You okay, Mik?"

Their mouth was too tight and their shoulders too high for the lie to be particularly effective, but they replied in the affirmative anyways. "Besides," they said, injecting some bravado into their voice, "if I'm facing my trauma, I'm at least glad I have two witches and two vampires to help me with it."

CZ nodded sagely. "Your friends," he confirmed.

Mik's shoulders lowered an inch. "You're not going to give up, are you?"

CZ walked over and wrapped an arm around Mik's shoulders, guiding them forward. "You're never escaping me," he said.

"Ward's on?" Abel asked Joan. She confirmed, placing a hand on the coin.

CZ plunged them between the trees.

On the other side, the market sprang to life. Despite them entering through the same patch of flora as last time, this section of the market looked new. It was still all multicolored tents, but Joan felt quite turned around.

Grace, Abel, and CZ had no such issues, demonstrating a clear confidence in their knowledge of the area. The line continued to stretch ahead of them, and Grace walked resolutely on.

Joan had to hurry to catch up, darting glances around like the witch who'd attacked her might strike again. "Why is the spell you cast on Mik not fading under the wards?"

"Small-area ward nullification," Grace said. "I had a hunch, so I baked it into the spell."

"You thought it would lead back to the market?"

Silence from Grace.

"Grace," Joan said, with a growing feeling of disquiet, "is there something you're not telling us? Something we should really know?"

"Let's see if I'm right first," Grace said. "Then I'll explain everything, I promise." She put on a surge of speed, forcing everyone to pick up the pace as they stepped through the tents.

The swell of wrongness increased.

A promise. Like they were children.

Grace knew her way around the market. She was a prodigious spellmaker. Her apartment was new and empty. She did not like the way power operated in the magic world, and she had been in the market when Joan had been attacked. Nearby.

Grace was thinking of leaving the magic world entirely. She loved spellmaking like an artist loved their craft. She'd made pancakes for them that morning. She had offered to help without a second thought. She kept looking at CZ when she thought no one was watching, and she could never remember her computer password, so she wrote it down on a sticky note.

The latter version of Grace was the one Joan wanted to believe in and the one she'd trusted in first.

But the former one seemed undeniable.

Grace had a secret.

Joan didn't know it.

"CZ," Joan breathed, so low that only the vampires would be able to pick it up. "Something isn't right about this. I don't know where Grace is taking us, but be ready."

CZ's response was a brush of his fingers against the small of her back.

Grace turned the corner and stopped in front of an entirely ordinary brown tent. "Joan," she said, a bit out of breath. "What do you see?"

Joan frowned. "A tent."

"Anything else?"

"Wards on it," Joan said, tracing a faint magic web. "Intricate ones, strong ones."

"Wards, in the Night Market?" Abel asked. "Most of us can't afford a witch who knows how to cast in here to set them up and keep them renewed."

Grace nodded once, as if proving something to herself. "It's pocket realmed in plain sight, which means it circumvents the magic rules of this realm." One slash of her hand, and a hole bloomed.

Grace stormed inside without waiting for them, and the thread coming from Mik vanished into the blackness inside.

Joan had no idea what was waiting in there, but she couldn't let her fear, overwhelming as it was, allow her to let Grace go in alone. She could be doing anything in there, and Joan wasn't going to let any of her friends go in next.

Idly, she wished she'd texted Molly before starting on this journey.

Joan stepped forward, crossing the threshold and feeling her own magic spring to life inside. She braced, like Grace might swing a vase at her head.

The tent was lit by the glow of a light floating above Grace's palm. The walls were dark blue. There was a bed. Two beds. An empty cage. In fact, the tent looked mostly abandoned, only a few small things left in disarray.

Grace did not attack her.

There was a sharp intake of air behind Joan. Mik had followed her in, one hand rising to their mouth in horror. "This is it," they said. "This is where I woke up."

Grace was inspecting every inch of the place, running her hands along the shelves, opening the cage to peer in. Putting on a very good show of acting like she'd never been here before. Joan desperately wanted to believe her.

"Scent's old," Abel murmured. "Whoever this was, they left the tent at least a day ago."

"Probably before they went into Joan's head," CZ said, sniffing the air. He stood at Mik's side, letting them lean on him. "Maybe even when Mik first escaped. Grace, are you going to explain what you're looking for?"

"I don't know. Anything," she said, whipping around to examine the cots. "Something to explain *that*." She pointed at Mik's thread, which was starting to fade but still bright enough that Joan could see it was now disappearing straight into the ground.

"Oh," Joan said. "What the hell does that mean?"

"I don't know, hence the ransacking," Grace snapped.

"Okay, before tensions escalate further," CZ said with a warning note in his tone, "can you explain what you mean for those of us who can't see magic?"

"Mik's thread disappears straight into the ground," Joan said.

"So, unless we're standing over the grave of whoever cast this spell..."

"It's probably showing us what the magic of the spell is tethered to," Grace finished.

"The *earth*?" Abel said. "Is that possible?"

Grace waved her hands. "I don't know! There's magic in everything. *Everything*. The air, the earth, the animals, chaos, order, *plants* as we've established, but it's always moving. It's not like there's a huge stockpile of magic beneath New York; we'd be able to feel that."

Joan paused in her rifling through the pillows on the cot, thoughts of Grace's betrayal temporarily abandoned—she was an *exceptional* actress if this was all a ruse—though Joan was confident that if there was some kind of magical clue here, she wouldn't be able to recognize it. "Wait, what if it's a metaphor?"

"The spell has learned language and decided to tackle metaphors?" Grace said incredulously. "My spells are a work of art, but they aren't poets."

"That goes so hard," Mik whispered, still unsteady against CZ. Magic sniffed them more curiously now that they were out of the market's direct wards, shielded by the tent's pocket realm. "'But they aren't poets'—someone write that down."

"Please focus on not throwing up on me," CZ replied. "Once was enough."

"I'll do it out of spite," Mik said, shoving away from him, but they were a bit too wobbly to stand on their own and leaned back against him moments later.

"Earlier today," Joan said. "Astoria and Wren—"

"You were hanging out with Astoria Wardwell?" Grace cut in.

"Yeah, big day—"

"Are you *ill*?" CZ added. "How did this happen?"

"I was tricked." Not that she'd ever forget Astoria in those glasses. "Can I finish my sentence?"

When no one else interrupted her, Joan pressed on. "They put together a map of New York, and you could see the whole city's magic. Like it was alive. It flowed like a bunch of currents coming together to form a singular tide, and when I channeled it, the whole city's magic, I felt like it was…I don't know. One thing. One entity, and I saw—" What *had* Joan seen, exactly? Eyes opening. A network of many somethings making one thing.

"CZ," Mik said very faintly. "Despite my big talk, I think I'm going to throw up after all, and would rather not do it all over you."

Magic kicked up a fuss, hissing toward Mik as they worked themself up.

"Bin! Is there any sort of bin or bag in here?" CZ asked frantically. Mik hunched over, palms on their knees, and dry-heaved, like a cat at three AM.

"Fuck, I don't actually know how to stop this on my own," Grace muttered, raising her hands to cast as Abel scrambled to try to find something, going so far as to pull the thin blanket off one of the cots and hand it to Mik bunched up like a bag.

Grace's tether spell stuttered and broke as Grace canceled it. Magic in here wasn't that thick, but there was enough that it was rapidly overloading Mik's system. It was like watching it shift in Astoria's map.

It was like Astoria's map.

And Joan had disrupted that by sucking all the magic in the air into herself.

She threw open the mental floodgates. *Come here*, she thought, and magic reversed course, passing into Joan instead.

All of it, all of you, come here.

Joan ripped the magic from the room, let it fill her up, and then released it in a thin stream that she looped back into herself, cycling it in three-second increments.

Mik straightened, frowning. "Grace, what did you do?"

"Not me," Grace said, face slack, looking at Joan. "Her."

"Mik, let me know once you've calmed down and I can let go," Joan said, her voice a strangled wheeze from trying to hold concentration. It took a shocking amount of brainpower to remember to let magic go again.

"You're casting?" CZ asked in blatant shock. "And you're still upright?"

"She is not casting," Grace said. "She's cycling the magic into herself so that Mik can't attract any. It's...it's very impressive to watch."

Joan laughed even as sweat broke out across her forehead, as she closed her fingers into a fist and dug her nails into her palms. It didn't hurt, but it felt like trying to levitate something with your mind alone, a full-body concentration. She was suddenly shy under all the attention. "Don't all sound so surprised; it's not useful for anything besides this."

"I'd disagree," Grace said, slipping into the scientist tone she used when talking about the intricacies of spellmaking. "You're essentially your own magic-nullification system—that's *fascinating*. I guess any witch could do it, but absolutely not at this volume. I mean, the baseline spell on Mik isn't cutting out; it's like it's effortlessly adapting to the new currents of magic to keep fueling itself. Joan would have to suck the magic out of a huge radius, for quite a while, for the spell on Mik to run out of steam and break..."

Joan wanted to hear every word of what Grace was saying, but listening ran counter to her concentration. Joan squeezed her eyes shut, Grace's voice fading out over the roaring of blood in her ears. Her theory, that Mik was tied to New York City itself, or something like it, meant that, just maybe, her strange visions today might indicate something other than an acute mental breakdown. If Abel, in his extensive understanding of magical folklore, indicated there might be stories of New York's sentience, then perhaps Joan was on to something.

Joan inhaled, sucking in more magic, and felt a weak flicker at the back of her head, that ancient thing rolling over.

What did you mean by "we see you"? she thought at it.

In the long silence that followed, magic danced along her bones, sparking against her marrow. Just a bit longer, just a little while.

Please.

The eyes opened, slowly, and where there would have been a mouth was really a maw, filled with a thousand voices in a thousand languages. They washed over her in a flood, too loud to decipher. If her body hadn't locked, she'd have fallen to her knees.

The jumble grew and spread, until Joan's own individual self felt a mile away, then five, ten. She was one of many, she was—

Joan, answer your phone.

Joan was shoved back into her body, and her connection to the magic vanished, like being dunked in the Hudson. When she opened her eyes, she was covered in sweat, and her friends were arguing in front of her. Her ears were ringing too badly to filter the information of their words in, and she groped in her pockets.

Joan, answer your phone.

She pulled it out to twenty-five text messages and five calls from Molly. Joan could only catch the top one in her notifications, the rest folded up in an accordion beneath it.

Joan, answer your phone.

Joan hit dial with a complete sense of detachment, body going through the motions, as a profound and overwhelming sense of wrongness settled on her neck like a too-tight scarf. Whatever had happened, it was big.

Molly picked up on the first ring.

"Where the hell have you been!" Molly screeched across the line. "Where are you right now? Did you read my texts?"

"I haven't gotten a chance to," Joan said, the tingling in her limbs fading. She looked up to catch the attention of her group, but CZ and Abel were already quiet, holding up hands to silence Mik and Grace as they listened in to her call.

"I tried to stall for as long as I could, like you said, and I don't know where you are or why you asked me to stall or really what you've been up to these last few days, because you haven't been home, and you haven't been staying with me, and you're leaving parties early and showing up to my house in old clothes—"

"Please jump to the point, you're freaking me out."

Molly took in a huge shuddering breath. "The market, Joan. Aunt Val gave the order to send a force in to search it thirty minutes ago. She asked Astoria Wardwell to lead it because of her training, that's what dinner was about. That's why Mom and Dad wanted you there so badly. We don't know how Moon Creatures might retaliate. If they'll come after the family. You need to get to the mansion, now."

Abel leaned down to say something to CZ, who replied urgently in a low tone.

"All of you get out of here now," Abel ordered, and ran out of the tent. Joan's heart was, approximately, in her ass. This could not be happening. She'd thought... naively, she'd thought she might have more time before her aunt did something this uncharacteristically asinine.

"Tell me where you are, Joan. I'll come get you," Molly said.

Joan looked around at the walls of the tent. "You're going to hate my answer."

"Don't be fucking funny right now, where the hell are you?" Molly's breathing on the line was ragged. "Tell me you're not in the market."

Joan hissed into the phone, her grip on it so tight, it pushed the blood from her knuckles. "Tell them to stop it, Molly. I'm serious, *get them to stop*."

She hung up, shoving her phone back into her pocket. "We have to go, now. They can't find Mik or we're screwed, and we can't let them attack the market."

"I'm going to break Valeria's kneecaps," CZ snarled, as he grabbed Mik's arm and ripped the tent flap open. "Take Mik and run. My family's here, Joan, I can't—"

"I know," Joan said, as they stepped outside.

"This is so messed up," Grace muttered.

"I know," Joan repeated.

"Stay and help," Mik said wildly. "I'll get myself out if I have to."

"Joan isn't safe here either," CZ said angrily, as they strode around a corner. "A Greenwood hostage is about to be priceless."

"I know," Joan said grimly, mind clicking through the possibilities and settling on one, just one, a horrible, horrible idea. "In fact, I'm hoping so. Mik and Grace, get back to the apartment. CZ, I have a plan."

"I assume it's terrible," CZ said.

Joan stumbled to a stop as a thunderous noise ripped through the air, the ground vibrating slightly.

A few rows ahead of them, a tent went up in a pillar of flame.

"Fuck," Joan said, grabbing Mik by the back of the shirt and yanking them in the opposite direction.

Grace stumbled and CZ caught her, setting her on her feet as she clutched his arm. Around them, a wide ring of fire lit up the boundary of the market, bright as the end of the world. Bright like betrayal.

"There go the wards," Grace said, as magic slammed back into them, rushing to fill the magical void in the area. "I'm not sure we can pass through that fire; they're probably corralling us in."

Screams filled the air, mixing with the ash starting to fall.

They were too late.

Around them, the market began to burn.

FIFTEEN

They sprinted back the way they'd come, trying to avoid the front of the assault, but the chaos was rapidly spreading.

Out, out, out, they needed Mik out. The rest of them falling into the hands of witches would be unfortunate, but unlikely to result in substantial personal harm.

Mik though, what they were was evident to any witch with sense in their head. They were everything the Greenwoods and Wardwells were hunting for.

"Joan," CZ began, distracted by people stumbling, confused, out of a tent down the aisle. He stopped, looking at her with wide, sad eyes.

"Go!" Joan screamed at him. "Help them!"

He reached out, squeezed her arm, and then he was gone.

It was pure instinct that brought Joan to a full stop, grabbing Grace and Mik so they stopped with her. Down the path, voices rose, and a group of people took shape, barely visible through the tents.

"I'm aiming for no casualties," Astoria Wardwell instructed. "Tents searched, no more. Whoever fucked up that barrier spell and set the market on fire is going to get their shit absolutely rocked as soon as we finish up here. No more fucking mistakes."

And then she turned.

And Joan made complete and perfect eye contact with her.

Astoria's eyes widened slightly, a cracking of her ever-present mask. She was dressed in tight-fitting black clothing with a sword strapped over one shoulder. Surrounded by a haze of magic, she was a vengeful goddess reborn.

Astoria opened her mouth slightly, closed it. She whirled, pointing in the opposite direction to distract her comrades, saving Joan and her friends.

Why?

Grace nearly ripped the sleeve off Joan's shirt yanking her to the side, down a path, before shoving her into a tent, Mik following a second later.

It was the one they'd just left, blue on the inside. The pocket realm.

"I have a plan," Joan blurted. "I need—I had to let CZ go help the vampires, but if someone wields me as a hostage, maybe they can get the New York witches to stand down."

"That," Grace gasped, "is a terrible plan."

"Wouldn't it make the witches angrier?" Mik countered, swaying a little. They sat hard on the bed, magic shifting toward them, and this time it was Grace who channeled, albeit more weakly than Joan.

"It would piss the Greenwoods off to no end," Grace said angrily. "Think, Joan. I know you don't have any self-preservation, but the witches are invading the Night Market on the rumor of its connection to Mik. What do you think they'd feel justified in doing if a Moon Creature took a Greenwood hostage? Or even if I did within the market?"

"I'm thinking short-term solutions," Joan shot back, jamming her fingers in her hair. "Do you have a better plan?" Joan surely didn't, every plan she could conceive of ended with Mik falling into the wrong hands and a swarm of witches ransacking the market.

Grace looked at Joan, her mouth a thin angry line. "No, but I do have *a* plan. We do this, what I'm doing to Mik, to the whole market."

"*What?*" Joan asked, peeking through the flap of the tent, letting in a thin stream of sound. Flames and breaking things. Snarls and howls and yells. Magic, booming.

"First thing they did was take down the wards, because normally witches in the borders of the market are nothing more than humans," Grace said. "You have proven that you can nullify magic by channeling it all into yourself. I need you to do that on a huge scale."

Mik spat up some bile on the floor. "Can you? You discovered this ability *today*."

"There's nowhere to put it," Joan replied. Gods, was a witch's heart meant to beat this fast? Joan was on the brink of throwing up herself. She leaned against a shelf, trying to get her heart out of her throat.

"I'm cycling it, but cycling that much magic in one place is only going to put it back into the air, and I don't know if I can suck it back in fast enough to make a difference, like I can in a very small area to help Mik. It needs a container, a spell or something to hold it long enough for witches to lose the ability to cast and be forced into a retreat."

"Then put it in a spell," Grace said.

"You *know* I can't do that," Joan argued. "You do it!"

"I can't suck in all the magic myself!" Grace yelled back.

"I fucking hate it here!" Mik shouted. "Why are we screaming at each other!"

Grace couldn't suck the magic in. Joan couldn't cast a spell.

Joan flashed, with sudden clarity, back to Molly's house that morning. Astoria and Wren had made that map together, Astoria pulling in the majority of the magic and Wren shaping it into a spell.

"Why does your face look like that?" Grace asked, luckily at a normal level this time.

"It's devious looking," Mik said.

"Grace, if I suck in all the magic and funnel it into you, can you cast a spell that holds it?" Joan asked.

Grace thought for one second, two. "It should be something simple so it's harder to break, but with unlimited depth so it can store a massive amount of magic."

"Which is?" Mik asked.

Joan's hand flew to her neck, clutching at the necklace there. "Mind ward," she said. "It scales with power, and the object holds magic." She nearly ripped her finger off tearing at one of her rings, a gold band with a small black pearl set in it. One of Abel's empty artifacts.

"Put it in this," Joan said, tossing Grace the ring.

Grace examined it, then stuck out her right hand as if for a handshake. "If this melts us both, I'm going to haunt your ass."

"Likewise," Joan said, and she took that hand.

"I'll tell your story," Mik said, taking a few steps back from them. "If I survive, I mean."

"Mik, if you at any point see an opening to run away and get back to the apartment, take it," Joan ordered.

"And if we really do die," Grace said, "your best bet will be turning yourself in to the vampires. In exchange for information about the original spellmaker, get them to use you as a bartering chip with the Greenwoods. Negotiate being sealed by going as public as possible. The LaMortes can put you in contact with the magical-world media—there are millions of everyday witches dissatisfied with the magical world's hierarchy who would protest if the Greenwoods or any other magical group experimented on you. And..." Her voice faltered; Grace swallowed hard. "Tell whomever you end up with that the spellmaker they're after... tell them to look into Fiona Ganon."

Joan's fingers loosened in shock, but Grace's grip was unyielding. "Do it, Joan. Every second we waste, Moon Creatures are being attacked out there."

"Fiona—"

"Just trust me," Grace said. "I know maybe I don't deserve it, but trust me one more time."

Joan looked to Mik, who seemed as bewildered as Joan. But they schooled their face into something resembling encouragement.

Joan closed her eyes.

She opened herself to the world, called its essence forth with a thunderous summons.

Magic poured into her in a wave, tumbling over itself in glee, and she concentrated on letting it out through her hand, toward Grace. Grace jolted, but that grip was steady between them as Grace channeled the magic, hard. Pulling from Joan just as greedily as Joan was pushing it toward her.

Joan opened her eyes to find Grace whispering over her hand, eyes golden suns, as the pearl began to glow an unearthly black.

"Faster," Grace said between words, and Joan pulled deeper.

Magic was a storm around them. A wind kicked up in the tent, blowing their hair about. Power sizzled in little lines of lightning, then froze, fell to the ground, shattered, and rose again. Water condensed on the cloth of the ceiling, dripping down on them steadily, every law of physics going haywire.

And still, Joan drew the magic in.

A grinding sound started up. Magic seized in glitches, making Joan feel like a video call with a bad connection.

"The tent's pocket realm is collapsing, that's good!" Grace said. "We need to connect to the magic around the actual market."

In stutters and bursts, the pocket realm collapsed like a black hole. For a breathless second, there was no more.

Then the whole world lit up, resplendent.

Grace was speaking faster and faster. The ring was a tiny star in her hand. Fire caught on the bottom edges of the tent, licking upward.

"Mik!" Joan screamed over the increasing wind. "Run!"

"I can't leave you guys in here—if the tent goes up in flames, you go with it!" Mik screamed back. They lurched, gripping the bed frame.

"It's magic, not real fire," Joan called back. "I can nullify it if it gets too close. All this magic is going to tear you apart, poison you. Run *now*, join the crowd, and get back to the apartment!"

"I can't—"

"Mik!" Joan roared. "If we were ever, for even half a second, kind of friends, trust me and go now!"

Mik stared at Joan, tears brimming in their eyes, for twenty-three seconds. Joan counted them, one by one, as the tempo of the magic increased. Twenty-three seconds Mik Batbayar held out for them, in an avalanche of magic that must have been tearing them apart. Twenty-three seconds, for people they'd met three days ago.

And then they wiped their tears, staggered against the wind, and ripped aside the tent flap to disappear into the world.

Joan turned back to Grace, who was throwing off sparks of gold. "I'm going to kick it up a notch," Joan said over the wind, and she wasn't sure if Grace could fully hear her, but her grip tightened anyways.

Joan shut her eyes again, threw open the doors of her brain.

Fireworks burst across the backs of her eyes, a luminous, never-ending array of glory. In them she saw the infinite swirl of time and space, bursting, fading, and bursting again. Skyscrapers rose from nothing to reach for nothing. New York City lay before her, its evening spread out against the sky, its streets an endless maze of possibility, the Hudson its spine. Along her back, life blossomed twentyfold, and death brushed slow feathery wings across the world. Joan was the cycle, and in the cycle, and the cycle's death as all the magic in the area poured into her. She became a god, shrouded in an incomprehensible amount of magic.

It grew and crested, every drop burning against her skin, licks of flame wisping across her face. It grew until she felt she could crack the world in two, suck the marrow from its core, and still she could go further. Still, she could reach for more.

Balance, Greenwood, a voice whispered at her, eight million voices condensed into one.

It didn't even slow her. Nothing could slow her when she was like this. She was made of the essence that ran the world. She could shape it with half a thought; she could break it with half a thought.

Joan brushed past the voice, stretching her seeking fingers beyond the borders of the city, because she could, because no one alive or dead could stop her now. Power, at last, an ambrosia that sloshed against her skin, filled her insides, the finest nectar ever created.

The world isn't yet yours, it said.

Open your eyes.

Your eyes.

Open.

Eyes.

Look, Joan.

LOOK.

The blackness vanished. Joan saw Grace in front of her, golden tears tracking down her face. She sagged.

Her grip loosened.

Blood dripped between Grace's teeth, slithered down her chin.

The magic was killing her.

Joan was killing her.

Joan was killing her and it felt *good*.

Stop, Joan wanted to say. *Stop the spell*. But her mouth was too big for her face, slow and hard to move.

Let go of me, she wanted to shriek, but Grace's eyes were rolling back in her head, the whites filling with red.

Don't leave me, Joan wanted to sob, and she didn't know if she meant Grace or the magic.

Feeling flooded her hand. This wasn't her. This wasn't Joan. She was not made for violence; she rebelled against its very presence. Joan made one finger twitch, then another, but only the first separated from Grace's skin. The magic churning through them glued their hands together, kept them locked.

I can't kill her. I can't let her die. Flames engulfed the entire tent. Joan cried, but the tears fell up instead of down. Physics twisted, a world unraveling in the fired forge of endless pure magic. Her body would shut down soon, completely. The unending magic kept her upright.

She matters to me. I can't kill her.

I can't let her die.

I am not a killer.

Another finger moved.

I am not a killer; I'm an artist.

Another finger, harder this time. There was a tiny pop as it dislocated under the torrent of magic. Joan didn't even feel it. Her pain melted away into a strange relief, its absence made her surge with more power.

I'm an architect.

And another. Flesh peeled away from it in a long strip, crisping and burning in the superheated air around them. The bed disintegrated into ash. The shelves around them atomized as her abilities accelerated.

I'm a sister and a daughter. Even when I'm at my worst, I'll never be a killer.

The last finger stuck. Grace fell to her knees.

I'll always be a Greenwood.

It wavered.

But there are so few things I've done that cannot be undone.

Please, let this be a thing I can undo.

The last finger shifted and broke, the bone snapping, and their hands fell apart.

Grace dropped to the floor.

Joan followed with her.

In magic's absence, Joan was nothing. Flames ate the tent, a halo around her vision.

She welcomed the darkness.

She met its lips with a kiss.

Sixteen

There was a woman in the shadows, and her skin was black as night.

Around her head, a halo of golden curls kissed her forehead. A staff, gnarled and pale, rested against her shoulder. She reached out a hand, and it felt like the passing of a meteor, skimming by, a kiss brushed across a cheek.

Daughter of the Bind, *she whispered, and her voice was every sunrise over the earth, every flame in the darkness of winter, every grain of sand on an endless beach.* God or woman, in your eyes I see stars.

Seventeen

⁓⁓

The slow beep of a hospital monitor pulled Joan from the thickness of her dreams.

Her body obeyed her mind in little fits. Fingers twitching slowly, one by one, but only on her left hand. She pried open her eyes to a blurry room and that steady beep, beep.

It was a hospital room, but a nice one. Fancy, which was how she knew her family had gotten their hands on her. Her second clue was Molly, asleep in an armchair that had been pulled next to the bed.

Joan blinked. Her eyelids stuck, so maybe she fell back asleep again for a second, because when she finally opened them again, Molly was in a slightly different position.

Her hair was loose and frizzy around her face. She wasn't wearing any makeup, and she was in a college sweatshirt, HARVARD emblazoned across the front.

She looked so tired. Why did Molly look so tired?

In her haze, Joan took slow stock of her body. She felt like she'd been strapped to the wheels of a plane during takeoff. Her mouth tasted kind of rusty. Her right hand was wrapped in bandages, but her left one was free. Joan painfully shifted her head on the pillow to look at her own monitor and noted with some satisfaction her blood pressure was excellent and her heart rate steady. She wasn't even sure why she was here. Had she had an accident?

She was still so sleepy though.

Another slow blink, too long.

There was no one in the room besides Molly. Joan turned her head back to look at her sister uncomfortably crammed in that chair. Her neck must hurt. But she was there anyways, and she'd been tired enough to fall asleep.

The blinds were drawn, but it was night. There was a vase of dahlias on the table, a riot of dazzling color. Beautiful. The thought was distant. A tear slipped from her eye at the radiance of their hue.

A last blink. There were stars imprinted on the backs of her eyelids.

She lost herself in them.

EIGHTEEN

The third time Joan woke up, it was with much more clarity. For one, she could move her right hand, which had two sets of splints. Molly was still there, in a new outfit, though one that was still worn and comfortable. Joan was pretty sure she'd seen Nate in that hoodie before, and there was Nate, in another armchair across the room, with a book of sudoku in his hands.

Joan shifted her head, and Nate's gaze snapped to her. She remembered his family owned a string of hospitals, stacking the ranks with hidden witches who could use healing magic. Perhaps they were in one of his own buildings.

He dropped his pen on the table. Sudoku done in pen, respect.

"You're awake!" Nate said.

Joan wasn't entirely convinced of that fact, but in perhaps the most herculean task ever devised, she unstuck her mouth and spoke. "Don't look so surprised."

She sounded like a chain-smoker had had a baby with a revving motorcycle.

Nate scrambled out of his chair. "I have to wake her, she'll kill me if I don't," he said apologetically, reaching over to gently shake Molly's shoulder. "She's been here the whole week."

A week?

That was too long... Wouldn't Joan have known if a week had passed? All time before her sleep was nothing but blackness.

Molly lurched awake, hand flying up to rest on Nate's. "Is she dead?" she gasped.

Nate laughed, which seemed a little cruel, because Molly sounded genuine. "See for yourself."

Molly looked confusedly at Joan, dashed a hand across her face, and when Joan didn't disappear, she burst into tears.

"You're not dead!" she wailed, reaching out to clutch Joan's forearm. "Joan, you're not dead!"

Her grip hurt, but Joan thought she'd let Molly have this one; she clearly needed it. "I feel dead," she said.

Nate went looking for a tissue box as Molly continued to open-mouth cry, snot coming out of her nose. Joan, in her saintly kindness, didn't point out how disgusting it was.

"I'm going to kill you," Molly sobbed. "Now that you're alive, I'm going to kill you. The market, Joan? Do you have any idea how dangerous that was?"

The market.

Her memory swung back around like a sledgehammer, careening into her head. The market. CZ running off. Mik, the magic, *Grace*. Their injuries had been bad, real bad, and magic couldn't cure all ills—it couldn't do anything the body couldn't naturally do, like grow new limbs, and the more severe the wound, the more magic was needed to heal it. Someone would have needed to get help very quickly for them both to survive. Very quickly and from a highly skilled team of witches who could blend their magic with human medicine.

Joan attempted to sit up and felt every fiber of her being protest the movement. Molly let out a little scream, reaching to push Joan back, and Nate yelped, running back over with the tissue box in hand, but Joan ignored them both.

"Grace Collins," Joan said, gripping Molly's wrist with her good hand. "Molly, is Grace Collins okay?"

"LIE BACK DOWN."

"GRACE COLLINS, MOLLY."

"Astoria got both of you out!" Molly screamed right back. "Grace is three rooms down, recovering. Mom and Dad wanted to keep a close eye on her. No one knows exactly what you two did in there, but we couldn't use healing spells on you for days; magic was corrosive to you both. You looked like humans with exposure poisoning. It was close, Joan."

Joan gaped at her sister. "Astoria *Wardwell*?"

"This reminds me, Nate, can you text our parents and let them know Joan is awake?"

"Sure thing," Nate said, unlocking Molly's phone and tapping out a message.

"Mol, *focus*. What happened with Astoria?" Joan asked.

Molly gave Joan a stern glare. A *you're not making demands here* glower, but she continued. "Astoria said she found you both in the market passed out. Grace was covered in blood, you barely had a pulse, and she brought both of you directly to the Greenwoods. Covertly," Molly added, like Joan gave a single fuck whether it was covert or not. She couldn't ask about Mik—gods, had Mik made it out?

"CZ and the market, what happened?"

"Can you lie back down and focus on not dying," Molly snapped. "I'm trying to be reasonable, but I'm like one second away from knocking you back out myself, you reckless fucking bitch."

"Don't call me a bitch, I'm literally on my deathbed."

"DON'T SAY THAT."

"STOP YELLING AT ME!"

"The LaMortes are fine," Nate said, putting a placating hand on Molly's arm. "For the witches, the Night Market search was a resounding failure. They lost the ability to cast and a huge fire started up before they could find anything. It's a miracle everyone managed to evacuate in time, but Owl's Head Park is looking a bit scorched. Not too bad—Wardwell is apparently a fire elemental and kept it mostly contained."

"On top of carrying out two unconscious bodies?" Joan said. Astoria was so insufferably perfect. "Did Wren help?"

Molly and Nate exchanged glances.

"There was...an argument at dinner that day," Molly said. "Wren vehemently opposed the plan and refused to partake. Astoria went alone."

"It was honestly pretty impressive, Wren was shouting at your father," Nate said. "Reminded me of you, Joan. I'm a little sorry you missed it."

Wren and Astoria had seemed inseparable, despite their apparently opposing moral viewpoints. For all Wren had said, she was still in New York, and she was still Astoria Wardwell's best friend. But she'd left Astoria behind rather than invade the market.

And for all Astoria had said about seeing the logic in both sides, she had still invaded the market.

There was a flutter at the door before it flew open to reveal their mother, who rushed in with a clatter. "Oh, baby, you're alright!"

She gathered Joan in her arms, and Joan let her, because it had been an embarrassingly long time since her mother had cradled her. She smelled like her signature perfume, and her silk shirt was soft against Joan's cheek.

"I'm fine, Mom," Joan said around the thickness in her throat, patting her mother awkwardly on the side.

Selene withdrew. "You are certainly *not* fine! What did the Moon Creatures do to you? Grace Collins still hasn't woken up."

"Nothing!" Joan said, horror gripping her. "Moon Creatures didn't do a single thing to us. Tell me you haven't spent the last week under that assumption."

"Astoria confirmed it wasn't them, Mom," Molly said pointedly.

Selene cupped Joan's face in her hands. "Then what on earth happened?"

Joan and Grace hadn't thought so far as to give a backstory; they hadn't thought of the aftermath at all. But the only other party who knew what had happened in that tent besides Grace was Mik.

Joan went with the truth, or some version of it. "I was in the market with Grace. She lives in the area and was showing me around. When it was attacked—"

"Don't use such charged language," Selene admonished.

Joan's heart rate monitor beeped faster. "When the market was *attacked*, viciously and without due cause—"

"Joan."

"Mom, if you're pissed off about me saying that, you're really not going to like what I say next," Joan said hotly, shaking off the haze of her coma with every jolt of rage that flashed through her veins. "And I'm not saying it to be contrary, I'm saying it so you stop falsely accusing Moon Creatures. I am the one who nullified the witches' casting magic. It was me."

Every lie Joan had ever told primed her for this next bit. "Grace tried to stop me and nearly died in the process. I knew that without casting ability, the witches would have to retreat, and the Moon Creatures would have more time to get somewhere safe."

Selene's hands dropped off Joan's cheeks, leaving them cold. "You don't know what you're saying. You can't even cast."

"I interrupted your big plan," Joan said. "It was me. I channeled without casting, enough that the other witches didn't have enough magic left to work with."

Selene's eyes were a set of lasers, boring through her youngest child. Joan had been incinerated by this look many times before, but she wasn't about to back off. She'd compromised so many principles in her life, being a Greenwood. Bent her head, borne her way through things, but the stakes had never been this high.

Joan didn't cower, and she didn't apologize. She straightened her spine and stared her mother down.

"Molly, Nate," Selene said, tone icy. "Give us a moment."

"Mom, you should really—" Molly began.

"Don't tell me what I should or shouldn't do, Molly Greenwood," Selene said. "Go get your sister some ice chips."

Joan broke eye contact with her mother to nod at her sister, but Molly hesitated another second. Her mouth shaped a word: *Uncle?*

But Joan didn't need Molly for this; she'd stand on her own feet. Or sit in her own hospital bed. She didn't regret what she'd done. The thought gave her a flush of strength.

She didn't regret what she'd done at all.

"Can you check on Grace for me?"

Molly withdrew. She turned once, like she had more to say, but Nate was there with a hand on her back, and whatever she saw on Joan's face didn't prompt her to say more.

Left alone with her mother, Joan had two seconds of silence before Selene exploded.

"Do you have *any* idea what you've done?" Selene snarled, pacing back and forth, hard enough that Joan feared her stilettos would pierce through the floor.

"I had to right our family's wrong," Joan said.

Selene scoffed. "Oh, so *noble*. Did you prepare that? Do you honestly think that's going to work on your aunt? Your father?"

Joan's willpower was enormous—somehow, she managed not to flinch at every word out of her mother's mouth. "I'm not trying to game Aunt Val or Dad. As hard as it is to believe, my actions don't revolve around either of them."

"Watch your tone. I don't care how old you are, you'll talk to me with respect and about your family with more care," Selene said, jabbing a finger in Joan's direction. "I know this family can be suffocating. I know the rules are endless and the eyes are always watching. But when you act out, it isn't just you who bears the consequences. It's all of us."

"Mom," Joan said, a bubble of some upset feeling rising in her chest. "Listen to me, please. You're not hearing what I'm saying."

"No, Joan, listen to *me*." Selene came to a stop at the foot of the bed. She hadn't ever been the one to yell at them as children; they had Merlin for that. But she'd always been stricter, because she paid closer attention. Joan had known exactly what Selene's lines were, what things her mother would hate: doing poorly in school, antagonizing Merlin, embarrassing her in public—all of it was a hard no. When she got pissed, she was Lawyer Mom, and she could out-debate any opponent on any circuit.

"You come back to town after I barely see you for seven years—*seven*, my own daughter—and promptly skip off," Selene said.

"No thought to check in with your parents, no sense of responsibility. I call and text, but you give me one-word answers. You were supposed to be at dinner a week ago; if you'd been there, you wouldn't have been in the middle of that market."

"Mom—"

"You wouldn't have nearly *died*, Joan," Selene thundered. She slapped a hand to her heart. "My daughter, my Joan. You nearly died because you insist on being so hardheaded."

Her eyes shone suspiciously, and that was enough to make Joan feel worse than she ever had. She'd made her own mother cry. What sort of monster did that?

"I'm fine, Mom, I'm good," Joan said.

"But you almost weren't, and now you're saying that the raid's failure was your fault." Selene leaned forward over the bed to grip Joan's ankles. "Joan, you don't know what it's like not to be a Greenwood, but I do. I was a Lacey before I met your father, and the life I lived then is worlds apart from the life I live now. Everyone's eyes are on us. Everyone's. People will use any excuse to try to unseat Valeria's rule. Our family's rule. You feed them ammo like it's nothing. You have no sense of consequence. You have no shame."

Joan looked at her splintered hand, the IVs trailing from it. She was no hero, but she did understand consequence. She'd always done that weighing: What could she do that wouldn't piss off her parents? How could she conduct herself in a way that made her as unnoticeable as possible?

"Is that what you want from me, Mom? Is shame your greatest wish for your child?"

"I didn't say that."

"You want me to feel ashamed—you just said that. Should I

be ashamed that I didn't go into law or finance like you, Dad, and Molly? Should I be ashamed that I can't cast? Should I be ashamed that I disagree with your opinions? I told you I channeled enough magic to nullify the entirety of Owl's Head Park, and your first thought is I should be ashamed. Which is it, do you want me to have magical prowess or not?"

The pressure on Joan's ankles lifted. "You're twisting my words."

Joan clenched her left fist in her blankets. "I don't think I am."

In the ensuing silence, Selene lifted a manicured hand and wiped a tear out of the corner of her eye before it could spill.

"If you won't listen to me," Selene said finally, "we'll see how your father fares."

"Great, because you know how we always see eye to eye."

"I can't deal with your attitude right now," Selene snapped. "We can talk when you're feeling more reasonable and I'm not feeling like I might say something I'll regret."

And like she wasn't in Joan's hospital room, like Joan hadn't just woken from a nearly weeklong coma, Selene left the room and her youngest child behind.

The quiet was punctuated only by the beep of Joan's monitor and her uneven breath. She leaned back on her pillows. She squeezed her eyes shut, and her own tears slipped out.

You did what you had to do, she sternly told herself.

You do not regret it.

You'd do it again.

They left her alone in that hospital room. At no point before she eventually fell asleep again did another person enter through that door.

NINETEEN

Two lonely days later, Joan had regained enough strength that they could bring in a healer to cast over her, and not long after that, she was cleared to go home, albeit with two of the fingers of her right hand still taped together for another week. Those injuries were resistant to magic.

Molly had come by frequently and smuggled Joan her phone, so she could at least text CZ.

Mik? Joan asked, once she'd confirmed CZ and his family were alright.

Not in Grace's apartment. I'm sorry, Jo, I haven't been able to find them.

Joan didn't want to ask her next question, but it felt like cowardice not to. Casualties from the market?

CZ's response was quick. No fatalities, some injuries and huge property damage. The market is shut down, which is going to completely screw the livelihoods of so many people, but we'll come together and rebuild. Mik didn't die there, but I don't know where they are.

Not dead. Not dead at least. Mik was not dead. Probably. Joan could find them as soon as they let her out of this godsdamn bed.

CZ: I'll come see you once you're out of the heavily guarded hospital

Joan: everyone keeps saying they're glad I'm not dead. It feels weird.

CZ: Being perceived? Please make no mistake, once I see you I am grabbing you in my arms and never letting go. I can't believe you were so stupid

Joan: can't you?

CZ: Hush

Jo, you're absolutely singular to me, I hope you know that. Idgaf about your family and what they think. I can't lose you, okay? It's all about me.

Joan: you're being sappy

CZ: I literally love u bro

Joan: bro

"If you're smiling like that, you must be texting CZ," Grace said, pushing open the door.

Joan nearly ripped her IVs out in her haste to swing her legs off the bed, sniffling back some tears. "Shit, Grace. I'm so sorry."

Grace was in street clothes, and there were no bandages in sight, but she looked absolutely exhausted. She strode over faster than Joan could stand and, to Joan's ever-loving surprise, threw herself into Joan's arms.

Grace squeezed, hard. "I'm really glad you didn't die," she whispered. "Thank you for doing that with me. Molly says we saved a lot of people. Though she also for some reason is under the impression I tried to stop you."

"Please tell me you furthered that lie," Joan said.

"I promptly refuted it. It was my idea in the first place, and we did it together."

Joan groaned. "Grace, you know they can't really get mad at me—I was trying to protect you."

"And who was going to protect you?" Grace said. "No, I know I've been harsh with you, but I'm not going to hang you out to dry."

Joan breathed slowly, trying to stifle the tears.

"Mik is missing," Joan murmured into Grace's shirt.

Grace stiffened. "We'll find them. I'm getting out today, and I can do a tracking spell once I get back to my apartment."

"You're always coming up with a plan."

"My last one nearly killed us."

"I brought half the idea to the table. Are you okay to cast?"

"I don't know," Grace said after a pause. "I apparently tolerated magic worse than you did but responded more quickly to healing spells. I'm tired. Bone-tired. And my job is probably so pissed at me for missing a week. We have to keep going, right? We already left them alone in the world for eight days."

Eight days with no phone, cards, cash, IDs, and they hadn't returned to Grace's apartment.

"I'll meet you at your place this evening," Joan said.

Grace was still hugging Joan. "I doubt your family is going to let you out of the house for a good long while."

Joan hadn't realized how badly she needed a hug, a real one, unconditional and fond, but judging by Grace's grip, Grace needed it too.

"Grace," Joan whispered into her hair.

"Mmm?"

"Let's never do that again."

Grace laughed. It sounded a little wet. Joan pretended not to feel the tears falling on the bare skin above her hospital gown. "Is it awful that it was kind of incredible?"

New York opening ancient eyes, the feeling of power, the whole city in her fist. "I felt invincible. And you—you were amazing. Who else would be able to adapt on the fly well enough to keep up with all that magic? I can't believe you're thinking about leaving spellmaking behind. You could do it on the side."

"As if anyone would leave me be if I did. Besides, I'm good, sure, but I wouldn't say *incredible* or *prodigy* or whatever; the world will be quite alright without my spells."

Joan tightened her grip. What was it with Mik and Grace that made them think they weren't important to the world? Joan had never met such tenacious, loving, generous people. "I don't know if it would be, Grace. I certainly wouldn't be."

Grace's breath in was long and shuddering. She drew back finally and dug around in the pocket of her jeans, before pulling out a ring. Joan's ring, with a black pearl inset into its gold band.

"I kept it on me," Grace explained, clearing her throat and blinking a few times to clear the sheen on her eyes.

Joan would let this go for now, but she had to find a way to get Grace to understand how extraordinary she was. "Does it... I mean, does it work?"

"I think so," Grace said. "There's magic in it, but I don't know if I'd put it on. That much magic in a mind ward? I'm not really sure what it might do to a regular person. I'll take it back to my apartment and hide it somewhere until we figure out what to do with it."

Joan swallowed thickly. "We?"

Grace put the ring back in her pocket. "What, you're gonna

ditch me now that we're in a ton of trouble with your family? No, we're a *we*, Joan. You and me and Mik, at minimum, but CZ and Abel too."

"At least until we fix this," Joan said.

Grace shook her head. "I don't know, I think I'll have your back as long as you'll let me. I'm sorry I was being such a secretive dick about things."

Joan lowered her voice, though the room was empty save for them. "Right, gods, I forgot. Fiona, what's that all about?"

"I started to suspect when I went in Mik's head... The spell there had a certain feeling to it. Spellmakers all have a kind of signature that they leave on the spells they create, and the memory wipe on Mik felt familiar," Grace said. "But it wasn't just that. Why could Mik cast in the market? How does the spell on them regenerate with such dedicated focus? It's a variation on a pocket realm—she changed the physics of magic around them so that the only function of the realm is to keep drawing magic into the spell, and in doing so made it possible for them to circumvent the wards in the market, just a little."

That was... genius.

"I thought about it forever, because I didn't want to make an accusation unless I was sure. But Fiona's always been fascinated by New York's Night Market, it's the biggest one in the country, it's why she lives in the city half the time. There's work to be found there, and when I got in that tent, I could feel the remnants of her magic, even several days old. She'd been there. She's good with pocket realms, like, really good. It's her specialty. And she's been researching a cure for magic poisoning for forever, which is not too far off the question of how to make a human a witch."

Before everything, Joan's growing suspicions about Grace had crescendoed. And she wanted to hug her again, believe in the best of the woman. But Grace's lifelong mentor being the latest suspect? It was too close to her. *I'd do anything to help her*, Grace had said once. Fiona was struggling to find work. Would Grace create a spell that was such a mystery, Fiona conveniently got called before the Greenwoods?

"There's one more thing," Grace said. "The night someone rifled through your head, Fiona was the friend I met in the market. She left an hour before you got there."

There were voices in the hallway, and it sounded like Molly and Nate were among them.

Joan's mind whizzed through the mental calculus. It didn't add up in Grace's favor, but Joan's gut was still a steady light in the darkness. Even if it was nothing more than wishful thinking, Joan wanted to trust Grace. She had to trust Grace.

"Tonight," Joan said quickly. "I'll meet you tonight; we can talk more then."

Molly and Nate entered the room with Joan's doctor in tow, rolling a wheelchair, their laughter dying down as they saw Grace in there.

"Glad you're okay," Grace said as goodbye, and then politely made her way out the door.

Molly gave her a quick smile before turning back to Joan with a suggestive look on her face.

Joan had forgotten Molly thought they were in love. "Leave off it."

"I didn't say a single word," Molly replied. "Ready to go home?"

Joan really wasn't, but it would be easier to break out of her family's house than this hospital. She slid off the bed. "Let's go." She pointed at the dahlias. "Can I bring those?"

"Of course," said Joan's doctor, a Black woman in blue attending scrubs. "They aren't the hospital's."

"I guess I never thanked you for them, Molly," Joan said, seating herself in the wheelchair.

"Not mine either," Molly said.

"Astoria dropped them off while you were both still asleep," Nate said. He leaned in and kissed the side of Molly's head. Joan decided not to gag and make fun of them, mainly because she was still trying to process that Astoria had brought her favorite flowers.

And single-handedly rescued her from a death of her own creation in the market.

Molly's eyebrows had rocketed up her face. "Is there something there? Was I wrong about Grace?"

"You are absolutely wrong about Grace, but there's also definitely not a thing with Astoria." Joan scoffed and attempted to wheel herself one-handed out the door, nearly running over Nate's toes in the process. *Astoria has a clear and unrequited crush on her best friend.*

Molly gained control of Joan's wheelchair before anyone could suffer further injuries. "Sure, Joan, whatever you say. Nate, please grab that vase of flowers."

"Yes, sir," Nate said, picking up the glass vase.

Molly teased her all the way to the taxi. Inside, Joan had an abysmally short amount of time to try and figure out what she'd say to her father and aunt.

She hadn't seen Merlin, Valeria, or Selene since Joan's argument with her mother.

Whatever was waiting for her at that house…it wouldn't be good.

TWENTY

At the Greenwood Mansion, Joan was fussed over by every member of the staff she'd grown up with, including George, who looked quite agitated and flickered in and out as he opened the front door for them, despite Joan insisting she could still use a doorknob. She felt tired and weak, and her hand kind of ached. The doctor, who Joan was pretty sure was both a witch who specialized in healing magic and someone with a human medical degree, had told Joan to try and keep the hand above her heart to reduce swelling and sleep with it elevated, which seemed like a hassle. But other than that, she was perfectly fine. The miracles of healing magic.

Selene, at least, greeted them at the door. Joan resisted the urge to duck and cover, a thousand possible arguments rearing ugly heads at her.

But Selene did not say a single word to Joan.

"The silent treatment, really, Mom?" Joan said, gobsmacked by this behavior. There had been plenty of times in life that Joan had pissed off her mother, and Joan had felt bad because she didn't want to get in trouble, and because she didn't want her mom to stop loving her, and because she could do the mental cartwheels that made her think maybe, after all, what Joan had done was wrong.

But Joan had spent her time in that hospital bed trying to do those cartwheels, and she could not fathom a universe where she was sorry for what she had done, except insofar as she had hurt Grace, which she did deeply regret.

Selene didn't look at her.

Deep in Joan, fear began to morph into annoyance.

"Come on, Mom," Molly said, hovering around Joan like she'd fall over at any minute.

"Indeed, Selene," Valeria said, coming out of her study to stand at the bottom of the staircase. "You can't expect an apology out of someone who isn't sorry."

"That is between me and my daughter, Valeria," Selene said. "Tell her what we decided. I'll be in the garden if anyone needs me."

Valeria's face was calm as Selene left.

"I assume you want to yell at me too?" Joan said, that ember of annoyance gaining heat at the mere sight of her aunt's stalwart face. Now was not the time for serenity.

Valeria stood there, neither leaving nor coming closer to greet Joan. Her ambivalence was infuriating.

The heat stoked higher.

"This family protects you because it must," Valeria said. "Do not take that as a blessing on your actions, and do not take that for granted. You won't do something like this again, Joan."

Joan's response was almost reflex at this point. "Don't invade the market again."

"Can you give it a rest for like half a second," Molly said.

But she couldn't. Joan couldn't. Standing in this house—surrounded by all their wealth and power, the soft scurrying of house staff, the relative quiet—all Joan could hear were the screams of the market, and the crackle of the flames, and her conscience leaping into action without a second thought for her own well-being. Pushed into a corner, the Greenwoods had done something horrific.

Pushed into a corner, Joan had responded in turn.

"You are not in a position to tell me what to do, and you lack the clarity to see what must be done," Valeria said. "That is why you do not rule, and that is why you are not heir."

"You don't have an heir," Joan shot back. Valeria neither had any children nor had named anyone to take over should she die. By default, the position would fall to Merlin.

Valeria, for a moment, looked every year her age. Growing old at the top of the magic world. So many layers of power and privilege and time and tradition kept her on top. "Because having no one is better than running the risk of having you, Joan. If you aren't careful, you will be the destruction of this family and its legacy." Her words reverberated through the world with all the force of a prophecy, settling like a noose around Joan's neck.

Molly wasn't looking at her. Neither was Nate. Only Valeria had the guts to actually say it and stare her down too.

In Joan's normal life, she was a creator. She was an artist and an architect. She made things from nothing.

In Joan's family, she did nothing but destroy.

There was a choice here somewhere, between who they thought she was and who she knew she could be, but she had never been strong enough to choose the right path.

She swallowed thickly, her throat tight, her eyes burning. She didn't want to be here; she couldn't stand to be in this room anymore.

Valeria stepped away from the stairs. "You will not appear as a member of this family in any capacity until such a time as I decide you are ready for that privilege again. Get some rest. I'm sure your father will have words for you."

Joan couldn't possibly have been grounded. That's what this was, her being grounded like she was eleven again and had accidentally smashed a vase while sliding on her socks down the hallway.

But she could be, couldn't she? They could all lock her in a room. She didn't have power here; she didn't have any true use.

There's a great magic in New York, and I spoke to it, and I called on it, and still I am grounded. Joan had spent a lifetime reaching for power in the hopes that it would earn her respect and acceptance. But now that she had some semblance of it, she saw it was the wrong kind of power. An unruly one her family didn't understand or believe in. One they couldn't control.

Molly hovered all the way up the steps and to Joan's bedroom, but the moment she tried to step in, Joan blocked her path.

"I'm going back to sleep," Joan said. "You should go back to your life. Thanks for hanging around."

Joan shut the door in her face.

Merlin did not make his appearance for several more hours, not until the sun had set, and Joan had cried herself out, and napped, and cried again, and taken a shower.

It was only when she was back in bed, counting down the

minutes until she might be able to sneak out to meet Grace and CZ to look for Mik, that Merlin deigned to visit his youngest daughter.

He knocked once, but didn't wait for a reply before stepping in. The top button of his shirt was undone; his sleeves were rolled up. If Joan were feeling nicer, she'd say he looked tired, but she wasn't, and she didn't care.

"Hi, Dad," she said bitterly, pulling her knees to her chest. "Finally decided to see me?"

"Right off the bat, snark from you," he said from the foot of her bed. "Stand up."

"I'm very comfortable—"

"Stand up, Joan."

Like a puppet on a thread, she stood. Unfolded, Joan felt terribly vulnerable, all soft belly, no hard shell.

"Since you've decided you're grown, and that you can shun this family, break the law, do whatever the fuck it is you want, then you can stand up and talk to me like the adult you are," Merlin said, voice rising in volume.

"I didn't break the law," Joan said, but her voice was small. Smaller than she'd like. She hated it. She hated how weak she sounded, how weak she felt. She'd managed to find some semblance of a spine with her mother and aunt, but Merlin knocked her right back on her heels.

"I am the law," he said, gripping her footboard. "I make the law, and when you hear your family intends to make a move and you defy it, that means you are defying me *and the law.*"

I don't set the moral code of the witch world, the Greenwoods do, Grace had said what felt like an eternity ago. *The rest of us are cogs in a machine; ethics don't factor into my ability to turn.*

"That was your last toe out of line," Merlin said. "That isn't a threat—I am telling you it was your last one. You will fall in your place now. When people ask, you will tell them that Moon Creatures forced you to nearly blow up the market. If you do a single thing more to defy us, I will bring the full hammer of the Greenwood family down on your head, daughter of mine or not."

The lie of it was outrageous. Disastrous, accusing the Moon Creatures of such a thing when they all knew it wasn't true. No, no, no. Not in a million years. Never.

That ember grew a flame.

"But you won't," Joan said, "You won't bring the hammer down, will you? Because it would reflect poorly on you. You'll lie your ass off to avoid that."

Merlin released the footboard to walk toward her, invading her personal space with his gesturing hands and his hot breath. "Call my bluff, Joan."

Joan was all cried out. No tears rose to the summons of her torn emotions; there was no more wobble left to her voice. She was calling his bluff, *she was*, because she had never once called it before. She had let herself get corralled. She'd gone to the parties they demanded she go to, and returned to the city when they said it was time, and chased after something she'd never have: their respect.

Joan stepped back, giving herself room. Carving it out for herself, since Merlin wouldn't grant it. "You were in the wrong," she said.

"And you are a naive child. Don't do this again."

"I had to try; they're victims, they deserve—"

"I don't give a shit, Joan," Merlin snarled, making a cutting motion with his hand, severing the air between them. "I don't give a single fuck what you think they *deserve*. Call them victims, call them pitiful sheep, call them evil, call them gods—whatever name you come up with for them, whatever story you spin to save them, they belong to New York, which means they belong to me, and I won't suffer them to hide this spellmaker for a second longer. You have no idea what's at stake here."

"You don't own shit, and even if you did, it's not you in power. You mean they belong to *Valeria*. Not you. Never you," Joan replied, her voice gaining heat. Ire prickled along her skin, raising goose bumps in its wake. "Even now, even *knowing you were wrong*, you can't for a second admit you may have made a mistake invading the market? Not even *you* can be so arrogant as to think you get to determine whether Moon Creatures live or die, whether anyone gets to live or die. Human or witch, man or *god*, I'm not bending to the whims of this family. I will not lie and blame the Moon Creatures for what I did."

"Then perhaps, Joan," Merlin said, and this was a guttural proclamation, a violent final ruling manifested between them as he jabbed a finger at her chest, "perhaps you aren't part of this family at all."

Silence gathered them both in her cruel fist, a trance broken only by Merlin's heaving breaths, the faint traffic outside. Joan's hospital bracelet was still on her wrist.

You aren't part of this family at all.

What a contrast it was to every loving thing ever uttered to her by CZ. Grace. Mik.

Jo, you're absolutely singular.

I don't know, I think I'll have your back as long as you'll let me.

Joan registered her tears only when they hit her collarbone.

"Oh, don't be dramatic," Merlin huffed, turning from her and taking a few steps away, embarrassed on her behalf.

Joan heaved an uneven breath around her tears, dashed them from her eyes with weak hands, and straightened her spine. "There," she said, only a little wobbly. "Was that so hard to admit?"

Merlin turned then, eyebrows rising in confusion, but Joan wasn't going to stand around here, frozen, like usual. She wasn't going to let Merlin's words spell her into paralyzed complicity. She wasn't going to let his anger hold her still, his yelling steal her will. She had a choice in front of her, a choice about what kind of person she wanted to be.

A week and a half ago, when CZ had first called to tell her he had Mik, Joan hadn't hesitated for a moment to run to him. It was a law of the universe—Joan and CZ against the world.

She knew that if she ran, people would run with her.

If she fell, people would catch her.

Joan strode for her closet, ripping open the door to grab her largest duffel bag before planting it on top of her dresser and yanking at her drawers, still mindful of her splinted fingers.

"What are you doing, Joan," Merlin ground out, and his tone was flat.

Joan bit her lip, hard. She could do no more than shovel her clothes into the duffel, fast, messy. Once she had the basics, she turned, brushing past him to toss in the sketch pads on her bedside, her pencil case, her phone charger, her laptop and headphones. She snatched a few of her favorite sweaters, a pantsuit Molly had given her, and one tailored suit—because who knew what she'd need in her new life—before opening a new compartment and shoving in a pair of shoes.

"Joan!" Merlin barked, but Joan was on a rampage, cataloging everything she'd ever owned, realizing how much of it, how much of this life, she was willing to leave behind. When it came down to it, she was willing to let it all go.

Merlin's hand on the scale wasn't enough to tip her back, his threats, everything. She'd looked up to him once—her dad was the most powerful man in New York City.

She saw him for what he was now: a coward riding the coattails of his sister's power.

Merlin moved to block the door as Joan slung her bag on her shoulder and made for it, but she ducked under his arm, fast, and sprinted, slipping through.

"JOAN GREENWOOD!"

Joan's socked feet thudded against the floor as she picked up speed down the hallway, sliding to the top of the stairs and then thundering down it in a way that had her afraid she was going to slip and die—and wouldn't that be pitiful—her breaths gasping out of her throat.

She was stupid for this; she had never been more of a fool in her whole entire privileged life. She saw nice apartments and expensive clothes and vacations flit by her eyes as she rounded the corner, heading for the front door. She saw family dinners, Molly nudging her beneath the table, her mother nearby, Valeria opening the door to her home with a gentle smile on her face, all gone.

"STOP IT THIS INSTANT, JOAN," Merlin roared from the top of the stairs.

Molly's voice drifted down too, faint behind the screaming in Joan's head. "What the hell is going on?"

"Merlin, what is this now?" Selene said.

Joan was too busy jamming her feet into her sneakers to turn.

The parties, gone.

The access, gone.

Her coven, broken.

And beyond the horizon, she could see CZ, where he always was, in his dusty Hell's Kitchen apartment. Grace waiting for her at the café for lunch, Billy appearing in the middle of Grace's apartment, Mik in a corner watching TV. A new coven, less likely, but kinder than the one she'd been born into.

Joan saw plants in windowsills, her own desk at a smaller architectural firm, freedom outside the bounds of New York City, an endless, ageless future waiting for her if she could just get out, if she could turn the doorknob and make it out—

You aren't part of this family at all.

The doorknob hummed with magic beneath her hand and resolutely refused to turn.

Joan let out a frustrated scream, half sob, half yell, as she turned to see Merlin with his hands drifting down, having cast the door sealed.

Molly and their mom were barely visible behind the veil of Joan's tears.

"Undo it," Joan breathed, but Merlin paid her no mind, animatedly talking to Selene. Joan caught snippets, her hearing fading in and out: *She's being unreasonable... It's time for her to face reality... Maybe if she stopped to think about how I feel in all this...*

Joan could not counterspell the door herself; they all knew that. She lived at Merlin's whims to leave, to stay. She was part of the family when he dictated, and she wasn't when he said so. Always, always she was under his control.

She tried to reach for magic and channel it in, snuff out the wards, but there were *so* many wards, and even as Joan tried to pull in magic, she felt winded far sooner than she used to. She tried harder, her concentration slipping, disappearing entirely.

Again and again she tried, but she couldn't focus well enough to cycle. She stopped, leaning heavily against the front door.

No.

She couldn't be trapped here. Why, why was this failing her *now*? She needed more time with this skill, more practice, more grace, more learning, and to be less magic fatigued.

The words ripped out of her, larger and harsher than she'd ever been with him. "UNDO IT," she demanded, loud enough that her voice shredded, and the snake plant by the door withered, and finally, they turned.

"Joan, go to bed," her mother said, a placating hand held out to Merlin. "We can talk about this tomorrow. You know your aunt and I already feel it would be best if you stepped back from family duties. You had to know there would be consequences."

Of course, Selene would soothe and make excuses. She'd say the same things Merlin had, in different words, in a different tone, and because it was gentler, Joan was supposed to forgive it. But Selene had said it as firmly as Merlin had: Joan was not part of this family. Joan was not a Greenwood witch. Joan had no place in this coven.

"You guys can't be serious," Molly said faintly. "You know what you're doing to her. It's akin to exile. A coven break in all but name. You can't make her lie about the Moon Creatures."

"This doesn't involve you, Molly," Merlin snapped. "Go back to your house if you don't like it in mine."

Molly looked like she'd been slapped.

Joan choked on a laugh, because if Molly couldn't command respect here, Joan didn't know why she'd ever, for even a second, thought *she* might. They weren't going to keep her here. She had made up her mind to run, she had made up her mind to destroy her own life before Merlin managed to do it, and she had all the self-preservation of a cornered rat now. She'd chew herself out of this cage if she had to; harm was an old friend.

Her fingers wrapped around the stupid vase in the entryway, one that was suitably expensive but wholly modern, at least. Did it deserve her ire? No. But everything was collateral damage now.

It hit the window with a sharp crack, and the entryway window had been spelled against damage, but the vase had not. It shattered beautifully.

A wordless roar greeted her from the head of the stairs, but Joan was on to the next thing. The hall table, tipped. She managed to throw the runner at the glass chandelier in a way that set it swinging precariously. Her right hand throbbed as she bashed it around, but it didn't matter. Another vase, launched at the wall. A potted plant kicked over, its leaves going limp. But, of course, Merlin couldn't stand a rampage for long. As she skittered to the hall closet, reaching for one of his precious golf clubs, her hand froze in midair.

Paralysis spread slowly up her body, enough so that she had time to look up and see Merlin red in the face, casting.

And see Molly bring one hand up, tears brimming from her eyes. See her other hand grab Merlin's, hard, stopping the spell in its tracks.

Her arm slashed down, and Joan was freed. Molly's fingers moved, and the door swung open.

In her sister's gaze, Joan saw every apology they'd never been brave enough to exchange. Every act of defiance they'd both snuffed. In her eyes, Joan saw Molly call *uncle* for her.

Chest heaving, Joan pulled her duffel bag on more firmly, her feet moving before her brain could fully catch up, seeing only the door and feeling the walls of this house fall away.

She paused, once, in the threshold, the infinite night at her back, the smallness of her family in front of her.

She faced down her father, incandescent at the top of the stairs.

"Fuck you, Merlin Greenwood," she said, "you spineless, worthless worm of a man. You will never be great. You will always be less than Valeria. And you live the narrowest life I've ever seen."

And Joan Greenwood, of the historic Greenwood witches of New York City, broke from her coven.

ACT THREE

TWENTY-ONE

~~~≈≈≈~~~

New York threw its arms wide to its favorite daughter.

Joan stumbled out onto the street, ignoring George's calls and Merlin's shout, picking a direction and running.

And when she couldn't run anymore, she jogged.

And when she couldn't jog, her heart beating too fast and her breath a painful lance through her worn-out lungs, she walked.

And when even that was too much, the shadows of the night beginning to reach across her vision, she leaned against a building and hoped distantly that no one mugged her.

She'd walked out. Out of the house. Out of her family's house. Out of their lives, undoing what she had begun the day she stepped across their threshold. She was not to appear as part of the family. She was not part of the family at all.

She didn't fully realize she'd dialed until he picked up.

"Hey, how's lockup treating you?" CZ said casually. "You need help breaking out to meet Grace?"

Joan breathed into the phone as tears dripped off her chin,

struggling to control the tragic hammer of her heart. It pulverized her ribs. She was raw, and empty.

CZ's tone flipped to something serious. "Jo? What happened?"

"I think I've run away," Joan said, dazed, into the phone.

"To me, right?" CZ said, and there was a clattering of keys being snatched from a table. "Tell me you're running to me."

Joan looked up at the street signs around her. She was only a block off Central Park and several blocks south of her house. Headed in the direction of CZ. "I think I am."

"I'll meet you, where are you? Don't bother answering; I have your location pin. I'm coming, Joan—stay right there."

"CZ," Joan said faintly. "CZ, what did I do?"

"I'm staying on the line," he said. "Keep talking to me."

Joan stood there for several minutes, murmuring nonsensically, listening to the swish of wind on CZ's side, feeling her heart rate slow, and slow, and slow, until CZ was there, putting a hand on her elbow.

He must have hung up the call, because the phone was dead against her ear. She lowered it slowly, and he took it from her limp hand. His face caught the shadows of the streetlight, and it was full of pity, but she didn't resent it from him. He knew what she'd done and understood the depth of it. How many times had Joan talked about shedding her family? And now here she was, alone in the night.

Not alone.

"What can I do?" CZ said helplessly. "I will do anything for you, Joan, give you anything. Ask me for anything."

Joan pulled the words out of the depths of her body. "Take me home, CZ."

CZ took her bag off her shoulder, slung it around himself. His arm was a solid scoop at her back. He picked her up, bridal style, and Joan let him without any quips, which was how she knew she really wasn't doing well.

The quick pace he set wasn't very comfortable, but Joan pressed her ear to his chest, listened to the slow thump, thump, thump of his heart, and closed her eyes to the world.

Joan had never slept in this bed or apartment before, so the first few moments of waking up were confusing.

Dawn was barely touching the tips of the city. She uncurled and felt a body at her back.

"Hey," CZ said softly, and when she turned, she saw he was scrolling through social media with earbuds in, likely at their lowest possible volume. He took one out. "You sleep okay?"

Joan's eyes felt puffy, and her nose was kind of stuffy, and her body was still achy, but she had slept deeply.

"You really do need those blackout curtains," Joan croaked, squinting at the strip of sun visible beyond his very thin, pale curtains.

Sun.

It was daytime.

Joan threw herself upright. "Fuck, we were supposed to meet Grace!"

"You fell asleep," CZ said, setting his phone aside in a rush. "I texted her and canceled."

"You have her number? Not the point." Joan twisted to face him, balancing her weight on her left hand. "CZ, we were supposed to meet her to *find Mik*. Who is missing, lost in the city."

"I know."

"They could be hurt! If they're upset, magic will keep coursing through them, and it could kill—" She choked herself off.

CZ gripped the tops of her arms. "I know, Joan. Take a second. You were completely worn out, and Grace wasn't faring that well either. We talked about it and felt it did Mik no good to have you two kill yourselves trying to find them. We'd have heard if they'd turned up dead, so let's assume they're alive, and we can head over to Grace's whenever you're ready."

Joan nearly tripped and went sprawling in her efforts to get out of the bed with the blankets tangled around her. She tore through her duffel bag for suitable clothes—she honestly hadn't done a half bad job packing—and was dressed and showered in a record fifteen minutes, nudging CZ out the door so they could hop on the subway.

"I'm thinking of getting a car," CZ said. "I know, I know, a car in the city? But I think it would come in handy."

Joan grabbed him and tugged. "I know you're as worried about Mik as I am, so why aren't you looking more panicked?"

CZ's stream of jokes died down as they crossed the street, heading for the 50th Street station.

His face was drawn. Joan said his name questioningly.

"I *am* panicked," he admitted. "I'm panicked about what we're going to find when Grace casts that spell. The two of you were hospitalized, and Abel had his hands full trying to help the displaced vampires who were run out of the market. It fell to me to find Mik, and I failed. Whatever happens next is my fault."

Joan pulled them to a stop and made CZ face her, squeezing their hands between them. "Cane," she said.

CZ groaned. "Not my legal name."

"Cane Aleczander."

A louder groan. "Am I being grounded?"

"This is not your fault," Joan said firmly. "Whatever comes next, it is not your fault. I'm the one who sent Mik out of the tent into the middle of the market. I'm the one who brought Grace in, which is how we did that tether spell. We're in this together, alright?" Joan was going all in on this. Her life was a pile of rubble, but Mik—Mik, she could still save. CZ, she could still protect.

CZ bumped his forehead against Joan's briefly. "You give a good pep talk."

Joan led him onward. "I mostly repeat stuff you've said to me before."

Once they made it to Brooklyn, the increasingly familiar walk from the Bay Ridge Avenue subway stop to Grace's apartment felt eternal. Despite her encouraging words, Joan was feeling the same concern as CZ. Mik would have had to escape through a fiery, chaotic market, and Joan had told them to go to Grace's apartment. The fact that they didn't surely meant they'd been picked up on the way, and the only people who would know to look for them, who had been looking out for them, who might have been able to help them, had been knocked out in a hospital or scrambling to help a wave of refugees.

They made it to Grace's building eventually, catching the door as someone walked out and making the trek up to the fifth floor. Joan was not feeling well enough to take the stairs, but she refused to admit weakness, so she kept dragging her feet up step by step, turning down CZ's repeated offers of a piggyback ride. She was shaking a little by the time they made it to Grace's door.

Luckily, Grace looked similarly awful. She didn't bother with pleasantries, leading them to the kitchen.

"Billy won't come out," Grace said miserably. "I wanted to ask her if Mik came and left, or never came. I went through their room, but I couldn't tell."

Grace picked up a mug of tea, sipping from it. "I assume you'd have heard from your parents if they picked Mik up though."

Joan wasn't sure anymore what they would have told her. That is, before she'd left in the middle of the night. "I'm kind of exiled," Joan admitted.

That woke Grace up a little. "Exiled? You coven broke?"

It was nice of CZ not to have told Grace last night.

"They wanted me to pin blame on Moon Creatures for what happened to us," Joan said with a shrug, playing off what a soul-rending event that had been. "I said no."

She wasn't sure what Grace would say here. She didn't want the easy comfort of platitudes. She didn't want someone else's condolences or their congratulations. Neither seemed right.

"Oh." Grace set down her cup. "We had better find Mik. And once we do, we're going to seal them, then set up some sort of audience with your family to get the blame off Moon Creatures and back on Fiona. If you trust Molly, we can call her in to help with the sealing. Or maybe we should take a leap of faith and try Wren if she declined to join Astoria at the market."

Joan let out a breath. "Do they know about Fiona? Did you mention her?"

"No one was interested in talking to me," Grace said. "And your family kept quiet from everyone that I was even hospital-ized. I assumed you told them?"

Joan had not. Somehow, she'd been too busy arguing with them.

CZ rubbed his face. "We're seriously the only people on earth who are on Fiona's trail?"

"The Greenwoods have been checking in with us both to see if there's been progress on recreating the spell," Grace said. "She texts me about it. I highly doubt they think it's her just on their own."

"Let's get Mik quickly, then," Joan said. "And maybe we go after Fiona ourselves."

"Absolutely not," CZ said.

"And do what with her?" Grace asked worriedly.

"We have more bargaining power if we get to her first," Joan said.

With a huff, Grace fished out a shirt Mik had worn, holding it in one hand as she put the other on top of it, rapidly casting a tracking spell. There was already a roughly drawn map of New York on a piece of paper on the counter, since she still didn't have a kitchen table.

Magic was a bit hesitant around Grace, and she grimaced a little when it funneled into her, but the spell glowed to life, the map's black ink shining with an intense white light before settling into a dull shine, an *X* appearing on the map.

"Is channeling tough for you too?" Grace asked Joan.

"Like I overworked a muscle," Joan replied, as they gathered closer to the paper. "I think it's faded from full poisoning to fatigue, but it isn't very pleasant."

Grace grunted. "I think it'll keep fading."

Think being the operative word. But maybe it was for the best Joan not touch magic like she had been lately. It was intoxicating to finally have some modicum of power, and she'd nearly committed a murder-suicide chasing it. "Best if I stay away from it for now, though I was just getting the hang of talking to New York."

Focus. Looking down at the map, Joan half expected it to

settle over Green-Wood Cemetery, as if Mik had been killed and neatly buried there.

But instead the *X* hovered over an area in Manhattan.

Joan frowned. "Why would Mik be in Manhattan? What's in that area?"

Silence.

She looked up to Grace and CZ exchanging very meaningful glances. "What?"

"Joan, my darling," CZ said, "what do you mean you're talking to New York? Are you feeling okay?"

"Is this related to when you asked Abel if New York was alive?" Grace added. Something clicked for her. "In the market, you said magic felt like one entity, but you didn't say it was sentient."

Had she seriously never told them? She picked over her memories, straightening. Yeah, that was right, she'd been kind of convinced she was having a breakdown, then the moment she was sure it was real she'd wanted to tell CZ in private, and she'd started to explain but hadn't actually said magic was aware, only that there was a kind of aggregate to the city, then the market had exploded, and in all that time since, she had never brought it up directly. "When I cycle huge amounts of magic, it's like I settle into the currents of energy in the area. Several times now it's felt alive and spoken to me. A sentient being that, since it comes from the magic across the city, I've been referring to as *New York*."

Grace leaned hard against the counter. "You've learned that you can not only nullify magic but also speak to magic itself? I've never heard of that happening. I've never heard of magic having a consciousness."

"Me neither! I'm having a late awakening," Joan said, maybe a little bit proud of herself. "Doing lots of things it had never occurred to me to do before. It's cool, isn't it? And I don't know that it's Magic, like worldwide Magic Itself, so much as it's magic within the city, like maybe Seattle has its own identity. I don't know, I need to have a long conversation with Abel."

CZ clapped her on the back. "You're such a little freak," he said endearingly. "Look at you!"

This was much more the reaction Joan was looking for. Her family hadn't seemed to want to dwell on her magic-nullification abilities, or at least they had been more concerned with convincing her to lie for them.

"Maybe we can seal Mik without anyone else," Grace murmured. She refocused on the map. "Maybe if Joan pulls in enough magic, I can do it solo."

"Last time you two were left to your own devices, you nearly died," CZ said. "We can get one more witch, to be safe. I really think we should consider Wren."

Joan got out her phone to pull up a map app, zooming in on the area that Grace's magic drawing was showing. The *X* was large, covering an area rather than a specific building, and Joan didn't want to strain Grace further by asking her to zoom in. "That's by the Diamond District, not far from Rockefeller Center."

"You're telling me what, that Mik fled a mass fire and decided to go diamond shopping?" CZ said incredulously. "With what money? They have no cash or credit cards, were working a publishing job for a frankly laughable salary, and they're still there a week later? Do they have a friend in the city who lives around there? I'd have assumed they'd go back to their parents, but I found their address, and Mik wasn't there."

"It's mainly shopping in that area, not apartments," Grace said, squinting at the map like it might cough up more secrets.

Something CZ had said was pushing at the building blocks of Joan's mind. Money. How would Mik survive in the city without a phone, cash, or cards?

"Oh! Oh, they do have a credit card," Joan said excitedly, exiting the map and opening up her banking app. "They have *my* card!"

Joan's fat fingers fumbled her sign-in a couple of times before making it through and checking her credit card transactions. Mik's full history was laid out here, purchase after purchase. Joan scrolled back to the beginning, one week ago.

"They got a cheap motel," Joan started. "Junk food, junk food, groceries—good for them, nutrition is important, I'm told. A phone, I think. Okay, the latest version of the iPhone, that feels like overkill. And then the regular transactions stop, and..." That didn't make a lot of sense. Joan paused, typed something into Google, went back to the app.

"Please stop with the dramatic suspense; the doctors say my heart is weakened," Grace said.

"Gods, is that true?" CZ said worriedly. "It sounds normal."

"Stop listening to my heartbeat," Grace said. "And it was a joke. I tell them sometimes."

"I enjoyed it," CZ said. "You should tell more."

Joan looked up. "Stop flirting."

CZ coughed suspiciously. "I wasn't— Shut up. Joan, the charges."

Joan's mischievous desire to tease him lost against the task at hand. She refocused. "Several days ago, room service charges for the Baccarat Hotel start popping up," Joan said. "But there isn't any sort of credit card hold for an actual room there, which is kind of nice, because that hotel is expensive as fuck."

"You have the money," CZ said.

"For now. I don't know what sort of legal, financial sorcery my dad might work to get my access removed, if he's pissed enough," Joan said.

"Isn't it in your name?" Grace asked.

"My family owns the bank it's held in; I wouldn't put it past him." The thought was admittedly rather sobering. Joan needed a job, and fast. She'd have to polish her portfolio, look for an architecture firm elsewhere. Another borough? Or another city entirely?

Now that she could actually leave the city, the thought felt hauntingly cold. She could leave New York behind. New York, whom she'd discovered like a long-lost friend.

"So, the Baccarat?" Grace prompted. "Should we go there?"

Joan corralled her mind into logical lines. "I think it's our best bet. Mik probably left us a trail on purpose."

"I think I'm going to kiss them full on the lips if they did," CZ said. He darted a glance at Grace. "Platonically."

Joan rolled her eyes at his hurried addition. "Platonically."

The three of them gathered themselves and stepped back outside. Because CZ was a vampire, they couldn't save time by taking the HERMES—an unfair barrier that Joan would disable if she were in charge.

But she'd never be in charge. She'd made sure of that when she left that house.

"See, a car would be great," CZ said, watching Joan closely.

"You want to drive on these hellish streets?" Grace said as they descended into the subway.

Joan snorted, pulled from the anxiety spiral of her bad thoughts. "See, no one thinks it's a good idea."

CZ grumbled all the way to Manhattan and was still grumbling when they got off and wove through the throngs to get to the lobby of the Baccarat. Joan had been to plenty of expensive parties here growing up, but Grace's mouth hung open a little as they stepped inside.

"What exactly is the plan here?" CZ whispered. "Do you know what room number it is based on the charges?"

"I do not," Joan said. She breathed deep. The lobby smelled expensive, like maybe they piped the air in from somewhere else to avoid the smell of the city.

Magic was the easy answer to finding the room here, but a quick glance at Grace's ragged form made Joan's heart pang. They relied on her too much.

"Plan A, I try to finesse my way into a key card. Plan B, a distant and last-case resort, Grace does something with magic."

"Like?" Grace asked.

"Tracking spell to figure out the floor? Sorry, I know you're not in good shape right now."

"I can manage, that's not what I'm concerned about. So I figure out the floor, fine, but I'm sure the elevators require a key card at a place like this."

"Magic the elevators," CZ said, wiggling his fingers.

"You are being a menace," Grace said.

Joan shook herself a little, altering her posture, trying to look like she belonged here, despite being dressed in flower-printed shorts and a black T-shirt. "Wait here," she ordered, and waltzed up to the front desk, shoulders back.

Mik was so close, or at least whoever had Joan's card was. Joan had to reach them.

The attendant did not look convinced by Joan's attire. "Can I help you?"

Be normal. You've been in places like this a thousand times. "Yes, I lost my key card and need a new one."

"Room number?"

Joan donned an air of apology. "I don't remember, I'm so sorry. But the room's charged to Joan Greenwood—here's my ID." Joan slipped it over the counter, hoping against hope it would work. Joan was pretty sure the room actually wasn't charged to her name, but maybe her card was in the system somehow based on the room service charges.

It was a long shot, a Hail Mary, and she'd already started trying to figure out what magic Grace could do.

The attendant straightened, examining the ID. "Of course," they said. "We were expecting you. Let me call up to the room."

Expecting her? Had Mik left some sort of note at the front desk? Hopefully Mik was behind that phone and not a dead body rotting in a fancy bathtub as someone ran up charges on Joan's account. Was Mik maybe a genius?

Was *Joan* going to kiss them full on the lips?

"We have a Joan Greenwood in the lobby for you," the attendant said into the phone. "Yes, we'll send her right up. Yes, I'll ask." They moved the phone from their mouth. "She asks if your friends are with you?"

"They/them pronouns," Joan corrected, looking over her shoulder to beckon Grace and CZ over excitedly. Only Mik would expect friends, not a random murderer who wanted to kill them. She was hopping a little in place. They'd done it. They'd done it! "Tell them Grace and CZ are here."

CZ made big, questioning, puppy-dog eyes at Joan, and Joan kind of shrugged and put her hands out, like a caricature of *I don't know what's going on either, but I think maybe it's really good news.*

The attendant spoke into the phone. "Right away, they are on their way up."

They hung up and stepped away from the desk. "If you'll follow me, I'll send you up in the elevator. Your friend is on the eleventh floor."

Grace, CZ, and Joan followed after them, Joan and CZ jabbing each other in the ribs with their elbows to get ahead while Grace whispered at them to knock it off, all the way to the elevator, where the attendant swiped the card and stepped in with them.

It was an agonizingly quiet elevator ride, a sharp contrast to the giddiness overriding Joan's system. Finally, some good news. The city was fucked, Joan's personal life was fucked, but Mik was here. Alive! Joan was going to kiss them *then* CZ *then* Grace *then* maybe the front desk attendant, as thanks.

Mik being alive made it all worth it. She hadn't fully understood how much she'd had riding on finding them. If she lost her family, then Mik, who had started all this—well, Joan wasn't going to go there. She didn't have to, not anymore.

The final chime of arrival was a sigh of relief. The group piled out. Joan let out a delirious giggle before CZ poked her in the shoulder blade. The attendant walked down the hall, stopped in front of a door, and knocked politely before stepping out of the way.

Joan prepared herself to leap into Mik's waiting arms as the door clicked open. They'd watch *Real Housewives* for days and spend so much money buying furniture for Grace's apartment. They'd be back together, a team, and they'd follow Grace's Fiona Ganon hunch and save everything and figure this out.

For a shining moment in Joan's mind, everything was exactly as it should be.

Then Astoria Wardwell opened the door, a pleased smile on her face.

TWENTY-TWO

~~~~~~

Joan blurted the words out before she could think, her vision of the future shattering.

"Oh, come on. Again?!"

CZ had yelped and ducked behind Joan. Grace had stepped rapidly to the side like she could hide from Astoria's line of sight.

Astoria's smirk grew, and Joan hated the way it pulled at the scar across her lower lip, how cute it all was. "Good to see you too, darling."

Darling.

Every alarm bell in Joan's brain clanged so hard, they started to crack. Was this payback for calling her *sweetheart*?

Astoria was still speaking. "Last I saw you, you were in a coma. Did you like my flowers?"

Joan had, tragically, had to leave them behind at the Greenwood Mansion, and damn Astoria, because Joan *did* like the flowers. "I hear you pulled us out of the market. I didn't know you were a fire elemental."

"And air," Astoria added. "I'm something of a double major. Is there a thank-you in there?"

Joan's mouth was running roughly three miles ahead of her brain, because her brain was still going, *Hello??? Mik???* and her mouth apparently was more than happy to verbally spar with Astoria. "There is not, seeing as your invasion was the reason I nearly got myself and Grace killed in the first place."

Astoria shoved the door wider, standing aside. "And Mik, don't forget about them."

Joan reached out, almost scrunching a fist in Astoria's shirt in her desperation, but she stopped short, kind of brushing Astoria's shoulder, like some sort of pathetic fool. "What did you do to them? Astoria, I swear to Circe—"

"Mik!" Astoria said loudly. "Your friends are here for your playdate!"

There was a crashing sound from inside the suite, and then a figure appeared at the end of the mirrored internal hallway.

Mik's hair was starting to grow in a little fuzzy, or maybe that was Joan's imagination, adding differences to mark their time apart. "You came back for me," they whispered. Their face transformed into a smile. "Guys! You found me!"

"Oh my fucking god," CZ said, which gave Grace a head start to duck around Astoria and sprint toward Mik, smashing into them in a hug. CZ wasn't far behind, sweeping them both up.

"I've never been happier to see another person," CZ said. "And Astoria called us your friends!"

Mik's reply was muffled by all the bodies. "My very best friends."

Joan felt like she couldn't turn her back to Astoria. Her body was torn in two, trapped between needing to keep her eyes on the Wardwell heir and throwing herself into Mik's arms, sobbing and blubbering.

She struck a middle ground by cautiously edging past, feeling the heat of Astoria's body. She looked up and found Astoria looking down at her from her precious few extra inches of height.

"They're fine," Astoria said softly. "This isn't a trap. Trust me, Wren would have my ass. She'll be back in a second." Astoria shut the door behind Joan and nudged her forward with a hot hand pressed briefly to Joan's back.

Joan resisted the urge to lean into it.

"Joan, hug me!" Mik said, shimmying out of the grips of CZ and Grace. This was enough to break Astoria's spell. Joan rushed to Mik, who wrapped their arms around Joan and squeezed.

"You saw my trail of credit card purchases?" they whispered in Joan's ear.

"You sure do know how to spend," Joan whispered back.

Mik stepped back, holding Joan by the shoulders. "When Astoria took me in, I was kind of sure it wasn't a trick, mainly because Wren seemed so genuine, but just in case it was, I thought maybe if I ordered some stuff, you guys would be able to find me? Astoria promised she'd tell you where I was."

Joan turned to glare at Astoria. "She did not do that."

"I was waiting for the hospital discharge," Astoria said, ushering them out of the hallway and into the living room. "It was the first thing on my agenda this morning, and then I heard you'd fled your family's house. Mik doesn't have your number, and neither do I, so texting was out of the question."

"If you want my number, ask for it, Wardwell," Joan said thoughtlessly. "And don't pretend some sort of message spell wasn't an option."

Joan expected Astoria to ignore her, but the woman held out her phone promptly. "Please give me your number, Greenwood."

When Joan hesitated, Astoria reached out, took Joan's hand, and put her phone in it. Why did Astoria's hands have to be so warm and nice?

A bark of laughter burst out of CZ's mouth, but he slapped his hands over it, and his hand was joined by Mik's in rapid succession, all before Grace elbowed him hard in the ribs.

Do it, Grace mouthed, miming typing into the phone.

Joan snatched the phone away, taking a step back for good measure before plugging in her number and practically throwing the device at Astoria's face.

"Good," Astoria said, catching it smoothly. "Now, the next time I discover a fugitive you've been hiding, I can text you directly."

"Mik, you're being very chill, so I'm giving her the benefit of the doubt," Joan said, shifting in place as Mik's hand slowly fell off CZ's face. "But I'd love an explanation as to what you're doing with the heir to California."

Mik sat on the arm of the couch and explained their desperate run from the tent, looking for anyone who could help Joan and Grace, slamming right into Astoria, directing her toward the tent, and fleeing.

"But not to my apartment," Grace prompted.

"I did go there at first," Mik said, pointing a finger of recognition at Grace. "But then I realized, if someone suspected you two, they might search it for answers. I thought maybe it wasn't safe there, so I got a motel. I was going to hole up until someone found me, but then four days ago, Astoria knocked on the door."

Astoria picked up the story. "I knew the Greenwoods were hiding something in Brooklyn. Then the market went to shit, and I found Joan at the center." Her gaze was piercing. It made Joan's skin prickle.

"Once I got the chaos under control, I went looking exactly where Mik thought someone might—Grace Collins's home. Though I couldn't get past the wards, I cast to see who had come and gone recently and followed a strange life signature to the motel, and Mik. We established I wasn't going to kill them, or Wren did, and that we wanted to help, then brought them here to keep them safe."

"See, that's what doesn't make sense to me," Joan said, joining in. "Why would Mik be safe with you? Why would you take them in? Is California sending a strike force to kidnap them right now? You can't be operating out of the goodness of your heart."

"Why?" Astoria challenged, an edge to her voice that Joan couldn't quite identify. "You think you know me so well. Why couldn't I be?"

Joan's voice was cold. "You invaded the market. I know why California was sent here."

"And so I can't ever change my mind?" Astoria said. "I have to be exactly what you assume I am? The market was complicated. I saved you, didn't I?"

That . . . was true.

How much of Joan's perception of Astoria was based on fact, and how much of it was based on who Joan thought she should be, considering her mother? She was easier to hold at arm's length when Joan could simply say they were on opposing sides. But Astoria was swimming in murky waters.

"If it helps," Mik said, looking between them, "Astoria and Wren have been nothing but kind to me."

"Listen to your friend, Greenwood," Astoria said, the edges of her mouth turned down, and the snarky tone she put on lost her whatever sympathy she had been gaining with Joan. What, was she hurt? Offended that Joan had used basic knowledge to draw a very clear conclusion about Astoria Wardwell?

Joan wasn't going to abide any more patronizing. She'd had enough of that from her family, thank you very much. A thousand comebacks filtered through her head, each more biting than the last. Joan had thrown a giant *fuck you* at her family for this, and Astoria got to change her mind willy-nilly, no questions asked?

It wasn't fair.

"Wren wants to give casting magic to Moon Creatures," Joan said, and her voice had gained its own level of heat. She failed to tone it down. "Did you know that? Did you know that's the real reason she's in New York? That she came to me privately at my family's party and asked for my help with that?"

"Of course she does," Wren said, closing the door at the end of the hallway with a bag of groceries in her hand. "Astoria knows everything about me."

Joan's heart sank inexplicably.

"If you want to know why I took Mik in," Astoria said, her voice a little uneven, pointing down the hallway at Wren, who was slipping off her shoes. "That's why. Maybe I don't have goodness in my heart, but I do have Wren. We aren't in agreement about the right thing to do with the spell that was cast on Mik, but I would never, ever, willingly hurt a human or witch, and Mik qualifies as both."

"No," CZ said bracingly. "You would just hurt my people. Vampires, the fae, ancients even."

Astoria's jaw ticked. "I'm not perfect, but I'm not naive enough to think the world is rendered only in shades of black and white. I'm in a gray area."

"And yet you still invaded the market," CZ said. "You could

have chosen to stand aside like Wren. Better, you could have chosen to stop it."

"It's not that simple," Astoria argued. "Valeria was going to have some brainless mercenaries run it if I didn't. At least I could run a clean, nonlethal operation. And you don't know my mother, the repercussions if I refused—"

"You are the heir to the second most powerful state in the US," Grace cut in. "The world is as simple as you make it."

Joan expected Astoria to yell, or get angry, summon that sword of hers or storm away—anything to avoid almost every person in the room calling her out. Joan, in her shoes, would have been on the defensive. Joan, in her shoes, would have told her aunt no, emphatically. She had done exactly that. But Joan would have hesitated too, because she knew what it was like to have an overbearing parent. A family name that tied you up in knots.

Astoria took in a controlled breath. "I'm here now, and I've been convinced not to turn Mik in to anyone."

"We'll help seal them," Wren said. "Then we can all work together to catch the original spellmaker. Mik mentioned Fiona Ganon, and we're looking into it. What we don't have is motive. Why do all this? Money? But then why not take credit for it publicly?"

"That's all well and good," CZ said, and Joan was endlessly grateful she wasn't the only one who was feeling untrusting here. "But it doesn't actually explain what you intend to do with the spell once you have it."

"I would still prefer to give it to Moon Creatures," Wren said. "After doing our best to complete it so it does not have the side effects it does on Mik. The magic poisoning needs to be resolved; even if you give a human or full Moon Creature the ability to channel, they have no natural ability to process magic in a way that doesn't make them sick."

Grace snorted. "You and every other witch on earth would love to cure magic poisoning. Doesn't mean it's possible. I'm years deep in that research, and so is Fiona. It makes sense that's where her spell fell apart. And you, Astoria?"

"I have agreed to help on the condition that all of you, including Wren," Astoria said, frowning at her best friend, "strongly and thoroughly consider the option of destroying all knowledge of the spell so no one can get their hands on it."

"Not even your mother?" Joan asked.

"What she doesn't know won't hurt her," Astoria replied. "That is the best I can offer." She was looking only at Joan. Her gaze was steady, hard. But her mouth told the rest of the story, still canted down.

Please, believe me, those lips said.

"And it's a deal I already accepted," Wren said, a warning note in her voice. "So, now that we have the requisite number of witches, let's seal Mik."

Mik popped to their feet. "I'm more than ready."

"One of you is still recovering from the brink of death," CZ pointed out.

"I'm fine," Grace said.

CZ looked unconvinced.

Wren's eyebrows were a clear question, gesturing at herself, then Astoria, then Grace, then Joan. She held up four fingers. "Isn't this more than enough?"

"Joan doesn't cast," CZ said, his voice overlapping with Joan's grumbled "I can't cast," which matched Grace's "Joan is strictly not allowed to cast."

"I can channel though," Joan offered. "Quite prodigiously, I'm told."

Grace flicked her arm. "Don't use *prodigiously*."

"Joan, you are also dealing with the effects of magic poisoning," CZ said.

"Having seen what Joan's channeling can do, I am not sure we need *quite* that much magic for this spell. Do you have some level of control over how much you pull in? How honed is this ability?" Astoria asked.

Underhoned, underdeveloped, and in fact brand-spanking-new. Joan scowled. "Can't I channel however much I channel and you all take in only what you need?"

"I don't think we want to experiment with that on Mik's sealing," Grace said, acutely betraying Joan.

"Wren and I can shoulder the magic channeling to minimize your reaction, Grace. We split casting and channeling all the time," Astoria said. "Just shape the spell."

Grace's eyebrows rose; she turned to look at Joan meaningfully.

"Yes, I got the idea from them," Joan muttered, flopping onto the couch.

Grace, in all her mercy, didn't say anything else.

Joan had never witnessed a sealing spell before, mostly because they were rather rare. Witches had to commit truly egregious crimes to be sentenced to such a fate, and Joan wasn't usually around to watch the judgment get carried out.

But it was, surprisingly, easier than she'd expected, which kind of frustrated her because Mik had been suffering all this time. If only Joan could cast or had realized sooner that she could channel magic for someone else to cast with and had a couple of weeks to practice. If only Joan had trusted Wren earlier, if only she'd had a better grip on things. If only all the world were in her control and did exactly as she said, when she said it.

Within two minutes of continuous casting, a seal formed in the air and settled on Mik's chest, over their heart, before sinking into their skin. Joan knew the theory—the spell would feed on the magic the witch would normally have attracted to themself, only now it was funneled into the seal. Every time Mik got upset, the spell would refresh itself.

Just like that, Mik was cured. Joan wanted to get past being put in time-out, but she had to admit it'd soured her mood.

Mik's smile was radiant the moment it was done. "Someone upset me," they said.

"Let me get a kitchen towel," CZ said, pretending to get up.

"You're such an asshole."

"It's one of my most endearing traits," CZ replied.

"Ignore them," Grace said to the Californians. "They've never been around company. Now—Fiona. Mik told you what I said about her? Joan's convinced we should get to her first, before we try to game out how we come clean to witch society and get the Greenwoods to leave Moon Creatures alone. Public outrage will be our best bet."

Wren subtly straightened, amusement melting off her face. "Astoria staked out her apartment, but she hasn't gone there in what seems like weeks."

Fiona. That, Joan had never seen coming. The *why* escaped her. Why would Fiona do this to Mik? How could the same person who'd taught Grace be behind this? Joan had been face-to-face with her and never suspected a thing.

"How wealthy is she? Could she have other property in the city?" Astoria asked, as the conversation continued around Joan.

"Not wealthy at all," Grace said. "So far from it. Fiona's well-known in the witch world, but I saw how she lived in Atlanta. All her money went toward giving the air of wealth, without actually possessing it. She's been aiming for the endorsement of the Greenwoods for years, trying to get them to secure her a job."

Joan remembered what her mother had said to Valeria the moment Fiona had left the room: *She wants a place in your employ.*

"So she's desperate for societal power and financial wealth," CZ mused. "Maybe that's motive—she develops this magic, sells it to the highest bidder, or uses it to establish a name for herself."

That was what Joan had always assumed, but Wren had been right earlier. "Like Wren said, why wait, then? The spell, even half finished, has sent everyone into a frenzy. She could have publicly claimed it and already made tons of money selling it. If it was just money, the moment Mik escaped and resurfaced elsewhere, Fiona would have been claiming to be the one behind it."

The room sat with that thought for a harrowing minute. *This must be hell for Grace.*

Grace stood in the corner of the room, fingers twisted together in what Joan was rapidly learning was a telltale sign of her agitation. She met Joan's gaze and looked away.

"Then she's probably hesitating because she needs the spell for something else and can't use it if it's defective, right?" Mik said slowly. "Her priority has to be fixing it, doesn't it?"

Astoria was flipping a little knife, faster and faster. She'd found Mik when the rest of them had lost them, saved Joan and Grace from the spell that should have killed them. For all her questionable morals, she was powerful. She could protect everyone in this room better than Joan could ever hope to.

Astoria spoke up. "Then does Fiona need Mik to perfect the spell, or are they a discarded failure?"

"Let's be careful of language here," Mik said. "I'm perfect."

"You're priceless in my heart," CZ said.

"Suck-up."

"We can use them as bait," Astoria said. "Set a trap, and have Fiona walk into it."

"And if she doesn't? I'm not a fan of putting Mik in danger," Grace countered. "Unlike some, I've never liked witches moving humans around like pawns for their own personal gain." Grace's parents were humans. It was an obvious fact of Joan's life and upbringing that witches used spells to manipulate humans for their own gain, but Joan herself had never had that power and so never much agreed with it either. Humans working in witch-owned factories, persuasion spells used on human politicians— there were no laws against that sort of thing in the witch world, beyond anything that might reveal magic to humans on a wide scale and prompt them to fight back.

"Okay, so we don't want to use Mik. Grace," Wren said, "do you know how to fix the spell? On Mik, you've gotten up close and personal. Can you perfect it?"

The room turned on her, but Wren threw up her hands as everyone spoke up at once. "Wait! I'm saying, if Fiona doesn't want *Mik*, we can bait her with *knowledge*. Grace knows her and has been in communication. But Fiona doesn't know Grace has her figured out. Grace might be able to set a meeting, either on her own or with the promise of a solution, even if it's fake."

Grace gave a hesitant nod. "Like I said, the issue with Mik is essentially magic poisoning, and I've been working on that for forever. I can fake something. But I ask only one thing—please, let's make absolutely sure she's the one behind it before we condemn her to some awful fate. We'll question her first, not just hand her over to the Greenwoods or whoever."

She took the room's agreements one by one, some more easily than others. Joan's voice was a quiet rasp, but she answered when called on. Thinking through Fiona's shadowy motivations had only unsettled her further. Her mood had continued to crash into the pits of hell after being unable to help seal Mik. She could recognize her inability to emotionally regulate in the wake of minor rejection as a standard symptom of her anxiety and depression, but in the middle of it, she could only sit there dully, running over every failure of the last week.

The group huddled together to hatch their plan for Grace's lure. Joan looked around: three witches, a witch-fae, a vampire, a human.

When Joan darted a glance at Astoria, she found the woman already looking at her, blatantly, without enough self-respect to at least drop her gaze when Joan met it.

She held it defiantly, and if Joan were feeling more generous, maybe she'd mark that look on the Wardwell heir's face as concern.

But she wasn't. She was feeling pitied. Joan hated that pity. She glared right back, something sizzling between them, before Wren caught Astoria's attention and pulled it away.

Twenty-Three

O ut on the street, CZ matched her pace.

"You good? You were kind of quiet in there." He didn't look down at her when he said this, like she was a frightened doe on the brink of running away. "Or maybe that's what Astoria Wardwell does to you?"

Joan might as well have been back in middle school, passing notes back and forth. She didn't want to follow that train of thought, not at all, because she couldn't deny the evidence of her eyes and ears—Astoria was very much in love with Wren. Joan had fallen for plenty of straight people she'd never had a chance with and her fair share of gay people interested in others. She wasn't going to make that mistake again here, and especially not over someone who was slated to head back to the West Coast in, hopefully, a matter of days.

The best defense was a strong offense though. "Tell me about whatever thing you've got going for Grace first."

Now CZ did look at her. "Not fair."

"I ship it," Joan said, spooling her energy. She boxed up her emotions and sank them to the bottom of a lake. The air outside helped cut through her turbulent mood. "You're a good, steady guy who could use someone to kick you in the ass sometimes; she's a brilliant, dedicated woman who needs someone to lean on. You'd have little witch-vampire babies who rage against the establishment, and they'd like me more than they'd like you."

"Do I need to be here, or do you want to monologue?"

"Every good orator needs an audience."

They'd left Mik with Wren and Astoria, partially on Joan's insistence, much to the confusion of the room. Mik had been safe there for several days, safer than they'd ever been with Joan and CZ, or even Grace. Joan could see that clearly, even if the rest of the room couldn't. Grace had asked to meet Fiona for an early lunch and stayed behind. Astoria and Wren would settle in nearby, and Grace would try to convince Fiona to go back to the hotel room willingly. Or if not willingly, the Californians would step in.

It was decided that Joan and CZ were better off not being seen by Fiona, what with their family connections and so they didn't reveal their full hand. They'd been ushered off, and it was just Joan and CZ now walking aimlessly.

"You're crying," CZ observed casually. "Does the thought of me being with Grace really bring you to tears?"

"They're happy tears," Joan said, wiping furiously at her eyes.

"Joan."

"I want to be useful," Joan said, maybe with more force than was strictly necessary.

CZ made a frustrated noise, grabbed her shoulder, and spun her around on the sidewalk, forcing her to look at him. "You *are* useful. When there are people better suited to a task, you let them work. When you know you can offer something, you stand and fight. You stood and fought when your parents told you to lie about Moon Creatures."

"*Very* low bar," Joan said wetly.

"And when I called you about Mik, you jumped into action. But you are not a trained fighter, you cannot bodily capture Fiona," CZ said. "So when it came time for people who do have that expertise to step up, you stood aside. That's not weakness, Joan. Don't try to be a hero. You need time with your fancy new power. I don't want to see you run headlong into something and get seriously hurt because your daddy issues made you so desperate to be useful."

"Hey!"

"I'm just saying, your family trauma is rooted deep, and you did a huge thing by walking out. Don't let your sense of helplessness in one area of your life drive you too far into a dangerous situation."

"You're therapizing me."

"I'm helping you because your mental illness matches mine," CZ countered. "Us second children, we develop complexes. And you always tell me I'm important, even if I'm not running my pack. I'm here to tell you the same. With or without the new powers, you are important."

Joan gently knocked her head against his shoulder, because if she said *thanks, you're right* out loud, then she'd have to face the fact that she'd thrown a minor temper tantrum at the age of twenty-five and her best friend had been forced to talk her down like she was a child. "Are you going to be mad if I ask to talk to Abel about my powers anyways?"

"No, I think that's a very good idea," CZ said. "I'd feel better if you were well armed with knowledge as you explored being a magic bomb. Let me ask him if we can meet him somewhere."

Unfortunately, Joan was no longer welcome at the LaMorte apartment building in Queens as a result of her family's actions. Which was completely and entirely fair, she knew that, but still felt like a loss.

Instead, Abel agreed to meet them in Brooklyn at Grace's apartment in an hour, and as Joan felt she needed to do something to avoid kicking a hole through a wall, she made CZ go to IKEA first.

With a couple of meatballs in her and CZ lugging along the table Joan had bought, Grace's thrifting dreams be damned—she could source her own chairs—they met Abel at the foot of the building.

He looked tired.

"Are you sure you're okay to talk?" Joan asked anxiously. "I didn't mean to pull you away from something important."

"I desperately need a break, and CZ's story about your new magic is, selfishly, hugely fascinating to me," Abel said, holding open the door so CZ could angle himself in with the table box. He grinned at Joan, eyes feverish. "It's true, then? The city spoke to you?"

"I feel better about being an object of curiosity and not an active burden," Joan said, approaching the lobby elevator and hitting the button. "And yes, it's true."

She wasn't entirely sure what you said to someone whose pack had been partially attacked by your family. "Abel, I'm sorry. Please let me know if there's anything I can do to help the displaced vampires or rebuild the market."

"You're always welcome to put your money where your mouth is," Abel said, sobering up. "And CZ says you left your family, so if you're feeling extra generous, we could use your insider mind on occasion. We're in talks with the fae to reestablish the market."

CZ punched his arm.

"What! She doesn't like them," Abel grumbled.

"I'll think about it," Joan said, feeling queasy at the thought. It felt like an irreversible decision if she went that far, but everything she'd already done was supposed to be irreversible. She was gone. For good. "Except the money thing, happy to do that anytime."

They entered Grace's peaceful apartment and set up shop in the kitchen. Joan plopped right down on the floor and started dumping pieces out of the box, her phone placed close by in case the group messaged about Fiona. The screen lit up with a text, but Joan looked away.

"Okay, so CZ told you about New York talking to me," Joan said, as CZ joined her in trying to read the instructions. "How freaked out should I be?"

Abel was practically vibrating with excitement as he settled against the counter. "*Freaked out* isn't the word. *Thrilled* feels better. It's the sort of thing that you hear about in our local folklore: A witch on a quest who bargained with a god, and the god is depicted as the city. A vampire on the brink of death, hallucinating from blood withdrawal, who thinks she hears a voice coming from the Hudson. What was always curious to me is that, as much as we can pinpoint the origins of this, these stories start in the late 1600s, which is after the city's founding. Normally fairy tales draw on some sort of naturalistic origin."

"The woods are big and dark, and so they're magic," CZ supplied. "The ocean seems alive, so it's secretly a god."

"Very happy to hear you listen to me on occasion," Abel said. "Also, Joan, I don't think those pieces go together."

Joan abandoned the two sections of wood she was trying to

jam together and grabbed a third one, trying to be mindful of her wrecked fingers. "But cities are man-made."

Abel nodded. "My theory? It's a little less about place and a little more about population density. Magic existed naturally and individually, but as more magical creatures, and particularly witches, settled in one place and started manipulating magic, it gathered and grouped together. Spells are like mini commands for magic, but what if it started to cobble together a will from all those little commands? The ability to think? And I highly doubt *those* pieces fit together either. Aren't you an architect?"

Joan nearly threw an Allen wrench out the window in her frustration at this stupid table. "I don't specialize in furniture design," she said back, "and I'm doing better than *him*."

She gestured at CZ, who was still attempting to piece together the instructions.

"Slow and steady wins the race."

The pieces in Joan's hands finally slotted together neatly. "That's something losers say," she said. She turned back to Abel. "So witches start using spells all in one place, magic wises up to us and starts to gain a sort of localized sentience? But is it one thing? It felt like...like a million different things that occasionally coalesce into one mouth." It felt really good to verbalize all this, and her shaky hands steadied on the furniture pieces.

"Sure," Abel said. "I mean, you're the only one I know who's actually gotten it to talk to you. I don't have answers here, just a lot of theories based on what you've told me and what I've read. Like I said, it was all fairy tale. But why you? Why not speak to any other random witch?"

"Who says it hasn't? I mean, who'd believe them?" CZ asked. "All we have is Joan's word."

Joan's responding glare was long-suffering. Her phone screen lit up once more, and her attention lasered in, but it was Molly again. There were a number of texts waiting for her from Molly. None of which she felt ready to open yet.

"Once again, I'm telling the truth," she ground out.

"I know that," CZ replied. "Abel knows that. But if a random witch on the street told you New York was occasionally talking to them, you'd do absolutely nothing with that information and probably see if you could call them some help. This is the sort of thing you tell a friend, and they whisper it to another friend, half joking, and thus superstitions and fairy tales are born over time."

"You have to stop before I burst with pride," Abel said, eyes alight. "You should audit one of my classes."

Joan handed CZ the table leg. "Help me attach this. Okay, so what do I *do*? I assume it's talking to me because of the magic cycling I'm doing, but is it dangerous? Am I about to be lured into a bargain with an eldritch god that damns my soul?"

"Is it asking you for anything?" Abel asked.

"No, if anything, it helped me."

"Next time you talk to it, maybe ask it why," Abel said. "Then report back to me so I can publish a paper."

"It's that simple?"

Abel shrugged. "Myth is a squishy thing. It seems to me like you're not doing anything to magic, you're just channeling it in such high quantity, and so rapidly, that you're establishing a mental connection. You're not hurting it, and it's not hurting you. Can you do it right now?"

"I can try," Joan said. "But I have to concentrate."

Joan had closed her eyes and settled her breath—and told CZ

to stop crinkling the instructions so loudly—ready to put on the performance of a lifetime, when Mik called.

CZ dove for her buzzing phone at the same time she did, but Joan came out on top.

"What happened!" she screamed into the phone at Mik. "Can we come back?"

"That is so loud, oh my god, Joan," Mik grouched over the line. "Don't yell at me. Everyone's being so crabby here. Fiona didn't show."

CZ grabbed the Allen wrench to throw out the open window, and Joan grabbed his fist to stop him. "What do you mean, she didn't show?" Joan asked, the dreams of the last two hours dying slow deaths. They were so close. "She told Grace she'd be there."

"Then she ghosted," Mik said. "You guys can head back, they're restrategizing. It's very intimidating, actually. Wren is like an evil mastermind, and Astoria can back up every one of her diabolical plans."

"I am not evil!" Wren yelled very faintly in the background.

"We're coming, we're coming," Joan said, gesturing furiously at CZ. "Be there in an hour, max."

Abel was already straightening. "I should head back to Queens anyways," he said. "Mom's already grumbling about CZ's attention being split. Keep me updated on Fiona, and I'll keep an eye out for her too. And the magical New York thing, Joan. I'm really serious about the paper. You could make my career. No pressure."

He left, and Joan and CZ surveyed the mess they'd made of Grace's floor.

"Figure it out later?" Joan offered, nudging a screw with her leg and watching it roll gently across the floor.

"Figure it out later," CZ confirmed, and they scrambled for the door.

They were almost out of Brooklyn when CZ's mom started calling him.

"She's going to ground me," he grumbled, letting the call ring and then checking his texts. It was incredible the calls were even going through on subway reception. "She wants me home. She probably heard Abel left Queens to see me and it reminded her that I should come home more often."

At least your mom cares enough to call. Joan bit her tongue to keep her first words in. They weren't children anymore. Even if Joan knew exactly what CZ meant by *she's going to ground me.* "Go home," Joan said. "Come back to the hotel when you can. We won't make any decisions without you."

The phone lit up again, and the train pulled into York Street. Joan nudged him with an elbow. "Go, your family needs you."

CZ's foot tapped. He let out a little groan, leaned over, and kissed the top of Joan's head. "I'll make it fast." He rose and slipped out the door at the last second, picking up his phone with a "hi, Mama, I'm on my way."

That had always been the difference between them, despite both having demanding families—CZ's actually wanted him around.

Joan rode the train in silence to the 7th Avenue Station and got off, orienting herself toward the hotel with ease. She felt CZ's absence like a cold void. His warmth had been keeping back the dark press of her thoughts all afternoon. Being back in Manhattan made her uneasy, like at any moment her aunt might pop out of a bush and have her dragged away. That was ridiculous. Right? She wasn't being hunted, not at all. They'd just . . . let her go.

How could that be such a relief and such a disappointment at the same time?

When they got their answers out of Fiona, either destroyed or finished the spell, and put this whole thing to rest, perhaps then her family would publicly disown her for her role in it all. Only once Joan had done something worth noticing.

The streets were busy, and Joan felt beautifully surrounded by people. It was what she loved about this city—it always felt like it was holding you. It was wonderful and shocking and maybe only a touch creepy to know it really was holding her. That it really was alive.

Joan reached for magic, pushing past the lingering fatigue that plagued her and trying to focus in, a trickle of magic snaking into her as she walked the block and a half to the hotel.

Talk to me, she thought at magic, at New York. *Why me?*

When there was silence, she pulled in more magic, squeezing her palms into fists, digging her nails into her palms. The entrance to the hotel was within sight. *More, more.*

Something began the slow swing of its head, directing its attention at her.

A clatter behind her broke her concentration. Someone had dropped their phone and was picking it off the ground, cursing to themself. Joan's nerves jumped and snapped, frustrated as she lost her concentration. She had been so close.

Joan swung around.

And walked straight into someone.

She opened her mouth, got halfway through her sentence. "I'm so sorry—" she exclaimed as the person bounced back, orange-brown hair spilling from beneath a ball cap.

It took her half a second to place the hair, even as large sunglasses obscured the face.

Joan stared Fiona Ganon down on the sidewalk, feet from the hotel entrance.

Fiona's expression was grim. "Nothing personal," she said, "I just couldn't waste an opportunity," and moving faster than Joan could react, she flicked her hands, fingertips trailing magic, and slapped a palm across Joan's mouth.

No, Joan had time to think as magic slithered down her throat and wrapped around her lungs. The effect was nearly instantaneous: The world tilted sideways. She slumped into Fiona's arms, limbs paralyzed, as Fiona cradled the back of her head, like they were old friends engaging in a loving embrace.

CZ, Joan thought distantly.

Her eyes rolled back in her head.

TWENTY-FOUR

Her wrists were killing her.

Joan registered that first as the slow fog of sleep slithered off her. Her wrists hurt, badly. They were stretched too far behind her back, fingers awkwardly locked together. The previously broken fingers on her right hand had tipped so far into pain that they were nearly numb.

She was bound to a chair, and when she opened her eyes, her vision blurred. There were wards chalked on the floor in a circle around the chair. It took her a second to read them upside down.

Magic nullification.

Joan could read her own name in the runes—magic nullification for Joan Greenwood specifically.

"I hear you've left the Greenwoods," Fiona said. Her voice was bouncing in from a hundred different directions. Joan squeezed her eyes shut. Shook her head, opened them again, and registered the other woman's shoes in front of her.

Joan's gaze climbed slowly to Fiona's face.

She had shed the ball cap and sunglasses and looked like a

perfectly normal middle-aged woman in a blouse and slacks. She looked perfectly nice.

"Oh, sorry, do you want some water?" Fiona asked, turning to step to the far side of the room, where a cot sat next to a bench covered in books and plastic water bottles. Joan's surroundings swam into focus. Construction lights lit up the space. There was ornate street art on the walls, and turnstiles stood not a dozen feet away.

An abandoned subway station, though the tracks weren't in sight.

Panic fought against the sticky lethargy of whatever spell Fiona had used on her, resulting in heaving breaths. Her neck felt empty. Abel's mind-ward necklace was gone.

"Here, here," Fiona said, tipping a water bottle into Joan's mouth, flirting with the edge of drowning her. Joan was forced to gulp some down to avoid choking, and even then half of it spilled onto her chest.

"I haven't quite figured out the grogginess side effect," Fiona said, a little shaky as she screwed the cap back on. "I made it for your aunt, that spell. An easy way to subdue someone. First, a paralytic, then a knockout, then they enter a dreamlike state so you can lead them anywhere you want to go and they retain no memory of it." Fiona noisily pulled up a folding chair and sat in it. "A piece of art. I thought it would finally get your aunt to show me at least a hint of gratitude."

A drop of water dripped off Joan's mouth and landed on the ground. "My hands," she gasped. "I can't think around it, please, free them."

Fiona looked so pitying. Joan didn't know how she could look so genuinely regretful after abducting her off the street. "I'm sorry, I'm so really very sorry, but I can't risk you getting free. You're never alone, you know that? I've been so hard-pressed to get you alone."

"I won't get free," Joan babbled. She couldn't think, she couldn't *think*. "Please, loosen my fingers."

She reached out, but magic was so thin around her, the wards flaring on the floor.

"Please stop doing that, Joan," Fiona said frantically. "I'll set you free soon, okay? I just need to finish up. You understand that, right? When this is done, you'll understand it."

She wasn't particularly calm or calculating; she looked genuinely nervous about this. Unsteady, oscillating between some weird mix of guilt and excitement.

"This is…revenge against my aunt?" Joan asked. She wasn't cool and suave like captured spies were in the movies. She was in pain; she would already do almost anything to make it stop. Both their pitches were skewing higher and higher.

"No, no, it's nothing as mundane as a personal vendetta against your family," Fiona said. She crossed her arms, tapped a finger against her bicep anxiously. "I'd have picked a more important Greenwood if it were about that."

Joan, even now, flinched.

Fiona's eyes gleamed in the dimness as she leaned in, a clear spark of interest transforming her demeanor. "It hurts? Being discarded? That's good, because I know how it feels, Joan. You can help me make it better. You can help me reshape the New York magic world."

Joan'd rather chop her hands off than keep feeling that pain. It rolled up her arms like cannon fire. Someone would realize she was missing, right? Not her family, but she'd been on the way to the hotel room. Mik—Mik! Fiona had been right outside. She knew where they were. "What do you want?" Joan croaked. "I won't give you Mik."

Fiona waved a hand. "If I wanted your friend, I'd have them," she said. "I'd have taken them when you were still in that poorly warded Hell's Kitchen apartment, the moment I saw them in your little memories. I'd have never let them go in the first place."

So it really had been Fiona in the market, but she . . . and yet—"You don't want Mik? You want . . ."

Fiona waited expectantly. Joan didn't know half as much about her as she seemed to know about Joan. They were strangers, total strangers; Joan could only remember their one meeting. Fiona didn't have a lot of money, she wore nice clothes, she had helped Grace, been like a second mother to her. None of that added up to a concrete personality. None of that helped Joan make sense of her situation, the musty air and the dampness. The chill of cold stone around them.

"Me?" Joan said finally.

"I want your magic," Fiona confirmed, steadying by the minute. "Or to study it. If I can watch the way you process magic, I can duplicate it. Grace told me about it, and then I saw what the two of you did at the Night Market. When I replicate it, you could be the great equalizer of this world. Any given witch could channel incredible amounts of magic. Any witch could be powerful, no matter their family or natural-born abilities."

She was a true believer, then. Some twisted version of Grace, whose passion never crossed lines. Grace, gods. How had Joan ever suspected her?

She scanned the room as best she could without making any obvious movements. Which way was out? *Keep her talking*, that would give the others time to find Joan. "Is that what you were after with Mik? Not making humans into witches, making witches stronger?"

"Both," Fiona admitted. She stood up, and Joan couldn't help but feel that was a bad sign. "I couldn't fully crack the human-to-witch transformation, humans are incompatible with magic by design. The early version of my spell killed them outright, except Mik, who probably has some witch ancestry, but then we had the issue of magic poisoning."

If I wanted your friend, I'd have them. Fiona's actions aligned with horrifying clarity. "You set Mik free," Joan said. "You wanted someone to find them and..." And what? If Fiona was working on something, why would she share it early with the world? Joan showed others her sketches only when she needed—help.

Fiona needed help.

"You wanted someone to find Mik and finish the spell for you. That's why you insisted Grace be called before my family. You wanted her to study it and finish what you started." How many people had she stolen from the market and killed before Mik survived?

"What the Greenwoods started," Fiona corrected. "Don't give me that look. You think no one's tried to figure it out before? Your aunt has employed so many spellmakers to pen a way to transform humans, but they never panned out. She abandoned it, I didn't. She wasn't willing to go far enough."

"Killing humans?"

"For a greater good. All great scientific leaps require sacrifice, Joan," Fiona said. They had been so wrong to assume money was the motivator. Fiona's mission was beyond wealth.

"Grace *is* a prodigy. No matter what scorn your aunt throws her way, that's true," Fiona murmured, putting her hands on her hips. "I knew Grace would catch on to me eventually, but I hoped, prayed, she'd finish the spell before she did. She's not motivated, you see. We've been tinkering with this research for years, but her heart isn't in it. I know she could cure the magic poisoning if she really tried. And then I could find humans with dormant witch genes and use the first part of my spell on them, allow them to channel.

"But Grace gave me you instead. The key to expanding the power of a witch. There's still time to figure the puzzle out, make a name off turning humans into witches, build a family reputation and a following off them, sure." Fiona continued. "But the priority is you. Amplifying my own abilities to become undeniable. Creating something witches want for themselves."

Fiona knelt in front of Joan, likely staining the knees of her nice pants. She was smiling a little, expectant. It disgusted Joan, so much so she felt her stomach heave.

"What do you need to gain more magic for?" Joan rasped, bile burning the back of her throat.

Fiona reached up, put a hand on Joan's cheek. Joan twisted her head in outrage. *Get off, get off.* Fiona's other hand rose, until she was holding Joan's head firmly still, fingers digging hard into her jaw.

"I'm not sure you'll live long enough to find out," Fiona said apologetically. "But do trust that we're aligned in sticking it to your family. Your legacy will be one of innovation and progress, rather than the staleness of tradition. And though, in the early years, this can't be tied to you and your death, I'll find a way to credit you eventually. I'll be a villain to many, but a hero to even more."

She couldn't be serious; she had her whole twisted logic and was prepared for people to condemn her for it, but she was rolling the dice anyways. Joan wouldn't be able to get through to her on any moral or ethical basis. The more room Joan gave her to explain, the more confident Fiona became.

"Grace will find me, or—"

"Astoria Wardwell, or Wren Dahl-Min, or CZ LaMorte, or maybe even Molly Greenwood. *Yes*, Joan, you have an army behind you, and they will come eventually," Fiona said. "But not fast enough."

She lit up with magic. The wards burned to ash.

Fiona plunged into Joan's mind, lodging in there like a rock splitting the flow of a river, and Joan was too slow, too stupid, too weak to stop her.

She tore open the gates to magic in Joan's head by triggering memory after memory of Joan channeling, so her body reacted on instinct to that input. Though Joan kicked and screamed mentally, magic still poured in.

Fiona wiped a tear from Joan's cheek, leaned in almost tenderly as Joan, paralyzed by the torrent of magic, felt it flow into her, filling her up, up, up until she thought she'd burst like a bloody, fleshy balloon. One second, two, Fiona flipped through memories like a deck of cards, before finding the one of Joan at the market and shifting from channeling into cycling right before Joan grew ill.

"I'm really sorry," Fiona whispered softly in her ear. "I'm only trying to right the scales. If not for me, then for the next spellmaker who comes along, someone like Grace, brilliant but born to the wrong family, who deserves a chance to succeed in this world your ancestors built."

Joan slurred Fiona's name; it was the best she could do. How could this happen to her, again? How could she need rescuing, *again*? Her gaze fixated on Fiona's desk. There was a snow globe on it, being used like a paperweight. New York City was capped with white inside. It was so tacky and beautiful. Joan could see nothing else.

She wished she'd black out.

But she was awake for every moment.

TWENTY-FIVE

Rest was brief and very far between.

Fiona made Joan cycle magic repeatedly, bringing her right up to the brink of blacking out before letting her go. Joan had long since hit her limits—magic was pain now, scraping against her skin. Her body was being poisoned, but Joan was in a delirious haze of reoccurring memories.

Fiona watched, at first, with a look of concentration, placing magicked glasses on her face to see the results.

Then she started to cast on Joan. Little spells. Joan was too out of it to parse their exact implications, but she felt them work or fail. Magic would shift around her, and in her, depending on the variable parameters Fiona placed on her.

One made magic funnel through Joan faster, but with less force. Another dimmed the pain of magic, at least temporarily. But then they broke, they all broke, and the pain was back, and magic still churned through her, and each draw was a fresh wound, her skin developing sores that trickled blood as magic poisoned her, slowly, slowly.

Joan didn't know if Fiona was making progress, but the empty bottles of cold brew were stacking up. Fiona was racing against something. Maybe Joan's impending death. Her fingers still hurt. She couldn't quite gather her thoughts well enough to care.

They'll come for me, she repeated to herself, over and over. *They'll save me.*

Twenty-Six

The sharp crack of shattering glass wrenched Joan from her fever dreams. Fiona had thrown something at the wall. A quick scan of her desk revealed the glass paperweight was gone.

"I don't understand it," Fiona said, head in her hands. "I don't understand why it doesn't work. It works for you!"

Joan made the mistake of shifting, looking for any kind of release from the stiffness of her limbs.

Fiona whirled, flashing with magic. "Oh, did I wake you? I'm sorry, you need to rest. Please, go back to sleep."

"No." Joan's tongue was thick in her mouth. "Not again, I don't want to...I don't want to...sleep..." Her words slurred. She went back under.

TWENTY-SEVEN

Joan's memories from before she was ten years old were fuzzy and indistinct, but she had one from her eighth birthday that was always crystal clear. She woke up with a stomach bug. She couldn't stop throwing up. She stepped out of her room, rubbing her eyes, to go tell her parents. They wouldn't be much comfort, but they'd at least make the house staff take care of her.

They'd been at the foot of the stairs, and it was early. They didn't hear her as she stood at the top. Something made her pause. Something made her listen.

They were arguing about her and her inability to cast. Selene wanted to give up; she was talking about a boarding school overseas, where Joan wouldn't be around anyone they knew.

But it was Merlin who insisted they not give up on their daughter.

"She's a Greenwood," he was saying. "She's mine, and no daughter of mine will be sent off in shame. Give her time, Selene."

Joan had thrown up a little pool of bile at the top of the stairs.

TWENTY-EIGHT

⟨~⟩

Give her time, Selene.

Fiona released the magic, and relief flooded Joan. *Give her time*, she mouthed to herself. It had always stuck with her. Merlin showing patience. Her memories were a muddy wasteland of lost concepts, things she hadn't realized she still remembered until Fiona took over and Joan's panicked brain tried to compensate.

She was eight and she was twelve. It was last year and a decade ago. Her first day of college, walking into the architecture building and knowing it was home.

Molly's sweet sixteen. They'd stolen a bottle of wine out of the wine cellar and gotten drunk together later that night, swigging straight from the bottle. *Sometimes I think this is all going to crush me*, Molly had said. Joan had such a headache the next day.

Fiona was casting. This was old news. Any second now Joan would channel the magic, and the pain would be so great, she couldn't even reach out to try and talk to the city. It looked past her. If it tried to call to her, Joan was sure she couldn't hear it.

She was dying. She knew that with a distant certainty, in the slowing thud of her heart, the piercing pain of her kidneys. She knew it in the wheeze of her lungs and the wetness in her chest. Death bent its head toward Joan, and some moments she begged it for release. *Kiss me and end it*, she thought. And some moments she was so hopelessly afraid, and she cried before her tear ducts ran out of water, and she begged, *Not yet, not yet, give her time, Selene.*

She had no idea how much time had passed; she only knew it was too long. *Too long*, and no one had come for her.

Fiona's latest spell settled on Joan like a coat, and she barely even jerked when Fiona waded into her mind, took control of her body, and forced her to channel again. She waited for the pain, and it erupted across her skin like starbursts, supernovas grinding her to ash.

Then it faded, smoothed over. The sores healed across her sticky, bloody skin. Her senses all returned, and clarity reached her for the first time in eternity. She was—free. She was—Joan. She could—see.

Fiona's eyes were shining in triumph. Joan was still channeling, but without pain. She was weightless, like gravity had reversed, and there was a blue sheen to her skin.

"Finally," Fiona breathed. "A loophole. And just in time, they're close."

A patch of runes, chalked to the wall, was glowing, slowly degrading into dust. A new patch lit up.

The clarity started to fade as the spell on her ebbed. All things were temporary in this world. Joan's thoughts began their slow slide back into the mud, and she scrambled for purchase.

"Let…me go," she whispered. Her mouth tasted like pennies. What a stupid thing to say. She skated further into the well of memories that stuck to her like grains of sand on a wet body.

She was untethered from the earth, something in her slipping from her body. She had no power here. Her demands went unanswered. Once upon a time, everything Joan had done had been to keep Mik from this very fate: being brutally experimented upon to reverse engineer their magic.

She wished she were dead already. She wished she were a ghost and magic would never touch her again.

"Maybe a few more hours before Astoria Wardwell hunts her way to me," Fiona said to herself, ignoring Joan. She turned to the desk and fished through the papers and books. "We'll leave her a present. She'll be a problem if I let her keep going. I can turn her into a message instead."

She pivoted back to Joan, a necklace of some sort in her hand. Her eyes were unusually kind as she draped it over Joan's head. "I wasn't sure you'd survive," she said. "It's strange, I'd have expected your ability to wane, but the more damage you take, the more magic you channel. What an odd dance between pain and power. I want to thank you, for everything you've given up."

"Fiona," Joan whispered, soft, needy. "Don't—" What, leave her? She should be praying for her to go. Don't what—do this? It was already done. *I'll be a villain to many, but a hero to many more.* Joan had never stood a chance of reasoning with that.

The thought of it made her so viciously angry. It was the first emotion in days clear enough that Joan could hold on to it. She'd never had a chance or a choice. She wanted—she wanted Fiona between her teeth, wanted to grind her to nothing, chew her to gristle. She wanted Fiona to feel even a fraction of what she'd made Joan feel.

Fiona was waiting, still pretending that all this had been done against her will. Forced into kidnapping and torturing by some higher calling, by some greater system. Did she think this was mercy, letting Joan utter her final words?

"Don't…look back," Joan ground out. "Don't stop running. If I catch you, you're dead."

Fiona jerked away as Joan's voice gained strength. She strained against her bindings, leaned forward in her chair, until her wrists screamed louder, until she thought her fingers might dislocate. It was all nothing to her now; pain was an old friend, death its strange and close cousin.

"Fiona," Joan growled, her voice half in singsong, and blood wound between her teeth, spilling over, out of her mouth. The necklace dangled from her throat, a heavy chain. "I'm going to ruin you."

Fiona's wide eyes betrayed her, even as she adjusted her shirt and brushed off her pants. Joan was a world-class expert in this woman's microexpressions now. "I thought we were coming to an agreement," Fiona said.

"Fuck. You."

Fiona withdrew, started gathering the things on her desk to pack them into a backpack. She was really leaving, and Joan was going to stay stuck in this chair.

Oh, Joan was all rage now, all frothing lips and gnashing teeth. She wasn't going to be left here; she'd break every bone in her body before she let Fiona get away. Her fingers popped.

A new patch of runes lit up, faded.

Then the whole wall burned white.

Fiona's attention snapped to it with a curse. She was messy now, throwing stuff into the bag, slinging it over her shoulder.

"What's wrong?" Joan called, her laugh a garbled curse. "Time running out?"

Fiona closed the bag in front of her. She didn't look back at Joan, just twisted her fingers together, still facing the wall. Her shoulders were slumped in a downward line. Joan wished, absurdly, for her sketchbook. She'd catch the dim light on Fiona's burnished hair and the manifold details of the abandoned room. It would be haunting, and beautiful, and on the cusp of something new.

The spell took shape, magic vibrating through the air. "Go to sleep, Joan Greenwood," Fiona said, voice heavy and resigned.

"Never wake up."

TWENTY-NINE

Fiona took the light with her.

Joan's eyes were half closed when it happened, slumped sideways in her chair. She had been immobilized. She wanted to sneeze. She couldn't move a single limb.

Fiona left in a rush, and she took the light with her.

Underground, there was nothing left. No hint of anything, just total, complete darkness stealing the sight from Joan's open eyes.

This was, maybe, the worst thing Fiona had done to her.

Darkness was no friend to Joan Greenwood. It was textureless and utterly dead here. She longed for something living, a plant to draw in air, confirm she was still alive, that this wasn't the afterlife, not yet.

I don't want to die. I changed my mind.

Tears dripped off her face.

Please, I want to live.

Fiona's last spell had done something to the necklace, which was growing hotter by the second. It'd scald her soon, even through her clothes. Burn a circle in her chest, right through to her heart.

Astoria was coming, that was what Fiona had said. Astoria was close, and Fiona had booby-trapped the room. Joan. Left her unable to warn anyone.

Her ears rang in the darkness, her thoughts locked in an ebb and flow and ebb of noise, building with a million voices.

I'm going to kill her, Joan thought. No, she wasn't a killer.

But for Fiona Ganon, maybe I am.

The necklace warmed further. Where would Fiona go next? And with what, a successful spell to amplify her own abilities? The potential cure or balm to magic poisoning to go with it? Joan had to warn—someone. Anyone. But she couldn't move.

Then she saw magic.

It glimmered faintly in the air, making its own light. The room was still silent save for the far drip, drip of some leaky ceiling, but magic moved. It shifted in the direction of where Joan thought the train tracks might be, behind the bend of the wall, opposite to where Fiona had exited. And where it flowed, it took on a silvery hue.

Joan knew that hue.

Hope was a violent thing inside her, sawing her organs in half. She was saved; they had found her.

The necklace burned.

They had found her, and Fiona had done something she'd seemed convinced Joan would never wake from. Joan was going to have to watch, paralyzed.

Astoria was too good at this to make noise, so Joan's only warning that the other woman was in the room was the area lighting up, and by then, it was far too late. By then, through the building scream in her throat, Joan could only watch as Astoria came into view, her sword out and magic flared around her in a protective air-based barrier, with Wren at her shoulder similarly armed with an array of knives, her fae eyes surely allowing her to peer through the dark tunnels.

When their gazes landed on Joan after a quick, practiced look around the room to confirm no one else was there, the horror was evident on Wren's face.

"Oh, Joan," she breathed.

Astoria promptly sheathed her sword down her back, face a flickering storm, but there was no pity on it, at least. Joan, dazed, her eyes so dry that they were blurring over with tears, appreciated that deeply as Astoria walked over swiftly.

No, turn back.

"I'll free her, Fiona can't be far. See if you can pick up a lead in the tunnel, but don't engage her."

"I can handle myself, you worrywart," Wren replied, but she moved to comply, setting off at a cautious jog.

"We don't know what she can do," Astoria called, gaze lingering on Wren's disappearing back. "See if there's a trail, do *not* engage, and don't wander too far."

"First priority is getting Joan to help, I know!" Wren called faintly, and she was gone.

The necklace was burning and Joan couldn't so much as wince.

Please don't come closer. She'd give anything for them to hear her thoughts, anything at all on this earth. She reached to channel and was met with a flash of pain she flinched away from. *No, no, focus, Joan.*

Astoria reached the brushed-away remains of the chalk circle Fiona had drawn on the floor, and the necklace's heat hit Joan's skin.

Astoria knelt in front of her. "Why aren't you moving?" she murmured. "Paralytic?"

GO AFTER WREN, ASTORIA.

She was frowning, with a perfect little crease between her eyebrows and her braids tucked neatly back up into themselves. Beyond the edge of the long-sleeve she wore under a sturdy-looking vest, hand-drawn tattoos peeked out, and Joan remembered what Wren had said about specializing in supplemental ink magic.

Astoria was quick on her feet, Joan knew that, dreaded that, because she cast a counterspell on the fly and Joan's limbs went loose.

Astoria's hand came to rest on Joan's knee.

The necklace reached a fever pitch.

The word burst out of Joan's mouth in a strangled cry: "RUN!"

Astoria's eyes widened, her lips moving in the beginnings of a spell.

The necklace shattered wholesale with a sound like a gong, and with it, magic burst into the air. If Joan had unwittingly stumbled upon it, she'd have been eviscerated by the blast, but Astoria caught the worst in her shield and was thrown clear across the room to smash into the wall with a sickening crunch, cracking the grimy tiles before falling to the floor. Magic fractured into shards of light, and one speared Astoria through the shoulder, narrowly missing her heart, her head. The tattoos vanished from her skin, used up.

Joan was—oh no, oh no, no, no. Astoria hadn't been casting over herself, she'd cast over Joan, and a thin, half-formed shield spell that burned with fire magic kept her alive through the initial blast.

But it wasn't over, whatever Fiona's spell was hadn't finished yet; the magic swirled into a compact ball, and time went breathless. Joan could see the spell's next move, it would burst again, a double shot, and Astoria was only barely leveraging herself back up, her shields obliterated. This time, it'd kill her.

It would kill her, and Joan, and it would be Joan's fault for getting snatched in the first place. She'd never live with that; she wasn't going to die taking Astoria Wardwell down with her.

In the infinite void between seconds, Joan breathed in.

THIRTY

Channeling magic was second nature to her now, and when the pain hit, this time she was prepared to push through. It was a familiar bed after a long night. She reached out, quick as a bird, and pulled that explosive spell's magic into herself, where it detonated in her body.

Joan, miraculously, did not turn into a pile of goo.

This remained, nonetheless, her breaking point.

Perhaps it was all the magic she'd already channeled, poisoning her body slowly but surely, weakening it far past what it had ever reached before. Or maybe it was too much magic for anyone at any time, but though she clung to the barest shred of consciousness, Joan was nearly 100 percent sure at least one of her internal organs popped.

Her ribs crunched in.

Joan threw up blood, so much blood, and it wasn't just that—she felt it seep out of her pores, ooze from her eyes.

Of all the ways she'd imagined her death, she'd never expected this, magic turning her inside out.

Hands fumbled at the ropes binding her to the chair, and then the pressure released, and for the first time in what felt like forever, Joan was free.

She fell.

Someone caught her.

"I have you," Astoria was saying. "Joan, stay with me, okay? Stay with me a little while longer."

The world smeared around them. Joan coughed and it was wet. She thought faintly that she was leaving a trail of blood on Astoria's vest. She was being lifted, maneuvered carefully into Astoria's arms.

Cradled, gently. She was so warm, and it felt so nice on Joan's torn skin.

"Don't die, you bastard," Astoria growled, huffing a little as they started moving. "You're not dying like this."

Blood dribbled out of Joan's mouth. This was really it. Astoria's temple was cut, her impaled shoulder slick, but she was moving, heading in the direction Wren had gone.

She looked so sad.

Joan hated that. "How . . . will I die, then?" she forced out.

Astoria shifted her higher in her arms, picked up the pace as they moved down the hall, an orb of light following them. "You'll die in your sleep when you're super old, in someone's arms, warm, with dahlias on your bedside. The last thing you'll say will be some stupid, taunting joke. You'll make someone laugh before you go."

More blood and spit foamed out of Joan. She thought maybe there was some dripping from her nose too, or maybe that was her whole brain, liquefied by the spell. "You . . . think about my death?"

"Shut up. The point is, it's not happening right now," Astoria hissed. "And it will not be because you saved my life. So it's not time yet. Say it. 'It's not time yet, I'm not going to die.'"

Joan shivered. Astoria's heat wasn't making a dent anymore; the cold was creeping too far into her. "You saved my life first." She coughed, almost choked on it. "Astoria, tell CZ... tell him to ask Grace out."

"We're almost to Wren," Astoria said, rounding a corner. "She's close, and she's good at healing spells. I'm shit at them. I only... I only destroy. Fuck. We can cast one together. Hold on so you can meddle in CZ's love life yourself."

The cold reached her lungs. They seized, and her breath skipped. Magic wasn't a cure-all. There were limits to its ability to heal.

Joan rather suspected she was past those limits.

"Stop channeling, Joan," Astoria hissed.

"I'm... not." She wasn't, was she? Magic slid through her as the world dimmed.

Astoria was screaming for Wren now. Oh gods, Joan never wanted to hear Astoria scream like that again, voice fraying, mask finally cracking into a look of genuine terror.

There was a distant answering call. The thundering of shoes. It sounded like hooves.

She was jostled. Oddly enough, the pain wasn't as bad as it had been a minute ago. Maybe a bad sign of her impending death. There was a hand on her face, flaring hot, cupping her cheek. Someone was talking at her, but she couldn't hear them. She was pretty sure her ears were full of blood. They felt wet.

The hand shook her face, harder, which was a terrible inconvenience. A thumb brushed across her cheekbone; she felt its softness with a jolt. Who would hold her like this? The curiosity alone was enough to get her to pry her eyes back open.

Astoria was sitting on the ground, Joan cradled in her arms, as Wren knelt over them both. Their exchange was rapid-fire, but it was all mumbles to Joan. She couldn't believe she was going to die in Astoria's arms. She couldn't believe she was going to die in Astoria's arms without ever having kissed her. That was so cruel. And homophobic.

Astoria's grip tightened; Wren's hands started to move over Joan. She couldn't see the magic. That was another shock to her system—where was magic? She'd always been able to see it, but it was no longer visible. All she could feel was a deep coldness coiling through her. And the distant pressure of Astoria's body against hers.

And then sensation lanced through her body like a white-hot brand. She wanted to scream, she opened her mouth for it, but it was so full of blood that she could only make a horrendous gurgling sound. Her ears burned, like someone was shoving pokers into them, and she heard the horrible noise she was making again.

She heard it.

Her hearing leaked back in, enough to pick up the edge of whatever Astoria was yelling at Wren.

"Keep going."

But the magic *hurt*; it was like someone was taking a cheese grater to her whole body. It was all salt in the wound. It was worse than whatever Fiona had done to her, a thousand times worse. *Stop it, please. Stop doing this to me.* They were pinning her spirit back into a wrecked body.

"She's magic poisoned." That was Wren, hands shaking. *"This is going to kill her, the damage is too extensive, Astoria."*

"*Keep going,*" Astoria ordered. "*She can take it.*"

She looked down at Joan. Her eyes were filled with tears. Joan didn't ever want to see that sight again. "You can take it, Joan."

She couldn't, she—

Her fingers knit back together with painful snaps. She convulsed, but Astoria held her firm. She kept saying it: "*You can take it, you can take it. You're strong.*"

"*Astoria—*"

"*Give her more time, keep* going, *Wren.*"

Joan didn't feel strong, Joan felt like a blade of grass being ripped in half lengthwise. Her vision blacked out as her eyes burned next. Magic might as well have scooped them out of her head raw, for the way it felt. The red haze was receding but slowly, too slowly, not fast enough to keep up with the damage magic was still doing to her body.

She blinked and magic was back, funneling into Astoria in massive amounts and getting shaped by Wren.

Blood trickled from Astoria's nose, but she didn't stop her mantra. "*You can do it.*"

It was so much magic, it was— Astoria couldn't process all of it. She was showing the same signs of poisoning that Joan had, that Grace had shown at the market. A sore opened on her neck, gently weeping blood. The more there was to heal, the more magic it took, and there was no witch on earth powerful enough to reverse the damage done to Joan's body.

But Astoria didn't relent. When Wren questioned her, worry so evident in her hesitation, Astoria told her to work faster, a snap to her tone.

Joan needed them to stop.

Joan needed them to stop because it was going to kill Astoria if they didn't, and then Joan was going to die anyways. The moment they stopped casting, Joan was going to die.

Their spell was the only thing keeping her alive.

Some ribs popped back into place. Joan's nose gradually stopped bleeding as the burst vessels of her body knit back together.

Bloody tears leaked from Astoria's eyes. The wound in her shoulder gushed blood harder.

Enough. "Stop," Joan gasped. "Astoria, you can't."

"You don't tell me what to do," Astoria said. Red spread across the whites of her eyes.

Joan wasn't going to let her do this; Joan would rather die herself than let Astoria tear herself apart for her. The spell slowed as Astoria struggled to keep channeling.

Darkness began to creep across Joan's vision again. She could see magic once more. It was a whirlwind around them, thick and cloying, close enough to taste on her tongue. Joan would do anything to reach it, strike any deal.

I know you're listening.

New York heaved around them.

I know you can hear me, Joan said, around the burning in her abdomen as the spell fought to regenerate blood as fast as Joan was losing it. *New York, don't touch her.*

The words were a faint laugh, wind over a lake. *She offers willingly. Don't. Touch. Her.*

Magic wiggled away. *She's ours. We could take her now, save her so much heartbreak. She'd be grateful for it, eventually, to avoid the pain coming for her.*

Wren's hands slowed; Astoria snapped at her again, but her voice was weaker this time. Wren wouldn't let this go on. Thank everything, thank gods Wren prioritized Astoria's life over Joan's.

But the spell kept going.

Wren looked blankly at her still hands, and then her head snapped up. "Stop it, Astoria. You're at your limit."

"Not yet," Astoria ground out, maintaining the spell herself. "She needs more."

"No one..." Joan coughed wetly. "No one can save me. Stop, Astoria."

Her heartbeat was a hummingbird against Joan's body. So fast, it'd burst.

"I'm not facing them without you," Astoria said. Her fingers loosened, her strength failing. "I promised CZ. I need...a little more magic."

Why wouldn't she give *up*? She needed more than *a little more* to fix Joan, more than any normal witch could bring in, more than Wren could give her in tandem. Maybe as much as Joan was uniquely capable of channeling.

She's not yours, Joan thought. Her hand came up; she wrapped it around Astoria's arm. *Don't touch her, she's mine.*

Joan reached for magic, and though its touch was a pyre, though its slide into her was a superheated knife, she wrenched as much as she could away from Astoria. Astoria's spell faltered, and she bled harder, like the effort of it was all that was keeping her conscious too.

"Heal us both, Wren," Joan hissed. Maybe the channeling would kill her faster than the spell, but maybe in the race, she could save them both. Being alive hurt more than dying, but it was life she'd be choosing.

"You fool," Astoria started, but Joan dug her fingers into her arm.

"Share, Wardwell," Joan said. *Let me in.* "Share it with me."

Astoria's eyebrows knit together in confusion.

"Split it with me, you dense, gorgeous, self-sacrificial woman, so we can *both* live."

Astoria stopped struggling.

Moments ago, you were ready for death, Green Witch. Now you fight against it. In your half-life state, the world unravels for you, New York murmured. *We enjoy the feeling.*

Come and get me, Joan snarled, and wrestled magic like a slippery fish, kicking it up a notch and releasing it directly into Wren. Astoria strengthened her when she faltered, took the edge off when it was too much, both of them feeding it into Wren's spell.

The skin began to knit back together on Astoria's shoulder. The red receded from her eyes; her nose stopped bleeding. It moved faster through Joan too, keeping up with the damage and then surpassing it, pulling her body back together quickly enough for her to stabilize. They locked eyes, Joan and Astoria, and Joan held the gaze, a lighthouse in the burning currents of magic.

It might have been seconds, it could have been hours, but finally, the spell stopped.

THIRTY-ONE

The three of them lay breathing on the filthy floor of the station for several long minutes.

Joan kept thinking one of the others would speak first, but time stretched out and they didn't. Perhaps they were each individually going over how close Joan and Astoria had gotten to a point of no return.

Joan was still in Astoria's arms, leaning into her as Astoria leaned into the wall. In another world, she'd be in a panic, because damn if she didn't really like this woman. In this one, she was too tired and achy to freak out. She curled closer into Astoria's arms, and it was likely just reflex that made the Wardwell heir tighten her grip.

Joan was safe. For the first time in what must have been two days, she was safe.

Her fist curled in the sleeve of Astoria's long black shirt. She licked her lips. "Fiona," she rasped. "She left."

"Her magical trail is faint," Wren said, voice cracking briefly before she leveled it out. "It heads to the surface, then gets lost up there in the crowds."

"CZ, Mik, Grace..."

"Are all fine," Astoria rumbled, chest vibrating against Joan's cheek. "Worried sick about you, but fine. I'm..." She swallowed, hard. "I'm sorry it took us so long to find you." Her hand twitched up, thumb brushing against Joan's jaw.

Joan's breath hitched.

"Her wards were good," Wren said, a voice at Joan's back, startling her back to the present. "Really good, confused all sorts of tracker spells."

"It took two hours for us to realize you were missing, then another forty to find you," Astoria said. "Too long."

"Grace cracked it, in the end, refined the map enough to tune it to your specific magical signature," Wren admitted. "We should get back to them; there's no reception down here, and they'll be anxious about not hearing from us. CZ wanted to come but we had to leave someone to guard Grace and Mik. We only have thirty minutes left on the clock before they call the Greenwoods and tell them where we went."

That was enough to get Joan to try and sit up. Astoria's grip was too tight for a second, but Joan must have imagined the hesitation, because a second later she helped Joan sit properly.

"I can walk," Joan announced. "But I might be a little slow, sorry." An understatement. She was fairly certain crawling was her best bet.

"*Don't* apologize," Astoria said, an undue harshness to her tone. Joan turned to her in surprise and found that they were nose to nose.

Astoria's eyes were a shifting tempest in Wren's hovering light. Tension pulled the corners of her mouth into an unhappy frown. She was grimy, but Joan could still detect hints of her cherry soap.

"Don't go soft on me, Wardwell," Joan whispered, and Astoria's gaze flicked to her mouth.

The fearsome woman swallowed. Again. "I'm not," she said roughly. "We need you alive to tell us what Fiona's after."

Joan knew a lie when she heard one.

Wren rose to her feet, breaking the spell, and Joan looked away to take Wren's outstretched hand, rising with a groan.

She was not well, not at all.

But she was alive when she was supposed to be dead. She'd do a little tap dance if she thought her feet would obey.

"Fiona set Mik loose on purpose to get Grace to solve the spell, or the magic poisoning part of it specifically," Joan said, as Astoria stood behind her. She was close. Really close or a normal amount of close, Joan couldn't tell.

Wren swore, rubbing the back of her hand against her temple. "And she went after you because . . . ?"

"She wanted my magic," Joan said, wincing as she took a step. Astoria was there instantly, slinging one of Joan's arms around her shoulder and guiding her forward. "Grace didn't help, so she used me as a guinea pig to test out magic-poisoning cures and to try to mimic my channeling ability so she could boost her own power.

"I said I can walk," she protested, Astoria's touch sending a riot of goose bumps across her body.

"Sure you can," Astoria said. "It was someone else who was almost exsanguinated a few minutes ago after being tortured for two days and then resurrected in a magical miracle."

"And then I was healed, and now—"

"I'm not letting go, Greenwood," Astoria said. "Walk. And explain more about Fiona."

Joan walked.

She laid out all the bits and pieces she had. Fiona wanted power more than anything, not just physically but in the witch world too. Her focus was on some level of systemic change, not solitary fame and fortune. She was smart and well resourced, at least in terms of knowledge of the city and spells. She had gotten whatever it was she needed out of Joan and set her trap.

Now she could be anywhere.

They climbed a set of old steps to a door, and when Wren pushed it open in front of them, the world was so bright, Joan had to squeeze her eyes shut completely. Wren murmured an apology, guiding them out onto a New York side street.

"I wish one of your friends had a car," Astoria grumbled. "We can't go on the HERMES or subway looking like this, and we're too worn out to portal."

"Walking's out of the question," Wren added, surveying the street. "And we need to figure out where Fiona's going next. If she's got a grudge against your family, Joan, I hate to say it, but it might be time to warn them. Your sister's been texting CZ a lot asking about you."

Molly. Gods, Joan had almost died ignoring all of her sister's texts. She'd helped Joan get out of that house, and Joan had repaid her by not even confirming she was okay.

They took a few more steps, Joan grimacing as each one shot pain up her body. They did need a car, and Joan knew only one person in New York with one. Her father.

She tugged Astoria to a stop. "Can I borrow someone's phone?"

CZ cried, unashamedly, when he heard Joan's voice. There was a fair amount of blubbering, and it became so much, he had to hand the phone off to Grace, who seemed kind of shell-shocked, and so it went next to Mik, who was the most coherent.

"I'll get him to call Molly," Mik confirmed. "Hanging up now to do so— Joan, holy shit. I am gonna hug the fuck out of you when I see you."

They found a bench in a nearby park to sit on and wait. The grass wiggled happily at Joan's feet, and she managed to discover they were in Queens. Not too far from CZ's pack headquarters. They could swing by and say hi to his parents.

Joan giggled, then smothered it at the odd looks from Wren and Astoria, who were sitting on either side of her like she might keel over at any minute.

The air was so delicious. Had air always been this delicious? *Gods bless you, New York City, and your dirty streets, and your car horns honking, and the way summer settles on you like a veil.*

Another giggle.

"Now I'm getting worried," Astoria said.

Everything had taken on a shiny new cast. Gorgeous Astoria Wardwell, worried about little old Joan! When was the last time she'd sat on a bench? Weren't benches a wonderful invention? And parks, they'd really done something when they'd invented parks.

"Californians," Joan said grandly, leaning back, "I may disagree with your way of life, but I adore you both right now."

Wren laughed, bumped Joan with her shoulder. "See, I told you we'd be friends."

Astoria looked suspiciously like she was blushing. Joan poked her side—why was she so muscular and firm?—and Astoria caught her hand before she could do it again.

"Enough out of you," Astoria said, but the haunted guilt had faded out of her eyes a little, and there was some amusement settling in there. "Is everything funny to you?"

"Everything is horrible to me," Joan said. "My dad always said I was too sensitive. *That's* funny to me."

Astoria's face darkened. "Merlin Greenwood is a fucking loser."

Joan couldn't help her shocked inhale. Wren was cackling madly.

"Wardwell! I didn't know you could curse," Joan said.

"I save it for the Greenwoods," Astoria said, a little pleased. "And don't worry, I have always found Merlin smarmy, so this isn't just because CZ explained that he's been a huge dickwad to you."

"Dickbag," Joan corrected. "CZ's partial to that term." Oh, CZ. She wanted to rub her cheek against his like a cat.

Astoria's rejoinder was cut off by a shadow that crossed her face. "Wren," she said.

Wren was already sitting forward, looking a bit less tense than Astoria was, but only marginally. "I know. No sudden movements, Story."

"Witches," someone said behind them, and Joan was the only one uncool enough to twist on the bench to see who had spoken.

A group of four people stood behind them, two Latino men and two Black women. Joan had no idea how Wren and Astoria had sensed them, because their appearance was sudden enough to startle her. Her eyes flicked across them. The predatory stillness, red-tinted eyes.

Vampires.

"We aren't doing anything but sitting," Wren said, casually leaning back. "Our ride will be here at any moment."

"Covered in blood?" one of the men asked. "We don't want trouble from your kind, and you're too close to vampire territory for your own good."

"You know those boundaries aren't official," Astoria said.

Wren shot her a sharp glare. "We understand and acknowledge your territory; we genuinely aren't looking for any trouble. Our friend here needs medical attention, that's it."

Not just any vampire territory—LaMorte territory. Wren and Astoria were clearly on edge, and while Joan had been ensconced in the world of witches for the last week and a half, she'd known tensions were high between species after the Night Market.

But Joan couldn't quite be afraid. One of the women looked familiar to Joan. Strikingly so. "Aunt Lila?"

The woman stepped forward, peering more closely at Joan. She had tied-back braids and the same cheekbones as CZ. "Joan Greenwood?"

Joan turned fully, going up on her knees on the bench, despite her screaming body. "Aunt Lila! It's been a while." Someone she knew! She'd thought for a while there that she'd never again see someone she knew, feel that flutter of recognition in her. This, too, was miraculous.

Lila shook her head. "I couldn't recognize you, you look terrible. You *smell* unrecognizable." Her face shifted. "Tell me CZ is okay. I don't want him caught up in your witch nonsense. We've had enough of you all."

"CZ's fine, he's in Manhattan right now," Joan said. She swung to the side laboriously, remembering her manners. "Astoria, Wren, this is Lila LaMorte, CZ's aunt." Joan had met his whole family a couple of times, though it had certainly been a while.

Wren relaxed more fully. "Pleasure to meet you."

Astoria was silent. Joan lightly smacked the back of her head in chastisement, and Astoria actually growled at her.

"Hello," she forced out.

"You're really waiting for a ride?" Lila asked suspiciously. "Girl, there's enough blood on you to drown someone in. We could smell you a mile away."

Joan opened her mouth to reassure Lila she was alright, but Lila put up a hand to cut her off.

"You know what, I don't need to know anymore. Tell CZ to get his ass back home. I'm sick of that boy's escapades, you hear me?"

"We can't let them walk away, not a Greenwood, not after the market," the woman next to Lila said. Her eyes flashed red. "That's livelihoods they fucked with, and all for some witch we don't even know."

News apparently still hadn't spread widely that Joan was coven broken, if people thought she had any sway in her family. The words were at the tip of her tongue, but she swallowed them. It would sound like an excuse. It *was* an excuse.

"We'll wait for this alleged ride," Lila said. "We aren't touching Joan. CZ *and* the witches would have my ass."

Thus passed an excruciating twenty minutes. Joan's attempts at small talk were batted away. CZ's family had never loved Joan, but they'd been friendly enough to her. This was something new, and it didn't spell good fortune for the magic world.

When Joan faltered, spirits tanking, Wren picked up the threads, trying to coax the group into some semblance of friendship, even as Astoria refused to do much more than glare at everyone.

That was as far as they got before a car rolled to a stop in front of them—Merlin's car—and the door was flung open for Molly to tumble out, dressed in a rumpled suit, and throw her arms around Joan, knocking her back into the bench.

"You can't keep almost dying," Molly said, squeezing hard enough that she was really hurting Joan, her charm necklace pressing into Joan's skin. "I don't— Why the hell didn't you tell me what you were up to? I could have helped. Kidnapped! For almost two days, kidnapped, and I didn't even know! You look so horrible."

Joan hugged back just as hard, breathing in the smell of Molly's expensive perfume, letting her eyes prickle and burn. "Thanks for coming," Joan said.

Molly pulled away, eventually, and greeted Astoria and Wren rather awkwardly, with unhappy looks at both of them. As their appointed babysitter, Molly likely wasn't pleased they'd been committing crimes under her nose.

Joan spun again to introduce Molly to Lila and the other vampires, but they were gone when she turned.

Wren gave Joan a little pat on the back and a sympathetic wince. "Sorry, I'm hopeful things will get better."

Maybe if they delivered Moon Creatures a complete spell that would grant them the ability to cast without magic poisoning, sure, but they still didn't have the spell figured out, and if they did that, witches would lose their collective minds. Or at least the Greenwoods and Wardwells would.

Molly ushered them all into the car, and they piled in, Joan in the front and the Californians in the back, before they set off for Manhattan.

"Okay," Molly said, waiting at a light. "CZ told me you'd been kidnapped by Fiona Ganon and needed to be picked up, and said you'd fill me in on the rest. Go on, fill me in."

Joan was too sore to look back at Astoria and Wren, but they were suspiciously silent, letting her take the lead.

Molly's eyes were focused on the road—she was not a very good driver, an endearing failure Joan much enjoyed. She tapped her fingers on the wheel. "No lying," she said. "I'm in too deep not to tell me the truth now."

She had a point. And Wren had one too, about Fiona's grudge. Though she'd claimed she wasn't specifically after the Green-woods, they seemed to represent everything Fiona found wrong in the magic world. As angry as Joan was with them all the time, she did not, for even a moment, wish the pain she'd experienced for the last two days on them. Not Valeria, not Selene, not even Merlin, and especially not Molly.

"You have to promise not to tell Mom and Dad," Joan said. "And Aunt Val."

"I'll make that judgment call after I hear this story," Molly said. "You were kidnapped, Joan, this isn't a joke."

"I'm not laughing," Joan replied. "I'm so dead serious, Molly. Not a word." This was why Molly hadn't been brought into the fold in the first place. Her sister was still loyal to the Greenwoods, still *believed* in them.

"Jo—"

"Uncle," Joan said.

Molly's gaze finally left the road to pass over Joan, bloody and covered in cuts and bruises, a half-healed burn on her chest, clothes singed, likely smelly as hell. Whatever she saw there was enough.

She bit her lip.

Joan started as best she could at the beginning—with the phone call from CZ, Mik, all of it.

By the time they made it up to the hotel room, Joan was finishing up the tail end of her story.

"So we're not sure if Fiona's going to go after the family. We were hoping maybe you could give Mom and Dad and Aunt Val a fair warning without actually revealing that we have Mik," Joan said, as Astoria unlocked the door.

Molly looked aged by a thousand years. "I need to process," she muttered to herself. "Gods, Joan, this is so bad."

Joan, still on the heels of almost dying, actually felt better about her situation than she ever had before. Maybe it wasn't helpful to say so to Molly, but she was going to anyways when she was bowled over by a moving body.

CZ kept them from careening into the wall, but his hug was still forceful, bordering on violent. "You're never leaving my sight again," he said into her neck, as Joan wrapped her arms around him and squeezed back. "Never ever ever. You'll come to work with me, come home with me."

"Go to the bathroom with you when you have to pee, like I'm a cat," Joan said.

"My tiny, helpless little cat who is *not* leaving my sight," CZ said.

"Cat people," Astoria said with derision, stepping into the room as Mik and Grace crowded out. CZ didn't let go of her, and that was perfectly fine with Joan, so the two of them piled into the group hug. Joan, convinced she had no more moisture left in her body, still managed to shed a few more tears. Grace sternly told her that she needed a shower, but she also wouldn't let go of Joan's hand. Mik climbed CZ's back to get closer.

"We ran into your aunt," Joan said at a lower pitch into CZ's ear, once the main fuss had died down and they'd started to migrate back into the room, leaving Joan and CZ, still attached, to trail after them.

CZ finally pulled back. Sniffled a little. "Out on the street? I'm in trouble, aren't I?"

"Big time," Joan replied. "I'm sorry you getting dragged into all this is pissing your family off. I think we all understand if you have to split your time between here and Queens a bit more."

"I left, and you were literally taken and almost killed," CZ said. "If there was any doubt in my mind about where I am most needed, this has squashed it. You needed me, Joan, and I left you."

"It is absolutely not your fault that Fiona kidnapped me," Joan said. "CZ, it's so important to me that you know that."

He wouldn't meet her eyes. "I wanted to be here. I *needed* to be here. And I was needed here. There's a place for me in my pack that allows me to make my life here," he said firmly. "I'm not turning my back on them, but I'm not turning my back on any of you either."

All words were inadequate, so Joan took his hand and folded him into this group, one that had never demanded more from him than he could give.

Joan endured their constant glances, even though sometimes someone looked too hard and she thought of Fiona's calculating stare. She allowed everyone to bump up against her to make sure she was still there, even though sometimes a rogue touch made her flinch, and she had to work to calm her heart down after. And she appreciated that they all scrambled to figure out dinner while she was in the shower and offered up various pieces of clothing she could sleep in because CZ had dashed home to get her underwear and regular clothes but failed to bring pajamas. She ended up in Astoria's big shirt and a pair of pants Mik had bought. It didn't matter what she wore, so long as it covered up her bruises.

Molly pulled her aside after dinner to confess she needed to go back home. There was another hug, luckily not as tight as the first one.

"I'll be back first thing tomorrow," Molly said. "I need to give them a broad warning about Fiona, check in on Nate."

"Do you know how you're going to phrase it?" Joan asked, not wanting to nag but needing a reassurance that Mik wouldn't become collateral anyways.

"I'll figure it out, while keeping you safe," Molly said with a lopsided smile. "I'll keep you all safe. Us Greenwoods, we have a way with words."

Once she left, it was Mik who proposed the movie and cuddle puddle, and Joan got put in the middle, CZ on one side, Astoria somehow maneuvering to end up on her other side, and before the movie even ended, Joan was fast asleep.

THIRTY-TWO

A noise woke Joan in the middle of the night, and she blinked awake with a pounding heart, straining to hear it again.

She must have been having a nightmare, though she couldn't remember it, because she was a little sweaty and a little wired, and the noise had not helped. In front of her, CZ had vacated his spot on the floor, and across the gap, Mik slept, mouth wide open.

Joan tried to turn and couldn't.

There was an arm around her waist. Someone's legs slotted into her own. Their body was recognizably warm, and so was the scarred hand limp across her.

Astoria was cuddling her.

She was also snoring, very softly. That had been the noise in Joan's ear; it was intermittent but there.

Very carefully, so very, very carefully, Joan turned incrementally.

Astoria's face in the darkness of the hotel room had all the drama of an oil painting, rendered in thick slashes of dark colors. Her hair was in a messy bun on her head, curls coming loose to brush her cheeks. Her eyelashes were a triumph, and breath fluttered out in those little snores.

This was now the second time Joan had ended up in the woman's arms, and she was so selfishly glad Astoria was sleeping and couldn't pull away and so wholly disgusted by herself at the thought, because she was being a creep. She was. She wanted something she couldn't have.

A soft cough made Joan tilt her head up to look past the back of the couch. CZ stood in the darkness, red eyes neon in the night, a little smile on his face.

"Be more obvious," he whispered.

She raised her eyebrows at him.

"Need to eat," he said. "Shockingly, there's no blood in this hotel room, and I ran out at home. I'm restocking."

Joan scrunched her nose.

"Don't be cute. I'll go to a bar nearby and be back tomorrow morning," he said. "I wouldn't leave if I didn't have to; I hate letting you out of my sight right now."

Go, Joan tried to make her face say. *I'm surrounded by people who will protect me.*

"Alright, sleep tight, little lesbian," he whispered, and pushed off the couch with a chuckle, striding for the door.

She was going to kill him, just as soon as she managed to get out of Astoria's arms.

Astoria, as if sensing the thought, curled her arm tighter around Joan, forcing her into her chest with a hand on her back.

Oh my. Joan's face was pressed to Astoria's neck. She couldn't help it, she breathed in. Why did Astoria have to smell so nice? Why did she have to smell so nice and be so deadly and have feelings for Wren? Why did she have to be from another state?

Another inhale. Drowsiness settled on Joan, her fingers curled between them, pressed to Astoria's chest, feeling the steady thud, thud of her heart. She'd give anything to press her lips to Astoria's skin, but that was a line she couldn't cross.

Joan matched her breaths to the other woman's. Let herself fade.

When dawn stretched her rosy fingers across the sky, Joan's eyes fluttered open again.

This time, to a chill.

CZ was still out, and as Joan took stock of her aching body, she realized there was an arm missing around her.

Astoria wasn't in bed either.

Mik was still sleeping. Grace had somehow secured a bonnet, and her braids were tucked away as she slumbered; even Wren had wrapped herself up like a burrito and passed out. Joan didn't much relish trying to throw herself back into dreams of dank rooms and orange-haired women. And she had to pee anyways.

She rose cautiously, stepping carefully over everyone's sleeping bodies, wincing when she made even the smallest noise, until she could tiptoe to the bathroom. When she exited, she heard the faint slash of something whizzing through the air coming from one of the bedrooms.

The door was closed save for an inch. Joan peered in.

Astoria had moved all the furniture she could to the side and was practicing with her sword. It swished as she twirled, her concentration absolute, wearing a sports bra and spandex. Her hair was still in that infuriating bun; she was glistening with sweat.

She spun to the end of a series of movements and then backed up to the start. "Couldn't sleep?" she asked in a low voice, and Joan's ruse was up.

She guiltily pushed the door open. "Apparently neither could you."

Astoria restarted her forms as Joan stepped inside. The twirling sword made Joan nervous, but Astoria wielded it so expertly that she was fairly sure she wasn't actually in danger.

It had switched, somehow, from Joan distrusting the woman to Joan trusting her with her life.

"I'm thinking," Astoria said.

"About how best to stab someone?"

"Funny." Astoria swung her sword extra hard. "Is that all you think I think about?"

"Hard not to make that assumption when you're...you know." Joan waved a hand at Astoria, trying to encompass both the fact that, in this day and age, the woman used a sword and that she looked so good doing it.

"You don't understand what it's like, in California," she said abruptly. "The way we run things—it's not to control Moon Creatures, as you say. We're the ones who get called when the ancients go berserk, when a banshee starts terrorizing a family, or when a rogue curse starts killing people off. Here, there's no central system. The people have no one to call on."

"We do," Joan argued back. "When one of the fae does something wrong, we leave them to the fae to deal with. Same for vampires and witches, and the ancients don't bother us much, but if it's bad enough, the Greenwoods will figure it out, or dispatch someone to. Like hiring private contractors to deal with individual issues."

"And it works, for you," Astoria said. "That's what I'm thinking about. That's what I don't get." She swung her sword a few more times. "Could it work for us?" she muttered, and lapsed into silence.

The kind of community self-governance that ruled here happened because the Greenwoods didn't usually spend their time squashing Moon Creatures completely, Night Market raid aside. Packs like the LaMortes could amass enough power and respect over time to establish their own systems. That didn't happen in California, where witches ruled with an iron fist.

But change could still come for them, slow as it might be, and Astoria was one of the few who had enough power to lead it. Maybe, just maybe, if Joan gave her room to evolve instead of assuming the worst about her, Astoria could start something new.

"Can I hold it?" Joan asked.

Astoria paused her footwork to smirk at Joan, and it was such a relief to see amusement back in the woman, rather than worry or guilt or whatever had her up exercising at six AM.

"I'm holding back so many jokes," Astoria said.

"Wardwell, you dog," Joan said, but she approached anyways, because Astoria was holding the sword out.

Joan wrapped her fingers around it, grip warm from Astoria's hand.

Astoria let go the moment Joan had a firm hold, and the sword nearly speared through the floor.

Joan let out a curse, but Astoria was back in a flash to lift the weight again, like she'd been expecting this.

"You didn't trust I was strong enough to hold it!" Joan accused.

Astoria looked meaningfully at how low the point of the blade had gotten. Looked back up at Joan. "You have other strengths," she said.

"A boatload of weaknesses, you mean," Joan snarked, but maybe it sounded a little pained. Their fingers were touching. Joan was a Victorian waif, and she'd seen an ankle. Her skin was all buzzing.

"No, Joan," Astoria said, and Joan's name on her tongue was velvet. "You have other strengths."

Joan tilted her head up. When was the last time she'd kissed someone? At least a year ago. Now was not the time to be fantasizing. "Like?" she breathed.

"Fishing for compliments?"

"Well, you're so insistent that I have strengths, I am waiting to hear what the great Astoria Wardwell might admire in another person."

"You can make anyone feel like they are the most important person in the world," Astoria said, surprising Joan with her ready answer. "Like they have indisputable worth. You listen so intently when other people are talking. I know all your friends feel it. They bend toward you. You love people and things and places like it's easy."

"Alright, I didn't mean it."

"Don't chicken out now, I'm not done," Astoria said. "Your ability to put people at ease is extraordinary. Your moral compass is striking. I understand you're also a very talented architect. Look, I don't care if you can't lift a sword or can't cast a spell. I will lift it for you. Cast it for you."

Perhaps this was what Agamemnon had felt like, leading his men to war. Or maybe Joan was Patroclus, donning a borrowed suit of armor to inspire false confidence. She wasn't the true hero here. She'd get struck down eventually.

And what a heady feeling it was, to think Astoria might follow her down.

Joan was a thousand things, with a thousand weaknesses, but standing in front of Astoria, she felt she had only one, and it was the strung bow of Astoria's lips.

She leaned in.

Their lips brushed, featherlight. Every atom in Joan shivered alive, like the stars were watching them now, like Fate had started back up at their loom and all threads bound Joan to this moment.

Astoria pulled away.

Her absence was a vacuum, she left Joan poised with her eyes closed, took the sword from their shared hands, and stepped back with a ragged inhale.

Joan's eyes fluttered open. She wished she'd left them closed, looking at the agony on Astoria's face.

"I'm sorry," Astoria said, voice rough. "I shouldn't have—"

"No, it was me," Joan assured, strangely calm. "I shouldn't have done that." *I was just... feeling so glad to be alive.*

Astoria's fingers squeezed and loosened on her sword in alternating beats. She wouldn't meet Joan's eyes. "I was leading you on. You're... I don't really know what I feel for you, but I do know I am in love with someone else. So I can't."

"Wren," Joan said softly.

Astoria jerked in surprise, and she met Joan's gaze again, but there was panic in her eyes.

"I won't tell," Joan said. "But she must know by now, you're so close."

Astoria loosed a breath, made her sword vanish into whatever little realm she normally stored it in. Joan was a million miles away from her own body. Nothing that was happening now surprised her at all, and still she had leaned in. Reckless.

Astoria tried again after a few false starts. "She does know, or she did. I confessed years ago, but she doesn't feel the same way. She loves me. She does." Astoria didn't seem to know what to do with her hands. She put them on her hips, and then that seemed wrong, so she dropped them again.

"But she loves you like CZ and I love each other," Joan offered. "Entirely platonic."

Astoria finally crossed her arms, muscles bulging. "I can't lose her. So we don't talk about it. And it doesn't even matter, because she's straight and I'm not out. Not to my mom, at least. Attraction, sexuality, they're things I've never wanted to look in the eye, I guess."

Joan closed her eyes and made herself draw in a breath, steady, steady.

"I really am sorry," Astoria said, so soft and pitiful, and Joan added it to the list of things she never wanted Astoria to do again. Her Astoria wasn't meant to sound like this, not because of *Joan.* "You deserve better than me."

Joan had called this from the start, from day one, hour one. Minute one, from nearly the first dazzling moment she'd laid eyes on the woman, Joan had known, deep in her bones, that Astoria was going to wreck her life. And still she hadn't seemed to be able to get off this path. Still, she'd driven this car right into a wall, pushed something she never should have touched in the first place.

She opened her eyes.

"I understand," Joan said. "I really do. And I guess I'll only say—you deserve better too, Astoria. Better than holding a torch for a woman who doesn't feel the same way, and better than wading through life afraid of your own ability to love."

The silence between them was excruciating, but Joan was

drinking her fill of the sight of Astoria like she'd never see her again.

Astoria cleared her throat, voice suspiciously gravelly. "I need you to know, there's a version of me somewhere who kissed you back."

Joan left the room so Astoria wouldn't see her cry.

Hours later, Joan was pretending to sleep, curled up with Mik, when CZ returned to the apartment. Grace and Wren were already up cooking, hashing out plans for Grace to return to Brooklyn to grab some stuff.

"Not alone, I hope," CZ said in a hushed voice.

"I might have an idea," Grace was saying. "About the spell, or about magic poisoning, I don't know. It's bugging me, and I think Billy could help me." There was the sound of her standing up from the table.

"Billy?"

"Or any ghost, really," Grace amended. "Joan said something strange about...dying. That New York commented on her being half dead, and that Joan longed to be a ghost so magic would run through her."

"Quoting Billy," CZ supplied.

"Was that exactly what Billy said?"

"Yeah, that magic runs through her like the wind and it can't hurt her. What are you thinking?"

"I don't know. Nothing maybe. Causation versus correlation. Again, just an idea."

"I'll go with you, we should have a buddy system," CZ said, standing too.

"You went out alone," Grace pointed out.

"I could kill half the room before one of you so much as raised a hand to cast," CZ said casually.

"Try me," Astoria said. Her voice squeezed Joan's ribcage.

"Astoria." That was Wren.

"The vampire is right," Astoria continued. "Buddy system for those who aren't trained in offensive magic." A pause. "Or eating humans."

"I can eat a witch too."

"Stop, stop," Grace said sarcastically. "You both have super huge dicks."

"Breakfast is ready!" Wren called. "Stop pretending to sleep! Mik! Joan!"

Joan opened her eyes and found Mik's eyes were also open. Mik put a conspiratorial finger to their lips. Despite herself, Joan grinned at them.

Mik stood, pulling Joan with them, then making exaggerated yawning movements. "Eggs?"

They headed for the table, Joan trailing after them and trying very hard not to make eye contact with Astoria, who had showered at some point and was back in one of her cool, tight-shirt, loose-pants outfits.

CZ planted a kiss on Joan's head as she sat down and then walked backward as Grace picked up her purse and headed for the door. He pointed a finger at Astoria, then Joan.

"She doesn't leave your sight until I get back."

"Come on—"

"Of course not," Astoria said, interrupting Joan's protest.

"I'll rip out your throat if something happens to her again," CZ said cheerily. Joan groaned his name. "Or maybe I'll rip it out for fun, for leading the raid on my people."

Mik whistled. "Guard-dog privileges from *two* predators," they said, sitting down too.

Wren was smiling into the scrambled eggs she was cooking. Joan hated them all.

Once CZ and Grace were out the door, Joan dug into the eggs Wren set in front of her. She was on her second plate, absently listening to Mik and Wren discuss the relative merits of making different kinds of eggs in different styles, when there was a loud knock on the door.

Noise cut off abruptly.

"Room service?" Wren said cautiously, looking around at the group.

Astoria cast under her breath, pulling her fingers apart to create a little magical window.

A window that revealed Valeria Greenwood at the door, with a team of five witches at her back.

Valeria, here. Joan shoved back from the table violently, her sore right hand protesting. Why was she here? It was Astoria and Wren's hotel room, that was normal, but why bring five extra witches? Wren motioned frantically for Mik to file into the bedroom, then tugged Joan's arm to get her out of her seat and herd her in the same direction, hissing furiously at her, but Joan's mind was a sluggish hellscape.

Yesterday, Joan had brought Molly into the loop.

Today, Valeria Greenwood was at the door of the place they'd been hiding Mik.

Wren had wrestled her halfway to the room when Valeria's patience apparently ran out.

With a pop, the door unlocked, and the witches poured in, leaving Valeria to take up the rear, stepping inside delicately. They were quick, well trained.

They'd come expecting a fight.

It was too late for all of them, Joan had known that the moment she saw Valeria at the door. No rush into a bedroom was going to save them from her.

Joan planted her feet. "Aunt Val," she called. "What do you want?"

Valeria was in a green satin blouse and black slacks. Her witches blocked the hallway. Astoria had edged in front of Joan, who was in front of Wren, and while her sword hadn't been summoned yet, her hand was out like it could be at any moment.

"Mik Batbayar," Valeria said, in the most frigid of all her cold tones. "You've been called to face witch questioning."

Wren was solid at her back, her hand wrapped around her bicep, lending her strength. Joan could ask all the obvious questions: *How did you know we'd be here? Who told you about Mik?* But the answer was obvious.

Joan had cried *uncle*. Molly had still betrayed her. At the end of the day, for all her decency, Joan's sister was Merlin's favored daughter.

"They're sealed," Joan said. "And of no use to you. You know about Fiona?"

"We were informed," Valeria said, looking interestedly around the hotel room. "Your friend can come out of that room."

"You can't haul them in against their will," Joan said.

"They're a human, I can do anything I'd like," Valeria countered.

"You think they're a witch, which means they have the rights of a witch and deserve protection," Joan replied.

"So pedantic. Fine, then, they can come with us so we can protect them."

Valeria always came out on top.

"Don't do this," Joan begged.

"Or what," Valeria said, and there was a rare note of impatience to her tone. "This can happen by force or by choice, but it *will* happen. Mik *will* come with me to the Greenwood Mansion. We *will* locate Fiona. If you'd like, niece of mine, you can set aside your tantrum and accompany us to discuss what comes next. You may make your petition to me there."

"They're innocent in all this," Astoria said. "The spell was cast on them against their will, and they have no desire to live as a witch."

"If that's the case, they will have no problem saying as much at the house," Valeria said. She gestured at the bedroom door, and her five witches moved like a bunch of cartoon goons to storm it.

Astoria's sword materialized. "Back up, Greenwood," she murmured at Joan.

This morning she had said *Joan* with such a softness to it, but now she was back to *Greenwood*.

The witches slowed, looking nervously at fearsome Astoria Wardwell and the murderous look on her face.

"Do you really mean to swing that at us?" Valeria said. "New York would consider it an act of war."

"And what, California is meant to roll over and show you our belly when you storm unannounced into our hotel room?" Astoria threw back. "You mistake us for cowards."

"I make no mistakes here," Valeria said. "You must honestly know you don't have a chance. Your mother would more than support this move. But I'll show you mercy." She beckoned her witches back, and they moved toward her again.

"Children," she said dismissively. "All of you, children, an unlikely coven of spoiled, naive creatures. As I said, you're welcome to make your case at my home. You can meet us there."

Us? Joan had time to think, before Wren swore, and Valeria reached out, making some quick hand movements.

With a yelp, Mik appeared next to Valeria, drawn by the spell the High Witch of Manhattan had cast.

Valeria faced the room. "Come home, Joan," she said, and a portal shimmered to life behind her.

Joan lunged as Valeria unceremoniously pushed Mik through it. Lunged and hit an air barrier that one of Valeria's henchmen had cast before they all filed through. She rebounded back into Wren's arms, and though Astoria's sword slashed down in fury, shattering the spell, Valeria was too fast.

The portal closed, popping them out of existence, and the hotel room returned to silence.

Every time Joan thought they might be in a reprieve, the universe stepped on her neck. For two weeks, Mik falling back into the hands of either Fiona or the Greenwoods had been her biggest fear, and now it had come to pass.

Joan hadn't been tortured for two days for this. She had not nearly died to let this go.

"Portal me in," Joan said in a strangled voice. "Take me to the Greenwood Mansion."

THIRTY-THREE

Wren and Astoria both started channeling, though Astoria's hand drifted up to rest on the wound from Fiona's magic bomb.

She was too stoic to wince, but Joan knew what it was like to draw in magic on the heels of a magic poisoning—that had to hurt.

Still, Astoria did it.

And despite it all, it was Joan who stopped her, grabbing her arms to break her concentration.

"I have it solo," Wren said. "Let me do this."

"I can help—" Astoria started, looking over Joan at Wren. Seeing past Joan.

"You worry too much." Wren laughed, and though a full portal was a clear strain on her abilities, she brought it to life within seconds. She gestured through. "Let's go get Mik."

Joan, still dressed in baggy pajamas, snatched a flannel she was pretty sure was Mik's off the couch, before pulling it on over her shirt as she jumped through first.

The portal took them two blocks over from the house, unable to break through the wards on the Greenwood Mansion or its direct vicinity, so Joan took off at a run, barely checking to make sure Wren and Astoria were behind her, her body a rusty machine.

Her mind flashed through the possibilities. Would Mik be treated as a curious guest or chained to a chair? What damage could the Greenwoods have done in the mere minutes of a head start Valeria had gotten them? Maybe they'd already removed the seal and were trying to make Mik cast; maybe magic was ripping through them at this very moment.

Joan slapped the gate open, registering faintly that it did indeed still open for her, despite the way she'd left.

Come home, Valeria had said. How absurd. They genuinely thought it was a temper tantrum. They couldn't fathom Joan leaving. Meanwhile, Joan had never once imagined she'd be able to go back after an outburst like the one she'd had. She'd assumed her exile would be mutual, and absolute.

"Miss Joan!" George called in alarm from where he stood by Merlin's car. Returned by Molly. That traitor. If they'd touched a hair on Mik's head, Joan was going to bite her sister's arm off.

She stormed up the steps, the Californians hot on her trail, and shoved open the front doors in a huff, ignoring every cut and bruise that protested at the action.

The lobby looked the same as always: Every vase Joan had destroyed was back in its place, seamlessly put together. The rug was spotless. The chandelier looked fine. It was all the same, like Joan hadn't even been here at all, save the audience of witches.

The Greenwoods were assembled at the far side of the room, Molly included, a hand around her father's forearm, eyebrows slanted down. In front of them were important witches Joan recognized from various functions, the wealthy families that held sway. All the High Witches of New York's boroughs were in attendance.

The room moved in surprise when Joan burst in, the crowd going concave to whirl on her, scandalized.

"So glad you could join us," Valeria called. "We were getting started with our line of questioning."

Mik looked terrified, standing up there facing a horde of witches, disheveled from sleep, but they seemed unharmed. For now.

"How the hell do you know about Fiona, what she did to me, and still feel it's a priority to grill Mik for answers?" Joan said, furious, pushing her way to the front of the crowd.

"We will find Fiona too," Valeria said calmly. "I can walk and chew gum at the same time."

"This is a circus to reassure your loyal followers," Joan said, throwing a hand wide to the room. She knew her family's games; they moved in public to solidify their reign. It would be a good look, the Greenwoods bringing in Mik before a crowd so no one could deny they'd found them first. They were staking a flag on Mik's body. They were squashing rumors of Greenwood weakness that people like Janet Proctor were spreading.

"Our daughter isn't well," Merlin announced loudly to the room. "She was viciously attacked, first by Moon Creatures at the market, then by a rogue witch."

"I'll escort her up to her room," Selene said, holding out a hand for Joan to take.

Joan looked at it in disbelief. Then up at her parents, the warning glimmers in their eyes, the triumph in Merlin's.

This wasn't just about Mik; this was a trap her family had set for Joan too.

They really thought she was going to come back.

They really thought that she was that pathetic, that they meant *that much to her*, that the Greenwood name meant more than anything.

"If there was any chance of me returning, Molly shot it in the head the moment she snitched," Joan hissed. "Go all the way to hell."

Molly's face had gained a look of horror Joan hated with every fiber of her being. "I didn't tell them," she said. "Joan, you think I told them?"

They could all act, the whole lot of them—it was a Greenwood trait. *Us Greenwoods, we have a way with words*, and Joan had fallen for Molly's act hook, line, and sinker.

"No one's touching Mik," Joan said, whirling and backing up toward them. "I swear to the fucking gods."

"No one wants to hurt them, Joan," Merlin said, with a sympathetic glance shared with the crowd. *Kids, am I right?* it said. *So unreasonable.* Every action of Joan's painted her as someone who needed to go under a mental hold. Joan could see it clearly—they were paving the road for her to disappear from public life. A mental breakdown in front of a crowd before her family shipped her off to get help—it was better than everyone knowing Joan had, in full control of her faculties, cut her family off and worked directly against their interests.

Merlin reached for Joan and, in her stunned agitation, got his hand on her arm.

He pulled up short at the sword to his throat.

"You're not going to touch her," Astoria growled, and a hot wind kicked up around her. A sword to her father's throat. Astoria Wardwell had put a sword to Merlin Greenwood's throat in front of everyone. She was so screwed, oh gods. Joan had screwed her; the room's collective gasp was proof enough of that.

But Astoria's hand was steady as a surgeon's. "Hands off her, Merlin."

Merlin put his hands up slowly, an exaggerated movement he paired with a nonchalant smile, a charming laugh. "Come on, now," he said. "I'm trying to help. Don't you think this is inappropriate? You hardly know her."

Astoria didn't waver. Merlin took a step back, then two.

"Joan, I think I hate your family," Mik whispered at Joan's back, hand twisted in Joan's flannel.

"I didn't tell them," Molly repeated, looking shell-shocked. "I swear I didn't, they called me down minutes before you got here."

Astoria's hand came down, sword pointing at the floor. Her chest was heaving; Joan knew her well enough now to see the panic in her eyes. So many times she'd insisted none of them understood how unreasonable her mother was, and now Astoria had threatened a New York Greenwood. For them. For Joan.

"How do you think this plays out?" Valeria said. "You hold the whole room hostage so that, what, we cannot question one human? You are more than welcome to petition for Mik Batbayar's release, *after* questioning."

The room murmured in agreement, polished witches looking appalled by all these unhinged moves. Damn witches and their respectability politics, and damn Aunt Val for sounding so reasonable. Joan wasn't entirely sure what her plan was here; she'd only known Mik couldn't be here alone, that she couldn't let her family get to them. But what, she was going to fight her way out and go on the lam? What now? Whatever Joan chose, she had the strong feeling Wren and Astoria would back her up.

That was the most frightening thing that had ever happened to her.

"I think I should answer the questions," Mik said, low in Joan's ear. "I don't think we can hide things anymore. I'll answer, and it'll prove I'm innocent, and then we can all go."

As if a justice system had ever operated that easily. Humans were nothing to witches; they didn't have rights in this world. They could easily be swept under the rug, as could witches without powerful families behind them. Merlin would find a way to twist Mik's confession. He'd have all of them strung up for harboring Mik, even if technically it wasn't illegal to have done so.

He was the law.

When Joan defied him, she defied the law.

Joan opened her mouth to speak to the expectant room, unsure what she was even going to say, how she was going to spin her way out of this one.

Then the wards popped.

THIRTY-FOUR

They snuffed out like a set of birthday candles, extinguished all around the Greenwood estate. Joan saw the magical haze normally present on the walls vanish.

The panic was instantaneous.

This was not a room full of warriors; it was a room full of sniveling rich people. Someone screamed as they felt the magic disappear, and several raised their arms as if they might cast something but were unsure what.

Astoria had her sword out, facing the door, head on a swivel, Wren next to her, having manifested a knife.

"Stay behind us," Astoria murmured, and Joan reached back to find Mik already reaching for her.

Valeria was a thundercloud of wrath; she raised her arms, and magic shot to her like a meteor, amassing faster than Joan had ever seen, faster than she herself had ever managed to make it. The wards went back up an instant later.

"Too late," Valeria murmured to Merlin, who was partially behind Selene, like the stupid-ass coward he was. "They're on the property. Whoever this is, I've never seen magic like it."

George flickered into being in front of them. "Mr. Greenwood," he said rapidly. "There's a woman here. Based on the description Miss Joan gave Miss Molly in the car, I believe it may be Fiona Ganon, and she's being bolstered by some immense magic."

In the car?

In the car, yesterday?

George hadn't been in the car.

Joan turned to Molly.

Had he?

Molly reached out as if to throttle George, but her hands passed through his incorporeal form. "You were eavesdropping on us?"

The front doors, heavy and wooden and so old, splintered into a million pieces.

Valeria stepped in before they could pulverize anyone, pulling out her signature time magic to slow the trajectory of the wood, then tossing all the pieces to the side. "Enough!" she shouted, and strode forward. "Your dramatics bore me, Fiona."

Fiona ascended the front steps of the house and crossed the threshold like a biblical plague, all rage and horror. The wards blipped out again, the magic sucked directly into her body. She was channeling an unbelievable amount, her hair whipping around her face.

"Valeria Greenwood," Fiona announced, stepping into the house, her foot hitting the floor and causing the hardwood to fracture. "I invoke Scales Law."

Valeria's face was a masterclass in wrath. No one had dared challenge a Greenwood witch to a formal duel in two hundred years. No one did it unless they thought they could actually *win*.

Another step, more fractures in the floor. Fiona was venting magic like it was nothing, cycling it back in to keep it close. Joan could see it all in brutal clarity. Maybe if they'd tracked her down instead of going after Mik, Fiona wouldn't even have gotten a chance to do this. Maybe if they'd trusted Joan, followed her lead, Joan wouldn't be staring down the woman who had copied her magic.

"She crossed our wards uninvited," Merlin was hissing at Valeria. "You don't need to answer the challenge, you can have her tried on those grounds alone."

"And have everyone say I am too weak and old to lead? I am not afraid of Fiona Ganon," Valeria hissed back, stepping forward as she darted a glance at the audience.

No! Fear was a jolt through Joan. Valeria had underestimated Fiona over and over again; if she did it here, they'd all be in danger. They never should have gathered witches for the spectacle of Mik's trial in the first place. Now they were the jury analyzing Valeria for weakness.

Joan reached past Astoria to draw her aunt's attention over the din. No matter what idiocy her family had wrought, she still didn't want them to die.

"Listen to Dad," Joan urged. "She's boosted her power by experimenting on me, Aunt Val. Not only could she outspell you, if she sucks in enough magic, there won't be any left for you to work with."

Valeria dislodged her niece's hand. "I don't have a choice here, Joan."

"Of course you do," Joan argued. "She kidnapped and tortured me—she doesn't have the right to call a duel. You're Head Witch, you make the rules."

Valeria took another step forward. Her words were partly

snatched away by the roar of magic. "There are some forces even I bend to." She raised her voice. "I accept your challenge, Ganon."

Ego. Stupid *fucking* ego.

Fiona's grim satisfaction was more infuriating than any glee might have been. Still, with all this drama, Fiona believed what she was doing was righteous. A reluctant soldier forced to walk a specific path.

The audience scrambled to the edges of the room, leaving a gap at the center for Valeria to face down Fiona. Valeria flicked her fingers, and a white chalk circle appeared on the floor. Joan had seen a duel only once in her life, between two minor families. You could win by forcing your opponent out of bounds, forcing them to yield, or killing them.

So many witches specialized in a certain type of magic. Molly's was luck, Mik's was light, Astoria's was air and fire. Valeria was particularly adept at time magics, a powerful and tricky subspecialty that should have won her any duel.

Still, Joan wasn't sure that'd be enough. She was herded, helpless, to the sides of the room as Fiona and Valeria entered the circle. It seemed the witches around them were fully prepared to fall in line with tradition and see how things turned out.

"What happens now?" Mik whispered in Joan's ear.

"Challenger goes second," Wren said, grim. "So Valeria takes the first move. It's turn-based: One witch mounts an attack that the other can defend against and reroute into a counterattack, then they swap."

There was no telltale show to Valeria; this wasn't some grand performance for her. Every second was a dalliance she couldn't afford, one where people, some of the most influential people in New York, watched her take on an out-of-state witch from a no-name family.

Fiona shifted, and the floor cracked further under the force of her magic, but the cracks were a slow creep. Valeria's first strike was brutal, an opening offensive meant to end the game. With her right hand, she grabbed time within the circle, slowed it to a fraction of its creep. With her left she formed an offensive spell, blasting Fiona with a shock of air meant to fling her out of bounds.

Fiona didn't move. Joan's first thought was that she couldn't, not with time moving so slowly for her, but as Valeria's left-hand spell struck, it simply dissipated across Fiona's body, a sheen of energy that rippled with an icy-blue hue.

Fiona lifted her own hands, moving at normal speed, and the force of Valeria's spell sucked into her.

"What am I looking at?" Mik prompted, fingers digging into Joan's side.

The room seemed just as flabbergasted. *Valeria* seemed shocked, though she handled it better than everyone else, revealing it only in a pinching of her brows. The moment she dropped her time magic, her turn was over.

Wren was shaking her head in confusion. Fiona had performed no visible counterspell, and Valeria's attack had clearly hit her head-on. It was mind-boggling. Joan flitted through everything she knew about Fiona's magic.

Grace had told Joan about Fiona's specialty, once.

"Pocket realms," Joan said from numb lips. The crowd around her, friends and strangers alike, swung toward her. Now that Joan looked, she could see a faint dark blue glow hugging Fiona's body. "Fiona specializes in pocket realms. She's encased in one. She's nullifying attacks by changing the magical rules right outside her skin. Aunt Val's abilities will need to adjust to cross a minor realm wall to actually hit her, and it's a realm Fiona controls completely."

"Can your aunt do that?" Astoria murmured.

Joan, quite honestly, didn't know. Maybe before, Valeria could have outlasted Fiona's abilities. Eventually, her pocket realm would have dissolved without enough magic to sustain it. But Fiona had the thing on magical steroids.

Valeria dropped her ineffective time spell, and Fiona launched her attack with a rapid, explosive force. Her hands danced, cobbling together pieces of half-recognizable spells. A blue cube formed around Valeria, glitching for a second, then stabilizing.

It shrank.

Rapidly.

Threatening to crush the older woman in a pressurized mini-realm.

Valeria flung her arms out, slowed the spell's execution, and reversed it until it burst open again. Triumph lit her body language, but it was Fiona Joan was focused on. Fiona and the little upward tick to her lip.

She'd expected that.

Astoria tensed, right hand kneading into her left shoulder in the phantom hint of pain.

Joan wasn't a fan of her aunt at the moment, but she couldn't watch Fiona kill her. "The shards, Aunt Val!" Joan screamed.

Valeria's attention flickered up to the still-formed blue shards, fast enough to shield against the first five.

Not fast enough to protect herself from the one that tore through her knee, sending her to the ground with a cut-off cry of pain. The shards flickered in and out of being, like Fiona was struggling to control them, and her brow furrowed.

"How do we stop them?" Mik said desperately.

"That circle's lethal to anyone not in the duel," Wren said, flinching away from the sight of Valeria's blood pooling on the floor. They traded turns rapidly now, Fiona pounding her with pressurized spells that burst, folded, ripped Valeria apart, Valeria desperately trying anything she could to avert them and only barely surviving.

Against logic, Joan had hoped her aunt might still win. She'd always seemed infallible.

But hope was a lead balloon, and it crashed at Joan's feet. Valeria was outmatched in every way, against a spellmaker with greater casting knowledge than her, wielding an unbelievable amount of power. Joan didn't know what Fiona had done to circumvent magic poisoning.

Fuck the rules. Joan reached out to channel.

She'd flirted with her limits too many times already; the shock of agony cut off her concentration. She folded with a stifled groan.

Valeria was fading fast, bleeding from a couple dozen cuts. Fiona managed to catch Valeria's left hand in a cube and crush it, the bones cracking, before the box vanished. Fiona's hand was still outstretched to control that spell when it disappeared. She looked down on it in confusion. Valeria's response was a muffled whimper.

Molly had a hand over her mouth in horror. Selene had her face turned away, tears spilling down her cheeks. Merlin had his hands laced behind his head, pulling at his own hair, watching wide-eyed. None of them moved to do anything. There was nothing to do; no one could stop the magic of the duelers inside the circle. Merlin's lips were mouthing something, and Joan had to watch them for several long seconds to understand it.

Yield.

Yield, Valeria.

"You stubborn old goat," he whispered.

Mik's fingers left Joan's ribs.

The blue haze around Fiona dimmed; Joan was probably the only one in the room who could even see it unassisted. Fiona's next spell was a bit wild, zinging around the circle, a shard of magic even hitting Fiona, though her pocket realm shield dissolved it. She was breathing hard now, hair sweaty around her temples.

"Give in, damn you," Fiona growled. "You can't win."

Valeria responded with another time spell, using up a turn by casting on herself, turning back the clock on her hand so the bones knit together. "What have you done to yourself, Ganon? You aren't supposed to have this much magic."

Fiona's betraying glance was less than a second long, focused in on Joan. "I am *supposed* to have anything I'd like," she said, and summoned a massive lance of energy, drawing in what must have been all the immediate magic in the room to form it. She launched it, but the trailing edge of the spell was unfinished, still attracting more energy. Unable to draw from the air, it pulled from the barrier magic of the chalk circle, snuffing it out.

"Shield the crowd," Joan ordered, hand coming down on Astoria's shoulder. Bless the woman's quick reflexes, because she reached for magic, Joan could feel it, but she was as magic fatigued as Joan. Astoria winced as she started channeling what thin magic was left, and in that hesitation, Fiona's bomb exploded.

The force rushed past the barrier, slamming the crowd, pressing Valeria so hard into the ground, she cracked the floor. They all skidded back a few feet, but as Joan brought her hands up to protect her face, she found she was entirely intact.

There was only one person still standing in their original spot by the circle, fingers splayed wide, panting under the force of the yellow shield she'd thrown over everyone. Molly's hands dropped, her breaths wheezing. She was looking at her sister.

"I didn't tell them," she gasped out, and then fell to her knees.

Joan slid to the ground next to her, propping her sister up. "How the hell did you do that in time?"

Molly slumped into Joan's shoulder. "Luck," she said, with a little smile, and one of the charms on her necklace dissolved. "I heard what you said to Astoria."

Merlin roared, storming back up to the circle. "Ganon! Not another move until the magic barrier can be reestablished. You could have killed us."

Fiona's hands were shaking, but her magic channeling hadn't faltered. Still it rushed into her, building up in her body until she released it in these huge bursts. "Not my fault," she said. "Nothing against it in the rules."

Valeria wasn't moving. She lay in a pool of her own blood, skin a deathly blue, but the chalk remained even if the barrier spell was down, which meant she was still alive.

Her wife wasn't even in the room. If Valeria died right now, they wouldn't even get to say goodbye. Ronnie would have been somewhere outside this house, oblivious.

This couldn't be how Valeria Greenwood died, on her back in her own home, felled by someone wielding an imitation of Joan's own magic.

Fiona raised her hand for a last spell. "Who knew the answer was right in front of me, all these years," she said, eyes shining at Joan. "Cycle the magic, don't channel it; holding it in speeds up the poisoning. Use the pocket realms to reverse the laws of physics and protect your body from the aftereffects. Amplify your ability to channel and cycle so much magic, you can use it to heal yourself faster than you kill yourself."

Legs blocked Joan's view from the floor, Molly still limp in her hands. Astoria looked down at them. Her face was pained.

"You shouldn't watch," she said.

No. No way, this wasn't how things ended. Molly let out a low cry.

Despite everything, Joan tried again, reaching for magic, grimacing past the aches that rippled to life in her body as she tried to sink desperate fingernails in. Pull it all to herself.

But Fiona's grip on the room was stronger, smoother. Joan was scrabbling against a glass wall, fingers leaving nothing more than smudges.

"Move, Astoria," Joan ground out. She wasn't taking the coward's way out.

Astoria hesitated.

"*Move*, Wardwell," she screamed. Astoria stepped aside in time for Joan to see Fiona bring her hand down.

And then fall to her knees in a shatter of porcelain, spell aborted, hands clutching her head and coming away red.

Mik stood behind her, chest heaving, eyes crazed as they grabbed another vase and launched it at Fiona too. It shattered on the woman, stunning her further.

"You stupid bitch!" Mik was screaming. "You stupid fucking bitch, you can go to hell! You ruined my life!" They dashed for another vase. "You kidnapped my friend!" Fiona dodged this one. "I'm not letting you kill another person!"

Fiona had taken down the barrier spell and left herself open to outside interference.

Outside, nonmagical interference.

Mik was reaching for something new to throw, tears streaming from their eyes, when Fiona finally gathered her wits well enough to counterattack.

"You should have died," Fiona growled, and magic swelled in her again.

Joan screamed, so high that it was nearly soundless, unashamedly leaving Molly so that she could scramble across the floor to Mik, who had just saved Valeria's life. Mik, who had never deserved this and had no magic to protect themself. Mik, who really had to stop watching so much reality TV, and folded kitchen towels into squares, and laughed just to make everyone else laugh, and held the dreams of their parents in them.

A sizzle of magic streamed through the air.

Fiona's hands froze. She looked down in shock at the fried hole in her chest.

Valeria's eyes, already swelling, had cracked open. Her hand flopped to the floor.

Fiona's body toppled sideways, lifeless, and the chalk circle dissolved completely.

THIRTY-FIVE

~~~

Three more people clattered through the gaping hole where the front door had been in a rush, coming to a harried stop in the shell-shocked silence.

On the floor of the Greenwood Mansion, Fiona and Valeria both lay still. Joan's momentum pushed her up to her feet, dashing to Mik, who was standing on the other side of the room with a hand pressed to their chest, like they felt the same blow that had killed Fiona.

"Are you alright?" Joan asked, shaking them slightly. "Mik? Mik! I can't believe you."

Mik's eyes finally met Joan's, brimming over with tears. "Can't believe I started throwing things like a toddler?" they said weakly. Then they dissolved into sobs. Joan pulled them tight to her chest, and she was joined by another set of arms, CZ looking wild on her other side.

"You weren't at the hotel," CZ said. "You weren't at the hotel, you were all gone."

Grace put a hand on Joan's back; Joan knew it was her, even

without turning. She reached for her, and Grace laced her fingers with Joan's.

"Fiona…" Grace said dully. "She's…?"

Joan couldn't say it. She looked back at Grace, who was unable to look at the body, and Grace's lip wobbled before she bit down on it. For as much as Joan hated Fiona, she had been Grace's mentor. Fiona had people who, despite everything, would still mourn her.

"Sorry," Grace whispered, wiping her eyes with her free hand. "I should be glad."

An anguished cry made Joan turn.

Ronnie had arrived at the same time as Grace and CZ, her black hair wired through with gray. She had sunk to her knees over Valeria, and she shoved Merlin and his paltry healing spell aside, her hands lighting up an icy blue. "She needs a hospital," Ronnie said. "I can put her soul in stasis to keep the damage from progressing, but we must move her to a team of actual healers." She smoothed a tender hand across Valeria's hair. "Oh, my darling, what have you done?"

From the crowd, one or two people rushed over to Valeria, glowing with healing magic.

Merlin hovered nearby. "Come on, Val," he murmured. "You won, now get up."

Grace's brow furrowed as she looked at Ronnie, then Joan, then Ronnie. She blinked, and a gold film fuzzed over her eyes. "She pulls in magic like you, Joan."

Joan realized she'd never actually seen Ronnie cast. She tried to concentrate, see what Grace was seeing, but though Ronnie was alight with magic, she wasn't the only one.

Joan swore. "Grace, tell me you see what I see, on Fiona."

Grace's breathing went shallow. "She's still channeling."

One of Fiona's fingers twitched.

She was gaining strength every second.

A hand jerked.

"She was dead!" Joan said. "I saw. She stopped channeling for a moment. I felt it."

"A resurrection spell?" Grace said fearfully. "No one's ever successfully written one."

"No one had done what Fiona did to Mik," CZ said grimly. "Until Fiona."

Astoria's sword was out, pointing at Fiona's body as the other hand spasmed, then the arm. "Is it one and done?" she asked, and Joan knew with a horrifying finality that Astoria would do it, she'd go over there right now and kill Fiona a second time.

Grace was furiously trying to yank some magic to herself to cast. "I don't know, I don't know, I don't know. She's hooked to some huge power source, so as long as there's a link, it might keep regenerating her. Is it New York? Is it the same thing as Joan?"

The flesh on Fiona's chest began to knit together.

"How do we deplete it, then?" Astoria asked, voice gaining strength, so practical, a good man in a storm.

Grace burst out another desperate "*I don't know!*" Then: "I can't undo whatever spell she cast on herself to increase her channeling ability without *seeing* it first, and it's buried under layers of whatever else she has on."

Fiona's head twitched.

The moment she came back fully, she'd attack again, and this time, without the bounds of a duel, she'd go after the whole room. She had that ability, whatever she'd done to herself to boost her magic, to imitate Joan—

To be just like Joan…

Joan stepped forward, closer to Fiona. She'd seemed so unsteady during the fight, barely able to control her spells, like they weren't strong enough containers for her abilities. Whatever she'd done to herself, she hadn't had enough time to hone it. She was like Joan, channeling huge amounts of magic into flimsy spells one wrong move away from going berserk, like the paper ball Joan had made with Mik.

If she was like Joan, then she was channeling New York too, cycling magic so fast that she was sucking it from across the city, moving quantities so vast, it was like touching a live wire. Shielding herself with manipulated pocket realms to circumvent her body's inability to process that much magic. Maybe Fiona didn't even know about its sentience. Did it speak to her like it spoke to Joan?

The thought triggered a hot burst of jealousy. How dare Fiona use ancient magic for her own selfish, human desires, paying it no respect, offering it no sacrifice? Joan had nearly given it her life, time and time again. It was Joan's city. It was *hers* and it was alive.

New York was alive. It would be nearly impossible to deplete, as Astoria wanted to, which meant Fiona could resurrect again and again and again.

Fiona's eyes drifted open. Astoria must have noticed at the same time as Joan, because she brought her sword up, slashing down at the woman to kill her again, to gain them more time.

The sword clanged against a blue cube.

Fiona sat up, shaking her head, magic flowing toward her faster now as she sat protected by the spell she'd cast over herself.

Selene's voice rose. "Run! Out of the room, everyone get out of here!" All the faces were a smear as people began to stampede.

The Greenwoods were still huddled around Valeria, trying to keep her tethered to life with their tiny spells. Joan's friends remained at her back, but the rest of the room evacuated in a flood of rushing feet, including the two healers who had previously been trying to help Valeria.

Joan had to do something. She looked down at her hands. How? Fiona now had the ability to suck in endless magic, without the limits magic poisoning placed on her. Limits Joan herself faced. If only New York could turn its back on her, use its mind to deny her.

Joan's head snapped up.

Fiona was rising to her feet with a groan.

Joan had bargained with the city before. She'd told it not to kill Astoria, made it funnel into her, split it so Astoria wouldn't get overloaded. If it had a mind, maybe it could make a decision. She breathed in, winced. Fiona's grip was getting stronger, and Joan's toehold was closing. She had to think past the pain, channel harder.

She tried again, tasted blood in her mouth.

"Stop that," Astoria snapped, grabbing Joan's shoulder to spin her to face the group. "Why the hell are you trying to channel? You'll kill yourself; you can't take in as much magic as Fiona in your current state."

CZ's face lit up. "Grace can help! Grace—help?"

"I can!" Grace cried in a burst of inspiration. "We left this morning because I had an idea about magic poisoning, and I needed to go home to—whatever. I think I can help shield you from the effects."

"Fiona's using pocket realms," Joan said. "And cycling."

"It's a loophole," Grace said. "A way to dodge the effects by never letting magic accumulate in her body. It's half the puzzle. She was looking at humans for a reason. She looked at Joan for a reason. Humans naturally protect themselves from magic by possessing a sort of barrier; it's what makes them sick and keeps them from channeling. Joan demonstrated how to channel more magic—by having little to no barrier around her. Or, by having less of the thing that keeps humans from magic, she can draw in more magic. But it's true for the poisoning too—curing it isn't about the symptoms, it's about removing that which makes us resemble humans. Making us *less* human and *more* magic. And who are the only creatures truly immune to magic, who are essentially just figments of magic themselves, and so spells don't work on them?"

"Ghosts!" CZ helpfully supplied. He tilted his head conspiratorially. "She explained all this to me already, with Billy. Repeatedly, because my brain is small and I didn't totally follow how she arrived at her conclusions."

"So your intention is...?" Joan asked.

"To kill you, just a little."

"Absolutely not," Astoria said.

"If I untether her from life, temporarily, and slowly, controlled, we'll boost her channeling ability and lessen the friction between her body and magic," Grace insisted, eyes lit with a feverish light. "She'll become magic."

Did Joan want to die? No, not even a little. She remembered what it was like to die. She'd almost died at the Night Market and in Astoria's arms.

And each time the pain in her body had faded right before she passed out. Each time, she'd channeled even more magic.

She'd assumed it was shock, but what if it wasn't, what if Grace was *right*?

"Greenwoods," Fiona called. She laughed, stumbled sideways. "Greenwoods, your time is up."

"Do it, then," Joan said.

"You don't even know what Joan's plan is here," Astoria argued, as Grace started casting. "It's likely reckless—"

"And stupid," CZ added.

"And terrible." Mik sniffled.

"But she's gotten us this far," Grace finished, yanking magic to herself hand over fist as she struggled to gather enough to cast. "And it's controlled, meant to mimic the very specific window between being alive enough to channel and too dead to channel."

"Here," Wren said, stepping up, and she started channeling too, drawing in magic and feeding it to Grace. "Astoria, help us."

Astoria's face warred between obeying Wren and stopping Joan.

Wren, as always, won.

Astoria channeled, the three witches attracting enough magic to let Grace pull off her new spell.

Astoria coughed and spat a bloody globule on the floor.

Grace's spell settled on Joan like the closing of a casket. Joan lurched to her knees, gasping as her heart slowed, her vision dimmed.

A shard fractured off Fiona's cube, whizzed for the Greenwoods, and was only just thwarted by Selene, who nudged it off course.

No time, no time. Grace didn't quite seem finished, but it was good enough. Joan was dead *enough*, and she didn't want to die more, because, gods, her body was moving slow and sluggish, her thoughts were coming to a stop. Before she faded too far, Joan let her panic carry her. She pushed past her fading discomfort and reached for the heart of magic.

"Not yet!" Grace yelled, but Joan channeled, hard.

Grace's spell stopped, incomplete, as Joan took the magic from it, from the air. Astoria and Wren were forced to leave off as Joan gained strength.

Joan dug her fingernails into the wall of magic swirling around Fiona and ripped off a chunk. Then another. *I am alive.*

I'm still alive.

Her head split open with a headache; it hurt, still, even with Grace's spell, it still hurt so badly, but Joan kept enough strength to keep going. Furiously, she waded into the stream of magic Fiona was stealing.

Come to me instead, she thought at it.

It shuddered, this uncertain magic, and began to diverge.

Fiona turned on her, abandoning her attacks on Joan's family. "What are you doing?!" she yelled, and Joan doubled down, pulling more magic in. She needed enough to talk to New York, just a bit more.

Fiona threw a magical attack at Joan, but Astoria was there to slice it away with her sword.

"I have you," Astoria said. "Keep going."

Joan channeled harder, fighting for every inch of purchase, wearing her mental grasp down to bare, stubby finger bones. Every inch she gained over Fiona was a triumph. All the practice she'd had under Fiona's experiments prepared her for this moment, this fight.

This magic's mine, she wanted to say. *This magic is* me. *You will never beat me at it.*

Fiona's face transformed with panic as she fought back, trying to gather the magic into her lap, her only defense. "I'm so close," she said, voice muffled, echoing strangely in the back of Joan's head.

Magic gave way like the opening of a dam, diverting to Joan in full. Joan sucked it in, and relished the pain, and leaned into the burn, until she felt the city shift.

New York! she called. *I've come to strike a deal.*

THIRTY-SIX

Joan's body was very far away from her.

New York's eyes opened, peering down at her in sets of two, then four, then a million. In the room around her, Joan knew Fiona was still leeching enough of a thread to both launch attacks at Joan and keep her own defenses up. Joan didn't have much time before her concentration was inevitably disrupted and Fiona gained the upper hand.

I need you to cut off Fiona Ganon, Joan pleaded.

Why should we turn from one of you? magic whispered, dancing around Joan's body. *What right do you have that she does not? Magic belongs to all of Circe's children; that was decreed long ago, when we were set free and given many names, and fractured into many pieces with many minds, and over time allowed to come back together as one.*

That was a bit hard to reason with. How did you convince magic itself, which was an impartial force, that it should stop working with one witch?

Then dismantle the spell she cast on herself to increase her magic capacity, Joan asked. *She isn't meant to use that much magic, you can see it in her casting. She can barely control her spells.*

Again, Green Witch, magic said. *We ask, why?*

Why, why? Because Joan said so, but who was Joan to decide such a thing? No, no time for self-doubt. She had only her heart and her wants, great enough to encompass the world.

What can I give you in return? Joan asked desperately.

What needs do we have? We are endless, magic replied. Its attention was fading, Joan could see that. *We care not if one witch can or cannot maintain control over how much of us she consumes. She should only pray she keeps a tight enough grip.*

Joan knew that fight well. All her life she had been unable to cast precisely because her spells would always break, but Fiona had managed to scale her spells to match her power.

Or... had she? Joan didn't actually know if the spells were more powerful, or if Fiona was merely regulating how much magic she was putting into any given one, toeing the edge of what it could hold without actually bursting it.

So long as she kept a tight enough grip, magic obeyed her.

But what if Joan could overload her enough that Fiona was forced to put more magic than she'd intended into a spell that couldn't hold it? Would it go haywire, burst, and backfire? That would put everyone in the room in danger; magic wouldn't discriminate if Fiona cast something lethal, it would rip everyone to shreds. It was a recklessly stupid move, which Joan couldn't risk. She had limits. Like Grace said, all spells had limits.

Even the one Fiona must have cast on herself to mimic Joan.

New York, if you won't turn your back on Fiona, will you channel into me? Joan asked. *I will give you anything.*

Magic's laugh was the distant ringing of a thousand church bells. *Your fate is prewritten, Green Witch. We see it. In this half-formed state, your ancestors dream of you. The world waits; if you want it, take it*, it sang, and vanished.

Joan could feel it like a massive wave on the horizon, just out of reach. All she had to do was throw out a hand and take it.

A deep breath in.

Joan tunneled deep, deeper into herself than she'd ever gone before, deeper into magic, and when her muscles screamed at her, when her ribs squeezed, she took it gladly, she let it kill her, she let it twist her into something less human and turned the pain into more magic.

She reached, and New York met her.

Magic tore through her system, galloping with the force of ten thousand horses, sailing with the might of a thousand ships, but Joan needed to hold on only long enough to do what she'd once done with Grace.

Grace's spell on Joan failed under the onslaught. Her heartbeat resumed a normal speed; her vision cleared. Magic turned to poison within her, wrapping like a serpent around her organs and squeezing, hard. But it was all a trick, because whether she died for a second by Grace's hand or she died under the magic, she was still untethering herself from this mortal realm.

Legs, I have legs. I need them. She searched for her body, plunging back into it. Magic sparked off her like an electrical fire. Joan pushed past Astoria and her startled protest. Fiona's projectiles shattered off the surge of power surrounding Joan. The woman's eyes were wide, furious, as Joan lunged for her, and her magic overloaded Fiona's barrier spell and fried the cube, taking it down, and Joan reached out, grabbing Fiona's face in her hands.

"I'm really sorry," Joan breathed, lips trailing magic in a fine green mist. "I'm only righting the scales."

She poured every ounce of magic she had into Fiona. Far beyond what Fiona had been channeling, far beyond what should have been in that one room. Joan pulled on all of New York, wiping out magic across the city as she drowned and drowned and drowned Fiona.

And Fiona, in all her greed, in all her stupidity, took it in.

"You ignorant girl," Fiona said, hands coming up to secure Joan's hands to her own face, sucking it in greedily. "What are you playing at?"

Joan kept going, stretching the limits, until she reached out of the city, her hands claws that raked across the state.

Fiona's face shifted in increments, from triumph, to confusion, to, finally, fear. Her hands dug into Joan's now, trying to pry them off, but magic glued them together, and Joan was as endless as the earth. She pushed harder, her vision doubling, tripling.

Not yet, not yet.

Not until— Then she felt it.

Something in Fiona popped.

Whatever spell she'd come up with to channel like Joan disintegrated, and without it, her pocket realm magic, the healing she was doing on herself, flickered and faded out. Fiona's tolerance tanked, wounds blooming like roses across her body. Red clouded her eyes; blood leaked from her nose. If Grace was right, there would be a small window between death making her more tolerant to magic and the magic killing her. Joan needed to surpass that window.

But right in that moment, Joan's own window closed. She tipped too far, and her vision blacked out completely. And she felt it; her heart paused on the edge of too long. She let go of magic with a gasp.

Fiona shoved her away, sending her flying in a magical burst that threw Joan into Astoria's waiting arms.

Fiona let out a wordless scream. "What did you do?"

Joan's legs were jelly, her breath wheezes. Astoria's arms were a protective cage around her. She whispered words of healing in her ear, and Joan's heart began to stabilize. *Don't die*, she sternly told herself. *Live. Live even though it hurts more than dying.*

"I bargained with New York," Joan said.

Fiona's face creased in confusion. "New York?"

She was lit up like a firework, staggering as her body overloaded with magic. She needed to let it out, fast, but the moment she did, she'd be back on everyone else's level, and someone like Astoria could subdue her.

Fiona's eyes darted around, and magic trailed between her and Joan, disintegrating, but in that connection, Joan could feel the edge of Fiona's thoughts.

I'm too close to fail. She tripped back, barely staying on her feet as blood sprayed from her nose. *They don't know what's coming for this city.*

I almost had it.

Almost.

Fiona's trembling body stabilized slightly. No, no no no. The window. She looked up, past Joan.

Grace. I'm sorry.

"Just let it out!" Grace shouted. "Fiona, you don't have to do this! Please, release the magic!"

But Fiona's face was defiant. "If I go down," she said around a mouthful of blood, "the Greenwoods go down with me."

There was no spell on earth powerful enough to contain that amount of magic; if she released it into a spell, it wouldn't explode as normal. It would turn Manhattan into a crater.

Did she know that?

Fiona's eyes were alight. "Grace," she said, "don't let them do to you what they did to me."

She must not *know*, or she wouldn't risk Grace like that. Still she thought she had the upper hand here, that she could control the magic.

Fiona released the spell.

It swirled as intended for one second.

Then it broke, magic losing its confines to expand out of control.

For the first time, Joan saw regret on Fiona's face. She was still staring at Grace; Fiona's hand came up like she could cancel the spell in time.

Joan knew better. She threw her hands wide, imagining a ring around Fiona. Magic nullification, Grace had said, that was what Joan was good for.

That was something she was willing to die for outright.

Fiona's spell incinerated the woman, turning her to dust, but where it stretched beyond the mental circle of chalk Joan had drawn, Joan sucked it in, nullifying the spell and releasing it instantaneously back into the air. But it was so much, and Joan knew this time she wasn't going to be able to gather it all.

She was going to fail.

Everyone, everyone she loved.

Joan gasped, tears filling her eyes. *Please.*

The air superheated, her friends crying out and shying away from Fiona.

Green Witch, New York said with some begrudging admiration. *You have proven yourself beyond death.*

A pause.

This, and this alone, we will aid you with at no cost.

The room shivered with power. The pressure lifted off Joan. Magic swept through her cleanly, dispersing neatly, defanged, into the world.

A hole opened in the Greenwood Mansion's ceiling. The debris rained down in the circle where Fiona had stood but disintegrated under the force of the magic trapped inside Joan's barrier.

Joan held on, magic tumbling through her painlessly, until the light began to fade, until the magic turned sluggish, until there was nothing left to channel.

She held on long after all the magic had died out, and the room had settled, and everyone started murmuring to one another to check that they were still alive. She'd have held on until the end of time, if it meant keeping everyone safe. Even as her lungs heaved, and her vision faded, and her ears rang with the rush of her own blood.

Joan kept at it until CZ stepped in front of her to fold her shaking fingers into his own fists.

"You can stop," he said gently. "Joan, we're all safe."

She looked into his eyes. He nodded encouragingly.

Only then did she let go.

THIRTY-SEVEN

Ash drifted like snow, down through the hole in the ceiling, raining on the people still inside.

CZ's grip on Joan's hands was firm. They all coughed in the dust, taking stock of one another. Joan, alive. Grace, Mik, Wren, alive. Astoria, gray with ash, but alive. CZ, as alive as he ever was.

And Joan's family, covered in Valeria's blood, with Ronnie holding Valeria in her lap, and Molly sitting next to them, shuddering, and Merlin and Selene standing over them all.

Valeria was blinking slowly, lips ashen.

Merlin let out a disbelieving breath, "Joan, that was—"

"Incredible," Selene finished. "We didn't know you could do that."

"She tried to tell you," Molly said. "At the hospital, she tried."

Ronnie's eerie blue eyes unnerved Joan, though the woman was silent, only clutching Valeria to her, both of them still shrouded in Ronnie's stasis magic.

Merlin brushed the dirt from his shirt, stepped closer.

Joan's step back was involuntary. The way her friends shifted closer to her, she knew, was not.

Merlin didn't seem to care; he was turning, inspecting the ceiling. "The Greenwoods come out on top again," he said with a little laugh. He laughed harder. Cleared his throat. Transitioned in an instant from grateful relief to something more businesslike.

"Valeria needs a hospital. In the interim we'll need to make some sort of public statement. Joan, everyone will want to talk to you about what you did, so we'll move into one of the other properties and make it our home base."

"This guy really doesn't change, does he?" CZ muttered.

"Dickbag," Astoria said firmly.

CZ looked at her in delight. "You listened to me!"

"I'm not giving any sort of statement or talking to anyone," Joan said over them.

Merlin had fished his phone out of his pocket and was texting. "I'll help you prepare what you'll say," he said, tapping away.

He had never understood *no*. That had always killed Joan—how did you fight against someone who just kept going? "Dad," Joan said. "I left this house and this family. I will not do it."

Merlin jammed his phone back in his pocket, and Joan could already see the argument stretching out in front of her. The same as it always was. But this wasn't Joan posturing; she was not like her father.

Merlin was cut off by Valeria's weak voice. "Listen to her, Merl," she said, struggling to sit up with copious aid from Ronnie and several admonishments. "I think she's serious this time."

"She can't be serious, that's ludicrous," Merlin said, arguing with his half corpse of a sister. "She can't leave, she knows too much. She's...she's *my* daughter. What would it look like if—"

"I will destroy this family before I come back here," Joan said. "Call my bluff, Dad."

Selene sat down on the floor, suddenly weary. "I can't believe you," she whispered. "You...how do you walk away?" She looked up, something strange in her eyes. "Is it really possible to walk away?"

Merlin was struck speechless.

Valeria drew in an unsteady breath. "Well, then. I suppose we will have to choose another path."

"Like?" Joan was shaking with rage and fatigue. She'd saved their miserable lives, and they were still going to end up on top, and the magic world would still keep wheeling on.

"You will no longer appear as part of the Greenwoods," Valeria said, focused entirely on Joan, the ends of her hair red and clumped with blood. "You will reside in the city, still, so no one thinks a major rift has formed in the family. Only that you made a personal choice to shift residences."

"I'm not going to play your stupid games," Joan said impatiently.

"We will not bother you," Valeria said, louder. "You will not join any rebellions against this family, and you will stick to whatever story we come up with to explain today's events."

"Aunt Val—"

"*Listen*, Joan, for Circe's sake, *listen* for once," Valeria snapped. "In exchange, we will not, in any way, shape, or form, go after or otherwise harass Mik Batbayar, Grace Collins, CZ LaMorte, or either of the Californians you seem to have befriended. We will pretend that your involvement never happened. None of you will ever speak of it—not even you, Wardwell. And Grace, you will not complete the spell on Mik and disseminate it." She heaved a breath. "Do we have a deal?"

Joan's silence in exchange for the safety of her friends. She barely had to think about it, but it wasn't just her silence she was promising. She looked around at her friends. No one contradicted Joan's aunt. The message from them was clear: *Your choice.*

"I won't blame Moon Creatures," Joan said, finding strength. "For this or the market."

"Fine," Valeria said.

"And you'll pay reparations to them, the ones whose market stalls you destroyed. You'll cover their lost wages, out of the Greenwoods' personal coffers," she added.

"This is ridiculous," Merlin said, throwing up a hand.

"And you will never again violate the sovereignty of the Moon Creatures by pushing into our territory and conducting a raid without permission from our individual governing bodies," CZ said firmly.

Merlin's face was the perfect picture of disgust. "We're never agreeing to this. Where do you even intend to go, Joan?"

"She's coming home with me," Grace said, stubborn chin held high. She addressed Joan: "Brooklyn is farther away from your family than CZ's place in Hell's Kitchen. One of my rooms is yours, if you want it."

Joan did want it. Badly. She wanted it more than she'd realized until right this moment. A quiet life in Bay Ridge with Grace and her enigmatic ghost roommate. She'd willingly get scared by Billy every day for the rest of forever for that privilege. She was too choked up to speak, so she only nodded at the offer.

"And Mik," Grace said, "the last room's yours, if you want it."

Mik, much less restrained, threw their arms around Grace, knocking the wind out of her. "Thank god," they said. "I was worried I was about to get left behind."

Grace hugged Mik back. "Never."

"Touching as this is, the point remains that we will certainly not be funneling money into the hands of vampires and fae," Merlin said. "All magical creatures fall under the Greenwoods' jurisdiction; there is no sovereignty to violate."

"Then you don't have a deal," Joan replied. "Astoria gets to go home and tell her mother all about how the Greenwoods nearly crumbled today and what she saw of Fiona's spell before we sealed Mik and Fiona eviscerated herself. CZ tells his parents, Grace finishes the work, and I tell everyone I can find every last dirty Greenwood secret." Abel had already asked for them.

"My mother will love this," Astoria said helpfully. "I can call her right now."

"I'm not going to negotiate with the lot of you," Merlin snarled.

"Then it's a good thing you aren't the one in charge here," CZ said.

"Dickbag," Mik chimed in. The room looked at them, and they held up their hands. "Sorry, got carried away, still not super fluent in magic-world etiquette."

Joan smothered a smile. "We're talking to Valeria."

Valeria's soft laugh cut the tension in the room before Merlin could go on. "You're a Greenwood to your core, Joan. You can leave us, but we'll never leave you," she said, and before Joan could find some way to violently refute that statement, Valeria seemed to decide something.

"I know you all think I'm unreasonable," she said. "But ruling isn't as easy as you think. You make tough decisions to protect people. I did not enjoy invading the market."

"Too little, too late," CZ snarled, his canines flashing.

Valeria sighed. "You have a deal. We'll be in touch with your family, LaMorte, along with the other leaders among the Moon Creatures, to discuss payment for those displaced."

Merlin started turning quite red in the face.

"Quiet, Merlin," Valeria said, groaning softly as she tried to sit up better. "They have us beat. We're in a precarious position, and they could ruin the family. Now everyone look away—I've nearly died, and I'd like to kiss my wife."

In the aftermath of that acquiescence, the group bumbled around for a few seconds, bumping into one another as they navigated the torn-up floor to flee before Valeria could change her mind.

Joan turned at the Greenwood threshold, looking back at her family trying to piece themselves back together. They'd be alright; they'd live. Molly met her eyes. Put her hand to her ear in the universal symbol for *call me*.

Joan smiled back.

THIRTY-EIGHT

~~~

Mik burst into giggles the moment the group hit the street.

"Is this a trauma response?" Astoria asked dryly.

"Definitely," Mik said. "I feel like we got away with murder."

Grace winced.

Mik's giggles ended. "I meant that as a figure of speech! I'm so sorry! Too soon, too soon."

CZ's arm brushed against Grace's with every step. She didn't move away from him. In fact, she leaned her head briefly on his shoulder.

"I'm not going to mourn a terrible person," she said, though she didn't sound that convincing.

"She was…" Joan swallowed hard. "She cared about you. That was always clear to me."

Grace lifted her head. "I don't think we should tell anyone that getting close to dying makes you temporarily more powerful. I think Fiona had the right question and the wrong answer. The magic world is unfair, but gaining more power to ascend its ranks isn't the way to go. You don't fight to overcome magic poisoning;

it's there for a reason. To protect us." She looked at each of them, swallowed hard. "You find a way to undo the system, a kinder way to live, and when you gather together, maybe then the world changes."

Joan sniffled pathetically. "Does this mean you're not hightailing it out of the witch world and leaving spellmaking behind?"

Grace scowled at her. "Let's take things one step at a time. I might consider keeping up with my spellmaking, carving a place for myself like you have—Joan, wipe that smile off your face—but not for any single High Witch, and still in tandem with my day job in the human world. And I hope I never have to use my death spell on you again."

Joan had no intention of poisoning herself again or slowly shuffling off her mortal coil, but she also suspected that talking to New York was a privilege she wasn't going to let go of lightly.

She smiled sweetly at Grace, who rolled her eyes. "Rascal," Grace said.

"I'm good, right?" Mik said suddenly. The group swung to look at them. "I mean...the sealing spell. I'll be good forever?"

"You should be," Grace said. "We could look into why Fiona's spell worked on you, at least partly, but to do that, I might need to undo the seal."

"No thanks," Mik said, swinging their head wildly. "Nope."

"Fiona's theory was that you have some sort of fairly recent witch ancestry that made you friendlier to magic," Joan piped up. "Oh! You said your grandmother made the hens lay good eggs. Maybe she had a little something to her she never told you about."

"That was a joke," Mik said. Paused. "Unless...? She did have double-yolk eggs all the time."

"Case closed," CZ said. "Though I suspect someone's going to find some way to recreate that aspect of Fiona's work eventually. Some sort of spell that'll at least make it possible for those with chicken-raising witch grandmothers but who aren't born with magic to gain it. Or people like Grace's mother."

Grace sighed. "It never ends."

They were two blocks away from the house when Joan realized Astoria and Wren had drifted behind the group. Joan slowed, waiting for them, a sinking feeling in her gut.

She turned to walk backward, confident she was going to trip over something shortly, but even more confident someone would catch her.

"You're leaving, aren't you?"

Astoria and Wren exchanged glances, and whatever they decided there, it was Wren who spoke. "Poppy's going to recall us the moment she hears the Greenwoods are closing the case on Mik. We'll have to come up with something to tell her, and it looks more suspicious if we hang around until she forces us to return, rather than rush back willingly."

"You'll lie?" Joan said.

"That's what the deal with your aunt required, isn't it?" Astoria said. Joan couldn't read her tone. Maybe she was projecting the bitterness in it.

"I appreciate you doing so to protect Mik," Joan said.

"To protect all of you," Wren added warmly. "All of *us*."

Joan couldn't help the way she looked to Astoria, though Astoria wouldn't look back.

Joan glanced at her constantly over the rest of the journey back to the hotel to pack up Mik's things. They parted at the door, the New York group heading back to CZ's place to grab Joan's belongings before they went to Brooklyn, where they'd help Mik figure out how to reemerge in the world after going missing for two weeks. Joan suspected her family would want to weigh in on that one.

Joan was the last one out the door after some surprisingly tearful goodbyes were shed. She'd gained Wren's number, promising to text her and go out to California sometime. Her friends were down the hallway, heading to the elevator, and Wren, with a knowing smile, stepped back into the room to give Joan and Astoria a last moment alone.

Joan didn't know what to say, staring Astoria down in the doorway. They were both filthy and scratched up. Against all reason, Joan still thought Astoria was the most beautiful woman she'd ever seen. She wanted to say something. Needed to. A real goodbye. But she feared if she opened her mouth, she'd embarrass herself by crying.

How to say *I wish I'd never met you, and I'm so glad I did*? How to say *I am going to think of you often and wish that I didn't*? How to ask her to stay, here, in New York? All of that was too much and not enough. Joan's mouth was always running a mile a minute, but here it failed her.

Astoria's thumb brushed Joan's cheek, wiping away a tear, so tender, with such care. Joan swallowed, hard.

"I meant what I said," Astoria whispered, and that hand withdrew.

Joan could think of only one thing she might mean.

There's a version of me somewhere who kissed you back.

Joan sniffled, wiped her tears away herself. "If you ever find her, call me."

She turned so she didn't have to see the woman's response, half raising her hand in a wave.

Down the hallway, Joan's friends waited for her, having let an elevator pass to call a new one. Their faces were sympathetic. CZ held an arm out to fold Joan in, hugging her tight. Mercifully, they did not say more.

Mik cracked a joke about the dirt they were tracking everywhere. Joan could see her future here among them, bright and endless, with room to grow into whoever she was without her family squashing her smaller. She turned as the elevator doors closed.

Astoria was still standing in her doorway, watching them move down the hall, until they vanished from sight. Until someone left someone else behind.

EPILOGUE

The abandoned subway station had been strongly spelled to ward off intruders, but in the coming days, the Greenwood family would crack it open like an egg and scoop out its double-yolk insides.

Fiona Ganon had left nothing of major importance there: Some books she owned or had stolen from various places. Empty bottles of cold brew. The mysterious glass-shard remains of something that looked rather like a snow globe.

They wiped Joan's blood from the scene, incinerated the rest.

But they never found the backpack she'd taken with her when she left Joan with a bomb around her neck.

A ghost with hawk-shaped eyes watched it sink, weighed down with heavy rocks, to the bottom of the Hudson. Billy had seen this coming, at least a flash of it, the remnants of her own magic giving her that much. These days she relied on her memory to know the future, but sometimes the universe still threw her a vision.

Fiona's research had gone deeper than they would ever know.

Water would pour in and destroy the papers, the journal, the scribbles, the passage about the end of an empire, stars crashing to earth, in a book of myths tracing back the lineage of witches.

Dead gods? Two years had been written and circled a few times. Billy had waited centuries, clinging to this half life and her mother's secrets, and still it wasn't enough time. Two more years until the anniversary of the Bind came again, and Billy learned if her vision would come to pass. Two years until the sweet, sorrowful end of Billy's afterlife.

The end of Joan, really.

Billy waited for the last bubble to emerge before she turned away. She couldn't do much to protect Joan from what was coming, but she could give her a bit more time to live obliviously. That was the greatest mercy she could offer.

She didn't know if it would doom them all. That was up to other fates.

Two years.

New York was opening ancient eyes.

They merely had to give her time.

The story continues in . . .

Book Two of the Green Witch Cycle

Acknowledgments

Joan would probably find it very easy to write these acknowledgments, because she is a person overflowing with emotion. One who isn't afraid to express it. I am a bit more guarded, but if there was ever a time to be sentimental, it would be writing the acknowledgments for my debut novel.

Many thanks to the boss, James McGowan—sometimes you're lucky enough that your agent is one of the best in the biz. I queried you on a whim and you dropped everything to read this book. Your enthusiasm breathed life into my publishing aspirations at a time when I was at my lowest. For that, my gratitude is unending.

Alyea Canada, my editor extraordinaire, gently told me I couldn't name the HERMES system the "witch subway" and had to get a bit more creative. I am always more creative at your prompting, and much of the texture of this book and world are due to you. Many thanks also to Jenni Hill, who saw the vision for bringing this book to the UK and made us global.

Indeed, the entire Orbit team has touched this book, and me, in immeasurable ways. Thank you to Rachel, Manu, Xian,

Bryn, Lauren, and the rest of the art, design, and production teams; thank you extra to Steph for my lovely cover and for putting up with all my tweaks; Natassja, Kayleigh, Angela, and the entire publicity, marketing, and sales team, every sales rep who advocated for me, every internal reader who built the buzz, and especially any and all assistants.

Thank you to readers everywhere! I don't know you yet, but I think we're going to have a great time together.

The Green Witch Cycle has been with me for at least six years now, so thank you to the agents and friends and writers and strangers who have seen it evolve and supported me. Those six years are only a portion of the decade I spent writing seriously in the hopes of publication, and they were filled with incredible highs and some very discouraging lows. The highs were brief, delirious, unreal. They fade in my memory, but I remember the lows with much more clarity. The despair, the waning hope, the insecurity. In these darker times, I pulled the Raft from the depths of the publishing ocean.

S. Hati, O. O. Sangoyomi, Casey Colaine, Amanda Helms, Sam Bansil, Shay Kauwe—I picked you up one by one by one. Each of you changed me with your writing. You shifted the axis of my life so profoundly, taught me lessons about mentorship and friendship and perseverance that challenged me, and encouraged me to be a better writer and person. Without that support, I doubt I'd have had the confidence to write this book. So, I gave this book to you.

And lastly, I keep my writing private from my family and most of my friends with one notable exception—Scrap. When I had to come up with the plot of this book, it was you who sat with me in front of a whiteboard. You're the one who wrote "homoerotic besties" on a sticky note and slapped it up there, giving me the guiding light for Joan and CZ. We have argued over my writing so many times, but you keep offering yourself as my first reader. That is one of my favorite ways you love me—by showing up for me even when you know we'll disagree.

If only all the world could be as lucky as I am.

extras

orbit-books.co.uk

about the author

AM Kvita is a speculative fiction writer, artist, and world maker who writes about restless gods and, if you're lucky, kissing. When they're not writing, they're usually loudly lamenting the state of their garden. You can find them online at amkvita.com.

Find out more about AM Kvita and other Orbit authors by registering for the free monthly newsletter at orbit-books.co.uk.

if you enjoyed

AN UNLIKELY COVEN

look out for

CITY OF OTHERS

City of Others: Book One

by

Jared Poon

*In the sunny city of Singapore, the government takes
care of everything – even the weird stuff.*

*Benjamin Toh is an overworked and underpaid middle
manager in a government department tasked with keeping the
supernatural population of Singapore happy and out of sight.*

*But when an entire housing estate glitches out of existence on what
was meant to be a routine check-in, Ben has to scramble to keep
things under control and stop the rest of the city from following
in its wake. He may not have the budget or the bandwidth, but
he has the best – if highly irregular – team to help him. Together,
they'll traverse secret shadow markets, scale skyscrapers and maybe
even go to the stars, all so they can just do their goddamn job.*

CHAPTER ONE

So there I was in the office, processing paperwork to register a batch of undead ducklings.

Four of the yellow fluffballs crowded the scarred table in front of me, the glint of malevolent intelligence in their beady eyes the only clue that they'd been raised through black magic to serve as familiars. Three were angrily testing the boundaries of the ward circle that kept them penned in, while the fourth fought valiantly to stay awake. None of them were having much success.

Across the table, Seng—short for Chong Jun Seng— watched me, smiling with irritating familiarity. He was a licensed necromancer and the CEO of one of the largest funeral services companies in the country, distractingly handsome, with the slight build and fine, classic features you'd expect from a leading man in a period drama. His charcoal suit and gold watch probably cost more than several months of my salary, their quality a sharp contrast to the worn-out conference room with its wheezing air conditioning and herd of broken office chairs in a corner. New money juxtaposed against the miserly prudence of the Singapore public service.

"Seng," I said, clicking through the Ministry's slow, outdated form system on my laptop and consciously unclenching my jaw. "You can't just walk in here. Appointments exist."

"Come on, Ben," he said. "Friends, right? Us against the world and all that."

Friends. That word. Our families had been neighbours and we'd played together as kids, gone to the same primary school. Back then, he'd made me help him with the most random things. Mosquito bites. Maths homework. Rehearsing talking to a girl he liked. Having his back when he—

I didn't want to think about that right now.

Later, we even served in the same unit in the army. Since then, we had drifted apart, perhaps because of his not-fully-legal use of necromancy to build his fortune, perhaps because that was just what happened to adults. You lose friends, to death or to life.

I hadn't heard from him in years, but some things, it seemed, hadn't changed. He was still making me fix his messes.

And this time, the mess was four baby birds giving me the stink eye.

The ducklings had apparently come to the conclusion that I was responsible for their predicament and were glaring at me with seething fury from inside the hastily drawn boundary of the ward. One of them was obviously trying to memorise my face for later revenge. Even the sleepy one was trying to join in, but its head kept drooping mid-glare, only to snap back up with a stiffness that didn't seem quite natural.

I ignored them the same way I was intently ignoring the notifications blinking in the corner of my screen—colleagues from my other meeting, I assumed, frantically messaging to ask why I wasn't there. But I couldn't very well leave Seng wandering around here unsupervised with this cargo.

"So, let me get this straight." I squinted at the screen and navigated yet another sluggish drop-down menu. "You want to transfer ownership of these... What are they even?"

"*Toyols*, technically," Seng said. "Used to be made from human fetuses, but I don't do those these days. Ethics and all that. Ducks are more loyal, anyhow. If you want, I can—"

"You're probably thinking of geese. Titus Livius actually credits them for saving Rome from the Gauls—which is apocryphal, obviously, but... You know what, it doesn't matter. You want to give these toyols to your nephew so he can... impress some girl?"

"It's not just *some* girl. Her family's important. Powerful."

"And you thought a set of postmortem poultry was the solution."

"The family," Seng said, glancing away as if embarrassed. "They're *jinn*. Wei Jie's got nothing compared to them. And her family..." He hesitated. "They're already talking about forbidding the match."

Of course. The jinn were big players, notoriously mercenary in all their dealings. I could see why they'd not approve of one of their own hooking up with some human nobody, and why Seng might have thought that a retinue of toyol servants would give his nephew some supernatural cachet.

And I could see why Seng would want this. A connection like this could mean security, legitimacy, maybe even a little respect. For Seng, these were worth almost anything.

I set my laptop aside and took off my glasses, already feeling the beginnings of a headache. "Look, I can do the paperwork to make sure these get proper IDs. The permits should come in within a couple of weeks. I can help you with the transfer forms after that, but I'm really not sure saddling the kid with zombie ducks is the way to go. Please tell me you asked him."

"No, but—"

Of course not.

"Listen." I slid my glasses back on. "This isn't going to solve your problem anyway. You think the jinn family is going to respect your nephew just because he's got a bit of power from his uncle?"

Seng started to argue, but I held up a hand to stop him. "And you know what's likely to happen? Wei Jie is going to do something stupid with these things—blow shit up or demonstrate his love or even worse. You remember what idiots we were back when we were teenagers. Someone's going to get hurt—maybe the jinn girl—and then the family will escalate, and then my Ministry will have to get involved, and then it'll end up on my desk next week as some sort of diplomatic incident."

I sighed, softened at the look on his face. The confidence he always wore like armour—it was cracked at the edges. He had looked like this, that one day when we were thirteen. He'd asked me for help then, too.

"Look," I said. "What we . . . what you need to do is have a little faith. Let the kids work it out themselves. In the meanwhile, I can reach out to the jinn side, see if there's a way to nudge them in the right direction. It's way above my pay grade, but I'll see what I can do."

Seng's shoulders relaxed a fraction, and he gave me a small smile. "I knew you'd come through for me."

"I haven't come through yet," I said.

"You always do, Ben. I don't know what I would do without you."

And there it was. He'd been saying versions of that since we were kids. Most of the time, I'd indeed come through for him. But we both remembered the one time I didn't.

He'd forgiven me. I hadn't.

Seng left without looking back, taking the ducklings with him. As the door clicked shut, I wiped the ward circle from the table and slumped back in my chair, a familiar tug of resentment twisting in my chest. It was a sharp-edged feeling, a thorned weed I had to burn out before it took root.

Seng shouldn't have put this on me. But he also knew I couldn't turn him away.

So that was one more thing on my plate. I eyed my laptop screen, the accusing blink of notifications, the column of tiny red flags marking out emails I needed to respond to today. A few from the Strategic Planning team, requesting inputs on the workplan slides and how our projects for the next year would fit into the key pillars of the Ministry's work. A couple from the Heritage Sites division, who were in charge of this year's Ministry-wide Sports Day, asking me to make sure the team signed up. More from our PS and DS—Permanent Secretary and Deputy Secretary, the head honchos around here—with PDFs of articles on psychology or philosophy or leadership they thought we should read. One from Rebecca, my boss, asking about the status of this email update I'd been working on.

I felt my headache get worse. The update was our quarterly report to the Minister, who for all intents and purposes seemed like a very nice, very reasonable man. The problem was that Rebecca was his gatekeeper, convinced that he would be scarred by any contact with inconsistently indented paragraphs, the active voice, or reality. We were now on our fifth round of edits, each iteration improving in elegance of phrasing but diminishing in actual content.

I thought I could catch the tail end of the meeting I'd missed, so I could at least know what next steps they'd agreed to. Then I could get those edits for the update to Minister done in an hour or so. After that, if I skipped lunch and really focused, I might be able to give everyone the replies and inputs they needed by five. Then I'd have the last part of the day to do the part of my job I actually cared about—what I'd done for Seng, if I was being honest with myself. Not bureaucratic bullshit but something more tangible.

On my list, there was a minor avatar of the goddess Annapurna, who'd put her pride aside to ask for help with racist landlords, and a goblin family who couldn't get their kid into any public schools but also couldn't afford the exorbitant fees for a private school. I could help them navigate the bureaucracy, get their issues seen by the state, as long as there were no last-minute interruptions—

A knock on the door of the meeting room, and then, without waiting, a young woman poked her head in. She was maybe twenty, short, her T-shirt printed with some anime thing and the tudung that hid her hair an alarming shade of pink. Her smile was bright but uncertain.

"Sorry! Mr. Toh? Ms. Saanvi from HR said to find you here."

"Wait, who are you?"

"Oh! Sorry, I'm Fizah. I'm here for my internship?"

Right. The new intern—jinni, if I remember her application correctly. *Jinni*, like the girl Seng's nephew is dating.

I blinked at Fizah, staring for a fraction longer than I meant to. What were the odds...? No, it couldn't be. There were enough jinn families in the city that jumping to conclusions would just make my headache worse.

Coincidence, I decided. I was overthinking things again. With all my other work, I'd forgotten she was starting today. Jimmy was supposed to be in charge of the internship programme, so it really should be him giving her the onboarding talk, but this poor girl looked frazzled enough as it was, and

I didn't want her first experience with us to be getting turned away. My day was probably shot anyway.

I set aside my headache and pushed my laptop away, composing myself, with some effort, into a semblance of friendliness.

"Come in," I said. "Let me tell you about the team."

My team was the Division for Engagement of Unusual Stakeholders, or DEUS—the post-colonial irony of a government team with a Latinate acronym was not lost on any of us. We were part of the Ministry of Community, the MOC, and I suppose it was a quirk of history that we were here instead of, say, the Ministry of Home Affairs or the Internal Security Department. Unlike most other developed nations, Singapore had quickly made it policy to count our spirit mediums and sorceresses, our *hantus*, our *devas* and *asuras*, as citizens to be served and regulated rather than monsters to be suppressed. This didn't spring from particularly liberal ideals about equality or moral community. Rather, it came from anxiety about Singapore's lack of natural resources and the pragmatic conviction that we needed everyone to work together if we were to survive. We could not afford to completely sideline our traditional gods and demons. We needed them to contribute to our nation's *actual* gods and demons—our government, our economy, our security, our new Leviathan and Moloch.

The job of DEUS was straightforward—keep the weird people content, get them to be productive members of society, and keep them out of sight. That is, don't bother the good, normal citizens of Singapore with disturbing things, and certainly don't bother your bosses (or other Ministries) with that stuff. They had more important things to worry about.

Thankfully, keeping the supernatural from normal human beings and senior management wasn't hard. People don't see what they don't want to see, and our minds are marvellous confabulators. That lady on the MRT with frangipanis growing where her eyes should be? Don't look at her face, don't remember seeing her, focus on your phone and the K-drama you're watching. That temple near your old house, where you've only seen people leaving but never entering, where you've seen something enormous and many-limbed and *holy* dancing inside? Well, it's usually dark, and it could have been something else. That canteen stall you went to all the time in primary school, where you could pay with promises and the food tasted like thunderstorms? Your friends don't admit to recalling anything like that, so you probably just misremembered. You know how fanciful children's imaginations can be.

So we whistle to ourselves as we walk deserted streets home at night, singing tuneless little songs, our brains protecting us from the horrors around us. Officially, this phenomenon is known as Deviant Occurrences Blind Eye Syndrome, or DOBES, following the British government's understated (and poorly chosen) name for it, but no one calls it that except in official reports, not even the Brits. They call it "the jumblies," I heard, and here in Singapore, we call it the DKP effect. Don't *kaypoh*, don't be a busybody, mind your own business.

The DKP effect did make life easier for those of us who

had to manage the supernatural stuff, that being the four of us on the team. Jimmy was our resident goofball and psychic—precognition, psychometry, all the usual. He spent an hour every morning, after his tea break, contemplating a printed map of Singapore and using a dowsing pendulum to sniff out neighbourhoods with unusual supernatural activity. Mei was our spell-slinging *bomoh*, always perfectly poised in her enchanted heels, and she had been doing this for a long time—don't let her pixie haircut and apparent youth fool you. Rebecca was our boss, the head of the department, but she also double-hatted with two other teams, so she was always at other meetings and never around. I was a Gardener and our ersatz field agent, for whatever that was worth.

And now, we also had a jinni.

"Technically, half-jinni, um. Sorry. My dad's just a teacher," Fizah said, fiddling with the edges of her notebook. "How old is Mei anyway? I mean, because…"

"Probably not the best idea to ask," I said.

"Sorry, sorry!" She flipped through her notes, her handwriting neat and perfectly aligned. Perhaps there was hope for the next generation yet. She looked up. "Um, so what do I, like, do around here?"

It was a valid question.

"For today, why don't you go check with Mei or Jimmy and see if they need any help." I knew real work was unlikely to get done—Jimmy would brag about his daughters, Mei would rant about third-wave feminism and the societal pressures forcing her to use magic to look young, and then they would all go out for cake. But hopefully that would give me the space to clear my emails, check in on Mdm. Annapurna and the goblin kid, and tackle that damned update in the evening.

Her face lit up at my suggestion. "Okay! Should I introduce myself, or—?"

Before I could answer, my phone buzzed. Against the sandy landscape that was my lock screen—a photo of Mars taken by the ill-fated rover Opportunity—notifications blinked. Missed calls from an hour ago from my father and from Adam, this guy I was seeing, and a message from Jimmy on the DEUS group chat:

Ghost cat! L3 pantry, come now!

We threaded our way out through the labyrinth of cubicles that made up the third floor. This close to lunchtime, every department had bifurcated into two camps. First: the sprinters, desperately trying to dash off their last four emails or final annex to a paper so they could leave. The second: the defeated, so far from the finish line they'd given up on leaving for lunch, picking at cold noodles while staring at their screens with dead eyes. They don't call it a rat race for nothing. By the time we reached the pantry, Jimmy and Mei had cleared the area, blocking it off along with a whole section of the adjacent corridor with signs that said: SENIOR MANAGEMENT FILMING IN PROGRESS.

Clever. There was no better way to make civil servants avoid a place than with the threat that their bosses might be there.

"Get me a cup," Mei said the moment we stepped in, her manner imperious. "Quickly. Water from the tap will do." She had her back to us and was spreading her scarf—peacock green and gold—on a table. Jimmy waved a broom around threateningly.

There had been rumours about this cat for months—gossip about scratching in the walls once the sun had set. How stationery on your desk would wind up in a different place from where you left it. How papers sometimes looked like they had been chewed on. Sok Ling, from Legal, was convinced that the perpetrator was the ghost of her cat's late best friend.

Hauntings like these were fairly common where we worked. We were in a heritage site that used to be a police barracks, and people said that terrible things happened here when the Japanese occupied Singapore during World War II. The occupation only lasted for about two years, but the pain, fear, and depravity that soaked into the brick and plaster during that time remained. Supposedly the building sat on a conjunction of ley lines and dragon meridians, and so the structure itself stayed, even as everything else around was torn down and rebuilt into shopping centres and skyscrapers, becoming a powerful node for spirits of the darker kind. Or so I have been told by those knowledgeable in such things. History speaks. Stones remember. Buildings accrete memories and excrete ghosts.

But now the inside of the building had been remodelled into air-conditioned government offices, rows of cubicles and meeting rooms, and it was civil servants instead of prisoners of the regular variety who spent their days there. The torture had gotten slightly more sophisticated, the shootings had become (for the most part) metaphorical rather than literal, and we had Wi-Fi. But the decor hadn't improved much, and now you had to buy your own snacks. So, you know, win some, lose some.

The cat didn't seem to think we were winners. It turned out to be a small tabby, one of those *kucintas* you'd find lounging around any housing estate—except this one was sitting very securely about two metres off the floor on absolutely nothing. It glared at us, slow-blinking with supreme indifference—at me, at Mei bent over her scarf and muttering, at Jimmy brandishing a broom, and at Fizah grinning with open delight. Then, as if to underline just how little it cared, the cat started licking a paw. It was a little insulting being ignored like that, to be honest.

I edged past Jimmy and got Mei her cup of water, which she placed on her scarf. The water gleamed momentarily, opalescent.

"Can we help?" I asked.

Mei shook her head, not breaking off from her chanting. Fizah came over to peer into the mug, then up at the cat, then into the mug again. She was practically vibrating with excitement.

"It's so cute!" she squealed. "And this is all so cool. Maybe it's not the only one—maybe there are, like, ghost kittens? Do you think there might be ghost kittens? Could we keep one? Like, what would we do with ghost kittens? Is there like an SPCA or...wait..."

She looked at Mei's water, a look of dawning horror on her face. "Are we..." she said, swallowing. "Are we going to exorcise it?"

All right, that was enough. Mei needed space to do her work.

"Hey, Fizah," I said. "Can you help guard the entrance? No, the other one. We need you to watch and see if PS or DS pass by, and distract them if they want to come in. Can you do that?"

We had to get this done under the radar. If Rebecca found out we were doing exorcisms without official clearance and a risk management plan, there would be hell to pay.

Fizah parked herself dutifully at one of the doorways, but she looked a little glum, her earlier enthusiasm for the work dampened now that she knew what Mei meant to do. All this on her first day. I'd have to find a time later to explain that ghosts were just echoes, not conscious things, and exorcisms were less like murder and more like wiping a cassette tape. Not that someone her age would even know what a cassette tape was.

Throughout all this, the cat remained unconcerned by what we were doing. It blinked slowly at us, then rolled over in mid-air, exposing a fuzzy white belly.

That was when Mei threw the cup of water on it, and all hell broke loose.

The cat yowled and shot straight up, tail rigid and bushy with indignation. It bolted through the air, landing on the back of a couch before springing to a table, Mei's scarf getting caught in its scrabbling claws. Then it launched itself onto a shelf, knocking off a tower of plastic cups and piles of mismatched paper napkins. Amidst all the clattering, the cat took a moment to turn and scowl at us before walking with injured dignity through the back of the shelf. We watched as the scarf disappeared behind it.

It was *definitely* a ghost.

"It is not a ghost," Mei announced. "It is something else."

"It walked through a wall!" Fizah said. "I mean, that's a ghost thing, right?"

Mei shook her head, patting her hair back in place. "It is not a ghost. If it were, my Working would have dealt with it. Few ghosts can ignore the blessed waters or have enough physical presence to tear up a couch like that. Jimmy, Fizah, come with me. We must figure out what it is.

"We will find it," she declared, her sharp glare making clear her new personal vendetta. "I *will* get my scarf back."

I was just about to add "scarf retrieval" to my very reasonably sized mental task list when Jimmy lowered the broom and turned to me, his expression serious.

"Hey, uh, boss," he said. "Since I have you here. I got a signal earlier. Clementi, Block 375. Energy spike. Ghosty one."

I froze for a moment. Jimmy's morning dowsings didn't catch everything, but what they did catch we couldn't afford to ignore. Especially not in a residential housing district.

"Define *ghosty*," I said.

"I'm not sure. Something dead and left over, maybe? It showed up for a few minutes, then disappeared. Not like a normal haunting. Felt…deep, but not strong. Not old, not big. You know what I mean?"

"Nope." I pinched the bridge of my nose. "I'll go over there tomorrow morning and take a look."

Fizah was still staring at the spot where the ghost cat had vanished, looking shell-shocked and lost. Her notebook was clutched tightly in both hands.

"How do you feel about coming along?" I said.

She blinked at me. "Me? For real?"

"Yes, for real," I said. "Clementi, tomorrow. Ghosts aren't dangerous, and it sure beats sitting in the office on your second day. You're just there to observe, but you might learn something."

Jimmy snorted. "You'll learn that Ben is entirely too chipper in the morning."

Fizah's grin was so wide I briefly worried that she might spontaneously combust. "Thank you, Mr. Toh! I'd love to!"

I sighed, already regretting my decision. "Ghosty" was new, and the last time Jimmy had invented a new word to describe something weird, it had cost me three nights of sleep, four email reports, and one pair of perfectly good shoes.

Surely this couldn't be *that* bad.